THE SECRET HISTORY OF
LUCIFER

By the same author

Mary Magdalene: Christianity's Hidden Goddess
The Encyclopaedia of the Paranormal (Ed.)
The Mammoth Book of UFOs

With Clive Prince

Turin Shroud: In Whose Image?
The Templar Revelation: Secret Guardians of the True Identity of Christ
The Stargate Conspiracy

With Clive Prince and Stephen Prior
(additional historical research by Robert Brydon)

Double Standards: The Rudolf Hess Cover-up
War of the Windsors
Friendly Fire: The Secret War Between The Allies

THE SECRET HISTORY OF
LUCIFER

The ancient path to knowledge and the *real* Da Vinci Code

LYNN PICKNETT

ROBINSON
London

ROBINSON

First published in Great Britain in 2005 by Robinson,
an imprint of Constable & Robinson Ltd

This paperback edition published in 2006 by Robinson

7 9 10 8

A CIP catalogue record for this book
is available from the British Library.

ISBN: 978-1-84529-263-8

Printed and bound in Great Britain by CPI Group (UK) Ltd, Croydon CR0 4YY

Papers used by Robinson are from well-managed forests
and other responsible sources

MIX
Paper from
responsible sources
FSC® C013604
www.fsc.org

Robinson
An imprint of
Little, Brown Book Group
Carmelite House
50 Victoria Embankment
London EC4Y 0DZ

An Hachette UK Company
www.hachette.co.uk

www.littlebrown.co.uk

For
Debbie Benstead, with love
Is there a tenth gate? Are we there yet?

Contents

List of Illustrations		ix
Introduction		xi

PART ONE: A STAR IS BORN

1	Satan: An Unnatural History	3
2	The Devil and All Her Works	35
3	A Woman Called Lucifer	63

PART TWO: LEGACY OF THE FALL

4	Synagogues of Satan	117
5	Pacts, Possession and Séance Rooms	165
6	Do What Thou Wilt	215

Epilogue: The Lucifer Key	251
Notes and References	263
Acknowledgements	289
Select Bibliography	291
Index	295

Illustrations

The Fall of Man, 1549 (oil on panel) by Cranach, Lucas the Younger (1515–86), © Museum of Fine Arts, Houston, Texas, USA, Edith A. and Percy S. Straus Collection
Courtesy of The Bridgeman Art Library

Glad Day or *The Dance of Albion*, c.1794 (etching with w/c) by Blake, William (1757–1827), British Museum, London, UK
Courtesy of The Bridgeman Art Library

The Egyptian god Set

Statue of the god Horus making a drink offering, Third Intermediate Period c.750 BC (bronze), Louvre, Paris, France
Courtesy of The Bridgeman Art Library

Diana Lucifera (Lucina)
A late Roman statue, she carries the torch symbolizing spiritual resurrection and illumination

Pan, c.1880 (bronze on stone plinth) by Thabard, Adolf Martial (1831–1905), private collection/Agra Art, Warsaw, Poland
Courtesy of The Bridgeman Art Library

Negative of the Turin Shroud

Aggemian's 1935 portrait taken from the cloth

Leonardo da Vinci (1452–1519) engraving by English School, (19th century), private collection/Ken Welsh
Courtesy of The Bridgeman Art Library

The Virgin and Child with St Anne and John the Baptist, c.1499 (charcoal, chalk on paper) by Vinci, Leonardo da (1452–1519), National Gallery, London, UK
Courtesy of The Bridgeman Art Library

Mary Magdalene, 1877 (oil on canvas) by Rossetti, Dante Charles Gabriel (1828–82), © Delaware Art Museum, Wilmington, USA/Samuel and Mary R. Bancroft Memorial
Courtesy of The Bridgeman Art Library

The Witches' Sabbath or *The Great He-goat*, (one of 'The Black Paintings'), c.1821–23 (oil on canvas) by Goya y Lucientes, Francisco Jose de (1746–1828), Prado, Madrid, Spain/Giraudon
Courtesy of The Bridgeman Art Library

Three Witches Burned Alive, pamphlet illustration (woodcut) by German School, (16th century), private collection/The Stapleton Collection
Courtesy of The Bridgeman Art Library

Edward Kelly (b.1555), a magician, and his partner the mathematician and astrologer, John Dee (1527–1608), raising a ghost, private collection
Courtesy of The Bridgeman Art Library

Sir Isaac Newton
Anonymous, Petworth House, West Sussex, UK
Courtesy of The Bridgeman Art Library

Introduction

Everyone knows what evil is. Everyone carries iconic pictures in their heads that symbolize the horror of real wickedness: smoke and flames pouring from the Twin Towers on the September 11 that stopped the world in its tracks; piles of emaciated bodies at the Nazis' death camps; thousands of grinning skulls in Pol Pot's killing fields; a naked little girl running screaming towards the camera, covered in napalm . . . Terror, agony, war, death upon death. Although entirely of humanity's doing, we use words such as 'satanic' to describe these deeds of historic atrocity, evoking the name of the Old Enemy, Satan, personification of all that is terrible, disgusting, beyond belief. Satan may or may not exist as a literal entity, but he is a potent metaphor for the worst of the worst. However, this book will sing the praises of another hugely powerful metaphor – *Lucifer* – who is emphatically *not* the Evil One, but the spirit of human progress, the fight to learn and grow, to be independent and proud, but also *spiritually* free. 'Lucifer' simply means 'the Light-bringer', the enlightener, and it is in that spirit that this book will examine the way that a belief in the values he represents has shaped our world, the Judaeo-Christian West, in which the very freedoms he seeks are fast becoming eroded.

As the great 19th-century French occultist and sage Eliphas Levi wrote 'What is more absurd and more impious than to attribute the name of Lucifer to the devil, that is, to personified evil. The intel-

lectual Lucifer is the spirit of intelligence and love; it is the para-
clete, it is the Holy Spirit, while the physical Lucifer is the great
agent of universal magnetism.'[1]

In the dire past, the days of witch burning and mass bigotry, there
were few recognizable freedoms. Today, when we are trying to
force-feed democracy to eastern cultures, it would seem that we
have all the freedom we want or need. Not so: the insidious fascism
of political correctness – with its chillingly Orwellian undertones –
and the growing threat of fundamentalism of all sorts mean that our
everyday freedoms are under threat. On both sides of the Atlantic
the radiant figure of the real Lucifer is being obscured by red tape,
yet rarely have we needed him more. With the breakdown of the
education system, ignorance, nihilism and the non-existence of self-
respect abound, turning into rage, violence and crime on the one
hand and dangerously rigid religious belief on the other. Both represent their own form of evil, both threaten the future of our culture –
but if we permit ourselves to be still, honest and objective for just a
few moments, we will be able to hear the rousing cry of the
Morning Star, Lucifer, all brightness and hope. Let the Light shine
in!

An unexpected sequel

When I began this book I had little idea how neatly it would follow
on from my previous work, *Mary Magdalene: Christianity's
Hidden Goddess* (2003), which examined the *real* role of one of
Christendom's most maligned saints, revealing her to be nothing
less than Jesus' lover and even his chosen successor. For two
millennia the Church has deliberately obscured the truth about her,
terrified that her status would inspire other women to fulfil their
own destinies as intelligent, spiritual leaders. In the light of all the
evidence, it is incredible that there is still heated debate among
churchmen about the validity of female priests – or, if 'stuck' with
them, of female bishops. Yet if the truth about Mary Magdalene
were widely known there could be no debate: she set the pattern for
women to be equal with the men in religious debate and leadership
– *and in that, she was Jesus' own choice*. And it is hugely significant that to her devotees in the south of France, she was known as
'Mary Lucifer' – 'Mary the Light-bringer'.

This was a time-honoured tradition: pagan goddesses were known, for example, as 'Diana Lucifera' or 'Isis Lucifer' to signify their power to illumine mind and soul, to create a mystical bond between deity and worshipper, to open up both body and psyche to the Holy Light. Of course to the ignorant all pagan gods and goddesses are still routinely dismissed as devilish, just as the great nature god Pan himself became the very image of Satan – with his horns and hooves – when Christians came to rule the known world with a rod of iron. Yet there is evidence to suggest very strongly that the Magdalene and even Jesus himself were highly influenced by pagan goddess cults, especially that of the Egyptian Isis (from which John the Baptist took his then new ritual of baptism).

Of course millions worldwide have now read about a Church conspiracy to defraud us all of our true spiritual inheritance via the Magdalene, from Dan Brown's publishing phenomenon, *The Da Vinci Code*. Until now, there has been far too much darkness in the world of the spirit for far too long, and whether presented as a worthy academic tome or a rip-roaring page-turner, letting a little light in can only change our culture for the better. Yet the truth is that his novel goes nowhere near far enough. The *real* Da Vinci code is considerably more shocking than merely suggesting that Mary and Jesus were man and wife with children.

Nineteen ninety-seven saw the publication of my book, *The Templar Revelation: Secret Guardians of the True Identity of Christ*, co-authored with my closest friend and long-term colleague Clive Prince, which first introduced the idea of heretical symbolism in the so-called 'religious' paintings of the great Renaissance genius, in a chapter called 'The Secret Code of Leonardo da Vinci'. Although this was to provide Dan Brown with the background for his thriller, he has hardly scraped the surface of what Leonardo was really trying to convey . . .

Leonardo (as 'Da Vinci' should properly be known) was the ultimate Luciferan hero: daring, shocking, challenging, endlessly questing without acknowledging any limits, ever pushing back the boundaries of human knowledge. Famously the inventor of flying-machines and military tanks, he also invented all manner of devices such as a sewing-machine, a bicycle (complete with chain and same-size wheels) – and even devised a primitive but effective form of *photography* with which he almost certainly created the world's most famous and baffling hoax, the Shroud of Turin, as detailed in our book *Turin Shroud: How Leonardo da Vinci Fooled History*. The 'holy' image even has his own face on it. In other words, incredibly, instead of a miraculous image of Jesus Christ, we have a 500-year-old photograph of Leonardo da Vinci, a fifteenth-century homosexual heretic who *hated Jesus and the Virgin Mary*.

The Church reserved a special loathing for those – and there were many – who tinkered with what we would call the early stages of photography, so it was a joke of particular viciousness with which Leonardo probably created the ultimate Christian relic, knowing it would be cared for by the priests of the very Church that he despised, perhaps until the day when it would be recognized for what it really is. But make no mistake, photography was believed to be 'occult' once, and there is no reason to doubt that Leonardo actually believed himself to be involved in a magical process when he created the 'Shroud'. If caught working with the 'devilish' photography, he knew his position on the top of a flaming pyre would be assured.

(For those who, despite all the evidence to the contrary, might be eager to declare the Shroud is genuinely the miraculously imprinted winding sheet of Jesus, may I draw your attention to certain glaring anomalies of the image – see page 179 – which conclusively prove not only is it a fake, but also that it is a *projected* image. Further details can be found in our first book, *Turin Shroud: How Leonardo da Vinci Fooled History*, 2000.)

And, of course, as Clive and I revealed in *The Templar Revelation*, it is our theory that Leonardo put Mary Magdalene next to Jesus in his *Last Supper*, forming a giant spread-eagled 'M' shape with the composition of their bodies as a clue. A brilliant psychologist, Leonardo knew that people only ever see what they expect or want to see. Quite what that says about my own mind, as the first person (as far as I know) to notice the giant penis on the head of Mary in the *Virgin of the Rocks* is open to question . . .

Leonardo da Vinci was by no means the only shining light of intellectual and spiritual Luciferanism throughout history, which included secretive alchemists such as Queen Elizabeth I's astrologer John Dee – who as her spy master took the code name

007! – and eminent pioneering scientists such as Sir Isaac Newton and Andrew Crosse. As well as the Freemasons, the backbone of British and American progress, still routinely accused of worshipping a *satanic* Lucifer . . .

However, because Lucifer and Satan are *very* wrongly assumed to be one and the same, this book will also examine those who have chosen to be Satanists or those whose magical operations have brought them perilously close to crossing the line into a much darker and bleaker world. But nothing could be darker or bleaker than the result of a *belief* in the existence of Devil-worshippers. For at least three entire centuries Europe (and then parts of North America) were ravaged by the craze for denouncing the most innocent of beings as witches, resulting in the devastation of whole communities, when the walls of village houses were caked in stinking human fat from the dreadful and seemingly endless burnings – even of tiny children. (Once a baby was actually born to a woman shrieking in agony among the flames. Somehow she managed to throw it free. The crowd threw it back, as an imp of Satan.) A *belief* in the Devil and his faithful has caused more agony, terror and evil in the world than even any true Satanism.

It was a madness that must never be forgotten, for like all historical abominations it holds a unique lesson for the future, should we be willing to confront and learn from it. This was not a vaguely interesting hiccup in European history that ought to be relegated to dry-as-dust text books – it was about the demonization of ordinary men and women just like you and me, by ordinary men and women just like you and me.

Yet while few of the hundred thousand or so witches caught up in this abomination were real Devil worshippers, most of their accusers could be said to be devils incarnate. It rapidly became a burnable offence even to question the existence of witchcraft. *That* is the price of a kind of fundamentalism. Lest we forget.

From the iniquities of the great ecclesiastical conspiracy to cover up the truth about Mary Magdalene and her 'Luciferan' predecessors, the goddess-worshipping priestesses and priests, through the astounding courage and intellectual magnitude of freethinkers such as Leonardo da Vinci and his brethren, we arrive at today, hedged around and threatened by censorship, political correctness and worse. But, paradoxically, our journey to the murk and high anxiety of the twenty-first-century West begins with the pernicious myth of very first humans and a certain talking snake . . .

LYNN PICKNETT
London 2005
Long live Lucifer – but to Hell with Satan!

PART ONE

A Star is Born

CHAPTER ONE

Satan: An Unnatural History

All cultures have their creation myths – the ancient Egyptians believed that the god Atum, deity of the solar disk and the sun itself, masturbated himself, exploding a life-giving burst of energy that seeded the dark unformed void with countless galaxies. In the land of the pyramids there was no impropriety in the concept that 'self abuse' created the universe, although millennia later Victorian archaeologists were predictably shocked to the core by the ancient Egyptians' melding of sex and divinity.

In the first act of creation, Atum was perceived as an androgynous figure, the hand that made the world being the female aspect, while his phallus represented the equal and opposite male principle. As the eminent American scholar Professor Karl Luckert writes: 'The entire system can be visualized as a flow of creative vitality, emanating outward from the godhead, thinning out as it flows further from its source'.[1]

However, this apparently primitive – if somewhat explicit – tale actually encompasses a highly sophisticated understanding of the cosmology, as Clive Prince and myself noted in our *The Stargate Conspiracy* (1999):

It literally describes the 'Big Bang', in which all matter explodes from a point of singularity and then expands and unfolds, becoming more complex as fundamental forces come into being and interact, finally reaching the level of elemental matter.[2]

Unfortunately our own culture's creation myth boasts no orgasmic Big Bang, no universe spawned unashamedly, even proudly, from the explosively virile phallus of the great Creator god.

What we have instead is the story of God's six-day creation followed by the myth of Adam and Eve – essentially the opposite of the Egyptian myth in its furtive, guilt-ridden attitude to nakedness and its emphasis on sexual sin, female culpability and divine retribution from a pathologically wrathful, tyrannical and petty God. Despite millennia of sermonizing and theological debate – in which the sheer nastiness and incompetence of Yahweh has been subjected to the damage limitation of philosophy by far greater minds, apparently, than his – arguably the story as told in the first book of the Old Testament, Genesis, has succeeded in inspiring more evil and more neuroses than Stalin and Freud could ever have dreamt of between them.

In the Judaeo-Christian tradition, all human woes supposedly originated in the Garden of Eden, the blissful earthly paradise that God created to provide innocent and unmitigated joy for the two creatures he made in his own image – the prototype man Adam and his critically wayward companion, the first female, Eve. Clearly unwilling to expend too much trouble, God frugally created the world's mother from one of Adam's ribs, although in fact this aspect of the story is a perversion of a myth of a Sumerian goddess who, more understandably, created babies from their mother's ribs in her role 'as the Lady of the Rib and Lady of Life'.[3]

Unfortunately one of the other creatures in the garden was about to become a little too intimate, as it slithered towards them with its burden of horror for the whole of mankind . . .

Inside Paradise

While 'Eden' itself may originate in the Sumerian *edinu*, simply meaning 'plain', the term used in Genesis for 'paradise' is a mixture of various near eastern words, including the old Persian *paradeida*, which may mean 'a royal park' or 'enclosed garden',[4] denoting a sense of exclusivity, even of luxury. Indeed, the Greek *paradeisos* was often used by writers such as Xenophon to describe the lush walled gardens of wealthy monarchs like King Cyrus, envied throughout the Near East for his opulence. Perhaps the old Mesopotamian belief in the 'king as gardener' underpinned the Eden imagery,[5] where God himself creates the garden, and Adam – a true human king-figure before the Fall – maintains it. (And it may be significant that the priests of several ancient Mediterranean religions, such as those of the Egyptian Osiris cult, were known as 'gardeners' and that Mary Magdalene, who, I have argued elsewhere, was a priestess of a goddess-worshipping religion,[6] believed the risen Jesus to be a 'gardener'.)

'Eden' may refer to the wider region in which the first garden was believed to be located, variously described in the Old Testament as the 'Garden of the Lord'[7] or the 'Garden of God',[8] a verdant place that was soon synonymous with peace, tranquillity and, above all, innocence. Four rivers gave the garden its lush fertility, providing abundant food for its teeming and diverse plant and animal life, inspiring generations of Christian artists and writers.

Many Jewish and early Christian chroniclers pursued a fruitless task of trying to locate the four rivers of Paradise. These are named by the Bible as the Euphrates and the Tigris – both of which are real and important features of the near east – together with the apparently mythical Gihon and Pison, although the first-century Jewish chronicler Flavius Josephus believed that one of the latter was actually the Nile, placing Eden in north Africa. Indeed, some early Church Fathers and late classical writers placed Eden in Ethiopia, Mongolia or even India. Others have located the earthly Paradise in eastern Turkey, where it would have been served by the Euphrates, Tigris and the River Murat, the north fork of the Euphrates providing the identity of the mysterious fourth river.

Many archaeologists and theologians had long believed Eden to have been situated in Sumer, the ancient area approximately 125 miles (200 km) beyond the northern tip of the Persian Gulf, but in the 1980s Dr Juris Zarins argued that the original Paradise had sunk beneath the waves as the waters of the Gulf had risen dramatically since the time described in Genesis. Zarin also suggested that the 'Gihon' is now the River Karun, which rises in Iran, flowing south-

west into the Persian Gulf. This is an exquisite irony – today's Iraq
is no one's Paradise!

However, it hardly matters where Eden may have been – always
assuming that it is a valid exercise to read the Old Testament so
literally – for, like the Holy Grail, its significance is so much more
potent if seen by the eyes of the heart, not the eyes of the head. Eden
may have had the geographical reality of, say, New York or Madrid
(or the comparative unreality of Las Vegas or Blackpool), but its
maps are really treasures of the mind, like Shangri-La or Atlantis.
In any case, Eden represents the Golden Age, when nature was at
peace with itself and mankind 'walked with God'. Unfortunately,
however, the loss of Paradise, even as a mythical concept, has
proved far more traumatic to the human race than any bitter-sweet
longing for the delights of Camelot.

'Eden' remains a synonym for the ultimate, unspoilt and
ineffably beautiful location. When Charles Dickens wished to
underscore the true vileness of an allegedly paradisical plot of
American swamp in his *Martin Chuzzlewit*,[9] he simply called it
'Eden' with characteristic irony. Surely it is one of the few instantly
recognized names of ancient myth that is as well known today as it
was millennia ago.

The curse of life

The story of Man's[10] abrupt expulsion from Eden – be it fiction,
metaphor or literal fact – has become etched too deeply on the
collective unconscious to ignore, for it has set in stone Judaeo-
Christian attitudes to men, women, original sin (and therefore
children), the Creator and his opposition, Lucifer/Satan/the Devil.
This all-powerful myth has imbued us all at some level of perception with a belief that life is a curse, that death is the end – a
collapsing back of the body into its constituent dust, no more – that
women are inherently on intimate terms with evil, that men have
carte blanche to do as they please with not only all the animals in
the world but also their womenfolk, and that God, above all, is to
be *feared*. Snakes come out of it rather badly, too, as the embodiment of evil, the medium through which Satan tempts we pathetic
humans. The Devil, on the other hand, is the only being in the tale
to show some intelligence, perhaps even humour, in taking the form

of a wriggling, presumably charming, phallic symbol through which to tempt a woman.

As both Judaism and Christianity depend so intimately on the basic premises of Genesis, this lost paradise of the soul is evoked several times throughout both Old and New Testaments. The crucified Jesus promised the thief hanging on the cross next to him 'Today you will be with me in Paradise',[11] although it is unclear how those listening may have interpreted this term. Did they see it as synonymous with 'heaven', a state of bliss that must remain unknowable to the living (and remain for ever unknown to the wicked)? Or did it somehow encompass the old idea of the luxuriant garden?

Images of the garden as Paradise recur throughout the Old Testament, assuming a highly sensuous form in its love poem, the Song of Songs – believed to be the erotic praise of the Queen of Sheba by her lover, King Solomon – in powerful phrases such as 'Our bed is verdant';[12] 'You are a garden locked up, my sister, my bride,[13] and 'You are a garden fountain/a well of flowing water streaming down from Lebanon'.[14]

(These blatantly sexual verses are still widely interpreted by modern churchgoers and theologians as 'an allegory of the great Christian drama of sin and redemption, affirming the love of Christ for both the individual soul and his Church',[15] which would be truly remarkable, for they were composed centuries before Jesus was born. Not only that, but the ripe lasciviousness which summons up sometimes disconcertingly vivid images of Solomon and Sheba's amorous activity in their tented boudoir seems a world away from the austere love of Ecclesia, the Christian Church. However, as we shall see, the Song of Songs does have some light to shed on a great Christian mystery, but hardly one that would feature in any sermon.)

As in all the best dramas, early harmony must be doomed – or there simply won't be much of a story – so the scenario described at the beginning of Genesis is not to last: after all, no state of earthly bliss can endure. It was to be all downhill after the creation.

Forbidden fruit

As the original naturists Adam and Eve frolicked among amiable animals, one of which had already evolved a remarkable talent. This was a talking snake, whose ability seemed to take its creator

by surprise, although this is by no means the last time his own
creations will catch Yahweh unawares.

Having created Adam and Eve 'in his own image' he then
ordered them not to touch the fruit of 'the tree of the knowledge of
good and evil' in the middle of the garden, on pain of death –
presumably a concept they had some difficulty understanding. But
along slid the loquacious serpent, who swiftly took the opportunity
to whisper with his flickering forked tongue to Eve: 'Did God really
say, "You must not eat from any tree in the garden?"'[16]

When Eve dutifully repeats God's proscription on 'fruit from the
tree that is in the middle of the garden', the serpent responds 'You
will not surely die . . . For God knows that when you eat of it your
eyes will be opened and *you will be like God*, knowing good and
evil'[17] [My emphasis]. While the humans seem to be enticed
primarily by the lusciousness of the forbidden fruit, the serpent
concentrates on making explicit the appeal of becoming like God,
with the implication of a potential challenge to his authority. If his
intention were simply to make mankind fall from grace – evil for its
own sake – there was no need to spell it out for them. 'Look at the
lovely fruit!' would have done just as well. Did the serpent actually
care about Adam and Eve's intellectual development? In any case,
there must be something special about the fruit because God put it
out of bounds so specifically. So they eat.

> When the woman saw that the fruit of the tree was good for food
> and pleasing to the eye, and also desirable for gaining wisdom,
> she took some and ate it. She also gave some to her husband, who
> was with her, and he ate it. Then the eyes of both of them were
> opened . . .[18]

They may have had only the taste sensation in mind – the fruit
being 'also desirable for gaining wisdom' seems something of an
afterthought – but in gobbling it down the damage is done. Their
guilty snack is a moment of pure cataclysm, for far from being the
equivalent of being caught with their hands in the cookie jar, it
opened the portals for evil – although of course in order to tempt the
woman Satan was already present, so presumably the Fall was only
a matter of time, fruit or no fruit.

The sensuous indulgence changes everything. The man and his wife realize abruptly that they are not only naked but that their nudity is a shameful thing – the implication is that this is actually *unnatural*, some kind of perversion – so they hastily manufacture clothes out of leaves, revealing if nothing else that sewing is apparently instinctive human behaviour in an emergency.

But as they cower in the bushes covered in fig leaves, they realize that all is lost: God is walking in the garden 'in the cool of the day' and calls out 'Where are you?' Adam tells the Almighty that he is hiding because he 'was afraid because I was naked'. God is outraged, demanding to know (without a flicker of irony) 'Who told you you were naked?' Like an irate schoolmaster trying to elicit a confession from a mulish class, he adds: 'Have you eaten from the tree from which I commanded you not to eat?'[19]

When God wrathfully demands to know how they knew they were naked, Adam pipes up disloyally: 'The woman you put here with me – she gave me some fruit from the tree and I ate it.' After the world's first sneak has finished blaming his wife, and in doing so also even implies that he blames God for giving him Eve as his companion, she, too, is keen to pass the blame on to the serpent, which God declares:

> Cursed are you above all the livestock and all the wild animals!
> You will crawl on your belly and you will eat dust all the days of your life.
> And I will put enmity between you and the woman,
> And between your offspring and hers;
> He will crush your head
> And you will strike his heel.[20]

Yet the symbolism of the snake is open to very different interpretations. In ancient Egypt it was used as the *uraeus*, the cobra that decorated the head-dress of the royal family as 'Lord of Life and Death',[21] the ultimate symbol of earthly power. According to the medieval Jewish Cabbalists, the secret or esoteric number of the serpent in Eden is the same as that for the Messiah: as the infamous – but extremely well educated – ritual magician Aleister Crowley wrote: '[the snake] is the Redeemer', noting 'the serpent is also . . .

the principal symbol of male energy'[22] and 'creator and destroyer, who operates all change'.[23] (He also amused and shocked by proffering 'the serpent's kiss' to women, especially those whom he had just met. Of course it was a more or less painful bite.) To the heretical Gnostic Christians, the serpent, coiled around the Tree of Life, was to be celebrated as the bringer of *gnosis*, of intense personal enlightenment of the spirit. And to the Tantrics, the eastern devotees of sacred sexuality, the snake represents the power of *kundalini*, the creative sexual force that is normally envisaged as being curled up at the base of the spine. When roused it produces intense heat and power – but woe betide the individual who has not prepared diligently for its awakening with rigorous magical and spiritual discipline, for it can become awesomely uncontrollable.

However, in the original Eden myth, as the serpent slithers off to a fate of humiliation[24] God rounds on Eve, cursing her:

> I will greatly increase your pains in childbearing;
> With pain you will give birth to children.
> Your desire will be for your husband,
> And he will rule over you.[25]

The culpability of Eve and the serpent may be endlessly debated, but those four short lines have proved only too influential over the minds of men, not only providing a divine blessing for wife-beaters and all manner of marital abuses, but also – as we shall see – even specifically and egregiously dooming generations of midwives to torture and death. As their medical and herbal knowledge eased the pains of childbirth, they were singled out by an outraged Church as heretics or witches who had deliberately flouted God's holy law. Thousands of midwives were duly hounded to an atrocious death.

(Although when God removed one of Adam's ribs with which to fashion Eve, at least he first mercifully put him to sleep, it is quite incredible that as late as the nineteenth century, Queen Victoria's doctors were horrified when she asked to have her pains relieved for the births of her last seven children by the new anaesthesia. These men of the modern era, the time of rail travel, photography and the telegraph, seriously objected that to kill the agony of child-birth was to risk offending the Almighty, who had made his views on this subject very clear in Genesis. Fortunately for Victorian women and subsequent generations of nervous mothers-to-be, the queen-empress won that particular battle.)

Marilyn Yalom, in *A History of the Wife* (2001), describes how early Christian Fathers such as Tertullian and Saint Augustine believed that Eve's Fall had 'conferred a moral taint on all carnal union, even that within marriage'. While Augustine declared that 'married couples should engage in sex only to beget children, and should scrupulously avoid copulating merely for pleasure':

Saint Jerome went even further. He considered sex, even in marriage, as intrinsically evil. He rejected sexual pleasure as filthy, loathsome, degrading, and ultimately corrupting. This linkage of sex and sin, with blame attributed to the daughters of Eve, became increasingly entrenched within the church, and by the fifth century was common currency among ecclesiastical authorities. It was also related to the rise of monasticism, which, by the sixth century, offered an alternative to marriage for Christian men and women. (Institutionalized celibacy has not been a part of Jewish or Muslim practice.)[26]

Back in a Paradise, trembling on the brink of disaster, Adam and Eve (wearing new suits of clothes made from animal skins for them by God himself) are then summarily expelled, prevented from trying to sneak back in for further helpings of delicious wisdom by 'cherubim and a flaming sword flashing back and forth to guard the way to the tree of life'.[27] In the words of the blind English poet John Milton (1608–74), Latin secretary to Oliver Cromwell and a fervent Protestant, in his epic religious poem *Paradise Lost*:

The world was now before them, where to choose
Their place of rest, and Providence their guide:
They hand in hand with wand'ring steps and slow,
Through Eden took their solitary way.[28]

Although weary and chastened, Milton's Adam and Eve seem on the brink of a great adventure as they resignedly turn their newly clad backs on Paradise. 'The world was now before them' –

anything could happen now they were no longer institutionalized and free to go and do as they pleased. They might be cursed and even damned, but they had a glimmering of *hope*.

Yet although, as the French writer Jean Markale notes of our progenitors, 'in discovering evil they also discovered good', he goes on to remark astutely: 'Men now felt guilty. Guilty of what? We have no idea.'[29]

After the Fall

It will not be an easy journey. Adam is condemned to a life of 'painful toil' with the brutal reminder 'dust you are and to dust you will return'. According to Christian theology, their Fall is the original sin with which we are all burdened, even – indeed, *especially* – newborn babies, who arrive in this world as kicking, screaming proof of Eve's curse, not to mention the very fact that their existence is the inevitable evidence of parental intercourse. Birth itself was shameful. (It was only in the 1950s that pregnancy was mentioned openly in polite society. Before that, euphemisms, such as being in 'an interesting condition' applied, and even then some blushes were expected.)

However, in the biblical account, there is no mention that the snake is the Devil, Satan or Lucifer. He is simply a snake, apparently doing what snakes do best – tempting women. The sexual connotations may be cringingly obvious to the post-Freudian world, but they were not necessarily so blatant to our Bible-quoting ancestors. However, it is not much of a leap from the story of the wicked snake to the notion of its being instructed or even possessed by the personification of evil, whoever or whatever that might be: Milton makes the point clear in his description of '. . . the serpent, or rather Satan in the serpent.'[30]

(The identification of snakes with evil is so ingrained that a serpent, tongue flickering horribly, simply had to be the symbol for Hogwarts' house of Slytherin, alma mater of all magicians who went to the bad, in J.K. Rowling's Harry Potter novels. Yet Harry's unconscious skills do set a boa constrictor free from London Zoo, who is polite enough to hiss 'Thanks', before slithering off.)

The unedifying story of the expulsion from Paradise is believed to be essentially about the arrival of sin among humankind – its fall from grace and future as the plaything of evil and the repository for all known pain and suffering. While the preferred modern view is to dismiss it as nonsense or at best see it as an allegory, a surprising number of Christians still believe that Adam and Eve literally existed and that we have since suffered from their sin.

However, perhaps the story is most revealing about God's own nature. He appears to be as much at a loss with Adam and Eve as they are in their new circumstances – and not much of a psychologist, despite having created the prototype man and woman in the first place. Did he really believe that banning a certain substance, the fruit of a tree – that one over there, look! – would mean that they would obediently steer clear of it? Clearly he has a great deal to learn as a father.

Not only does God seem taken aback by the whole episode, but also he seems neither to have understood that he has created intellectual curiosity and a desire for sensuous satisfaction nor that the snake, too, was his handiwork, saddled with a set of characteristics that inevitably led him to tempt the woman. Like Judas in his role as catalyst for Jesus' sacrifice, the snake was doomed from the first. And both are seen as literal embodiments of, or at best, servants of evil. And – after Eve's calamitous fall – traditionally women have been seen as not much better.

Perhaps, too, the myth also contains an element common in modern science fiction, the fear of the robots' rebellion. Just as medieval and Renaissance Jewish legends told of the horror of the golem, a magically animated man, in the story of the Fall God's robotic creatures seize the initiative, revealing an inherent – and potentially dangerous – intelligence that their creator did not want to acknowledge. The creation myth is famously parodied in Mary Shelley's *Frankenstein*, although perhaps it may be less of a travesty and closer to the original than is usually thought.

However, although it might seem a pointless exercise to question or read such a modern interpretation into what is essentially a group of ancient myths, even today's most sharply sophisticated cultures are still heavily influenced by them and their potent ramifications. Even in the twenty-first century, much of the Judaeo-Christian legacy informs the way that even most materialist sceptic thinks and behaves. Whether we like it or not, that legacy has built the history that spawned us, and shaped the attitudes that linger, often unpleasantly, in the dark recesses of our minds.

Perhaps, though, God did have a psychological understanding of Eve, knowing she would inevitably fall prey to the serpent. Perhaps the whole episode of the Fall was set up to test the loyalty of the first man and woman. But, in that case, surely their banishment was somewhat harsh? Perhaps a stiff talking-to, literally to put the fear of God into them, and another chance to prove themselves, would have made more sense? It is only too easy to liken God's reaction to that of a spoilt child taking out his spite on his new toys, the rather mindless Adam and Eve, when they failed to work according to the instructions. Indeed, if he had never experienced any other being standing up to him, a spoilt child is pretty much what he would have become. But was he ever challenged – apart from Adam and Eve in what was to prove their critical act of rebellion?

According to the Old Testament, Yahweh was confronted by one of his own leading angels, Lucifer, in a sort of explosive palace coup – which, of course, failed spectacularly, ending with the rebel leader's banishment to Earth, and beyond, into the nightmarish realms of hell.

To the Jews, the infernal regions were ablaze with Gehenna, a river of fire, although the name was often applied to the whole area. The concept of Hell as a fiery pit, so beloved of medieval theologians and witch-hunters, actually originated in ancient Egyptian wall paintings of 'the wicked' being consumed by fire, although in fact these tormented souls were not meant to represent human sinners, but elemental spirits, enemies of the sun god Atum.[31] However, that religion never laid any emphasis on eternal punishment for sin, the afterlife being instead a sort of assault course of monsters and demons that could be overcome with the right spells.

Although Egyptians spent their entire lives, and often their fortunes, trying to escape death – which they called 'an abomination' – an essential aspect of their belief was that the dying-and-rising god Osiris had saved humanity from death through the process of rebirth.

But in the West, the concept of Hell has long proved useful to keep the vulnerable in terror of God. Although this subject will be discussed in detail later, the following extract from the nineteenth-century Father Furniss' *Sight of Hell*, an improving tract for young people, will suffice to convey these sadistic fantasies:

> Of two little maids of sixteen, one cared only for dress, and went to a dancing school, and dared to disport in the park on Sunday instead of going to mass: the little maid stands now, and forever will stand, with bare feet upon a red-hot floor. The other walked through the streets at nights and did very wicked things; now she utters shrieks of agony in a burning oven. A very severe torment – immersion up to the neck in a boiling kettle – agitates a boy who kept bad company, and was too idle to go to mass, and a drunkard; avenging flames now issue from his ears. For like indecencies, the blood of a girl, who went to the theatre, boils in her veins; you can hear it boil, and her marrow is seething in her bones and her brain bubbles in her head. 'Think,' says the compassionate father, 'what a headache that girl must have!'[32]

Surely no comment is necessary.

As we shall see in a later chapter, some of the worst excesses of hellish punishments were invented by patriarchal societies to terrorize women. Barbara Walker notes, for example, that in this male-dominated Hell:

> Women who scolded would be forced to lick hot stoves with their tongues. Women who showed disloyalty to men would be hung up by one leg, while scorpions, snakes, ants and worms dug their way in and out of their bodies.[33]

'Disloyalty to men' is a conveniently loose term open to a wide variety of interpretations.

We are not told whether Hell existed before the war in Heaven, but it certainly existed afterwards, when Lucifer lost his heavenly status. Isaiah apparently describes this landmark event:

> How art thou fallen from heaven
> O day-star, son of the morning! *(Helel ben Shahar)*
> How art thou cast down to the ground,
> That didst cast lots over the nations!

And saidst in thy heart:
'I will ascend into heaven,
Above the stars of God *(El)*
Will I exalt my throne;
And I will sit upon the mount of meeting,
In the uttermost parts of the north;
I will ascend above the heights of the clouds;
I will be like the Most High *(Elyon)*.'
Yet thou shalt be brought down to the nether-world,
To the uttermost parts of the pit.[34]

While the putative existence of this once-great, but apparently anonymous, hero of Heaven provides the opposing force to God's goodness – and to a cynic an excuse for the evils of the world – in fact the passage quoted above may well simply be an allusion to a Phoenician or Canaanite myth about Helel, son of the god Shaher, who, coveting the almighty god's throne, was cast down into the abyss. But while in northern Syria there is an ancient poem about Shaher (dawn) and Shalim (dusk) – two divine offspring of the god El – no mention is made in the Canaanite sources of a Lucifer figure or a revolt against God.

Lucifer was also associated with the Assyro-Babylonian light-ning god, Zu the Storm Bird, sometimes known as 'the fiery flying serpent'. He was condemned for seeking Zeus' Tablets of Destiny, given to him by his mother, the goddess Tiamat. Zu cried: 'I will take the tablet of destiny of the gods, even I; and I will direct all the oracle of the gods; I will establish a throne and dispense commands, I will rule over all the spirits of Heaven!'[35]

However, the description of the fallen one in the passage quoted above is seen as a clue to his identity by many Apocalyptic writers and Christians, particularly evangelicals or fundamentalists. 'How art thou fallen from heaven O day-star, son of the morning!' is taken as a reference to Lucifer, whose name means 'Light-bringer', and therefore by extension is associated with the radiant Morning Star, the perfect symbol of hope that comes with each bright new day. Lucifer is identified as the former hero of heaven who chal-lenged God, lost, and, together with his faithful angelic hordes, was exiled to Hell. Milton writes of the agonies of the fallen being, once

God's favourite, now the personification of evil as Satan: 'Apostate Angel, though in pain/Vaunting aloud, but rack'd with deep despair'.[36]

The first book of the apocryphal book of Enoch refers to the falling angels as stars, listing them by name as 'Semiazaz, Arakiba, Rameel, Kokabiel, Tamiel, Danel, Ezeqeel, Baraqijal, Asael, Armaros, Batarel, Ananel, Zaqiel, Samsapeel, Satarel, Turel, Jomjael and Sariel'.[37] Perhaps this passage was the origin of the confusion between the story of the Watchers – the angels who were overcome with lust for human women and fathered a race of giants with them – and Isaiah's story. Later Christian writers such as Saint Jerome also associate the fallen being described in Ezekiel 28: 13–15 with Lucifer:

You were in Eden, the garden of God;
Every precious stone was your adornment:
Carnelian, chrysolite, and amethyst;
Beryl, lapis lazuli, and jasper;
Sapphire. Turquoise, and emerald;
And gold beautifully wrought for you,

Mined for you, prepared in the day you were created.
I created you as a cherub
With outstretched shielding wings;
And you resided in God's holy mountain;
And walked among the stones of fire.
You were blameless in your ways,
From the day you were created
Until wrongdoing was found in you
By your far-flung commerce
You were filled with lawlessness
And you sinned.
So I have struck you down
From the mountain of God,
And I have destroyed you, O shielding cherub,
From among the stones of fire.

Here a great anti-hero's dazzling radiance is emphasized: he is hung about with the world's greatest riches, resplendent with the most fabulous jewels and gold. But he transgressed through his 'far-flung commerce' apparently suggesting an unpopular trading deal – which is a little odd but meaning 'social relations' or even 'sexual intercourse', – and lost it all. Worse than bankruptcy by far, however, was the fact that he has been *struck down* 'From among the stones of fire', brought to the lowest state imaginable, apparently both materially and spiritually. Superficially this story seems to reinforce that of the fallen angel in Genesis, stressing the terrible dynamics of Luciferan exile.

Once again, though, there are other interpretations: it has been argued that this passage actually refers to the proud king Nebuchadnezzar, who suffered a dramatic fall from grace.[38] But the associations with Lucifer persist, although not always in the context of evil. The Morning Star god, the Canaanites' Shaher, is still commemorated in the Jewish Shaharit or Morning Service.[39] His twin brother, the Evening Star Shalem, announces the daily death of the sun and utters the Word of Peace, *shalom*. The twin gods were openly worshipped in the 'House of Shalem' – or Jerusalem.

Their female parent was the Great Mother goddess Asherah, or Helel, the pit. The Canaanites believed that Shaher sought to usurp the glorious sun god, but was defeated and cast down from heaven as a lightning bolt. A seventh-century pagan dirge to the fallen one reads:

> How hast thou fallen from heaven, Helel's son Shaher! Thou didst say in thy heart, I will ascend to heaven, above the circum-polar stars I will raise my throne, and I will dwell on the Mount of Council in the back of the north; I will mount on the back of a cloud, I will be like unto Elyon.[40]

The prototype for the story of Lucifer's fall originated in the Persian myth of Ahriman, the Great Serpent or Lord of Darkness, who challenged his rival, the sun god, Ahura Mazda, the Heavenly Father. ('Ahura' was once a feminine name.[41] As Jean Markale notes: 'Ahura-Mazda was originally a luminous being who materialized in the form of a female goddess.')[42] Being cast out of Heaven, Ahriman tempted the first man and woman in his guise as the Serpent, and prophets declared he would be defeated for ever at the end of the world. But he was Ahura-Mazda's *twin*, from the womb of Infinite Time, the Primal Creatress, not his inferior. In fact, Ahriman is honoured for having created the physical world, and became a major influence on the cult of Mithras – another dying-and-rising god – as 'Armanius', the secret god of magic. The Persian emphasis on opposite-but-equal gods of Light and Dark enjoyed a renaissance in the beliefs of the Christian Gnostics, as we shall see.

In some versions of Lucifer's fall, Lucifer fought and lost to the archangel Michael, who remains for ever his personal enemy. (Both angels had shared similar characteristics, being associated with light and fire.) However, some of the angelic host refused to take sides and – somehow – managed to remain neutral, and will resurface later as central characters in the myths surrounding the Holy Grail.

In the last book of the Bible, the New Testament Revelation, the story is told thus:

> And there was a war in heaven. Michael and his angels fought against the dragon, and the dragon and his angels fought back. But he was not strong enough, and they lost their place in heaven. The great dragon was hurled down – that ancient serpent called the devil, or Satan, who leads the whole world astray. He was hurled to the earth, and his angels with him.[43]

Revelation also tells us that 'the dragon's tail swept a third of the stars out of the sky and flung them to earth,[44] which is taken to mean that a third of Lucifer's angelic followers fell with him.

Later versions of the Fall describe Lucifer being angered because God created a brother for him, Jesual the Son, from whose head sprang Sin, who in turn gave birth to Death. It was only after suffering this extra humiliation that Lucifer was ejected from his heavenly home.

According to Milton, the heavenly hosts – presumably slightly ruffled by Lucifer's dramatic exit from their number but no doubt rather smug at having made the wiser choice to remain in Heaven – were divided up into the following hierarchical categories: Powers,

Seraphim, Cherubim, Thrones, Dominiations, Virtues, Princi-
palities, Archangels and finally, angels. Although much favoured in
recent years, especially by the New Age, angels were originally
merely God's messengers, and often took the form of ordinary men.

However, in the first century CE the account of the Fall in Genesis
was not the only story of mankind's earliest days that circulated
among both Christians and Jews. Certain apocryphal tales loosely
based on Genesis 6 began to circulate.

> When men began to multiply on earth, and daughters were born
> to them, the sons of God saw the daughters of men, that they
> were fair.[45]

The 'sons of God' being angels, their subsequent enthusiastic
coupling with Eve's descendants was a blatant transgression of
God's law, but in any case their offspring became the half-human,
half-angel 'giants' (or 'heroes' in some versions) in the 'earth . . .
the mighty men of renown', whom later writers had no compunction about categorizing as demons. (The early Christians believed
they were constantly at the mercy of attack from demons of all
sizes, often quite literally. Saint Paul ruled that women's heads
should be covered in church 'because of the angels',[46] for there was
a real fear that female hair attracted *daemones* (other-worldly
entities), much as jam attracts ants. The veils were therefore seen as
sensible precautions, a sort of holy mosquito net.)

Another, non-biblical, myth has God calling his angels together
to admire his latest creation – Adam. The archangel Michael
obediently enthused, but Lucifer was horrified, demanding to know
'Why do you press me? I will not worship one who is younger than
I am, and inferior. I am older than he is; he ought to worship *me*!
[My emphasis].'[47]

Us and them

As Elaine Pagels points out in her excellent *Origin of Satan* (1995),
all the stories of the Fall, both biblical and non-biblical, 'agree on
one thing: that this greatest and most dangerous enemy did not
originate . . . as an outsider, an alien, or a stranger. Satan is not the
distant enemy but the intimate enemy – one's trusted colleague,

close associate, brother.'[48] Just like Judas, who was to bring about Jesus' torture and death according to a heavenly script, Satan brings about mankind's freedom of choice, although – as we have seen – he may have done so from almost altruistic motives.

Pagels notes that

Whichever version of his origin one chooses, and there are many, all depict Satan as an *intimate* enemy . . . Those who asked, 'How could God's own angel become his enemy?' were thus asking, in effect, 'How could one of us become one of *them*?'[49]

But while an eagerness to divide the world into rigid categories of 'Us' and 'Them' is nothing new – the Greeks called foreigners 'barbarians' and, tellingly, the Egyptians' word for themselves was simply 'human' – the western Christian tradition degraded its enemies as primarily nonhuman: if they challenged Christianity *they were God's enemies*.

(Yet of course God himself had behaved reprehensibly in the story of the Fall. As Jean Markale writes:

. . . the Eternal God is bad-natured and horrendously jealous, and . . . he behaves like a rich capitalist who has no intention of sharing his eternity with anyone else. For what pleasure would there be in it if everybody had it?)[50]

While sadly it seems to be a human failing to dismiss those outside the tribe or church as unworthy of the same rights and considerations, the Christians made this a moral and religious issue, which gave their later persecutions a fanatical edge as they used this attitude 'to justify hatred, even mass slaughter'.[51] As we shall see, this justification was used to extremes by the Inquisitors, largely against 'heretics' – free thinkers, Christian dissenters, or women – but 'revulsion at this doctrine is one of the main reasons for the decline of belief in the Devil since the eighteenth century'.[52] However, while the Jews have tended to dismiss the importance of the Fall as simply an allegory of evil, for many Christians the story of Lucifer remains potent.

Lucifer is also depicted as the immortal serpent Sata, ruler of lightning, who takes on the Hebrew name Satan in Jesus' words: 'I beheld Satan as lightning fall from heaven'.[53] However, 'Satan' as a synonym for 'Lucifer' became 'official' among Christians in the late first and second centuries, with the theological writings of Church Fathers Origen (born 185 CE) and Saint Augustine (354–430) – indeed, some theologians argue that Origen was the first to make this connection.[54]

To the famous Greek philosopher Plato, the god associated with the Morning Star was Aster (which means simply 'Star'); Plato realized that it had a strange, dual personality, for it also appeared in a different celestial position in the evening. Plato lauded Aster as the ultimate dying-and-rising god, exclaiming: 'Aster, once, as Morning Star, light on the living you shed. Now, dying, as Evening Star, you shine among the dead.'[55]

Adversary and obstructor

A major tendency of Judaeo-Christian thought is that God's opposite is a *Satan*, an 'obstructor' of his will – which becomes, in New Testament Greek, *diabolos*, the Devil. But while the New Testament and the early Christians became increasingly concerned with building up Satan's role as they themselves fell prey to the barbarians and executioners, the Jews were, in the words of the American scholar Jeffrey Burton Russell 'moving decisively in the other direction'. He explains: '[To the Jews] evil results from the imperfect state of the created world or from human misuse of free will, not from the machinations of a cosmic enemy of the Lord'.[56]

In the older Jewish traditions Satan is known as Sammael, a

high angel who falls, uses the serpent to tempt Adam and Eve, and acts as tempter, accuser, destroyer and angel of death . . . Satan has no existence independent of the Lord, who uses him as tester of hearts, an agent who reports our sins to the Lord, and an official in charge of punishing them.[57]

Satan continued to lose his personal glamour where the Jews are concerned: by the 1940s he had dwindled to 'little more than an allegory of the evil inclination among humans'.[58] This sophisticated interpretation remains fairly constant today, certainly among

Liberal Jewish congregations. Christianity was, and often still is, rather different in this respect.

In the New Testament, Satan is *Antikeimenos*, the Adversary or enemy, the 'archon of this age' – *arction ton aiomon touton* – or 'ruler' of the early Christian era, according to the Church Father Saint Ignatius, Bishop of Antioch. Since the Fall, the Devil had held sway over humanity, but now the incarnation of Jesus, God's son, has shaken his influence, which will finally be exploded by the 'Parousia', or Second Coming of Christ. In the meantime, however, the individual can ensure a place in Heaven via the doctrine of Atonement, a phrase first used by William Tyndale in the first English translation of the New Testament, in 1526. In fact, he had to invent the word – meaning 'at-one-ment' – to convey the now-familiar idea of reconciliation, itself a term that did not exist in his day.[59] This is also found in the later King James' or 'Authorized' version of 1611, in New Testament passages such as 'We also [have] joy in God through our Lord Jesus Christ, by whom we have now received the atonement'.[60]

However, Jesus became the man-god substitute for a much older idea of the Jewish scapegoat, when the chosen animal was ritually heaped with the sins of the people and sent off into the wilderness to die. But as Barbara Walker explains, 'The Jews' Yom Kippur, Day of Atonement, was based on the Sumero-Babylonian *kupparu*, an atonement ceremony in which a sheep was ceremonially loaded with all the community's sins, and killed.'[61] Jesus was symbolized as the sacrificial Lamb of God – although certain heretics, as we shall see, had a startlingly different version of this concept.

The New Testament declares 'Thanks be to God, who gives us the victory through our Lord Jesus Christ:'[62] that is, victory over 'sin, death, and Satan'.[63] This triumph was accomplished by Christ's willing death upon the cross, and the spilling of his holy, redemptive blood. As it says on posters outside countless churches: 'Christ died for your sins.' Jesus *atoned* for the sin of Adam and Eve by his sacrifice, and in dying became our *saviour*. After the doors of Paradise were slammed shut, his blood was the price that re-opened them. However, to non-theologians this presents a complex and rather contradictory conundrum, for if Christ has already died for our sins, why do we need to be baptized, live a good life, and die in a state of grace to hope to reach Heaven? This scenario had not bypassed the Church Fathers: as Barbara Walker notes:

> Among medieval theologians there was a general opinion that Jesus' sacrifice was not really effective; only 'a few' were saved by the Savior's death. St Thomas Aquinas and others claimed the vast majority of people were still doomed to eternal suffering in hell.[64] Thus the theory of atonement for all time or for all humanity was actually denied by the same church that pronounced it as a basis for worldly power.[65]

Take the concept of Atonement out of the picture, however, and it makes more sense, for baptism is an outward and visible sign of the individual's cleansing of sin and commitment to lead a good Christian life and deny the Devil. In fact, the early Christians were exorcized before being baptized – no doubt a considerably tougher and perhaps even more traumatic ritual than today's polite dips and modestly clad dunkings. This was hardly surprising, as the precursor of the Christian rite also took that form, the Egyptian baptisms in grand temples dedicated to Isis and Osiris on the banks of the Nile were preceded by public confessions of sins, and dramatic exorcisms.[66]

Exorcism was necessary for, as we have seen, demons were genuinely believed to be everywhere, in the food the good Christians ate and the wine they drank, in the sidelong glance of a young woman at the well, even in the uncovered tresses of a nubile girl. To the early Christian, everyday life was beleaguered by Satan, a paranoia that in a sense was justified, for who knew which kindly seeming person was actually a spy, about to deliver them up to their pagan persecutors?

Of course all pagans were deemed to be inherently heretics, followers of the Devil, although, according to the Church Father Irenaeus, a heretic was any individual whom a bishop had singled out as a heretic. As Jeffrey Burton Russell remarks dryly, 'Since no objective definition of "heretic" is possible, this definition was almost inevitable.'[67]

The pagans were clearly satanic, for their gods had even dared

mimic Christ's life and death. The Egyptian Osiris, the Persian
Tammuz and the Roman Mithras – not to mention several other
dying-and-rising gods, such as the Greek Orpheus and Dionysus –
were born at the winter solstice around 25 December in humble
surroundings such as caves, their nativity attended by new stars,
shepherds and Magi. They all died (on a Friday) in spring, to be
resurrected miraculously a few days later. Incredibly, even today,
some Christians explain away this awkward fact as a sort of diabolical parody on the part of the pagan myth-makers, even though this
stretches blind faith rather thinly as most of these stories predated
the life of Jesus by hundreds, perhaps thousands, of years.
Sometimes it is suggested that at best these stories were invented as
a *rehearsal*, a sort of feeble dry run for the real thing.[68]

Even membership of the Church was no guarantee of a pristine
soul. Bishop Ignatius declared that anyone who acted without
the approval of his bishop was a Devil worshipper, although he
admitted to being tempted himself by Satan to shirk his 'duty' of
martyrdom – an interesting theological and moral point. Here we
have the Devil tempting him to save his life and the good God
requiring him to commit a form of suicide, although of course that
is a modern view, for which, no doubt, some wretched demon
would have been blamed, had it been voiced in those far-off days.
Ignatius wrote 'I long to suffer, but I do not know whether I am
worthy . . . I need the meekness in which the prince of this world
[Satan] is undone'.[69] As Jeffrey Burton Russell notes: 'Torture and
death were [Satan's] work, and even kindness on the part of the
pagans was a diabolical snare, since it might weaken the martyr's
resolve'.[70]

Distasteful though this holy masochism may seem to most
modern eyes – although Catholics are still encouraged to 'offer up
their suffering to God', who surely must be hoping for someone to
offer up their joy and pleasure by now – it must be remembered that
these zealots firmly believed that Christ was about to return at any
moment and claim his own. (In fact, it is highly unlikely that Jesus
ever intended to found a church for posterity, being apparently
firmly of the belief that the end of the world was imminent.
Certainly his disciples expected him to return in glory, signalling
the end, at any moment. Ironically, Saint Peter's founding of the

Church of Rome can be seen as the direct result of Christ's failure to return as promised in the Apostle's lifetime.) In the meantime a martyr's death would guarantee the early Christians eternal bliss.

Perhaps it was one way of glorifying, even simply of coping with, the persecutions that took the willing and unwilling alike and had them disembowelled by wild animals in the Colosseum or used as human torches. The arena became a potent metaphor for the battlefield between good and evil – indeed, an early Latin sermon depicts Satan as a gladiator attempting to ensnare the good Christians in his net,[71] a perhaps unfortunate analogy, reinforcing the image of the enemy's virility at their own expense. (And ironically, this early Christian insistence on those who cause pain and humiliation being evil – and who can doubt it? – sits uncomfortably with later Inquisitorial justification for its institutionalized sadism.)

Yet for at least the first two centuries of Christian belief there was no coherent set of articles of faith, not even a shared set of holy writings, a New Testament. Attitudes to the Fall of Adam and Eve and the nature of God and the Devil differed massively from Christian group to Christian group throughout the Roman Empire. This confusing state of affairs only ended when Constantine created a state religion out of Christianity, the old slaves' faith, in the fourth century CE. By then, of course, any individual or group who took a different line from that of the Catholic Church was anathema.

Lords of light and dark

Although most shared the view of Church Father Polycarp that 'Anyone who twists Christ's words to suit his own desires and says that there is no resurrection, or judgement is the first-born child of Satan',[72] there were always dissenters, who were inevitably accused of 'twisting Christ's words' to suit themselves. By and large, these were the Gnostics, who were to lose out to the Roman Church and, by doing so, become persecuted almost to extinction as the perceived servants of Satan. Certainly, they were to entertain some extremely thought-provoking notions about good and evil, even daring to reverse the usual role of God and Satan . . .

'Gnostic' derives from the Greek *gnosis*, which means knowledge, referring to a sense of personal relationship with the deity, maintained by intuition, revelation and incremental initiation.

Gnosticism was basically a knowledge of *self* – *Gnothi sea uton* – 'know thyself': 'what united the various Gnostic sects was the belief that the world is completely evil and cannot be redeemed.'[73] To them the world was so terrible that it could only be a shadowy, inferior realm, a grotesque parody of something far finer, more spiritual, which existed beyond our material senses.

Even the less extreme Gnostics assumed that the Creator himself was formerly a benign spirit who had fallen, like Lucifer. Indeed, they often identified this blind, ignorant and evil entity with the Devil, and, after the Greek Gnostics, called him the 'demiurge' or 'partial mover', the opposite to the prime mover, God. Robert McL. Wilson writes: 'The Demiurge of Gnostic theory is simply the Satan of Jewish and Christian theology . . . transformed by the dominant Gnostic pessimism into the creator of the world, its present ruler.'[74]

To the Gnostic it made no sense to debate the likely outcome of the battle between Good and Evil – or as they frequently symbolized it, Light and Darkness – if, as most Christians believed, the Devil was already known to be doomed to defeat. Like the ancient Persians, most Gnostics were dualists, seeing the world in a constant state of flux between the powers of equal but opposite forces of Light and Darkness. The only problem, to put it bluntly, was knowing which was which . . .

Although colourful, with their wild prophecies and speaking in tongues, the Gnostics' cosmology – apart from being immensely, not to say ludicrously, complex – was ultimately somewhat depressing, as acknowledged in the passage quoted above. They saw men and women as vulnerable slivers of spirit trapped in a gross fleshy package: to them originally mankind had been pure spirit, but had been caught by the evil aeon. Of course by espousing the idea that Yahweh was Satan, they were doomed to a not very peaceful future among the flock of the emergent established Church, the Roman Catholics.

It was usually left to the heretics to point out that there was a basic and disturbing discrepancy between the harsh, tyrannical Almighty of the Old Testament and Jesus' loving Father of the New Testament. Indeed, John Milton, who sought in his poem *Paradise Lost* famously to 'justify the ways of God to Man' – and only succeeded in firing up luminaries of the Romantic Movement such as Percy Bysshe Shelley and William Blake with admiration for Lucifer, who saw him as the hero of the work – wrote of a truly sadistic Yahweh:

Almighty . . .
Have left us this our spirit and strength
Strongly to suffer and support our pains
That we may so suffice his vengeful ire.[75]

He seems little better, and because of his status and omnipotence even worse, than the Inquisitorial torturers who revived their victims so they could suffer further agonies, even (as we shall see) pulling them half-consumed from the flaming pyre to writhe for an hour or two before returning them to the fire. God has ensured that Adam and Eve had enough 'spirit and strength' with which to suffer, to appease his own pathological anger. Yet even here, Milton seems unwilling to have the first man and woman wholly and irretrievably tormented, for although they were condemned 'to work and suffer' the situation was '*not without hope*'.[76] And while Satan was to suffer 'torture without end', this somehow represented 'Eternal justice'.

Indeed, many early Christians (and some more recent thinkers) became exercised over the vexed question of whether a just God would leave even Satan to languish in Hell for eternity – although gradually they came to accept that even the average sinner would be condemned to the infernal regions for ever. The Church Father, Clement of Alexandria, believed that in the fullness of time, all sinners – even Satan himself – might be saved. To Clement, the existence of free will meant that even the Devil retained the right to repent. But it was left to Origen to develop the concept of *apocatastasis*, 'the ultimate return of all beings, including Satan, to the God from which they sprang'.[77] Today the Vatican proclaims that even the most dyed-in-the wool sinner can be forgiven *by the Church*, if he is genuinely repentant.[78]

However, the Gnostics with their intense anxiety about the real nature of God, had not plucked the idea of a good Lucifer out of thin air. Their sympathy for the Fallen One was similar to the ancient Greeks' admiration for Prometheus (whose name means 'Forethought'), who stole fire from Zeus and gave it to mankind, only to be condemned to be chained to a mountaintop where his liver was torn out by 'his own totemic eagle and nightly restored to be devoured again'.[79] The wretched Prometheus lamented: 'I rescued mankind from the heavy blow that was to cast them into Hades . . . Mankind I helped, but I could not help myself.'[80] Admiring this altruistic anti-hero, and seeing in him true Luciferanism, Gnostic icons depicted Prometheus creating the first man out of clay – according to the Greek legend. Perhaps they saw behind the myth, for, like Lucifer, Prometheus, who gave Man the 'fire' of intelligence, was ultimately the loser. With his fellow Titans, the giant spirits who roamed the earth even before Zeus and his pantheon took up residence on Olympus, Prometheus lost the ensuing battle for supremacy, and was chained in bondage under the planet.

This story was one of the inspirations for the Judaeo-Christian 'war in heaven' and the fall of Lucifer,[81] although Prometheus seems also to have been the prototype for trickster gods, such as the Scandinavian Loki. According to Barbara G. Walker he played a trick on Zeus that also surfaced in the Old Testament in another guise:

> . . . Prometheus tricked Zeus into accepting the less edible parts of sacrificial animals, such as the fat and bones, on behalf of the gods, while human beings were allowed to consume the meat. This was not what Zeus intended, and he swore vengeance on both Prometheus and his human friends.[82]

Zeus was forced to accept the offal because he had made a sacred oath to take the sacrifice, but when the similar thing happened to Yahweh – the priests being instructed that they 'shall remove all the fat . . . and burn it on the altar as an aroma pleasing to the Lord'[83] – 'the Jews simply claimed that Yahweh preferred it'.[84]

Significantly, however, it was 'Prometheus' excessive contribution of rationalism'[85] that effectively brought the Olympian religion to its knees. Intuitive and mystical religious sentiments fade like the morning dew under the bright solar glare of too much thought, too much 'right-brain' logic. (We will also see this in action when the scientific Age of Enlightenment of the eighteenth century helped sweep away the religious dogma and superstition of the ages, although some claim that science itself has become the modern bigotry.)

To Christians, Lucifer fell because of his wicked presumption. Yet to an objective eye, the Church's story is all too neat, Lucifer's transformation being suspiciously swift. Somehow during the fall, between being God's favourite angel and arriving on earth/in hell, the radiant Son of the Morning had acquired much nastier characteristics than mere pride. The shining Lucifer had become *Satan*, the literal embodiment of all imaginable evils, a dark creature of mind-freezing horror, who knows no mercy or compassion. He presides over his hellish college of demons amid the eternal flames of punishment and conspires with them to lure mankind into their foul embrace. He is the ultimate vampire, the soul-sucker *par excellence*, whose chief triumph is to make men evil like him. His underlying *raison d'être* is to *kill hope*, although, as the 'Father of Lies', he will first deceive by offering whatever the seeker desires.

Despite Milton's best intentions, his Satan, compared to a God seriously in need of anger management, is comparatively normal. Once forced down to Hell – or 'Pandemonium', the abode of devils – Satan seems determined to make the best of it, as a sort of diabolical pioneer, declaring 'Here at last we shall be free',[86] and, classically: 'Better to reign in Hell than serve in Heav'n'.[87] And Milton depicts Hell as a sort of Parliament (perhaps he should know, having worked for Cromwell!), where the demons debate whether or not to try to recover Heaven, which sounds really rather democratic.

The early Christians themselves were often confused by the nature of evil and the character of God. Marcion, who was expelled from the Christian community in Rome in 144 CE for musing on the big question 'Whence is evil?' came to the conclusion that two gods must exist, the Old Testament demiurge, whom he also called the *conditor malorum*, 'author of evils', and *auctor diaboli*, 'maker of the Devil'.[88] The benevolent deity, on the other hand, was all-merciful, but – presumably because there is not much evidence of this characteristic in most people's lives – his ways must be hidden from humankind.

To the Muslims, the Devil is either 'Iblis' or 'Shaytan', a pagan Arabic term 'possibly derived from the roots "to be far from" or "to [be] born with anger".[89] He was originally one of the morally ambiguous, shape-shifting *djinn*, created by God out of fire. These impish beings are associated with graveyards and the underworld, and on occasion they can be 'trapped' into servitude as sorcerers' servitors. Satan himself can only tempt, never force, but he is remarkably successful, leading the righteous astray – specifically into apostasy, heresy and blasphemy.

Red god of the desert

Traditionally, the Hebrew *Shaitan* – who acted as arch-tempter in the Book of Job – is seen as deriving from the ancient Egyptian god Set,[90] but there is another, more unsettling and controversial association. Although this would hardly sit comfortably with traditional Judaism or a literal form of Christianity, Hebrew scholar Professor Karl W. Luckert notes an interesting parallel between the Old Testament God and the ass-headed Set (although he is often depicted as a jackal-like mythological beast), the ancient Egyptians' nearest equivalent to the Judaeo-Christian Devil. Once ruler of the pantheon, Set (or Seth) villainously killed and dismembered the good god Osiris, consort of Isis, the mother goddess. In some versions of the story, he also sexually abused both Isis and her son Horus. However, the Egyptians had no out-and-out Satan figure, no irredeemable evil god with no function or purpose except to torment and entrap humans. To them, all their gods were aspects of the one God, so in a sense Set was an equally valued part of the Creator with the likes of Osiris, or Thoth, god of learning and healing. Even Set had his uses, to balance the usefulness and goodness of the others, and therefore should not be blamed for it. (His was also a useful name to utter in spells, as in *The Book of the Dead*, where the soul uses it to pass by afterlife snares and obstacles, saying '. . . for I am great of magic, with the knife that issued from Seth, and my legs are mine for ever.')[91] Set also appears in the Old Testament in human form as Seth, 'the supplanter' of the Good Shepherd Abel.[92]

Nevertheless, Set ruled over a physical realm – an actual, geographical location – that the Egyptians knew from their everyday experience to be nightmarish. With only their narrow strip of verdant land hugging both banks of the Nile, on which they were totally dependent for food, they were vulnerable to famine and recognized the hellishly inhospitable nature of the surrounding 'red' desert – which was Set's kingdom. The Egyptians hated anything red, as can be seen from an invocation to Isis: 'Free me from all red things'.[93] In his *alter ego* as Typhon, Set was called 'the red-skinned one'.[94]

Yet Set's desert was exactly the same environment that the Old Testament God Yahweh seemed to favour, as he led Moses and the Israelites out of Egypt, as a cloud by day and a pillar of fire by night. Indeed, he seemed curiously loath to let his nomadic people escape from the never-ending wilderness, managing to keep them wandering on its sand for 'forty years' (usually taken to mean simply 'a long time'), while they managed to travel just as many miles, apparently going round in circles. And like a typical desert dweller, in the story of Adam and Eve's fall, Yahweh prefers to walk 'in the garden in the cool of the day'.[95] Luckert writes:

> As a desert god, Seth was known among Egyptians as the god of foreigners, of thunder, lightning and earthquakes . . .
> It has been told that Moses spoke to the Pharaoh in the name of the God of the Hebrews. (*Exodus* 5:3). To an Egyptian pharaoh that meant in the name of Seth.
> [...]
> The God who killed the firstborn sons of the Egyptians would have been Seth to them, the very god of desert-dwellers.[96]

It is interesting that Set combined the characteristics of both Yahweh and Lucifer, especially his association with lightning. The Egyptian pharaohs also descended into the earth as the serpent Sata, father of lightning, before their triumphant ascent into the heavens as the resurrected Osiris, where they literally became a star. The devout believed they could become immortal like Sata, by repeating the prayer in which they identified with him:

> I am the serpent Sata, whose years are infinite. I lie down dead. I am born daily. I am the serpent Sata, the dweller in the utter-

most parts of the earth. I lie down in death. I am born. I become new, I renew my youth every day.[97]

In the Gospel according to Luke Jesus describes Satan 'as lightning fall from heaven.'[98] Yet the nearest Egyptian god to the bright star Lucifer was the hawk-headed Horus, magically conceived by Isis and the murdered Osiris. Horus was Set's sworn enemy – so reminiscent of the Israelites' Yahweh, was no benevolent deity. But although he delighted in human folly, as we have seen, he had his uses. The Gnostics, like the ancient Egyptians – who rejoiced in the ultimate balancing triad, their Trinity of Father, Mother and Child – also saw a sort of essential balance in Good and Evil, the glue that kept the cosmos together. The Gnostic *Gospel of Philip* (rediscovered after nearly 1,500 years at Nag Hammadi in Egypt in 1945)[99] makes the point that: 'The Light and the Darkness, life and death, right and left, are brothers one for another.'[100]

A contemporary of the heretic Marcion, the Egyptian Valentine, arrived in Rome in 139 CE and caused an enormous stir, not least because of his 'complex, cluttered, emanationist mythology aimed primarily at the problem of evil'.[101] Yet running beneath all his babblings about eight 'higher aeons' and at least twenty-two lower ones that in his fevered world view encompassed the nature of the deity, was a straight challenge to the notion of original sin. He believed that Adam and Eve's rebellion against the evil Creator god was a gift to humankind, and the snake its benefactor for making us wise to the principles of good and evil, which Yahweh was intending to keep from us.

Largely because of this concept, other Gnostic groups, such as the Ophites (from the Greek *ophis*, 'snake') developed the tradition of the 'fortunate Fall' (*felix culpa*). Because of original sin, man could transcend puerile ignorance – or perhaps foolish innocence – and begin to make progress towards his own god-like status. But to most Gnostics, the snake remained the evil 'dragon', as in the New Testament Book of Revelation:

And there was a war in heaven. Michael [the archangel] and his angels fought against the dragon, and the dragon and his angels fought back. But he was not strong enough, and they lost their place in heaven. The great dragon was hurled down – that ancient serpent called the devil, or Satan, who leads the whole world astray. He was hurled to the ground, and his angels with him.[102]

However, although Luckert notes that both Set and Yahweh were associated with the hated colour red[103] it has been argued that the 'Scarlet Woman' of the New Testament's apocalyptic Book of Revelation owed her inspiration to a *female* Egyptian deity, the lioness-headed Sekhmet. Goddess of flame and destruction (like the Hindu Kali), her very fearsomeness seems to have inspired particular terror in the heart of Saint John the Evangelist, who is generally believed to have written the last book of the Bible. Although his authorship is by no means certain, there would have been a certain irony for – as we shall see – perhaps he had his own reasons for appreciating the archetypal Feminine.

The myth of Eve's fall came to associate all women and the concept of evil, but there are good reasons to link a certain historical woman with the powerful attraction of Lucifer . . .

CHAPTER TWO

The Devil and All Her Works

Sacrilegious and bizarre though it may seem to believers, arguably even the Bible does not claim that God, the Heavenly Father, created the world – or at least, that he did so alone and unaided. Although carefully obscured by both Jewish and Christian priests in the millennia since Genesis was compiled, the Hebrew that has been translated as the singular 'God' in the creation passages is actually the plural *elohim*, just as cherubim means more than one cherub. And by implication *elohim* encompasses both male and female – gods and goddesses.

However, *elohim* is often shortened to *El*, or God (*Ale* or *Allah* in Arabic), giving the spurious impression of one male god as ruler and creator of everything, while apologists continue to protest that the plural is merely used to indicate a plenitude of might. Be that as it may, the fact remains that even the familiar Yahweh was *not* alone at the beginning of all human life, for even that alpha and omega of male supremacy once had *a wife*.

Not only that, but in some versions of the story, she gave birth to Lucifer, while in others she had taken him as her lover. Worse, she herself had tumbled terribly from grace in men's eyes, becoming a demon, and metaphorically carrying all women with her. Together with Eve's fondness for fruit and snakes, the apparently shameful exit of God's wife from her exalted place as his consort and help-meet underpinned the collective unconscious of the Jews, followed by that of the Christians. The concept of women as unreliable, unpredictable pawns of the Evil One (and Eve at least had yet to experience premenstrual tension) informed their treatment of wives and daughters even up to the present day.

Wives were a problem for God from the beginning. According to Hebrew legends, Adam's first spouse was not the infamous Eve grown from his spare rib, but the even more troublesome Lilith, although she began life as the Canaanites' revered Baalat ('Divine Lady'). The story goes that as poor Adam was bored with having to take his pleasure with the beasts of the field he was compelled to marry Lilith (who must have been very flattered). It was not to be a marriage made in heaven, especially as she refused to obey the rules of Yahweh because she knew his secret, ineffable name.[1]

The new husband was appalled by Lilith's assertiveness in bed: she refused to lie beneath him in the 'missionary position' (anything other than the man-on-top position has traditionally been denounced as 'accursed' by both Muslims and Catholics). Unimpressed by Adam's declarations of male supremacy in which he cited God as his authority, she taunted his sexual technique before using her convenient wings to fly away. Then when God's angels arrived to take her back, she cursed them and threw herself enthusiastically into orgiastic sex with 'demons', who apparently knew a thing or two about pleasing a lady, producing a hundred children a day – all, of course, devilish.

Eve was much easier to cope with, although being a woman she still managed to get expelled from Paradise for bad behaviour. (But, as Jeffrey Burton Russell notes, although 'The story of Eden readily lent itself to an attack on women . . . In fact no good reason existed for blaming Eve for original sin any more than Adam.')[2]

Lilith is no longer found in the Bible, but she resurfaced in medieval times as nothing less than the Devil's mother, 'In parody of the Blessed Mother and the angels, she joins the ranks of demons singing praises round the throne of her son.'[3] In another version of her later myth, she and her daughters, the *ilim*, continued to wreak havoc in men's lives as lustful she-devils whose nightly attacks caused nocturnal emissions, against which medieval Jews carried talismans. (Like their notorious mother, the *ilim* always squatted on top of their male victims, apparently adding to the horror.) Christian monks lived in terror – or so they claimed – of an attack from 'the harlots of hell', or *succubae*, and slept with hands holding a crucifix uncomfortably crossed over their genitals to ward them off. 'It was said that every time a pious Christian had a wet dream, Lilith laughed . . .'[4] We may be amused at such an unsophisticated interpretation of a natural physiological phenomenon, but it must be remembered that to good Christian men, this was a truly terrifying attack, for they believed their souls were being sucked out of them together with their semen. Lilith's daughters – also called Lamia, Hora, Daughters of Hecate among other titles – caused 'men to dream of erotic encounters with women, so the *succubae* can receive their emission and make therefrom a new spirit.'[5]

In fact, one common name for the *succubae* was *Brizo*, after the Greek goddess of dreams whose title, in turn, came from *brizein*, 'to enchant'. 'Like Babylon's dream-goddess Nanshe, Brizo brought prophetic dreams which were subsequently identified as "wet" dreams.'[6]

Lilith and her brood were also designated as 'night hags', actually beautiful *succubae* whose lovemaking expertize was so exquisite that once mortal men experienced it they could never be satisfied ever again by coupling with ordinary human women. But she-devil though she may be, Lilith's continuing power over both Jewish and Christian imaginations was clearly intense. As A. T. Mann and Jane Lyle write in their classic *Sacred Sexuality* (1995): 'In the Pyrenean cathedral of St-Bernard-de-Comminges, Lilith has found her way into a church: a carving there depicts a winged, bird-footed woman giving birth to a Dionysian figure, a Green Man.'[7] Dionysus was a middle-eastern rustic wine-god whose ceremonies included drunken orgies in which his priestesses, the Maenads, tore men to pieces.

The same area in the south of France where Lilith may be found in church has legends of Herodias – the wife of Herod who made Salome ask him for John the Baptist's head – having ended her days by drowning in a local stream. After which, she joined her sisters, the night hags, and still waits to swoop down on the unwary male traveller.

Of course there was a male version of the *succubae*, the *incubae* which lay with women as they slept. In medieval times it was often said that nuns awoke 'to find themselves polluted as if they had slept with men'[8] – in many, if not most, cases because they actually had. Some quick-thinking nuns claimed they had slept with Christ (possibly many believed that they had), but this was swiftly denounced as blasphemy resulting from demonic possession, despite the fact that they were known as 'Brides of Christ'.

Predictably, women who were believed to consort with demons – as we will see – caused more fear and horror among the God-fearing than the imps of Hell themselves. An Anglo-Saxon book suggested the use of magic potions – or rather 'holy salves' – not against the incubi themselves but against the women with whom Satan had allegedly fornicated. In Toulouse in the south of France in 1275 a woman of 56 was tortured until she confessed to nightly romps with an incubus and having given birth to 'the demon's child, which was half wolf and half snake'.[9] But as Barbara Walker notes grimly: 'Perhaps the ultimate irony was the church's official opinion that all the activities of *incubi* were performed "with the permission of God".[10] But what God allowed, men punished.'[11]

All that was in the bleak future, when men had discovered how to deal with the daughters of Eve and Lilith. Back at the beginning of all things, however, even Yahweh clearly had no idea how to cope with the latter bad girl – it seems never to have occurred to him to adopt the smiting mode that distinguished his later career – and his angels appear to have been similarly impotent in the face of her feisty response. Perhaps the Lord should have sought advice about how to deal with Lilith from his wife, who was already a force to be reckoned with in the ancient world. American Scholar William G. Denver wrote in 1984:

> Recent archaeological discoveries provide both texts and pictorial representation that for the first time clearly identify 'Asherah' as the consort of Yahweh, at least in some circles in ancient Israel ... We cannot avoid the conclusion that in Israel Yahweh could be closely identified with the cult of Asherah, and in some circles the goddess was actually personified as his consort.[12]

Excavations at Ras Shamra (ancient Ugarit) have unearthed 14th-century BCE tablets on which it states that the 'wife of El', the

'Progenitress of the God', or Asherah, was one and the same as most Mother Goddesses, including the Sumerian goddess Astarte[13] and the Phoenician Tanit, whose temple in Carthage was called the Shrine of the Heavenly Virgin, while the Greeks and Romans referred to it as a 'temple of the moon'.[14] Elath, on the coast of the Gulf of Aqaba, may have been named after the great goddess, who was clearly celebrated as the personification of the Feminine Principle throughout the Near and Middle East. Walker writes:

In Egypt [Asherah] was also a Law-giving Mother, Ashesh, an archaic form of Isis; the name meant both 'pouring out' and 'supporting', the functions of her breasts. Her yonic shrine in Thebes was Asher, Ashrel, or Ashrelt. Some called her 'Great Lady of Ashert, the lady of heaven, the queen of the gods.'[15]

The Canaanites called her Qaniyatu elima or 'She Who Gives Birth to the Gods', or Rabbatu athiratu yammi, Lady Who Traverses the Sea – in other words, the Moon.[16] All three major manifestations of the Great Mother were associated with the three phases of the Moon: the Virgin goddess with the New Moon, the Mother with the full Moon, and the crone or older wise woman with the dark of the Moon. Significantly, too, as Barbara Walker notes, 'Rabbatu was an early female form of rabbi'.[17] Wife of God *and* a rabbi! To the grey-bearded patriarchs this situation could not be allowed to last, whatever God's own views on the subject. (There is archaeological evidence that it was common for blessings to be invoked 'by Yahweh and his Asherah',[18] a turn of phrase that implies a touching, even tender, closeness.) Clearly Asherah's days of power were numbered.

Walker writes dryly: 'For a while, Asherah accepted the Semitic El as her consort' – a nice reversal of the usual situation with females in the Near East, especially in ancient times. Walker continues: 'She was the Heavenly Cow, he the Bull.[19] After their sacred marriage, she bore the Heavenly Twins, Shaher and Shalem, the stars of morning and evening . . .'[20]

As noted in Chapter One, the Morning Star was none other than Lucifer – and in this legend, literally the son of God. As the heir to the divine dynasty, his challenge to paternal authority can be seen in the context of the sacred kings of the Near and Middle East. The outgoing priest-king, possessed of magical powers and totemic representative of his tribe is ritually challenged – and often slain – by his successor. But Yahweh's priesthood was disinclined to permit its King-god to be challenged, and in any case rapidly buried the idea that God had a wife, let alone a child or children. Everything about Asherah soon became anathema – even the cooking of a kid in its mother's milk,[21] which was believed to have been involved in her marriage ceremony to Yahweh.

Yet not only was Asherah Yahweh's consort, but also, magically and paradoxically, his creator, sometimes honoured by the title 'Holiness', which later became her husband's (and, of course, the Pope's). She reigned jointly as supreme deity with Yahweh for 600 years, together with other lesser pagan gods, after the Israelite tribes arrived in Canaan.[22]

Had her star not waned, presumably Asherah might have been in a position to have had sharp words with Yahweh about his treatment of Eve – for originally she had the Law on her side. The Semitic 'Asherah' probably derives from the Old Iranian *asha*, meaning 'Universal Law', which some take to be synonymous with matriarchal law, 'like the Roman *ius naturale*'[23] (literally 'natural law'). Yahweh would have had to defer to her judgement.

Once, Asherah's influence was great among the ordinary Israelites, although they were soon to be denounced for her worship. In the Old Testament her name is often translated as 'grove', a reference to the sacred tree-lined places where the Great Mother was worshipped in the prior matriarchal period: 'They also set up for themselves high places, sacred stones and Asherah poles [carved fetish objects] on every high hill and under every spreading tree.'[24] However, the later Yahwists wasted no time in hacking the goddess' holy groves to pieces and even summarily burning her priests and followers on their altars – presumably not simply because they represented the goddess whose power they had come to hate and fear, but also because her devotees included the *qedishim/qadishim*.

These were cross-dressing young men, elaborately made-up and bejewelled who serviced the temple pilgrims, just like their female counterparts, as sacred prostitutes. Indeed, legends of Asherah tell of her special servant, 'Qadesh wa-Amrur', which is traditionally, but inaccurately, interpreted coyly as 'fisherman of Lady Asherah of the sea'. However, confusingly, 'qedesh' can also mean 'holy' or 'divine', presenting an intriguing dilemma in Biblical interpretation, especially where certain passages in the New Testament are concerned – as we will see . . .

There was even a shrine to Asherah in the Jerusalem Temple, as Hebrew scholar Raphael Patai points out:

> Of the 370 years during which the Solomonic Templae stood in Jerusalem, for no less than 236 years . . . the statue of Asherah was present in the Temple, and her worship was part of the legitimate religion approved and led by the king, the court, and the priesthood and opposed by only a few prophetic voices crying out against it at relatively long intervals.[25]

One shrine was raised by King Manasseh, in the form of an Asherah pole,[26] which the writer of the Old Testament book of 2 Kings utterly abhors as sacrilege both to the Lord God and to the memory of King Solomon, who had built the Temple. This was somewhat hypocritical, as Solomon himself was not averse to goddess-worship, as his biblical critics were fond of pointing out: 'As Solomon grew old, his [foreign] wives turned his heart after other gods, and his heart was not fully devoted to the Lord his God, as the heart of David his father had been. He followed Astoreth the goddess of the Sidonians . . . So Solomon did evil in the eyes of the Lord . . .'[27]

Solomon's fondness for the goddess was also singled out for condemnation by John Milton in his *Paradise Lost*:

> . . . Astoreth, whom the Phoenicians call'd
> > Asarte, Queen of Heav'n, with crescent Horns;
> > To whose bright image nightly by the Moon
> > Sidonian Virgins paid their Vows and Songs,
> > In Sion [Jerusalem] also not unsung, where stood
> > Her Temple . . . , built
> By that uxorious King, whose heart though large,
> > Beguil's by fair Idolatresses, fell
> > To idols foul.[28]

'That uxorious King' is the much-married Solomon, whose most politically ambitious union was with a daughter of a Pharoah who worshipped 'the Goddess of the Sidonians' – and of course this divinity was none other than Asherah.

Almost certainly one of Solomon's foreign women who 'turned his heart after other gods' was his lover, the legendary Queen of Sheba, whose fabulous kingdom of Sabia with its great city Marib formed part of the Yemen. Not much is known about her, apart from her fabulous wealth and her dazzling beauty – but she was apparently a black woman, 'dark, and comely', according to the erotic poem, the Old Testament Song of Songs.[29] But it is known that she carried the traditional title for Sabian queens of Makeda or Magda ('Great Lady'), and disappeared from history in Ethiopia, where it is believed she gave birth to Solomon's son. And she was a worshipper of the Sun (primal God) and Moon – a Mother Goddess, presumably a version of Asherah who, as we have seen, was called by the Canaanites *Qaniyatu elima* or 'She Who Gives Birth to the Gods', or *Rabbatu athiratu yammi*, Lady Who Traverses the Sea – in other words, the Moon. Whatever the source of his inspiration, Asherah would certainly have figured in Solomon's pantheon, despite defensive Israelite claims that he converted Sheba to the monotheism he himself notoriously failed to follow.

As the grip of the fiercely patriarchal Yahwists tightened, officially God no longer had a wife – indeed, to claim the contrary, or to honour her in any way, was to invite dire penalties. Because of the hatred of Yahweh's priests, Asherah, like the other goddesses who bore her archetypal stamp, was literally demonized, although a second – and arguably more vicious – cycle of diabolization of the ancient deities would take place under the later auspices of the Christian Church. From being creator and bride/mother of God and mother of Lucifer, the great goddess Asherah/Astarte/Isis/Ishtar became inherently evil. It is no coincidence that the Old Testament emphasizes the fact that four hundred of her prophets ate at the table of the wife of King Ahab (873-852 BCE), the loathed Jezebel – clearly they considered this sort of association to be typical of Asherah's devotees.

'Now I am nothing at all . . .'

The Great Mother also becomes a metaphor for Hell, although there is another, more intriguing, interpretation. When the Biblical writer tells Lucifer 'Thou shalt be brought down to hell, to the sides of the pit', according to Barbara Walker,

'this "pit" was a metaphor for Helel, or Asherah, the god's own Mother-Bride; and his descent as a lightning-serpent into her Pit represented fertilization of the abyss by masculine fire from heaven. In short, the Light-bringer challenged the supreme solar god by seeking the favors of the Mother.'[30]

The church fathers may translate Lucifer's sin – hubris – as 'pride', but, as Walker points out, 'its real meaning was "sexual passion".'[31] Although the Greek word does carry the meaning of 'pride', this also involves 'lechery', 'both words [being] associated with penile erection . . . Patriarchal gods especially punished hubris, the sin of any upstart who became – in both senses – "too big for his breeches".'[32]

Originally there was an Argive festival called Hubristika, or a 'Festival of Lechery' in which ordinary men 'broke a specific taboo' by dressing in women's clothes in order to assume their acknowledged magical powers. With the advent of Christianity, this festival was denounced as devil-worship, together with any other practice that implied a belief in the power of women.[33] Tellingly, Goddess-worshippers in the area now called Switzerland were compelled with the dominance of Christianity to desecrate the Great Mother's statues while reciting 'Once I was the Goddess and now I am nothing at all.'[34]

With the radical demotion of the goddesses, all things feminine were fair game. A version of the apocryphal Old Testament Book of Raziel tells how 'witchcraft and sorcery were imparted to woman by the fallen angels of Uzza and Azail, and also the use of cosmetics, which were ranked as wicked enchantments.'[35] Goddesses such as Isis-Hathor and Astarte were believed to impart all feminine secrets to their devotees, from using camel dung as contraceptives to casting spells to secure lovers.

However, Yahweh and his prophets did not suffer alone: other testosterone-fuelled deities had trouble with the Feminine. We have seen how the Greek Prometheus, like Lucifer, brought fire – symbolizing both civilization and intellectual inquiry – to humankind, against the will of Zeus, the all-powerful Olympian god. Empathizing with the sad fate of mankind, Prometheus acted out of compassion, to be rewarded by the eternal torture of having his liver eaten by his own totemic eagle, only to have it restored every night so the horrendous cycle could begin again. In Aeschlus' *Prometheus Bound* Prometheus mutters: 'Mankind I helped, but I could not help myself', and reflects bitterly on 'The mind of Zeus [that] knows no turning, and ever harsh the hand that newly grasps the sway.' However, he foresees a karmic punishment for Zeus at the hands of 'the Fates triform and the unforgetting Furies' – the children of Io, the Moon-cow goddess (like Isis-Hathor in Egypt), who had also suffered at the hands of Zeus.

However, while Zeus the all-powerful will be brought low by the feminine he has oppressed, unfortunately – or so it seems – the converse is true where the almighty Biblical Yahweh is concerned. Although there remain strong undercurrents of the Feminine in modern Judaism, it is not usually recognized, certainly among the Orthodox.

In this light, the Biblical description of Lucifer, the fallen one, as a 'shielding cherub' is particularly interesting. From the Hebrew K'rubh, which in turn is thought to derive from the Akkadian *karibu* – the *cherubim* were intermediaries between God and humanity, and not the morbidly obese infants with implausibly tiny wings so favoured by sentimental Victorians. In fact, a 'graven image' existed in the Jerusalem Temple that graphically depicted two Cherubim engaged in a sexual embrace, representing a sacred mystery. Interestingly, there is not a hint of condemnation of this image in Jewish literature, even though the people fornicated orgiastically after seeing these statues carried before them in religious processions. As Patai notes of this custom,

'Since one of the two Cherubim was a female figure, we find that, in addition to the Canaanite goddess whose worship was condemned by the Hebrew prophets and Jewish sages [Asherah], the Temple of Jerusalem contained a replica of the feminine principle which was considered legitimate at all times.'[36]

When Asherah was banished, the female cherubim lived on,

unmolested – although, eventually, only with their femininity obscured and forgotten.

Much as the Israelites were loath to admit it, they carried a great deal of Egyptian thinking away with them when Moses led their flight from slavery in the land of the pyramids. Not only did Yahweh himself evince characteristics of the Egyptian destroyer-god Set, but the Israelites also seem to have absorbed some of the feminine imagery of the dynastic age. Archaeologists excavating the palace of King Ahab of Israel (873-852 BCE) in Samaria discovered an ivory stele depicting two crouching female entities wearing distinctly Egyptian-style collars and clothes, and apparently holding the ceremonial lotus.

Raphael Patai suggests that they were really 'female genii', similar to the equally female Shekhina, who survived incognito as the Christian 'Holy Spirit', or the more blatantly feminine 'Sophia', the Gnostics' embodiment of wisdom. Patai writes:

> The Talmudic term 'Shekhina' denotes a tangible – visible and audible – manifestation of God on earth – yet originally 'the Shekhina concept stood for an independent, feminine divine entity prompted by her compassionate nature to argue with God in defense of man. She is thus, if not by character, then by function and position, a direct heir to such ancient Hebrew goddesses . . . as Asherah . . .[37]

Although the Shekhina as such do not appear in the Bible, they are represented there metaphorically as Hokma or 'Wisdom'. Intriguingly, Hokma may originate in one of the ancient titles of the Egyptian Isis, *Heq-Maa*, 'Mother of Magical Knowledge', which dates back to the days of the powerful *heq* or tribal wise woman. Its derivative, the later Greek Hecate, or Wise Crone, was associated with the dark phase of the Moon and women's mysteries, including the secrets of life and death. The Neoplatonist scholar Porphyry (c. 234-305 CE) wrote in praise of her: 'The moon is Hecate, the symbol of her varying phases . . . Her power appears in three forms, having as symbol of the new moon the figure in the white robe and golden sandals, and torches lighted; the basket which she bears when she has mounted high is the symbol of the cultivation of crops which she made to grow up according to the increase of her light.'[38]

With historical inevitability, the much-loved Hecate was to become one of the Christians' names for the Queen of Hell, while her threefold power was absorbed into Christianity by the medieval clergy who metamorphosed it into 'The threefold power of Christ, namely in Heaven, in earth, and Hell.'[39] But, as we will see, Hecate was especially singled out for anathema by the Church because of her alleged conspiracy with midwives to subvert the natural order by helping women, either by easing their pains or aborting unwanted foetuses – in other words, helping women to empower themselves.[40] In a garbled version of this, in one old tradition, Satan's wife Lilas was supposed to hover about the birth-bed and kill newborns.[41]

In the Old Testament Book of Proverbs Hokma/Wisdom, the predecessor of Hecate, has a major role to play:

> Does not wisdom call out?
> Does not understanding raise her voice?
> . . . she takes her stand . . . and cries aloud:
> 'To you, O men, I call out;
> I raise my voice to all mankind.
> You who are simple, gain prudence;
> You who are foolish, gain understanding.
> Listen, for I have worthy things to say;
> I open my lips to speak what is right.
> My mouth speaks what is true,
> For my lips detest wickedness . . .
> They are faultless to those who have knowledge.
> Choose my instruction instead of silver,
> Knowledge rather than choice gold,
> For wisdom is more precious than rubies,
> And nothing you desire can compare with her.'[42]

The section of Proverbs known as the Proverbs of Solomon reinforces Wisdom's gender: 'Wisdom reposes in the heart of the discerning/and even among fools she lets herself be known'.[43] Proverbs also states that Wisdom, with her Aphroditean symbol of the dove, was God's first creation, and ever since as the Shekhina, in Patai's words, 'she has been God's playmate'.[44] Seemingly a Tinkerbell-like creature[45] of darting intelligent light, the Shekhina was believed to possess a mind of her own, which she never hesitated to use in performing her function of influencing, even opposing, God. Clearly a feisty being capable of being tough with Yahweh had no very rosy future. As Patai notes:

> From about 400 BCE to 1100 CE the God of Judaism was a lone and lofty father-figure, and whatever female divinity was allowed to exist in his shadow was either relegated to a lower plane, or her femininity was masked and reduced to a grammatical gender, as in the case of the Shekhina.[46]

Too like Christ for comfort

With the spread of Christianity, the old gods – both male and female – of the Mediterranean and Middle East were rapidly and hysterically demoted to the rank of demons, often because their legends were too similar to Jesus' story for comfort. The dying-and-rising god Tammuz, whose consort was Ishtar-Mari, had reached Jerusalem via Babylon and before that, Sumer, as 'Son of the Blood' or 'only-begotten Son'. As a dying-and-rising god with a major cult centre in Jerusalem, Tammuz is believed by some to be one of the prototypes of Christ: his cradle was made from a grain basket, similar to Jesus' manger, for example.[47] He was the sacrificial Lamb of God, Heavenly Shepherd, Man of Sorrow, and sometimes bore the name 'Usirir', a variation of 'Osiris', the hugely influential dying-and-rising god of ancient Egypt, who was dismembered by the evil Set, who in turn was arguably the prototype for Yahweh. Osiris, together with his consort Isis and son Horus, formed the great Egyptian Trinity of Father, Mother and Child, revealing a much more psychologically balanced psyche that the Church's apparently all-male 'Father, Son and Holy Spirit' – although the latter was in fact the feminine Shekhina, or Sophia. (This is yet another example of a fact that theologians have long known and seminaries taught generations of priests, yet the average church-goer remains in ignorance of what would no doubt prove a comfort in a largely male-dominated organization.) The Egyptians sought balance above all things: the beneficent Isis was balanced by her dark aspect, the goddess Nepthys, while opposite to the 'Good Shepherd' Osiris was Set, Yahweh's apparent prototype.

Ruler over the afterlife and human and agricultural regeneration, Osiris possessed over 200 divine titles, including 'King of Kings', 'Lord of Lords', 'the Good Shepherd' (a title shared with his consort Isis), and 'the Resurrection and the Life'. The great Egyptologist Sir E. A. Wallis Budge wrote: 'From first to last, Osiris was to the Egyptians the god-man who suffered, and died, and rose again, and reigned eternally in heaven. They believed that they would inherit eternal life, just as he had done.'[48] According to ancient Egyptian writings: 'As truly as Osiris lives, so truly shall his followers live; as truly as Osiris is not dead he shall die no more; as truly as Osiris is not annihilated he shall not be annihilated.'[49]

Disconcertingly for Christians, the ancient god Osiris' advent was heralded by the sound of an angelic choir and by the Three Wise Men, although they took the form of the stars Mintaka, Anilam, and Alnitak in Orion's Belt, pointing to Christ's equivalent of the Star of Bethlehem. Originally the Israelites acknowledged this as 'Ephraim', or the 'Star of Jacob', whereas to the Persians it was nothing less than the Messiah – Messaeil. As Barbara Walker notes, Osiris'

flesh was eaten in the form of communion cakes of wheat, the 'plant of truth'. Osiris was truth, and those who ate him became truth also, each of them another Osiris, a Son of God, a 'Light-god, a dweller in the Light-god'. Egyptians came to believe that no god except Osiris could bestow life on mortals.[50]

Like the rites of Tammuz, the annual Osirian mystery plays required the priestess playing the widowed Isis to lament his murder on the Egyptian Good Friday, setting the scene for the miracle of his resurrection two days later. Bizarrely, Osiris as Un-nefer, 'the Good One', was actually canonized as a Christian saint.

In Ezekiel's day, women sat by the northern gate of the Temple weeping for the annual death of Tammuz, the 'Christos' (simply 'Anointed One'), the sacred king ritually sacrificed each year at Jerusalem. The women first dedicated him to his mother/bride Ishtar-Mari, Queen of Heaven,[51] another manifestation of Asherah.

As his female devotees gathered annually at the temple gates they raised ritual howls that the Greeks called *houloi*, crying 'All-Great Tammuz is dead!' and lamenting:

'For him that has been taken away there is wailing; ah me, my child has been taken away . . . my Christ that has been taken away, from the sacred cedar where the Mother bore him. The wailing is for the plants, they grow not . . . for the flocks, they produce not; for the . . . wedded couples, for . . . children, the people of Sumer, they produce not . . .'[52]

(The concept of the death of the god causing the land to be infertile resurfaces in the quasi-Christian legend of the Fisher King.)

Like all the other 'Good Shepherds', 'Saviours' and 'Fishers of Men', Tammuz was diabolized by the Church, even becoming Hell's ambassador to Spain, where he was still worshipped by certain Moorish sects in medieval times.[53] (His name, which means 'twin', transmutes into Jesus' disciple Thomas, suggesting a cultic link with the ancient dying-and-rising god – and possibly, an intriguing clue to a secret about Christ's family.)

Tammuz and Osiris were not the only much-honoured ancient deities to be assigned to Hell with the coming of Christianity. John Milton in his epic poem *Paradise Lost* exults over their demise, declaring:

> Old gods confused with incubi/evil spirits
> Of Baalim and Ashtaroth [sic], those male,
> Those Feminine. For spirits when they please
> Can either Sex assume, or both; so soft
> And uncompounded is their Essence pure.[54]

Milton lists the names of the fallen gods with some relish, including: 'Astoreth, whom the Phoenicians call'd/Astarte, Queen of Heav'n, with crescent horns', together with Adonis and 'Thammuz yearly wounded', and not forgetting 'Osiris, Isis, [H]Orus and their Train/With monstrous shapes and sorceries abus'd/Fanatic Egypt and her Priests'.[55] Together with the golden calf of Moses' apostate followers and a huge tribe of gods and idols, they are all swept away into the infernal regions with the coming of Jesus Christ.

Et in Arcadia Ego

Astarte's horns, representing the new moon – as they did in the iconography of many other lunar goddesses, including Isis and Diana – were important evidence of devilish influence to the later Christians. However, it was a male deity of the ancient world who was to provide the physical model for the medieval Satan – horns, tail, cloven hooves and all the trappings of Hell. This was the once 'all-great Pan', the king of Greek satyrs, the ultimate woodland god – perhaps Arcadian – whose limitless libido, once so admired and envied among his devotees, became a source of terror for Christian women. The Goat-God, sometime mate of various forms of goddess such as Selene, Athene and Penelope – and, apparently, *all* the ferocious Maenads – his furry thighs, curly hair growing luxuriantly around budding horns and lascivious, almond-shaped eyes, was seen as the epitome of lust. Many of his idols were even impressively, and shamelessly, ithyphallic. No fig leaves obscured Pan's proud masculinity, probably because no fig leaves could possibly cover it.

In his essay on the Tarot card 'The Devil', Aleister Crowley notes tellingly '. . . the card represents Pan Pangenetor, the All-Begetter . . . the masculine energy at its most masculine.'[56] He describes the function of Pan, even in his less-than-acceptable mode: 'All things equally exalt him. He represents the finding of ecstasy in every phenomenon, however naturally repugnant; he transcends all limitations; he is Pan; he is All.'[57] Undoubtedly the worship of Pan required a strong stomach and a feverish libido, but as challenger to the staid and small-minded he exemplified a true *Luciferan* spirit, while never being, as so widely believed, the embodiment of *Satan*. Horns and hooves alone do not the Devil make.

The Greeks believed the Egyptian solar god Amen-Ra to be another version of Pan – the Masculine Principle being almost universally associated with the Sun, just as its opposite and equal Feminine Principle was usually (but not exclusively) personified by the lunar goddesses – calling his sacred city 'Panopolis', city of Pan. Its sacred processions became our modern English *panoply*, meaning 'Any imposing array that covers or protects,'[58] such as complete armour worn ceremonially. 'Panoply' comes from 'Pan' and *hoplon*, meaning weapon. Pan's own name in turn possibly derived from *paein*, pasture, and also carried the meaning of 'bread' (as in the modern French *pain*) and 'all' (as in 'Pan American Airlines'). Other 'all-fathers' such as Osiris and Tammuz were symbolized by sacred bread, eaten in order to ingest wisdom. In their sacramental meals, the bread also represented the flesh of the god, and wine symbolized their blood. In an ancient legend concerning the dying-and-rising poetic divinity Orpheus, finding only water to drink, he turned it magically into wine.

Like those of his brother gods, Pan's holy drama of death and resurrection was celebrated annually, providing the original Greek *tragoidos*, or 'Goat Song', as he fertilized the land. Pan-inspired sexual revels lasted well into the Christian era, together with elements of worship from the cult of the Maiden, as the May Day festivities where maidens danced around the phallic maypole before coupling – perhaps indiscriminately – with the local lads, much to the Church's impotent disgust.

Cromwell's Puritan Protectorate banned maypoles, along with virtually everything else that made life worth living. To the Puritans, the sexual licence involved in the festivals was bad enough, but in some areas the 'Mai', or Maiden who gave her name to the month, was even associated somewhat confusedly with the Popish Virgin Mary! The crude symbolism of the maypole was understood, if not accepted, by Cromwell's co-religionists, such as the writer Philip Stubbes, whose detailed description of the festivities seems a little fevered:

Young men and maids, old men and wives, run gadding overnight to the woods, groves, hills, and mountains, where they spend all night in pleasant pastimes; and in the morning they return, bringing with them birch and branches of trees to deck their assemblies withal. And no marvel, for there is a great Lord present amongst them, Satan, prince of hell. But the chiefest jewel they bring from thence is their May-pole, which they bring home with great veneration . . . two or three hundred men, women and children following it with great devotion. And this being reared up . . . they strew the ground about, bind green boughs about it, set up summer halls, bowers and arbours hard by. And then they fall to dance about it, like as the heathen people did at the dedication of Idols, whereof this is a perfect pattern, or rather the thing itself.[59]

May Day was so indelibly associated with ancient pagan rites across Europe that in France church bells were rung all that month 'to protect the city from flying witches'.[60] And although May itself is still regarded by the superstitious as unlucky, it is especially inauspicious to marry on a Friday in May, Fridays traditionally being sacred to goddesses such as the Nordic Freya, who gave her name to the weekday.

The goat-footed one also gave his name to our 'panic', 'originally the terrible cry of Pan, who dispersed his enemies with a magic yell that filled them with fear and took away all their strength.'[61] True panic is believed to be only experienced in wild woods or the wilderness, a theme that was portrayed in the haunting Australian movie *Picnic at Hanging Rock* (1975),[62] in which schoolgirls and a teacher disappeared mysteriously on a trip to Hanging Rock (a thinly-disguised Ayers Rock) amid a heady atmosphere of repressed sexuality, simmering neurosis and something darkly paranormal lurking subliminally under the plot – something elemental and lusty . . .

Pan is also intimately associated with satyrs, originally so timid that their animal totem was the hare, but later widely seen as a rapacious goat-like being, with hooves, hairy legs, bare human chests and horns. That they have assumed archetypal qualities of challenging sexual repression can be seen from the description of the 'deep, secret wound' in the mind of Dorothy Hare, the eponymous heroine of George Orwell's *A Clergyman's Daughter* (1935), who found 'that sort of thing' exceptionally distasteful after witnessing 'certain dreadful scenes between her father and mother' as a child:

> . . . And then a little later she had been frightened by some old steel engravings of nymphs pursued by satyrs. To her childish mind there was something inexplicably, horribly sinister in those horned, semi-human creatures that lurked in thickets . . . ready to come bounding forth in sudden swift pursuit . . . The satyr remained with her as a symbol . . . [of] that special feeling of dread, of hope-

less flight from something more than rationally dreadful – the stamp of hooves in the lonely wood, the lean, furry thighs of the satyr. It was not a thing to be altered, not to be argued away.

Orwell adds with a touch of irony – and perhaps vivid memories of personal frustration: 'It is, moreover, a thing too common nowadays, among educated women, to occasion any kind of surprise.'

Artemidorus (whose name suggests a link with the cult of the goddess Artemis), the late-second-century dream interpreter, implies strongly that Pan makes regular appearances in the dreams of humankind, and is most often glimpsed at night. The classical poet Horace wrote with pride and gratitude that Pan protected his farm, and occasionally even visited him, although he never saw him properly.[63] Occult lore has it that Pan is perceived at 'crossover' places and times – the edge of the wood at noon or midnight, for example – and should never be conjured immediately after lunchtime, because he will be enjoying his afternoon nap and, ominously, will be rather cross.

In his *Pan: Great God of Nature* (1993), the occult scholar 'Leo Vinci' notes that 'In the Authorized Version of Isaiah the word "satyr" is used to render the Hebrew *se'rim* ('hairy ones') a demon or supernatural being ... that lives in uninhabited places.'[64] He cites Isaiah: 'But wild beasts of the desert shall lie there; and their houses shall be full of doleful creatures; and owls shall lie there, and satyrs shall dance there.'[65] Again, Isaiah repeats the satyr/desolation *leitmotif*: 'The wild beasts of the desert shall also meet with the wild beasts of the island, and the satyr shall cry to his fellow.'[66] Vinci points out that the allusion to 'devils' in the following passage from Leviticus refers to satyrs: 'And they shall no more offer their sacrifice unto devils, after whom they have gone a whoring.'[67]

As in the annual mysteries of Tammuz, Pan's mourners would lament 'Great Pan is dead!', but soon that ritual phrase was taken to mark not simply the end of another year, but the final chapter in a whole religious era, the death of the supremacy of Pan – and, by extension, all the great pagan deities – with the advent of Christianity. As Stephen McKenna has his mysterious 'Mr Stranger' say in his little-known book, *The Oldest God* (1926):

The world . . . is too timid . . . for paganism; and so mankind remains suspended in mid-air, higher than the beasts and lower than the angels, miserable in the void between animal satisfaction and celestial bliss . . . The rule of Pan came to an end on the day when a fanatic preached that the kindly, joyous, savage Pan was in truth the embodiment of original sin!'

When the stranger leaves, 'the baffling animal-scent had departed'.[68]

The profound and unsettling concept of a great being who was simultaneously 'kindly' and 'savage' usually proves too strong for modern folk, often even New Agers who follow their own form of neo-paganism. (Pan becomes a sort of bar-room decadent, while the old uncompromising destroyers such as Sekhmet transmogrify into solicitous friendly figures, almost furry pets. While few would want their home town to be laid waste by a ferocious lioness-headed Egyptian goddess breathing fire, the cuddly modern version is so inauthentic it would be unrecognizable to her ancient devotees.)

Yet with the collapse of the Roman Empire – which in any case was increasingly sceptical and atheistic – few of the old gods remained popular. However, metamorphosed into the horned Devil in his dark form as the Goat of Mendes, and all his attendant satyrs transformed into demons from the pit, ironically Pan remained foremost in Christian minds. As Geoffrey Ashe notes in his classic, *The Virgin* (1976): 'During Rome's long decline, almost the last thinking believers in the old gods were their Christian enemies. A pagan might laugh at Apollo as a fable. A Christian would shudder at him as a malignant spirit.'[69]

Far from his Arcadian woodlands, Pan became the Devil, and – as we shall see – his European adherents of the Middle Ages were accused of worshipping him in the depths of the countryside. And in Europe, the horned god of the West, Cernunnos, lord of fertility and the underworld – similar in appearance and characteristics to Pan – was also assimilated to the Devil, while the Norse Thor, dressed all in devilish red, drives a cart pulled by goats – very suggestive to the Christians. Saint Paul had no doubt that all pagan deities were actually demonic, writing to the Corinthians:

Do I mean . . . that a sacrifice offered to an idol is anything or that an idol is anything? No, but the sacrifices of pagans are offered to demons, not to God, and I do not want you to be participants with demons.

You cannot drink the cup of the Lord and the cup of demons, too; you cannot have a part in both the Lord's table and the table of demons.[70]

Tellingly, Paul adds, a little nervously: 'Are we trying to arouse the Lord's jealousy? Are we stronger than he?'[71] Perhaps Paul knew to be particularly wary of Pan, for he ruled over the countryside, the *paganus*, which gave its name to the hated pagans. And his association with lusty, assertive goddesses could only blacken Pan further in Paul's eyes, if that were possible.

Apart from the Maenads, one of Pan's more distinguished female associates was Artemis, 'uninjured, healing, vigorous', who 'grants health and strength to others'.[72] She was also known to her worshippers at Ephesus, in Turkey, under her Latin name of Diana – 'Goddess-Anna' – where her monumental golden statue was covered in breasts, to symbolize her succour for all. Yet she also had a dark and terrible aspect, being known in Sparta as Artamis, 'the Butcher', a Kali-like destroyer whose wrath was akin to Yahweh's. One of her many animal incarnations was as a she-bear, called by the Celtic people 'Art', the mate of the great Arthur, whose totem animal was the bear. The medieval King of the Witches was known as 'Robin, Son of Art'. With their usual mixture of fear, superstition and reluctant reverence, the Christians both denounced Artemis as a demon and canonized her as Saint Ursula, from her Saxon name, Ursel.[73]

(As Liz Greene remarks in her haunting and important novel about the alleged secrets of the Merovingians in France, *The Dreamer of the Vine* [1980] '. . . how different these gods were . . . What the one demands, the other abhors. Yet though our poor minds cannot comprehend it, I often suspect these gods are the same.' Then she adds sagely: 'I think too much of any god can drive one mad.')[74]

The shaggy outline of the Goat-God hung over the years of the witch trials: now the Devil incarnate, he had free rein to ensnare the unwary – mainly women – and seize their souls.

Even the gentle 'sylvans and fauns' of lost Arcadia were believed – by the Inquisition and even their much later co-religionists, not the least the Catholic zealot the Reverend Montague Summers (who died in 1948), of whom much more later – to be 'commonly called *incubi*', or sexual demons.[75] In this as in much else, Summers is toeing the long-established party line: in fact, satyrs, fauns and the Gaulish nature spirits called *dusii* (from *deus*, 'god') were listed in the Inquisition's official handbook as *incubi*:

> who had intercourse with witches in front of witnesses . . . Women seem unaccountably willing to copulate with their demons under the eyes of 'bystanders'; the latter reported that, while the demon remained invisible, 'it has been apparent from the disposition of those limbs and members which pertain to the venereal act and orgasm, [that] . . . they have been copulating with Incubus devils.'[76]

Summers demonstrates his quirky contrariness when discussing the Devil as represented on the medieval stage: 'He is, in fact, the Satyr of the old Dionysiac processions, a nature-spirit, the essence of joyous freedom and unrestrained delight, shameless if you will, for the old Greek knew not shame.' Strangely, Summers appears grudgingly to admire the 'joyous freedom' of the Satyr, and even goes on: '. . . in a word he was Paganism incarnate, and Paganism was the Christian's deadliest foe; so they took him, the Bacchic reveller, they smutted him from horn to hoof, and he remained the Christian's deadliest foe, the Devil.' The Rev. Summers seems to be oblivious of the fact that a good proportion of his book is devoted to describing the horned and cloven-hooved Devil as a reality. In any case, he notes that in Euripedes' classic play *Medea* dating back to the fifth century BCE, there is the passage: 'She seemed, I wot, to be one frenzied, inspired with madness by Pan or some other of the gods',[77] adding 'Madness was sometimes thought to be sent by Pan for any neglect of his worship'.[78]

Although to certain groups of country folk, Pan never really died, it was with the rise of the Romantic Movement in the early nineteenth century that saw him enjoy a comeback, although again, perhaps a little diluted in character. The grounds of countless country residences became littered with follies in the form of temples or even classical tombs, and statuary evocative of Pan – satyrs, nymphs and the god himself. Ideas about a long-lost Arcadia, a gently wooded Golden Age, permeated society as a whole.

Perhaps the poet Shelley had the Romantics' more sentimental and vivid images in mind when he wrote to his friend Thomas J. Hogg: 'I am glad to hear that you do not neglect the rites of the true religion. Your letter awoke my sleeping devotion, and the same evening I ascended alone the high mountain behind my house, and suspended a garland, and raised a small turf-altar to the mountain-walking Pan'.[79] Shelley's reverence for the supremely pagan Pan seems to have filled the gap left by his rejection of Christianity. In a recently discovered letter from the poet to Ralph Wedgwood – dating from around 1811 when Shelley was expelled from Oxford University for publishing a tract entitled 'The Necessity of Atheism' – he wrote: 'Christ never existed . . . the fall of man, the whole fabric indeed of superstition which it supports can no longer obtain the credit of Philosophers.'[80] It is interesting that Shelley felt more comfortable with the ultimate archetype of the pagan god than with the Christian deity. The high priest of decadence, Lord Byron – who had an intimate relationship with his own sister among countless other dalliances – wrote regretfully:

> The Gods of old are silent on their shore
> Since the great Pan expired, and through the roar
> Of the Ionian waters broke a dread
> Voice which proclaimed 'The mighty Pan is dead.'
> How much died with him! False or true – the dream
> Was beautiful which peopled every stream
> With more than finny tenants, and adorned
> The woods and waters with coy nymphs that scorned
> Pursuing Deities, or in the embrace
> Of gods brought forth the high heroic race
> Whose names are on the hills and o'er the seas.

Oscar Wilde, perhaps genuinely, or simply ever mindful of his reputation for excess and perversity – after all, he did insist on playing Salome in his play of the same name on its first, and only, night – lamented: 'O goat-foot god of Arcady! This modern world hath need of thee!'[81]

Less predictably, Pan appears anonymously in the great children's classic, Kenneth Grahame's *The Wind in the Willows* (1908) when Rat whispers, awed, 'as if in a trance': 'This is the place of my song-dream, the place the music played to me . . . Here, in this holy place, here if anywhere, surely we will find Him!'

Lucifer and all her tribe

We have seen how Plato called Lucifer 'Aster', simply meaning 'star', after his identification with the bright Morning Star. But Plato and countless others in the ancient world knew that the Morning Star had another incarnation – moving round in the heavens as the Evening Star, or Venus. In his classic *The Golden Bough* (1922), J.G. Frazer wrote:

> Sirius was the star of Isis, just as the Babylonians deemed the planet Venus the star of Astarte. To both peoples apparently the brilliant luminary in the morning sky seemed the goddess of life and love come to mourn her departed lover or spouse and wake him from the dead.[82]

Like the lesser-known Astraea or 'Starry One',[83] the Libyan Goddess of Law who dispensed the fates of man, the beauty and truth of the deity Venus was believed to be visible in the Evening Star, the opposite and equal to the Morning Star, Lucifer. However, this distinction was too subtle for the pagans' new Christian enemies, and a great blurring between the Feminine Principle and the Evil One rapidly took place, eased in its passage by the tendency of the Romans to refer to Venus as 'Lucifera', the enlightener. Venus, the archetypal goddess of the arts of love and women's secrets, an unashamedly sexual deity, gave her name not only to 'venereal disease' and 'venery', but perhaps, some claim, also more courteously to Venice, the city of her element as 'Stella Maris' ('Star of the Sea', a title she shared with Isis, and much later, the Virgin Mary). Originally, like Diana, Venus was a huntress, a 'Lady of Animals', whose horned consort was Adonis – 'both the hunter and sacrificial stag – became *venison*, which meant "Venus's son".'[84] Once again the line becomes blurred between horned gods and their consorts. And once again the goddess is associated with animality, sexual secrets, lust – and Lucifer. Barbara Walker describes a predictable reaction:

> Early Christian fathers denounced the temples 'dedicated to the foul devil who goes by the name of Venus – a school of wickedness for all the votaries of unchasteness'.[85] What this meant was that they were schools of instruction in sexual techniques, under the tutelage of the *venerii* or harlot-priestesses.[86] They taught an approach to spiritual grace, called *venia*, through sexual exercises like those of Tantrism [the eastern cult of sacred sex].[87]

This aspect of Venus-worship was not uncommon among goddess cults: as we have seen, God's wife Asherath had both female and male 'temple prostitutes' – although this is a derogatory term first employed by disapproving and uncomprehending Victorian scholars. To the culture itself, these workers in sacred sex rituals were known as 'temple servants', a role that was acknowledged with reverence. Both the females and cross-dressing males were there to give men ecstatic pleasure that would transcend mere sex: the moment of orgasm was believed to propel them briefly into the presence of the gods, to present them with a transcendent experience of enlightenment. Only men went with the temple servants because it was believed that women were *naturally enlightened* and therefore had no need of such rituals – a diametrically opposed attitude to the repressive misogyny of patriarchal Judaism and Christianity.

To these male-dominated religions, sex was evil because women enticed men to lust after them – often, it was claimed, against their better judgement: the unwilling gentlemen were literally 'enchanted' by their 'glamour' (literally their ability to cause hallucinations or actually shape-shift). Women were inherently evil because of Eve, who let Satan into the world and got mankind expelled from Paradise.

Worse, goddesses were often explicitly associated with serpents – indeed, the Egyptian uraeus snake, worn in pharaonic headdresses, was a hieroglyph for 'goddess'.[88] Cleopatra took the title

'Serpent of the Nile' after all Egyptian queens who represented the Goddess, who took the king into their life-giving embrace. The Egyptian serpent goddess Mehen the Enveloper enfolded the ram-headed Auf-Ra – Phallus of the solar god Ra – every night, as he travelled in the underworld, symbol of their sexual union. Isis and her dark-aspect Nepthys were associated with the Serpent mother of material life and the afterlife, their knowledge specifically aiding the post-mortem traveller in the region of ferocious snakes. In ancient Crete before the Bronze Age the objects of veneration were women and snakes. Even with the later dominance of the bull cult, the priest was inferior to the snake-wielding priestess. The literal interpretation of the ancient Akkadian word for 'priest' is 'snake charmer'.[89]

Perhaps that is too cerebral a connection, for to the clergy pagan goddesses were inherently evil, basically because they were pagan and goddesses. They notoriously encouraged both men and women to worship the Feminine Principle that they so gorgeously and flagrantly embodied and taught their female devotees the mysteries of life and death, of sex, contraception and abortion. And, like Adam's first wife Lilith, goddesses notoriously took their pleasure with their consorts in the superior position, believed by the Judaeo-Christian priesthood to be profoundly wicked as a deliberate over-turning of God's law. (To them, the only godly way of intercourse was the 'Venus observa', or 'missionary position' – so called because Christian missionaries insisted that their native converts use it exclusively in their marriage beds. The natives thought it was hilarious.)

Despite the fact that the clitoris is the only human organ whose function is exclusively to give pleasure, sexual delight was frowned upon, especially for women, whose sole sexual purpose was to breed. Isis, Diana-Lucifer, Artemis, Asherah, Venus and all other manifestations of the Great Goddess would have difficulty in comprehending this: to them, every aspect of womanhood was there to be experienced and celebrated, from virginity through motherhood to a dignified and wise old age, with everything in between from warrior queen and sacred whore. Schooled in such an attitude, pagan women were often unsurprisingly assertive and independent – especially in Egypt, where in the first century they were permitted to own property and initiate divorce. Learned women were also celebrated: an inscription as early as the Fourth Dynasty (*c*. 2600–2500 BCE), approximately contemporary with the building of the Giza pyramids, refers to a woman in the Temple of Thoth as 'Mistress of the House of Books'.[90] Hypatia, the first great woman mathematician and philosopher, a native of Alexandria, was torn to pieces by an angry mob in 415 CE, some say, inspired by the Christian bishop Cyril, through envy.

Eve had acted on her own initiative, Lilith taunted both God and his angels, and Asherah had taken Lucifer as a lover. Women were clearly Satanic, the spawn of the Devil, and must at all costs be prevented from thinking or acting unless under male orders. Barbara Walker notes another historical link between goddesses and western notions of evil:

> A triple six, 666, was the magic number of Aphrodite (or Ishtar) in the guise of the Fates. The Book of Revelation called it 'the number of the Beast' (Revelation 13:18), apparently the Beast with Two Backs, the androgyne of carnal love. Solomon the wizard-king made a sacred marriage with the Goddess and acquired a mystic 666 talents of gold (1 Kings 10:14). Christians usually called it Satan's number, yet the recurrences of this number in esoteric traditions are often surprising. For example, the maze at Chartres Cathedral was planned so as to be exactly 666 feet long.[91]

Today's Christian hell-and-damnation fundamentalists and vast numbers of conspiracy theorists see the devilish '666' in everything, as evidence of satanic influence in the government, the Freemasons or whoever they have decided to demonize. The saddest and most disturbing consideration is that even if they knew about the true background of Christianity's most notorious number, like their predecessors, they would still regard it as evil. To them, as a pagan goddess Aphrodite was clearly demonic, yet in fact she was truly *Luciferan* – in the sense of being an enlightener to her followers, just as were her sister goddesses. Some of Aphrodite's works were too strong even for the traditionalist ancient Greeks, to whom women should be confined to a narrow domestic life. When the lesbian poet Sappho petitioned the goddess for help in winning the favours of a particular girl, she replied: 'Who/O Sappho, does you justice?/For if she flees, soon will she pursue/and though she receives not your gifts, she will give them/and if she loves not now, soon she will love/even against her will.'[92] Somehow one detects Sappho's own hand in this convenient response from the deity.

As we have seen, some of the pagan goddesses, such as the huntress Diana, even took the title 'Lucifer/Lucifera', the bringer of Light into the darkness of human woe.

Another reason that the old goddesses became synonymous with the Devil is that many of them were depicted wearing lunar horns. Isis-Hathor wears a pair of magnificent cow's horns, as befits that animal's patron, and must have seemed truly diabolic to the early Christians as her cult persisted in Europe as a rival until the fourth century CE – into the fifth century in parts of Italy. God's wife, Asshereth, gave her name to Ashteroth–Karnaim in Gilead, or 'Ashteroth/Asshereth of the horns'. American researcher David Lance Goines believes that the goddesses' horns are not lunar at all, but reflect their association with Venus, a planet that also produces a visual crescent shape in the night sky.[93] If so, this merely reinforces the sense that the early Christians associated the Feminine Principle with horns and venery – the Devil incarnate.

No doubt it will be assumed that Christianity, like Jesus himself, sprang from a divine state of chastity with no breath of the loathed contamination of sex. But like Yahweh with his Asherah, Venus and her Adonis and Osiris with his Isis, Christ also had his sacred consort, a woman who even received the title 'Lucifer' from her devotees – and who, apparently, taught the mysteries of sacred sex not only to the chosen one, but also his followers . . .

CHAPTER THREE

A Woman Called Lucifer

In the twenty-first-century West, all our ideas about right and wrong, good and evil, come from our culture's Judaeo-Christian tradition. But, as we have seen, Yahweh's credentials as a noble or even particularly intelligent deity fail to match his capacity for jealousy and smiting, and the story of humanity's fall from grace – and the subsequent subjugation of women – is a sad tale of garbled myth and blatant bias. However, none of that compares with the deliberate reworking of the original Christian story, apparently often *in direct opposition to Christ's own wishes*. This chapter will deal with a quite different view of Christianity, pieced together from long-forbidden texts, obscured identities and the reinsertion of passages from the flagrantly edited gospels. The result will be shocking and thought-provoking, and implicitly reverses many Christian assumptions about sacred figures, and even about their basic understanding of what is devilish and what is righteous.

In 1958 a discovery was made by Dr Morton Smith (later Professor of Ancient History at Columbia University, New York) in the library of an Eastern Orthodox closed community at Mar Saba near Jerusalem. It was a copy of a letter from the second-century Church Father, Clement of Alexandria, which, as we shall see later, includes potentially explosive material taken from a 'Secret Gospel of Mark', apparently an esoteric version of the biblical Gospel, but for initiates only. Clement's letter is in reply to a Christian called

Theodore who wanted to know how to deal with a heretical group called the Carpocratians who practised their own – extreme – version of the ancient sacred sex rites referred to in the previous chapter, allegedly based on a secret Gospel of Mark.

The Carpocratians were second-century Gnostics led by one Carpocrates, called by author Michael Jordan in his highly revisionist *Mary: The Unauthorized Biography* (2001) 'a Christian pioneer who did much to advance the cause of Gnosticism'.[1] The modern scholar *par excellence* of Gnosticism, Tobias Churton, calls Carpocrates 'a proto-Communist . . . [an] intellectual anarchist, who coined the dictum, "Property is theft".'[2] However, this modern, if muted, admiration is a far cry from the ancients' horror at what they perceived as the Carpocratians' penchant for radical licentious behaviour. Predictably, the dogmatic and uncompromising Bishop Irenaeus of Lyon fired off a broadside at these offensive libertines, singling out their leader Marcus:

Marcus, thou former of idols, inspector of portents,
Skilled in consulting the stars, and deep in the black arts of magic,
Ever by tricks such as these confirming the doctrines of error,
Furnishing signs unto those involved by thee in deception,
Wonders of power that is utterly severed from God and apostate,
Which Satan, thy true father, enables thee still to accomplish,
By means of Azazel, that fallen and yet mighty angel,
Thus making thee the precursor of his own impious actions.[3]

Irenaeus leaves us in no doubt as to his views on Marcus, whom he declares to be 'really the precursor of Antichrist'. The Bishop attacks the Carpocratian leader for a litany of sins and crimes, including an 'addiction to philtres, love-potions [drugs], "familiar demons", prophecies, the defiling of women, numerology . . . and Satanism'.[4] However, Irenaeus[5] soon leaves aside the fire-and-brimstone ranting and knuckles down to specific accusations. Not surprisingly, they concern alleged sexual misconduct – 'the defiling of women' – the usual accusation against rival cults throughout the ages, which may or may not have a basis in fact. He declares with a critic's, not to say bigot's,[6] certainty:

Marcus devotes himself especially to women, and those such as are well-bred, and elegantly attired, and of great wealth, whom he frequently seeks to draw after him, by addressing them in such seductive words as these . . . Adorn thyself as a bride who is expecting her bridegroom, that thou mayest be what I am, and I what thou art. Establish the germ of light in thy nuptial chamber. Receive from me a spouse, and become receptive of him, while thou are received by him.[7]

Although Irenaeus seems only to have heard rumours rather than first-hand knowledge of these practices, he may have been quite right about Marcus's leadership, for there was indeed an early Gnostic initiation known explicitly as 'the Bridal Chamber', a form of sacred sex. But sex in any form appalled the early Christians – indeed, even modern Catholicism only just tolerates it even in marriage[8] – and the Carpocratians were renowned for their licentiousness and the use of female prophets who channelled their powers of clairvoyance and divine inspiration for the benefit of the cult. However, as Benjamin Walker writes:

The practice inevitably led to abuse. Marcus was accused of seducing many of his young female 'prophets'. Irenaeus writes that by various suggestions he makes his deluded victim believe that she has the power of prophecy. Full of false pride, and excited by the expectation of using her gift, she ventures into oracular utterance. With pounding heart she articulates any ridiculous nonsense that enters her head. Henceforth, stimulated by vanity she audaciously considers herself a veritable sibyl.[9]

(Nothing is new under the sun: the above passage could have been written about the legion New Age channelling cults, often run by a quasi-spiritual male leader with a libidinous personal agenda.)

Once the prophetess was established and her vanity persuaded her to continue in her new role, Marcus made his move and seduced her – or so Irenaeus and other Church fathers claimed. Perhaps they were right and Marcus was simply helping himself to the traditional cult leader's perks, or perhaps there really was a serious ritual side to their coupling, as indeed seems to be the case from the words Marcus is supposed to have uttered, quoted by Irenaeus above.

Indeed, the founder of the group, Carpocrates of Alexandria (78–138 CE), had based what was essentially a pagan-Christian hybrid religion on the cult of Isis, absorbing the complex rites of initiation – complete with secret passwords and handshakes – and baptism as an important rite. And, incredible though it may seem to Christians, Carpocrates' practices may not have been too dissimilar to those of John the Baptist's following, as we will see . . .

Carpocrates travelled with a woman called Alexandria, with whom he had a son, Epiphanes ('Illustrious'), the author of the influential treatise *On Justice*. Dead by his late teens, Epiphanes was revered as a Gnostic 'aeon' with his own temple and museum complex. Carpocratian beliefs were a mixture of the teachings of both father and son.

Apart from worshipping the great Egyptian gods (with especial emphasis on the ancient Trinity of Isis, Osiris and Horus), the cult also revered the famous Greek philosophers, such as Plato and Pythagoras, besides Jesus whom they saw as partly divine. To them, there was no miraculous Virgin birth and no immaculate conception of Mary herself: Christ had been born naturally. It was rumoured that the Carpocratians possessed a sketch made of Jesus on Pilate's orders, on which they based the statue they carried in sacred procession – becoming the first known Christians to venerate a cultic image of Christ.[10]

The cult scandalized the more ascetic Christians on almost every level: disbelieving in both the concepts of adultery and property – they had everything in common, including sexual partners – they also banned procreation. Clearly this prohibition was more theoretical than practical, as the very existence of the holy Epiphanes proved. However, sex of all sorts was deemed obligatory, and a way of honouring the gods, as semen was the divine life-force – an aspect of Luciferanism (by any other name) that was to assume various guises over the centuries. The inborn itch of sexual desire must be honoured: 'By thus sinning, the divine light of God's grace was provided with a chance to operate, a fact that was eminently pleasing to God. Sin thus became a way of salvation.'[11] (However, interestingly, the Carpocratians were still conventional enough to think of sex as *sinning*.) After the group's lavish communal meal, the room would be plunged into darkness and an indiscriminate orgy followed: as Church Father, Clement, sniffed: 'uniting as they desired and with whomsoever they desired'.[12]

The irrepressible Reverend Montague Summers thunders: 'Carpocrates even went so far as to . . . [make] the performance of every species of sin forbidden in the Old Testament a solemn duty, since this was the completest mode of showing defiance to the Evil Creator and Ruler of the World'[13] (the Gnostics' Demiurge or *Rex Mundi* – or the Old Testament's Yahweh).

However, Summers is – perhaps wilfully – missing the point, although even if he had grasped it totally, he would still hardly have approved. As Tobias Churton writes matter-of-factly:

> Sex might be used either allegorically or in fact as part of Gnostic ceremonies. Semen could be regarded as a sacramental substance, as an image for the *logos spermatikos* (the spermatic *Word* cast into the world) or pneumatic spark: the fugitive fragments of spirit, diffused in Nature. Fertility was seen as a metaphor for spiritual growth. (This was how some Christian Gnostics interpreted Christ's parable of the sower who sowed seed in barren earth.)[14]

Of course this would have seemed like an intellectual version of making a silk purse of a sow's ear to the Church Fathers. The Carpocratians and their apologists could dress it up as they wished, but they were still filthy heretical radicals who wallowed in sin.

The Carpocratians believed that the concepts of good and evil were invented by mankind, and that everyone must suffer or enjoy the whole gamut of human experience, including the loftiest and noblest and the most humiliating and sordid acts. Every individual would be reincarnated until they had finished the immense number of possible permutations of human life. A recording angel was assigned to each person and each act, and must be invoked consciously while performing them in order to ensure that a fair karmic record is kept.

Clement's sensational slip

However, by far the most significant aspect of the Carpocratian beliefs is that they claimed to possess a secret Gospel of Mark that preached sexual rites *in the name of Jesus*. Highly compromising references to this were what Professor Morton Smith found in the library at the Mar Saba monastery in 1958. Ironically in his denunciation of the Carpocratians, Clement had unwittingly preserved material that possessed the potential to undermine seriously the whole concept of Christianity – not to mention the image of an eternally chaste Christ.

Of course the first objection must concern the authenticity or otherwise of the copy of Clement's letter, which Smith found written on the end-papers of a book dating back to 1646 – a common practice at that time when volumes began to disintegrate with age.[15] Understandably, in the case of such a potentially sensational discovery, there will always be suspicions that Smith was deceived, perhaps by the Mar Saba monks, or that a disaffected seventeenth-century copyist was merely enjoying a bit of grim heretical humour – or even that the professor himself perpetrated an outrageous hoax. However, paleographers have established from an analysis of the letter that it was indeed written by Clement, whose stylistic idiosyncracies are well known. And as Clive Prince and myself noted in our 1997 *The Templar Revelation: Secret Guardians of the True Identity of Christ*:

There are also peculiarities in the extracts from the 'Secret Gospel' quoted in the letter that make it probable that they are genuine. (For example, it describes Jesus as becoming angry. Of the canonical Gospels only Mark attributes normal human emotions to Jesus – the others excised such elements from their accounts, and it is hardly something that the Church Fathers such have Clement would have invented.)[16]

Indeed, it is extremely unlikely that any conventional Christian could even have imagined what Clement claimed, for he stated that the Carpocratians' 'filthy' sex rites came via Saint Mark from Mary Magdalene – and ultimately from Jesus himself. Predictably Clement – who was later canonized – huffs and puffs with outrage that the cult 'polluted the spotless and holy words of scripture to accord with their blasphemous and carnal doctrine, and by doing so wandered from the narrow road into the abyss of darkness',[17] yet he also acknowledges that the alternative Gospel of Mark was *authentic* . . . Therefore he tacitly agreed that originally Christianity *did* practise sexual rites, although they seem to have been reserved for an inner circle of high initiates.

Of course, the implications of this are truly momentous and provide a double blow to Christianity: not only was, and is, the whole idea of sex rituals abhorrent, but also it has always been believed that the religion is primarily open to anyone, with no secrets and hidden mysteries, but here there is evidence that there was such a thing as *a sexually-initiated elite* of adepts.

Certainly, Professor Smith himself believed, largely on the basis of this long-lost document, that Jesus may have headed a 'libertine circle'. What prompted him to make such a remarkable statement is another passage from Clement's letter, a different version of the story of the raising of Lazarus, the brother of Martha and Mary of Bethany (also known as Mary Magdalene)[18] which puts quite a different complexion on the original Jesus movement. Found in the Gospel of John in the New Testament, it famously tells how Jesus received a message that his beloved friend Lazarus was grievously sick at his home in Bethany, a village only two miles from Jerusalem. But Jesus deliberately waited four days, by which time Lazarus was not only dead but stinking in his rock tomb. As soon as Jesus arrived on the scene, Mary fell at his feet, sobbing: 'Lord, had you been here, my brother would not have died'[19] – which perhaps contains more than a hint of bitter accusation. Jesus told Martha: 'I am the resurrection and the life. He that believes in me will live, even though he dies; and whoever lives and believes in me will never die.'[20] Then he commands that the stone be removed from the mouth of the tomb and, raising his voice, orders Lazarus to step forth. It must have been a remarkable moment when the corpse immediately shuffled out, still in the 'strips of linen' that comprised his grave bandages. It was this event that finally prompted the Jews to take action against Jesus, for they would have seen this as a clear example of necromancy, devilish dealings with the dead. (Anything connected with the grave was and is abhorrent to Orthodox Jews.) It was after this, too, that a woman bursts into a house in Bethany and anoints Jesus – in one of the strangest and most misunderstood rites in the New Testament, which will be discussed below.

However, the raising of Lazarus in the secret Gospel of Mark owned by the Carpocratians and quoted by Clement, has 'a certain woman' approaching Jesus for help because her brother has died. But when Jesus arrives at the tomb he hears a loud cry from within, clearly indicating that the young man is not dead, at least not in a literal, physical sense. Jesus then rolls away the stone and raises the youth from the ground. 'And the youth looked upon him and loved him and began to beseech him that he might be with him.'[21]

Together they went into the house, where Jesus remained for six days, instructing the young man in the ways of the kingdom of heaven. On the last day the two men spent a sleepless night together, 'naked [man] with naked [man]'.[22] Perhaps this apparently compromising scenario was an invention of the unknown real author of the secret Gospel of Mark, who might well have been out to vilify Christianity with heavy hints about sexual practices. However, there does appear to be some circumstantial corroboration for that offending passage, ironically in the New Testament itself. This episode is in the otherwise mysterious verses in the authorized Gospel of Mark about 'a young man wearing nothing but a linen garment'[23] who followed Jesus after his arrest – when all the others fled to save their skins. He then suffered a traumatic embarrassment: 'When they seized him, he fled naked, leaving his garment behind'.[24]

But does spending the night unclad with a religious teacher automatically imply that some kind of homosexual activity took place? Of course not, but Professor Smith himself had no doubts about Jesus' 'libertine circle', and the possibility that his followers were admitted, 'singly and by night, to the mystery of the kingdom, by certain ceremonies derived from ancient erotic magic'.[25] Based on his knowledge of this tradition, Smith conjectures that the young man's thin linen garment was removed and his naked body immersed in a baptismal pool or bath to a background of prayers 'and some kind of rite of manipulation' – presumably masturbation, possibly prior to other sexual rituals – accompanied by a breath control technique that induced ecstasy, and possibly a hallucination of heavenly bliss. 'The disciple was possessed by the spirit of Jesus and so united with him.'[26] Professor Smith surmised that 'Freedom from the [Jewish] law may have resulted in completion of the spiritual union by physical union.'[27]

Perhaps it is significant that, as Marilyn Yalom points out in her *A History of the Wife* (2001): 'As for Christianity, Jesus said nothing on the subject of homosexuality – and this in contrast to numerous condemnations of adultery.'[28] (While discussing the pressure on Sr Buttiglione to stand down from the European Commission in November 2004 because of his traditionalist values, *Daily Mail* columnist Andrew Alexander also noted: 'For myself, I would delight in debating with our Italian friend why homo-sexuality is not singled out for condemnation in the gospels. Was it due to the gospels' authors failing to take proper notes, or divine incompetence or what?')[29] Yalom points out that the criticism of same-gender sexuality originated in the Christian movement with Saint Paul, who 'explicitly condemned both male and female homosexuality (Romans 1:26–27, I Corinthians 6:9, and 1 Timothy 1:10)'.[30]

Of course a zealous Christian will simply deny the authenticity of this secret gospel and carry on believing as if it had never been drawn to his or her attention. After all, there is a distinct architec-ture to the faith: significant constructs are made that surround the character and the traditions of Christ; dogma that then becomes immovable, and the whole carapace hardens with time and belief. But *what if* the implications of the secret gospel are sound? *What if* Jesus' movement was really based on initiation and mysteries – including rites of a strongly erotic or even homosexual nature? Suddenly what was considered demonic, devilish, satanic, would be inexorably linked with Jesus Christ, hitherto the very epitome and literal embodiment of noble chastity. It is surely unthinkable.

In fact, there is considerably more evidence, albeit for obvious reasons circumstantial after all this time, that Jesus and his initiates were involved in the sort of cult behaviour that modern Christians would not only condemn as filthy and immoral, but actively seek to have banned from their community. This is where polarized notions of good and evil, the godly and the Luciferan, or outright Satanic, become merely the stuff of bias and therefore fair game for debate.

Lazarus, the youth involved in some kind of ritual rebirth or sexual initiation into the mysteries of the Kingdom, had two sisters – the house-proud Martha and the mysterious Mary, also known as the Magdalene, whose character and role have been discussed in detail in my previous book, *Mary Magdalene: Christianity's Hidden Goddess* (2003).[31] She is 'mysterious' because she appears only rarely by name in the New Testament, her identity also being obscured as 'Mary of Bethany', 'a certain woman' or 'a sinner of the town'.

Although any church goer will be quick to describe her as the reformed prostitute who foreswore her wicked ways to follow Jesus, in fact her alleged career as a street-walker was an invention of Pope Gregory I in 691 CE, based on the biblical description of her as 'a sinner'. He simply put two and two together and made five: the original Greek word was *harmartolos*, a term taken from archery meaning 'one who falls short of the mark' and was applied to those who, for whatever reason, failed to keep the Jewish Law. One major reason for not doing so, of course, was not being Jewish – a foreigner – or perhaps a follower of another type of Judaism. As discussed in my previous book, there is evidence to link Mary Magdalene primarily with Egypt, and possibly with the ancient goddess cults of Ethiopia.

Not only did the Church vilify her as a whore, but the writers of the canonical gospels clearly set out to marginalize her. In the canonical gospels she only really comes into her own at the crucifixion, when she heads a team of Jesus' female disciples who come to show their solidarity with and love for their stricken leader, when the famous men – apart from the young Saint John – have fled. She, too, takes a major role in the story of the resurrection, where she meets the risen Jesus in an almost exact re-enactment of the Egyptian mystery plays of Isis and Osiris. Yet her abrupt appearance as a significant player in the great drama seems odd until it is realized that she had been deliberately edited out of the story until it reached the point where she *had* to take centre-stage, perhaps simply because her part in the story was too well known to leave out. But why was her role demoted and degraded in this way? What did the writers of the gospels of Saints Matthew, Mark, Luke and John have against one apparently harmless and devout woman?

Many people would answer that the men of the early Church were too biased against an ex-prostitute to permit her to take the limelight, or that, being basically still patriarchal Jews, they were just too sexist. In fact, the answer is almost certainly rather different – and considerably more far-reaching. Mary Magdalene committed what to the early Christian men of Judaea must have been an act of blasphemous presumption, for anyone, let alone a woman who was probably foreign and possibly black (as noted previously,[32] racism was not invented by the British Empire). *She anointed Jesus.* It happened in Bethany at the home of a man known to history simply as Simon the Leper – probably fictitious – as described in Mark's Gospel:

> . . . a woman came in with an alabaster jar of very expensive perfume, made of pure [spike]nard. She broke the jar and poured the perfume on his head.
>
> Some of those present were saying indignantly to one another, 'Why this waste of perfume? It could have been sold for more than a year's wages and the money given to the poor.' And they rebuked her harshly.[33]

In Luke's Gospel, the unnamed woman anoints his head and feet and also dries them with her hair.[34] But if the men's objection was intended to provoke praise and gratitude from Jesus, it failed utterly. Instead of congratulating them on their wisdom and concern for the poor, their leader says vehemently:

> Leave her alone . . . Why are you bothering her? She has done a beautiful thing to me. The poor you will always have with you, and you can help them any time you want. But you will not always have me. She did what she could. She poured perfume on my body beforehand to prepare for burial . . .[35]

The last sentence contains a clue to the real significance of her action. It was not, as has been suggested, merely a kind of *ad hoc* aromatherapy, a compassionate and pleasant thing for the townswoman to do to show her devotion to Jesus. This was a *ritual anointing* and as such is of enormous significance: for Jesus' title of Christos/Christ means 'Anointed One' – and as the only anointing mentioned in the whole of the New Testament is *performed by a woman*, surely it should be celebrated as a major rite of Christianity. Indeed, Jesus says forcefully, 'She poured perfume on my body to prepare for my burial', but that burial, Christians believe, was unlike any other interment, for Jesus triumphed over death and the tomb to fulfil his destiny as the incarnate deity, the risen sacrificial king. In anointing him she *Christened* him, and marked him out for his fateful death. The true meaning of the ritual was completely lost on the other disciples, but Jesus tries hard to impress Mary Magdalene's importance on them, saying sternly: 'I tell you the truth, wherever the gospel is preached throughout the world, what she has done will also be told in memory of her.'[36]

Put simply, then why isn't it? Jesus' prophecy failed dramatically: even the first disciples to hear it were to make sure it never came to pass. What Christ himself wanted clearly counted for nothing in their zeal to create a Church in their own image, or rather in the image of the Gospel that they chose to approve. This would not be the only example of even the first Christians reworking the message of Christ to accord with their own agenda, especially where the Magdalene was concerned.

So far from the anointing being celebrated – there is no Catholic feast day dedicated to this event – the Gospel writers were careful even to obscure the name of the performer of the rite. However, John's Gospel[37] makes it clear that the anointing actually took place in the house of Martha, Lazarus and Mary at Bethany and it was the latter who performed the ritual. And while Luke[38] is careful to describe its initiatrix as 'an unnamed sinner', he immediately goes on to introduce the Magdalene for the first time, as if the association of ideas was too strong to ignore.

Mary Magdalene may never have earned her living on the Judaean streets as is still so widely believed – despite the fact that the Pope officially recanted this 'fact' in 1969, although in a whisper rather than a shout – but she was profoundly associated with quite another kind of 'Whoredom'. Spikenard, the ruinously

expensive perfume that she used to *Christ-en* Jesus, was used extensively in the sacred marriages and other sexual rites of the ancient
Oriental systems of Taoism and Tantrism, being especially reserved
to anoint *the head and feet*. As Peter Redgrove acknowledges in his
The Black Goddess (1989), in his discussion about Taoism:

> It is interesting to compare this with Middle-Eastern religious
> practices, and the image of them which we have inherited. Mari-
> Ishtar, the Great Whore, anointed her consort Tammuz (with
> whom Jesus was identified) and thereby made him a Christ. This
> was in preparation for his descent into the underworld, from
> which he would return at her bidding. She, or her priestess, was
> called the Great Whore because this was a sexual rite of *horasis*,
> of whole-body orgasm that would take the consort into the
> visionary knowledgeable continuum. It was a rite of crossing,
> from which he would return transformed. In the same way Jesus
> said that Mary Magdalene anointed him for his burial. Only
> women could perform these rites in the goddess' name, and this
> is why no men attended his tomb, only Mary Magdalene and her
> women. A chief symbol of the Magdalene in Christian art was
> the cruse of holy oil – the external sign of the inner baptism expe-
> rienced by the Taoist . . .[39]

'Horasis', the sacred whole-body orgasm is mentioned only once
in the New Testament, in the Acts of the Apostles, although
Redgrove believes it is mistranslated as 'visions',[40] in a passage in
which the writer quotes from the prophet Joel: 'In the last days, God
says, I will pour out my Spirit on all people. Your sons and your
daughters will prophesy, your young men will see visions . . .'[41] It
would give a remarkably different flavour to Acts if rendered as:
'Your young men shall enjoy the sacred sex rite of horasis . . .'

In the traditional form of sacred marriage, the *hieros gamos*, the
priestess/queen/goddess also anoints the priest/king/god with oil on
the genitals as a preparation for ritual *horasis*. Behind the male
disciples' concern for the wasted money and the plight of the poor,
was there another reason for their distaste at this ritual? Clearly the
anointing of Jesus' feet – the singling out of the sacrificial king –
took place in front of them, but the climax of the ceremony might

have been a matter for closed doors (and a great deal of muttered conjecture). The woman with the alabaster jar may have been making a sacred king, but she was also making herself some powerful enemies.

Apostle of the Apostles

In the most recent translations of the Bible, 'Mary Magdalene' is rendered as 'Mary *called* Magdalene', quite a different form of words for example, from 'Simon from Cyrene' or 'Saul of Tarsus', implying something over and above her place of origin. (Although even if 'Magdalene' did refer to her home town, it is unlikely to be the 'Magdala' on the shore of Lake Galilee that is usually cited, because according to Josephus it was called Tarichea in her day. However, intriguingly there was a Magdolum just across the border in Egypt, and a Magdala in Ethiopia.)[42] 'Magdalene' – as in '*the* Magdalene' – is almost certainly a title, meaning 'great lady', possibly originating in the Queen of Sheba's title *Magda*, accorded to her for her devotion to the Moon goddess.

Even the New Testament writers tacitly (and reluctantly) acknowledge the Magdalene's status, almost always naming her first in any list of Jesus' female followers – although they are given short shrift by Luke, who sniffs dismissively 'The Twelve were with [Jesus], and also some women who had been cured of evil spirits and diseases: Mary (called Magdalene) . . .'[43] Unlike most of the other women in the Bible – including the Virgin Mary – she is never defined by her relationship with a man. Whereas they tend to be the 'mother of the Saviour' or 'Joanna, wife of Chuzah',[44] she is simply '*the* Magdalene', as if too important, famous and independent to be otherwise. Indeed, there is a distinct sense that if they could have got away with it, the writers of Matthew, Mark, Luke and John's Gospels would have excluded her altogether, so keen are they to marginalize or obscure her when she does appear in the story, despite Jesus' absolute insistence that her role in his anointing be celebrated throughout history.

However, as many people know today – usually excluding Christians, who are deliberately kept in the dark by their own clergy – the New Testament books are not the only Gospels in existence. Before the Emperor Constantine adopted Christianity as the state religion of the tottering Roman Empire in the fourth century CE, there were hundreds of diverse 'Gospels', poems, songs and epistles doing the rounds. However, after Constantine's Council of Nicaea in 325 CE[45] decided what books would be included in the very new New Testament, the dozens of other candidates were instantly declared anathema, together with anyone foolish enough to claim they had equal claim to be 'authentic'. Cyril of Jerusalem (315–386 CE) declared dogmatically:

> Of the New Testament there are four Gospels only, for the rest have false titles and are harmful . . . receive also the Acts of the Twelve Apostles; and in addition to these the seven Catholic Epistles of James, Peter, John and Jude; and as a seal upon them all, and the latest work of the disciples, the fourteen epistles of Paul [now acknowledged to be chronologically the first of these Christian writings]. But let all the rest be put aside in secondary rank. And whatever books are not read in the churches, do not read these even by yourself, as you have already heard me say concerning the Old Testament apocrypha.[46]

David Tresemer and Laura-Lea Cannon point out how the New Testament came about in their 2002 Introduction to Jean-Yves Leloup's 1997 translation of *The Gospel of Mary Magdalene*:

> . . . the Council of Nicaea . . . decided which texts would become the standards of the Church . . . and which would be suppressed. Those not chosen as standard were attacked – sometimes violently – for many years. Indeed, the bishops at the Council of Nicaea who disagreed with Constantine's choices were exiled on the spot.[47]

One wonders what Cyril and his fellow Church Fathers were so afraid of. A clue may lie in the fact that although the New Testament gospels only reluctantly mention the Magdalene, her role in many of the forbidden books is so major as to be positively stellar. And we know about at least some of these other books because they were hidden from Constantine's vengeful clergy, only to resurface in much more recent times – for example, the *Gospel of Mary* (Magdalene) (thought to have been written in the second century CE) was found in Cairo in the 1850s, while a large cache of lost gospels was found at Nag Hammadi in Egypt in 1945, including *The Gospel of Thomas* and *The Gospel of Philip*. These are routinely dismissed by most modern biblical scholars as being of dubious theological authenticity or worth, which is allegedly the reason that they are never even mentioned from pulpits or in Bible study groups. The fact is, however, that although many of the recovered gospels are fragmentary or incomprehensible, others present a coherent and consistent picture of Jesus and Mary Magdalene that is wholly unacceptable to the churches, and if a fraction of their congregations ever took these gospels seriously enough to read them carefully, grave questions would be asked about the historical authority of the Christian religion.

While the canonical books are resolutely from what might be termed 'mainstream' Christianity, or Saint Paul's version, these other works are mostly Gnostic in origin and outlook. The biblical Gospels try almost too hard to sound authentic, piling on detail upon detail of Christ's travel schedule, the people he met and healed, the accusations of his critics, the chronology of his arrest, torture and death. The Gnostic gospels are usually much more concerned with the teachings and the mysteries, with a distinctly transcendent, intuitive feel to them. More significantly perhaps, the biblical texts are very masculine in tone and outlook, while the Gnostics are considerably more feminine – largely because of their reverence for their heroine, Mary Magdalene. Her role becomes clearer: indeed, even a cursory glance through the Gospels of Philip, Thomas and Mary, and the later *Pistis Sophia* (*Faith-Wisdom*) will present an almost explosively different picture of Jesus and his mission.

Mary comes across as feisty, intelligent, and perhaps a little too assertive and even controlling for her own good. In the *Pistis Sophia* – almost comically – she insists repeatedly on taking centre-stage in Jesus' lengthy question-and-answer session with his disciples, asking 39 of the 42 questions. Although other women such as Salome, Martha and Mary the Mother do occasionally participate, the text is littered not only with the phrase 'and Mary continues again' but also with the increasingly bitter complaints of the men, who feel humiliated and angry at her pre-eminence. One disciple in particular feels dangerously irate. Peter explodes to

Jesus: 'My Lord, we will not endure this woman, for she taketh the opportunity from us and hath let none of us speak, but *she* [my emphasis] *discourseth many times*.' Any mild suspicion that Peter may have actually loathed the Magdalene is substantially reinforced by another passage from the *Pistis Sophia* in which Mary herself says to Jesus:

My Lord, my mind is ever understanding, at every time to come forward and set forth the solution of the words which [thou] hath uttered: but *I am afraid of Peter, because he threatened me and hateth our sex.*[48] [My emphasis.]

Peter, the bluff hot-tempered 'Big Fisherman' clearly absolutely detests Mary, saying to Jesus, 'Lord, let Mary leave us, for women are not worthy of life'[49] – although Christ's own reaction, as we shall see, is perhaps at first sight not as female-friendly as it might have been. But does Peter (and perhaps the other men in the mission) hate the Magdalene simply because she is a woman? Although married,[50] Peter had no compunction in abandoning his wife to follow Jesus – he may have been glad to escape an unhappy home life – although in any case misogyny was a way of life to the Jews of his time and place.

The days of wine, roses and Asherath had long gone, the *shekhina* were desexed and Yahweh ruled with an impressively male rod of iron. Goddesses belonged to the louche foreigners, such as – or perhaps especially – the sophisticated Egyptians, and were therefore an abomination to the Lord. (When the Greeks tried to foist the new dying-and-rising god Serapis on them, the novel religion only took hold when the people's beloved Isis was restored to power and set at his right hand, a situation that was to be echoed, albeit feebly, when the Christians made Mary their Virgin goddess.)

To the likes of Simon Peter, women should know their place: in the home behind the cooking pot or washing the men's clothes, going submissively and silently about their business with their hair modestly tied up and veiled. On the other hand, the Magdalene was known to flout Jewish Law (being *harmatolos*) and custom, audaciously wearing her hair unbound in public – so grievous a social and religious sin that a man could divorce his wife for doing

so. (Her unbound hair, with which she dried Jesus' feet, was probably a major reason for the male disciples' distaste at the anointing.)
She unhesitatingly spoke up, even in the company of the 'superior'
men, and was one of the women who funded Jesus' mission.
Clearly rich, independent and articulate, possessed of secrets the
dim Peter could only guess at, the Magdalene was riding high
among the cult members. In the *Pistis Sophia* she even permits
herself the verbal equivalent of a sly wink at Jesus as she says with
something approaching mock humility: 'Be not wroth with me if I
question thee on all things.' Jesus says 'Question what thou wilt',
so, seizing on a particular point of theology, she says with an
unmistakable air of condescension, as initiate to initiate: 'My Lord
reveal unto us . . . *that also my brethren may understand it* [My
emphasis].'[51] Peter was ill-equipped to deal with a woman who was
clearly already so well-informed about Jesus' secrets and who occasionally succumbed to the temptation to rub it in. But worse, it was
she who was Jesus' favourite – and absolutely not Peter himself, as
indicated in the New Testament. And her role in the resurrection
was something of a stumbling block for the Church, which –
unbelievably – claims its authority from the 'fact' that its founder,
Peter, was the first person to see the risen Christ. Even a brief
glance at the story in the New Testament will reveal this is arrant
rubbish, although the truth would have been considerably easier to
keep from the flock in the days before widespread literacy.

The Gospel of Mark states plainly: 'When Jesus rose
early on the first day of the week, he appeared first to Mary
Magdalene.'[52] The Vatican still tries to wriggle out of this by
explaining that Jesus had no female disciples: basically a spiritually
inferior woman, Mary Magdalene didn't count. And as the argument about female bishops rolls on unedifyingly in the ranks of the
Anglican Church, the old prejudices emerge with some degree of
viciousness – of course women should not be bishops, or even
priests, for it is a known fact that Jesus chose his disciples only
from among the male population.

Yet even the male-oriented New Testament not only lists the
women on the mission – always beginning with the Magdalene –
but also describes them as 'disciples', although unfortunately this
telling term has traditionally been translated as 'disciples' of the

men, but the more derogatory and inferior 'followers' in a female context. In reality, it is the same word for the same role. In any case, according to Luke's Gospel, the women 'were helping to support [Jesus and the men] of their own means',[53] or basically funding the men's mission. (The women must have been somewhat taken aback at Jesus' teaching 'Consider how the lilies grow. They do not labour or spin,'[54] about not worrying about the future because God would provide. If he did, his bounty took the form of the purses of the daughters of Asherah.) The Magdalene and the other women essentially *kept* the men, and proved loyal to the end, while Peter got drunk, denied three times that he even knew Jesus and, like his brothers in the Gospel (apart from young John) was nowhere to be seen at the crucifixion. Surely the women had earned the right to be called disciples.

However, the Gnostic Gospels make explicit what was lurking implicitly in the New Testament about the status of the women, especially Mary Magdalene. These forbidden, anathematized books make it very clear that not only did Christ welcome women into his mission, but they were members of his inner circle of initiates rather than the slower-witted and unimaginative men, who time and time again 'knew not what he meant', and even showed no sign of comprehending the significance of Christ's death. The impression is that Peter in particular had no idea what was going on: all he knew was that he loved Jesus and spent much of his time in a red-hot passion of envy and anger at the – to him – incomprehensible status of the Magdalene. Of all the women, *Magda*-lene, the Great Lady and anointing priestess, even earned the title 'Apostle of the Apostles',[55] which implies that Jesus acknowledged she stood head and shoulders above all other apostles.

In the *Gospel of Mary*, even Peter is forced to acknowledge her closeness to Jesus, saying 'the Saviour loved you more than the rest of the women',[56] but not before he had suggested that she had invented the story of meeting the resurrected Christ, thundering incredulously: 'How is it possible that the Teacher talked in this manner with a woman about secrets of which we ourselves are ignorant? Did he really choose her, and prefer her to us?'[57] When Peter calls her vision a lie, naturally:

... Mary wept, and answered him: 'My brother Peter, what can you be thinking? Do you believe that this is just my own imagination, that I invented this vision? Or do you believe that I would lie about our Teacher?' At this, Levi spoke up: 'Peter, you have always been hot-tempered, and now we see you repudiating a woman, just as our adversaries do. Yet if the Teacher held her worthy, who are you to reject her? Surely the Teacher knew her very well, for he loved her more than us ... Let us grow as he demanded of us, and walk forth to spread the gospel, without trying to lay down any rules and laws other than those he witnessed.'[58]

Unlike the canonical gospels, several of the Gnostic texts make Jesus' love for the Magdalene crystal clear. Despite the tendency of the *Pistis Sophia* to indulge in the usual excessively impenetrable Gnostic ramblings about complex realms of heaven and hell, the passages concerning the personal relationships among the disciples read with an unusual clarity and confidence that strongly suggests a single tradition – perhaps beginning with authentic memories of the individuals on the Jesus mission. Christ makes this unambiguous statement to the Magdalene, which must have made the irascible Peter seethe: 'Mary, thou blessed one, whom I will perfect in all mysteries of those of the height [the highest mysteries], discourse in openness, thou, whose heart is raised to the kingdom of heaven more than all thy brethren'.[59] Later in the same Gnostic text, Christ announces: 'Where I shall be, there will also be my twelve ministers. But Mary Magdalene and John the Virgin, will tower over all my disciples and over all men who shall receive the mysteries ... And they will be on my right hand and on my left. And I am they, and they are I.'[60]

Mary and young John are Jesus' closest apostles who will sit on his right and left throughout eternity – and John the Beloved/Divine/Evangelist will have a special part to play in this investigation. But Mary is more obviously Jesus' favourite, being dubbed 'The All' or 'The Woman Who Knows All' by him. A clue as to the depth of their relationship is found in this explicit passage from the Gnostic *Gospel of Philip*:

. . . And the companion of the Saviour is Mary Magdalene . But Christ loved her more than all the disciples, and used to kiss her often on the mouth. The rest of the disciples were offended . . . They said to him, 'Why do you love her more than all of us?' The Saviour answered and said to them, 'Why do I not love you as I love her?'[61]

It has been suggested by Christian traditionalists that Jesus was merely kissing Mary in the spirit of *agape*, or spiritual love – indeed, the Gnostics celebrated their religion at 'love-feasts', which were more or less chaste depending on the group. (Of course the Carpocratians' love-feasts were somewhat more colourful.) But if he only meant to give her an affectionate spiritual peck, why did Jesus choose to kiss her on the lips, and why would it have 'offended' the others so blatantly? Actually, no one knows where Jesus kissed her because, frustratingly, the ancient gospel is missing that particular bit of papyrus. 'On the mouth' is merely a scholarly speculation, but of course it is extremely interesting that even scholars thought fit to suggest the mouth and not the hand or cheek. Of course the original may have said something quite different, such as 'on the Sabbath' or 'on the Sea of Galilee'! Another passage from the *Gospel of Philip* is even more intriguing:

Three women always used to walk with the lord – Mary his mother, his sister, and the Magdalene, *who is called his companion*. For 'Mary' is the name of his sister and his mother, and it is the name of *his partner* [My emphases].[62]

The word for 'companion' is the Aramaic *koinonos*, a Greek loan word meaning 'partner'. Previously[63] when I claimed that this means 'sexual partner' there were howls of outrage from certain quarters. I remaiṇ unrepentant. I maintain that *koinonos* means 'partner' in exactly the sense of our modern word, which depends almost entirely on context for its nearest definition. If someone is introduced as 'partner' in an office setting, it will be assumed this means business associate. If at a party, 'lover' is more likely to fit the bill.[64] Here we have the Magdalene, who elsewhere in the Nag Hammadi texts is described as being repeatedly kissed, presumably on the mouth, by Jesus. She may have controlled the purse strings, but somehow she hardly sounds like a business partner – nor would the modern British 'good mate' match the context. (In which case she would probably have been described as 'disciple' or 'follower'.) *Koinonos*, in this context, can only mean lover.

The phrase 'who is *called* his companion' is also slightly stilted, perhaps as if some kind of euphemism, as in 'who *they say* is his companion', and Mary is specifically called his *partner*.

Despite the belief fostered worldwide by Dan Brown's block-busting thriller *The Da Vinci Code* that Jesus and the Magdalene were man and wife – a concept that first reached the Anglo-Saxon public in 1982 in Michael Baigent, Richard Leigh and Henry Lincoln's *The Holy Blood and the Holy Grail* – there is little to support this view, either in the Bible or, more tellingly, even in the Gnostic writings. The miracle of the turning of the water into wine at a marriage at Cana, said to be the wedding of Jesus and Mary, originally – as we have seen – came from the myths of the dying-and-rising wine god Dionysus.[65] And the single most important piece of evidence for their *not* being married is one of glaring omission: simply, there is no mention of a 'Miriam, wife of the Saviour' or 'Mary, Christ's spouse' in either the New Testament or *any* of the known Gnostic writings. Although there was a conspiracy to marginalize her in the Gospels of Saints Matthew, Mark, Luke and John, it seems that it did not extend to air-brushing out her marital status. Indeed, the obvious distaste the male disciples feel for her may partly arise from the fact that her relationship with Jesus was not sanctioned by Jewish Law.

In any case, Jesus' disciples were forbidden to marry – although John the Baptist's followers were not – and there are other possible considerations that would prevent Christ 'making an honest woman' of her. Unacceptable and unthinkable though such consid-erations may be, either or both of them could already have been married, or they may have been close blood relatives – too close to make their love legal. Or one or both of them could have been dedi-cated to chastity, most likely as priest or priestess of a foreign cult. (Even temple 'prostitutes' or servants were expected to remain unmarried and observe the sexual rites only within the temple walls.) The thirteenth-century citizens of Béziers in the south of

France – all 20,000 of them – willingly died martyrs' deaths rather than recant a belief that Mary was Jesus' 'concubine', which they probably gleaned from Gnostic gospels that were circulating in the area at that time, but which have since been lost.[66]

The Magdalene's closeness to Jesus, her relationship with 'John the Beloved', and Peter's hatred, are all significant factors in her emergence as 'Mary Lucifer' – for better or worse in the minds of future generations. And in order to piece together her true significance, we need to fast-forward to the late fifteenth century, where one of the world's most famous figures was concocting works of the most outrageous blasphemy.

Discovering the code

In the early 1990s Clive Prince and myself were busily researching the secrets of the great Florentine Maestro Leonardo da Vinci, for what became our first joint book, *Turin Shroud: In Whose Image? The Shocking Truth Unveiled* (1994), its subtitle becoming the more self-explanatory *How Leonardo da Vinci Fooled History* for the 2000 paperback. Our discovery of a mass of circumstantial evidence that suggested strongly he had created the allegedly miraculously imaged Holy Shroud of Turin using a primitive photographic technique will be discussed later, when analysing Leonardo's Luciferan credentials. For now, suffice it to say that as we became convinced of Leonardo's intimate link to the 'Shroud', our homes rapidly disappeared beneath a mass of Leonardo reproductions, which we habitually scrutinized minutely for any clues as to what he really stood for. Concentrate as we might, however, our eventual discoveries seemed always to operate on an unconscious level – apparently spontaneously – as if a coiled spring was released explosively in our minds as a reaction to hours of intense staring. We 'suddenly' saw the most astonishing things in what are, after all, the most famous works of art, and therefore the most familiar images, in the world. However, these were not simply the equivalent of imagining faces in the fire or animal shapes in cloud formations: gradually the features we had noted and our discoveries about Leonardo's own particular brand of heresy came together as an utterly consistent, coherent whole.

That he intended posterity to notice his hidden clues is certain, and reflects his attitude, as revealed in his contempt for the typical poet because 'he has not the power of saying several things at one and the same time'.[67] One of the first of the 'hidden' symbols we discerned in *The Last Supper* proved astonishingly blatant, yet like everyone else for 500 years we had succumbed to the blanket of assumption that veiled our eyes. In 1994 we wrote:

> Look at the figure of Jesus with his red robe and blue cloak and look to the right where there is what appears at first glance to be a young man leaning away. This is generally taken to be John the Beloved – but in that case, should he not be leaning against Jesus' 'bosom' as in the Bible? Look yet more closely. This character is wearing the mirror image of Jesus' clothing: in this case a blue robe and red cloak, but otherwise the garments are identical . . . [and] . . . as much as Jesus is large and very male, this character is elfin and distinctly female. The hands are tiny, there is a gold necklace on show . . . This is no John the Beloved: this is Mary Magdalene. And a hand cuts across her throat, in that chilling Freemasonic gesture indicating a dire warning.[68]

Yet if we thought we could safely leave *The Last Supper* behind us, we were sadly mistaken. Its symbolism proved central to our next co-authored work, *The Templar Revelation: Secret Guardians of the True Identity of Christ* (1997) and was of enormous significance for my own *Mary Magdalene: Christianity's Hidden Goddess* (2003): with each book we had something new, exciting and disturbing – like all Leonardo's secrets – to present. This trend continues here, with a major new revelation. But first, the essential background:

In the *Last Supper* the young 'St John' leaning as far as possible away from Jesus to make a giant 'M' shape with him, indicating the real identity of the character, appeared in our second book, and has also reached a huge international audience through *The Da Vinci Code*, which used our work as the inspiration for the whole concept of Leonardo's codes and secrets. Yes, clearly this is Mary Magdalene, her mirror-image clothes revealing her to be Christ's 'other half', taking what many heretics would have believed to be her rightful place at his side as he initiates the great Christian sacrament in which the wine represents his sacrificial blood and the bread his body. And, as I noted in *Mary Magdalene*, the hand that makes the vicious slicing motion across the woman's neck belongs to Saint Peter, whom the Gnostic gospels make clear actually had threatened her . . . But how was a 15th-century Italian painter to know about the fraught relationship of those two long-dead disciples? Did he have access to the forbidden books that were circulating in the south of France a few centuries before his birth? (Certainly he understood the value of secrets, writing about 'truth and the *power of knowledge*'.) And why did Leonardo believe she ought to be sitting at Jesus' right hand during the Last Supper?

Perhaps he knew something about the original gospels that remains elusive even to the twenty-first century. In their book *Jesus and the Goddess: The Secret Teachings of the Original Christians* (2001), Timothy Freke and Peter Gandy claim that the biblical *Gospel of Saint John*, 'if it is to bear any name at all, should be *The Gospel of Mary Magdalene*.' They explain that although it claims to be written by 'an unspecified "Beloved Disciple", it is attributed to John *solely* on the basis of . . . Irenaeus, at the end of the second century, claiming he had a childhood memory of being told that the gospel was written by the disciple John.'[69] Noting that the late first-century Gnostics attributed it to their master Cerinthus, they add

> Modern research suggests that the 'Beloved Disciple' he makes the narrator of the story is not John, but Mary Magdalene . . . The Gospel of the 'Beloved Disciple' has been modified . . . in order to turn the 'Beloved Disciple' Mary into the male figure of John, who was more acceptable to misogynist Literalists.[70]

Taken in this context – however speculative – the following passage describing the biblical Last Supper after Jesus announces that one of his followers will betray him has a particular significance, if 'Mary' is substituted for 'the disciple whom Jesus loved':

> One of them, the disciple whom Jesus loved, was reclining next to him. Simon Peter motioned to this disciple and said, 'Ask him which one he means.'
> Leaning back against Jesus, he asked him: 'Lord, who is it?'[71]

It is interesting to note that Peter tacitly admits the status of the Beloved by asking him/her to ask Jesus for information – recall how Mary hogged the floor during the question-and-answer session reported in the *Pistis Sophia*, and how she and Jesus clearly enjoyed their mutual and no doubt intimate secrets. And in this version of the verses the Beloved is leaning familiarly against Christ at the dinner table. (However, if this really were the Magdalene, such a flaunting of her intimacy with Jesus would have flown totally in the face of what was considered decent behaviour in that time and place. Far from cuddling up to Jesus in front of all his male colleagues, even a legal wife would have kept her distance and modestly supervized the preparation of the meal in the kitchens.)

The originator of this intriguing hypothesis, Ramon K. Jusino, (largely based on the research of Raymond E. Brown,[72] although the controversial conclusion is Jusino's own) argues that as 'there was a concerted effort on the part of the male leadership of the early church to suppress the knowledge of any major contributions made by female disciples' . . . 'much of Mary Magdalene's legacy fell victim to this suppression', ascribing the Fourth Gospel's alleged authorship to John the Evangelist to the crafty work of an early 'redactor' (or editor) who basically wrote her out, changing the grammatical gender. He comments that 'there is more evidence pointing to her authorship of the Fourth Gospel than there ever was pointing to authorship by John'.[73]

Jusino cites certain tantalizing structural inconsistences in St John's Gospel as evidence of reworking to an anti-Magdalene agenda. Arguably the most convincing example is the following passage, which has Mary and the anonymous male Beloved Disciple together at the foot of the cross: 'Near the cross of Jesus stood his mother, his mother's sister, Mary the wife of Clopas, and Mary Magdalene. When Jesus saw his mother there, and the disciple whom he loved standing nearby, he said . . .'[74]

Suddenly there is the mysterious Beloved, although he is not listed with the Marys by the cross, implying that 'he' is actually one of them. American biblical scholar Raymond E. Brown, while not agreeing with Jusino's radical conclusion, does admit that the mother of Jesus 'was specifically mentioned in the tradition that came to the evangelist [John] . . . but the reference to the Beloved Disciple . . . is a supplement to the tradition', adding that the 'Beloved Disciple' appears strangely incongruous in this setting.[75]

Perhaps more excitingly, following Jusino's line of evidence, we can now compare certain passages in the Gospel of St John that depict a distinct sense of 'one-upmanship' between Peter and Mary with those already discussed above from the Gnostic Gospels. As we have seen in the *Gospel of Mary*, Peter is jealous of Mary's vision of Jesus, claiming that she fabricated it;[76] in the *Gospel of Thomas* he demands of Jesus 'Let Mary leave us, for women are not worthy of life';[77] and in the *Gospel of Philip* the close relationship between the Magdalene and Jesus is compared to his relationship with the other disciples – to their detriment.[78] Jusino lists five episodes in St John's Gospel that match the Gnostic passages. As we have seen, 'the Beloved Disciple leans against Jesus' chest while Peter has to petition the Disciple to ask Jesus a question for him';[79] 'the Beloved Disciple has access to the high priest's palace while Peter does not';[80] 'the Beloved Disciple immediately believes in the Resurrection while Peter and the rest of the disciples do not understand';[81] 'the Beloved Disciple is the only one who recognizes the Risen Christ while he speaks from the shore to the disciples in their fishing boat',[82] and 'Peter jealously asks Jesus about the fate of the Beloved Disciple'.[83]

However, while acknowledging that of course there was a conspiracy to marginalize the Magdalene on the part of the Gospel writers, even to the open-minded there must remain objections to Jusino's theory. As we have noted, if Mary were indeed the 'Beloved' disciple who leant against Jesus at the Last Supper, her behaviour was extraordinarily provocative, even for an Egypt-trained priestess of particularly assertive character! (And although she is present at Jesus' side in Leonardo's great work, she is actually leaning as far away from him as possible – although this may be simply a composition-driven necessity, to create the clue of the 'M' shape.) Then again, even in the Gnostic texts, where one might expect the biblical censorship to have considerably less influence, there are references to 'the *youth* whom Jesus loved' – Lazarus, Mary of Bethany/Mary Magdalene's brother – about whom the offending Mar Saba verses concerning some kind of sexual initiation with Jesus appear to have been written. Clearly there was something about *both* siblings that the Gospel writers perceived as so distasteful that whenever they could they reduced them as much as possible to vague and dismissive phrases such as 'a certain woman', 'an unnamed sinner', 'the youth whom Jesus loved'. But in Leonardo's painting it is *John* and Mary who are wrought as one, not Lazarus and the Magdalene, almost as if *both* were somehow equally Jesus' 'other half' in *The Last Supper*.

The answer could be simply that, as far as Leonardo was concerned, this was literally so: the Magdalene and young Saint John both participated in secret sacred sex rites with Jesus, from which the other disciples were barred and perhaps of which they only had the faintest notion. One can imagine that they knew something sexual went on behind closed doors with the favoured two, and deep down, hated it, but their respect and love for the obviously charismatic guru meant they were willing to put up with it, if only on the surface. We know what the men – especially Peter – thought of the Magdalene, and in the Gospel of John he also extends that irritation or downright enmity to young John. Although once again Lazarus is not apparently in the frame, the situation begins to make more sense when it is realized that there is evidence that John and Lazarus were in fact one and the same . . .

In fact, 'Lazarus' is Greek for 'Eliezer',[84] a version of 'Elijah' or 'Elias', the Old Testament prophet strongly associated in Judaea of that time with John the Baptist –, indeed, many ordinary people thought he was Elijah/Elias reincarnated. In this context, Lazarus is essentially called 'John' twice over by the Gospel writers, although they are careful to obscure his real relationship to Jesus. 'John' was often taken as a baptismal name to honour the Baptist, and usually denoted one of his disciples: one of the women who followed Jesus was Joanna, wife of Herod's steward, who was probably originally a 'Johannite' – a devotee of John the Baptist: 'Johannine' more usually being a follower of John the Evangelist.

Then there is the evidence of another Mar Saba verse, from the *Secret Gospel of Mark* that Clement referred to in his outraged letter about the wicked Carpocratians, a passage that apparently caused grave displeasure among the Church fathers because, for some reason, it excited enormous interest in that disgraceful cult.

Yet superficially it seems totally innocuous, even pointless, although it does provide the missing link between two apparently unconnected but chronological passages in the canonical Gospel according to St Mark, which read: 'Then they came to Jericho. As Jesus and his disciples, together with a large crowd, were leaving the city, a blind man, Bartimaeus . . . was sitting by the roadside begging . . .'[85] The passage seems utterly futile – Jesus goes to Jericho but then suddenly leaves: clearly something interesting must have happened in between, something that the heretical Carpocratians found especially intriguing. Yet the missing episode simply reads: 'And the sister of the youth whom Jesus loved and his mother and Salome were there, and Jesus did not receive them.' At first glance this passage may seem rather dull – hardly worth the build-up – but it contains implications of the most tantalizing sort. For it suggests by inference that *Lazarus* was Jesus' male 'Beloved', and therefore that he was also John. Note, too, that here 'Salome', like the Magdalene, is not defined by her relationship to a man, as wife, daughter or sister. Why? Is it because she was also too well known, or that her status was too impressive for the writer to need to explain her in any detail? We will return later to the vexed question of Salome.

But if Lazarus was the *youth* whom Jesus loved, and his sister Mary was the *woman* he loved, and they both lived at Bethany with their sister Martha, why was everything about that place hedged around with obfuscation and deceit by the New Testament writers? Was it the association of sex rites, which the other disciples must have been reluctant even to consider, either from a sense of offended morality or just a confused sense of jealousy at not being one of the lucky inner circle?

St Luke's version of the anointing stands out from the other three New Testament gospels for several compelling reasons. Unlike the accounts in Matthew, Mark and John's Gospels, his is set in Capernaum, not Bethany, and at the start, not the end, of Jesus' mission. The woman remains anonymous, unimportant. The incident seems to have been included only to emphasize Christ's power to forgive sinners, as in his defence of the anointress to the householder, Simon:

'Do you see this woman? I came into your house. You did not give me any water for my feet, but she wet my feet with her tears and wiped them with her hair.

'You did not give me a kiss, but this woman from the time I entered has not stopped kissing my feet. You did not put oil on my head, but she has poured perfume on my feet.

'Therefore, I tell you, her many sins have been forgiven – for she loved much. But he who has been forgiven little loves little.'[86]

The last sentence – as several libertine Gnostic sects firmly believed – seems implicitly to approve of those who have a great deal to forgive, such as the unnamed woman who 'loved much'. The greater the sins, the greater the forgiveness. But why should Luke fight shy of giving any details that would link the milestone event of the anointing with the Magdalene or indeed the last and climactic part of Jesus' mission? And why does he insist on calling it 'a certain village?' The other gospel writers obviously knew it was Bethany, so presumably so must Luke, although he did everything he could short of excluding the episode completely to obscure the fact. Why?

Some scholars, such as Hugh J. Schonfield, admit that there was something about Bethany and the family whom Jesus visited there that appears to be deliberately withheld by the Gospel writers. Yet this seems odd, for the 'Bethany family' actually make the necessary arrangements – to put it more cynically, stage-manage – the lead-up to the crucifixion. For example, as Schonfield points out in his closely argued *The Passover Plot* (1965), they are the key characters who provide the donkey on which Christ rides triumphantly into Jerusalem, apparently deliberately ensuring that the Old Testament prophecies about the Messiah are fulfilled. However, if that was their *raison d'être*, the ensuing arrest, torture and crucifixion of Jesus must have come as a traumatic shock, for the Jewish Messiah was never expected to die – at least not before liberating his people from the occupying Romans. And he emphatically was not supposed to suffer the shameful death of a common criminal, nailed to a cross in a public place, reviled and spat at by the dregs of society.

But whatever the underlying motivation behind the Bethany family's involvement in the furthering of the mission, there was another link that may explain why Luke avoided mentioning the village by name, and why the disciples generally felt a great distaste for it and everything it stood for. And this also provides a major link with the real 'Da Vinci code' and a crucial 'Luciferan' current that drove many heretics, even up until the present day.

Leonardo's legacy

Christians might be horrified to learn of the true extent of heresy that my colleague Clive Prince and I have discovered in the allegedly 'pious' paintings of Leonardo da Vinci. First, there was a giant 'M' shape in the painting of *The Last Supper*, created by the figures of Jesus and the 'Beloved', indicating that 'he' is actually a she: none other than Mary Magdalene.

Then there is a distinctly homoerotic undertone in his *St John the Baptist*, one of only two of his works which had pride of place in the room where he died in 1519 – the other being the *Mona Lisa*.

The peculiar *St John* is not well liked among art historians, and one can easily see why. The young man leers knowingly at the observer, a pretty boy with luxuriant curls and fur hanging negligently off one polished shoulder, apparently the keeper of deep and probably dark secrets – judging from his wicked smile, a knowledge as old as sin. (A considerably less well-known work, a sketch of *Bacchus*, is unambiguously phallocentric: another young man smirks at the observer, but he is naked, his phallus unavoidably – and impressively – aroused. As we have seen, Bacchus was associated with Dionysus and Pan, gods of the wild woods and shameless sex rites, and in Leonardo's more finished depiction of this pagan deity the resemblance to his *John the Baptist* is striking. Indeed, both may have been based on the artist himself as a young man: Leonardo loved including himself in his own works.)

St John the Baptist almost appears to be 'camping it up', while raising his right index finger across his body to heaven, in what Clive and myself had dubbed 'the John gesture'. Although this appears in many medieval and Renaissance works to indicate the significance of heaven or generally the 'higher things' of spirituality, in Leonardo's works it always indicates, or is actually made by, John the Baptist – whom he clearly appears to revere intensely. Leonardo's devotion to the Baptist is promoted through sly allusions and half-hidden symbols, even at the expense of the Holy Family. . Although Clive and I have detailed Leonardo's heretical – 'Johannite' – symbolism elsewhere,[87] I shall provide a summary here to illustrate my argument.

In *The Last Supper* a disciple is thrusting a finger raised in the unmistakable 'John gesture' into Jesus' face with a rough intensity, although Christ ignores him and stares serenely down at his outspread hands – between which there is no chalice of wine, as one might expect, no 'Holy Grail'. What does the gesture mean here? Is it, as Clive and I suggest, a terse and even hostile '*Remember John* . . .'? But why should Jesus need reminding of his forerunner, the wild man from the desert – his cousin – who apparently fell down at his feet and declared him to be 'the Lamb of God'? And why is there the implicit warning in the gesture? Should you think that we are reading too much into this, our examination of Leonardo's other works proved surprising, even shocking.

The 'Cartoon' (or preliminary drawing) of the *Virgin and Child with St Anne and John the Baptist*, which is now displayed in London's National Gallery[88] shows an apparently masculine St Anne raising a massive John gesture at her daughter, the Virgin, who smiles slightly, totally oblivious. (It has been suggested that St Anne is really intended to depict St Elizabeth, the Baptist's mother.) The young St John gazes up without expression at the baby Jesus, who seems almost to writhe forward in his mother's arms, in order, apparently, to bless him. Yet the infant Christ has a strangely serpentine or maggot-like body (complete with sectioned torso) and appears to be an extension of his mother's arm, almost like a glove puppet. And although supposedly chucking John under the chin with one hand while blessing him with the other, it takes no stretch of imagination to notice that the one hand could equally well be steadying the boy's head to take a blow. To those who are impatient with this sort of heretical interpretation, may I advise caution, an open mind, and an open book – as large as possible – of Leonardo reproductions. It is surprising what the 'uneducated', non-art historian will find – such as the following, a new revelation.

With a mind cleared as far as possible of preconceptions, look

with a child's unsophisticated clarity at the Cartoon, specifically at
the tree-covered hill in the top right-hand corner, above John's
curly head. Actually, the 'hill' serves a double purpose, for its elaborate foliage also forms the distinct outline of the severed head of a
bearded man, with closed eyes. (Once seen, he can never be unseen:
some friends admit that they continually expect the man in their
reproduction suddenly to open his eyes any day now.) Why would
Leonardo depict a severed head? A clue lies in its position over
young John – according to the biblical account, John the Baptist
was beheaded while in King Herod's jail. He had been arrested for
denouncing the Roman puppet's illegal marriage, and suffered
death because Herod's wife Herodias had persuaded her daughter –
who remains anonymous in the New Testament – to ask the king for
John's head.

The astonishing, half-hidden theme of the Cartoon is also played
out in Leonardo's other works, as we shall see – even in the finished
painting based on the Cartoon, although the hovering head disappears in the transition. Even a cursory glance reveals that *The
Virgin and Child with St Anne* has changed considerably since its
haunting preliminary sketch was created. Mary is still sitting somewhat awkwardly on her mother's lap, but John the Baptist has
completely disappeared, to be replaced by a lamb. Yet in the New
Testament it is *Jesus*, not John, who is symbolized by the Lamb,
and it is the Baptist who memorably hails him as such. In
Leonardo's painting the lamb seems in imminent danger, for baby
Jesus boisterously hangs on to its ears – almost as if intent on
pulling its head off – while a chubby limb cuts across the lamb's
neck, creating the visual illusion of decapitation. But why would
Jesus at any point in his life want to harm the saint who proclaimed
his divinity to the world?

There are other, considerably more offensive examples of this
Johannite sub-text in Leonardo's works. In his unfinished
Adoration of the Magi, the Virgin and child occupy the lower fore-
ground, where they are honoured by the visit of the Wise Men, as
the title indicates. Yet, like all the great Florentine heretic's works,
it repays closer scrutiny. The worshippers adoring the Holy Family
are hideous, so gaunt, ugly and ancient – with their shrunken eyes
and skull-like heads – that they appear to be like ghouls or vampires

from the grave clawing at Mary and Jesus. And of the three famed gifts, only frankincense and myrrh are being proffered: gold, symbol of sacred kingship and perfection, is missing.

A second group of worshippers occupy the top half of the picture, beyond the Virgin's head. These are in marked contrast to the 'undead' around her and the infant Christ – vigorous, youthful, attractive, they appear to be adoring the roots of a tree. Bizarre though this may seem, there is a message here: the tree is a carob, traditionally associated in Catholic iconography with John the Baptist – and as if to reinforce the point, a young man raises the John gesture close to its trunk. Another man lurks at the bottom right of the picture, turning almost brutally away from Mary and Jesus. This is acknowledged to be a self-portrait of the artist, and here he is blasphemously turning his back on God incarnate and the Immaculate Conception. And as the model for Saint Jude in his *Last Supper*, Leonardo also has his back to Christ. There is a wry joke here – Jude is patron saint of lost causes!

There is considerably worse blasphemy in *The Virgin of the Rocks* (the Louvre version: the painting in London's National Gallery is less obviously heretical), which was originally commissioned by a religious organization, who certainly got more than they bargained for, although they seem not to have realized quite what they *did* get. The painting shows a scene from Church fable, in which the baby Jesus meets the equally infant John in Egypt specifically to confer on him the authority with which to baptize him in later life. The fact that to perform *any* rite on Jesus Christ implies greater authority than his had to be explained away in this cumbersome manner (although of course in the case of the anointing Magdalene the Gospel writers simply edited out her identity and made her act random, virtually meaningless).

The painting shows the Virgin apparently with her arm round John, who is kneeling submissively to Jesus, who in turn blesses him. Christ appears to be in the care of the archangel Uriel. Yet there is something wrong here: Uriel is traditionally the protector of *John*, not Jesus, and obviously Mary should be holding her son, not John. But suppose the children are with really their usual guardians, everything suddenly makes sense and Leonardo's fervent Johannitism shines through once again. For then it is John (now properly with Uriel) who is blessing Jesus (now with Mary), who in turn kneels submissively . . .

Leonardo also made his feelings about Mary's status very clear. The reason this painting is called *The Virgin of the Rocks* is because almost the whole of the top half is given over to apparently random shapes of dark, looming stones. But nothing is truly random in Leonardo's works, especially when he has the opportunity to pour ridicule on Christ and his mother. For rearing up out of the rocks virtually out of the Virgin's head is a remarkable pair of testicles topped by a huge upright phallus – right to the skyline – complete with tumescent central vein and impudent spurt of weeds. Clearly, once seen in this light, *The Virgin of the Rocks* will never quite have that pious aura again. This astonishing interpolation was presumably intended to be a savage attack on the alleged virginal status of Mary the mother, possibly inspired by the organization that commissioned the painting – the Confraternity of the Immaculate Conception.

But why did Leonardo so clearly adore the Baptist, while despising Jesus and his mother? What is it about John that inspired so much devotion – and why should it be heretical?

The Baptist: behind the myth

It is curious that John the Baptist is not celebrated as the first Christian martyr – that honour fell to the young Saint Stephen. Even when John was arrested by Herod and then beheaded on the wishes of Herodias and her unnamed daughter, the New Testament is silent about whether he cited Jesus Christ as his inspiration and Saviour with his last breath. Nor are we told in whose name John baptized . . .

This odd but implicit reticence on the part of John to acknowledge Jesus' superiority is dramatically at odds with the explicit scene in the New Testament where John apparently makes sense of his entire life by falling at Christ's feet, declaring him to be the chosen Lamb of God, whose sandals he is unworthy to untie. Jesus is baptized in the Jordan, and God appears in the form of a dove, announcing his Son's divinity. This is splendid, inspirational stuff, but unfortunately it is almost certainly complete and utter nonsense.

If John had really been so overcome at the very sight of Jesus, it was a passing phase, because not long afterwards, as he languished in jail he sent a message to him asking 'Are you the one who was to come, or should we expect someone else?'[89] But while the scene at the side of the Jordan is enthusiastically read out from the world's pulpits, the clergy keep tactically silent on the matter of John's subsequent doubts.

In fact, we now know that although Jesus must have been baptized by John – because thousands flocked to join the movement to repent and be baptized – in reality there never could have been any of that rather sickening 'Gosh, you're so wonderful and I'm so unworthy' declaimed by the Baptist. For it is now acknowledged that Jesus and John were rivals, and so were their respective cult members. In fact, despite the biblical depiction of John as a sort of mad desert hermit who enters the story briefly to bolster Jesus' image but apart from that hardly makes a wave, he and his movement were huge. The Baptist's following extended from Egypt, where he had his headquarters at the port of Alexandria, as far as Ephesus in Turkey. In fact, it might more properly be called a church. Indeed, its very existence startled Paul on his first visit to Ephesus and Corinth, especially when some of the Johannites told him they had never heard that John had prophesied the coming of any Messiah, let alone this Christ. It was Jesus' group that more closely resembled a cult, most probably a breakaway movement from the Johannites. And it was Jesus who was never mentioned in the only secular chronicles of the day, by the Romanized Jew Flavius Josephus in his *Antiquities of the Jews*, whereas the Baptist's celebrity is given a glowing report. In fact, there is now a rather gushing passage that celebrates Jesus in the *Antiquities*, but it was a medieval insertion by a monk, specifically invented to cover the embarrassing non-appearance of Christ.

Clearly, John would never have grovelled at Jesus' feet: the New Testament being really little more than propaganda on behalf of the triumphant Jesus sect, this was an audacious fabrication. But as the Gospel writers had no wish to waste too much effort on John or build him up in any way, they stopped short of actually making him a Christian martyr, or, even given his fulsome welcome to Jesus, any kind of Christian at all.

Yet they did go to *some* trouble in rewriting the Baptist, but unfortunately causing a lasting confusion in the process: scholars are now convinced that certain passages from the New Testament originated in Gospels dedicated to *John*, not Jesus at all. They have isolated, for example, the opening passage of the Gospel of John (although the name is probably a coincidence) as belonging to the 'John literature'. And the Virgin Mary's famous hymn of praise to God when she discovers she is pregnant with Christ known as the Magnificat was originally *Elizabeth's* song – John the Baptist's mother. Similarly, Herod's massacre of the Innocents was originally intended to rid himself of the threat of a blue-blooded *John* growing up and challenging his authority (although even so it was only ever fictitious – no chronicler reported such an atrocity). In other words, the late first-century followers of Jesus took over the Baptist's gospels and basically just changed the name of the hero. But the Gospel of John is also the one about which it is claimed that the Magdalene was its author . . .

Let us revisit that strangely disturbing village, Bethany, where Jesus' two 'Beloveds' – the Magdalene and Lazarus/young John lived with their sister Martha. Although Martha is usually associated with mundane household chores, the compromising letter found by Professor Morton Smith at Mar Saba in 1958 states that the Carpocratians believed that the sacred sex rites were secrets practised and handed down by 'Mary, Martha and Salome'. Clement of Alexandria, who fulminated against the filthy heretics, also, however, implied strongly that *he knew Jesus and his circle had indeed practised these rites*. Clement was in the business of sweeping all that under the carpet and deliberately changing the basic tenets of Christianity to accord with his own view of what it should have been, and therefore must be for ever – even if that meant actually transforming both the Christian message and the character of Jesus himself.

There was something else about Bethany that the gospel writers sought to obscure. It was where John the Baptist's mass baptisms took place, although the New Testament tries hard to imply that of the two Judaean Bethanys John's base was at the other one, 'Bethany across the Jordan.'[90] Was this an attempt to dissociate 'Jesus'' Bethany from his rival, the Baptist?

But was the Baptist in some way affiliated with the Bethany

family? Such an association would hardly have endeared the place to Jesus' disciples, who were constantly at loggerheads with John's followers, although Christ himself was obviously drawn to the place like a magnet, if only because his two Beloveds lived there. However, the biblical accounts of the raising of Lazarus and the anointing take place well after John's death, when Jesus had taken over a large part of his following. Had Christ also appropriated the initiating Magdalene and Lazarus/John for his own cult?

It might be objected, reading between the lines, that the Baptist was nothing short of a holy terror about anything connected with sin and therefore would never have contaminated himself by contact with louche foreign priestesses. But the real John, too, proves very surprising.

Despite the implication of the New Testament account that the Baptist was merely a local holy man, who spent his lonely days and nights in the Judaean wilderness living frugally off the land on locusts and honey, he was actually based in the great Egyptian sea-port of Alexandria – presumably in its flourishing Jewish colony. His movement, which has been described as 'an international following',[91] was taken to Ephesus by an Alexandrian called Apollos. As we noted in *The Templar Revelation*, this was 'suspiciously the only reference to Alexandria in the whole of the New Testament'.[92] That city was also home to the great Serapeum, the museum-and-temple complex dedicated to the new god Serapis, whose consort was the considerably more venerable Isis. Serapis was a riverine deity, most commonly associated with Dionysus/Bacchus/Pan – all wilderness gods, who seem almost interchangeable in Leonardo's works with the Baptist. (In 395 the alleged ashes of John's headless body were buried in the gorgeous new basilica in Alexandria, on the site of the famous old temple to Serapis.)

The usual image of the Baptist is as an apocalyptic ranter – such as might star in the insane forum of religious fanatics depicted in *Monty Python's Life of Brian* (1978) – and a zealous puritan along the lines of the much later Scottish fire-and-brimstone preacher John Knox, fulminator against 'the monstrous regiment of women'. Certainly, with his camel-hair garments, desert retreats and constant call for the masses to repent of their sins and be baptized, the

Baptist does seem the archetypal righteous teacher, disapproving of all worldly delights and normal human relationships. But that would be very wrong, although the truth about him can only be approached by piecing together non-biblical evidence about his life.

According to John's surviving cult, the Gnostic Mandaeans – of whom more later – the Baptist was a married man with children, leader of a much-persecuted religion *that had both priests and priestesses*. As it seems that young John/Lazarus was originally a disciple of the Baptist, presumably he was an officiating priest of the sect. Presumably, too, his sister would therefore have been a high-ranking Mandaean priestess . . .

Their holy books recount the clash of the two messianic titans, John and Jesus, on the banks of the Jordan. They claim that Jesus had to beg John to baptize him, and that when he acquiesced, the dark goddess Ruah (similar to the Jewish Holy Spirit) threw a black cross over the water to indicate her disapproval. John sends Jesus off with the abjuration, 'May thy staff be as a dung-stick.' Clearly no love was lost between the two, despite the picture painted in the New Testament of a sickeningly obsequious Baptist, grovelling at the Messiah's feet. The triumphant Jesus sect felt confident not only to hijack the Gospels dedicated to the Baptist, as we have seen, but also to rewrite his relationship with Jesus so that Christ emerges as by far the superior. In real life, however, this does not seem to be the case – quite the reverse, in fact.

Rehabilitating the Magus

If there was one New Testament character whom the early Church loathed, it was not so much John or the Magdalene, as their 'first heretic', Simon Magus, who allegedly aped Christ. Yet if true, his very imitative success deserves acknowledgement. According to French occult historian André Nataf, 'As a rival to Christ, Simon the Magician is a historical character without equal.'[93] Nataf notes 'He attained legendary status within his own life time: "he made statues walk, could roll in fire without burning himself, and could even fly" . . .'[94]

The Acts of the Apostles, in what is clearly an attempt at damage limitation, have him trying to buy the Holy Spirit off Peter, and later losing his life in a dramatic magical battle. He embodied everything the Christians hated (and continue to despise to this day), claiming to heal and raise the dead just like Jesus. As he was clearly a spectacular exorcist and healer, one might be forgiven for thinking that he must have got his powers from Satan . . .

The Magus was also known as 'Faustus' – 'the favoured one' – in Rome, giving his name to the overweeningly ambitious Renaissance legend Dr Faustus, whose pact with the Devil went oh-so-predictably wrong, as he slid screaming down to Hell at the appointed hour for him to pay for his material success with his soul. Like the Magus, Faustus consorted with the beautiful Helen of Troy (or rather, Simon considered his lady to be her reincarnation, see below). However, the most significant aspect of the Faustian pact was that it was not sought primarily for wealth or sex, but *knowledge – and therefore power*. As we shall see, the search for the forbidden fruits of the mind was, and is, the real Luciferanism.

The usual Christian view of Simon Magus is summed up by Rollo Ahmed: 'He imitated Christianity in the reverse sense, affirming the eternal reign of evil'.[95] He also claimed to be a god – which was taken seriously as far away as Rome, where a statue was raised to him. Almost worse, 'his sect welcomed women and held that the world-creating power was as much female as male.'[96]

According to Epiphanius,[97] he was an unrepentant practitioner of sex magic, or sacred sex, travelling with a black woman called 'Helen the Harlot', whom he believed to be the incarnation not only of the legendary beauty of Troy but also of the great goddess Athene – just as the Magdalene came to be associated with Isis – and the Gnostic 'First Thought'.

Yet Simon the Samaritan, or sorcerer (Magus) had another role to play, which the gospel writers carefully avoided mentioning while at the same time blackening his name as vehemently as they could. However, the third-century *Clementine Recognitions* once again provide us, however innocently, with an astonishing admission:

It was in Alexandria that Simon perfected his studies in magic, *being an adherent of John* . . . through whom he came to deal with religious doctrines. John was the forerunner of Jesus . . .

. . . Of all John's disciples, *Simon was the favourite*, but on the death of his master, he was absent in Alexandria, and so

Dositheus, a co-disciple, was chosen head of the school [My emphases].[98]

Here we have the apparently puritanical John the Baptist's favourite disciple being *Simon Magus*, the one man so utterly loathed by the Church that he was deemed to be the very pattern of heresy. And a sorcerer and sex magician . . . It is interesting that references to John's inner circle include a disciple named Helen – presumably Simon's travelling *koinonos* or sexual companion. Suddenly, once again, the New Testament's presentation of the Baptist seems flawed to the point of deliberate misrepresentation.

Simon's reputation was and is truly unenviable. Of course the infamous Catholic bigot Montague Summers had plenty to say in typical uncompromising style, calling him 'one of the most famous figures in the whole history of Witchcraft', whose 'Devilish practices' were undone, unsurprisingly, by Saint Peter. As the man who notoriously tried to buy the Holy Spirit, the Magus gave his name to the sin and crime of simony, or trying to buy spiritual preferment – ironically a favourite mode of corruption of the priests of Peter's Church. But perhaps his greatest crime was being John the Baptist's official successor and a sex magician and admirer of the Feminine. In many ways he also seems rather modern. As Tobias Churton remarks in his *The Gnostic Philosophy* (2003): '. . . it would seem that Simon was as humourous a figure as the magus Aleister Crowley two millennia later, with a magician's taste for ironic symbology.'

Yet Simon Magus was also hated because he was *feared*. As Karl Luckert in his landmark *Egyptian Light and Hebrew Fire* (1991) remarks:

As the 'father of all heresy' he must now be studied not merely as an opponent, but also a conspicuous competitor of Christ in the early Christian church – possibly even as a potential ally . . .

From the fact of their common Egyptian heritage may be derived the very strength of Simon Magus' threat. The danger amounted to the possibility that he could be confused with the Christ figure himself . . .[99]

Like Jesus and the Magdalene, Simon seemed keen to return the Jews to a form of goddess worship, based on the Egyptian system. Luckert goes on: '[he] saw it as his mission to fix that which . . . must have gone wrong; namely, the estrangement of the entire female Tefnut-Mahet-Nut-Isis dimension from the masculine godhead.'[100]

Presumably, then, Simon's beliefs echoed, at least in part, those of his master, the Baptist – an almost incredible thought when seen against the inevitable background of Christian propaganda. Simon himself wrote in his *Great Revelation*:

Of the universal Aeons there are two shoots . . . one is manifested from above, which is the Great Power, the Universal Mind ordering all things, male, and the other from below, the Great Thought, female, producing all things. Hence pairing with each other, they unite and manifest the Middle Distance . . . in this is the Father . . . This is He who has stood, stands and will stand, a male-female power in the pre-existing Boundless Power . . .[101]

In the light of Simon's Egyptian-style sexual egalitarianism – he first learned his magic in Alexandria – it is particularly interesting that his great antagonist was Saint Peter, who also hated Mary Magdalene and 'all the race of women', and who went on to found the misogynistic Church of Rome.

The true nature of the Baptist's movement – once again, though, perhaps only the chosen inner circle – prompts another thought about young John the Beloved/Lazarus, whose later titles include John the Evangelist and John the Divine (or holy). As the late occult historian Francis X. King noted in his Introduction to *Crowley on Christ*:

Incidentally, the Hebrew word 'qedesh', applied to St John, which [Aleister] Crowley sarcastically claimed should be trans-lated 'the divine' and had been 'grossly mistranslated' in the past, is normally translated into English as 'sodomite'.[102]

(Even the ritual magician and rabid showman Aleister Crowley, the so-called 'Wickedest Man in the World', may usually be quoted with confidence. Although he was said to be many things, most of them physically impossible, he was a shrewd scholar of ancient languages and customs.)

As we saw in a previous chapter, the *qedeshim* were elaborately cross-dressed and made-up male prostitutes who offered their services to pilgrims at the gates of the great Jerusalem temple, like the female 'temple servants'. Although the word does also carry the meaning 'holy/divine', clearly the two interpretations must have originated from the same custom. And as young John is associated as Lazarus with his sister the sexual initiatrix, he falls foul of Peter repeatedly in the Gospel of John, and was also perhaps the naked young man in the Mar Saba passages, it is interesting to speculate that he was *quedesh* in *both* senses of the word. How Peter must have hated both brother and sister.

However, trouble must have existed well before Peter came on the scene. It is not difficult to imagine the tensions in John's group between the two charismatic, talented and ambitious would-be cult leaders, Jesus and Simon Magus. Indeed, the very fact of Simon's association with the Baptist's movement must have worried and disgusted Christ's own devoted followers as the rivalry between the sects escalated. Perhaps it is no exaggeration to suggest that Jesus' anointing, his becoming a *Christ*, the chosen one, was stage-managed to be at least partly very public so that news of it would be sure to reach the Magus. To be called '*the* Christ' in days when even minor Roman officials were anointed or 'christ-ened' into their jobs, is a rather enormous statement of intent – not to mention ego. And far from 'aping' Christ, perhaps Christ 'aped' Simon Magus, probably the elder of the two and certainly John's favourite – an early role model, perhaps.

Deadly rivals

Jesus Christ may have begun his religious adulthood as one of John's disciples, but he soon became a sneering schismatic. This may seem a radical statement, but incredibly, the evidence is there in the New Testament, where we read that Jesus utters the following apparently contradictory statement: 'I tell you the truth: Among those born of women there has not risen anyone greater than John the Baptist: yet he who is least in the kingdom of heaven is greater than he.'[103] On the one hand, Jesus seems to be saying no one can be greater than John, but on the other the least impressive of Jesus' own followers is greater than him. However, once it is realized that 'born of women' does not mean 'everyone', as Westerners might suppose today but is an ancient Near-Eastern *insult* meaning 'fatherless', 'bastard' (in both the literal and derogatory sense), perhaps 'son of a bitch', then the passage makes sense – if a somewhat uncomfortable one. (Its meaning is reinforced by the fact that John's followers, the Mandaeans, use a similar insult of the hated Christ, calling him 'Son of a woman'.) Jesus is publicly taunting the Baptist in the worst kind of a way – perhaps from some deep wellspring of personal hurt, for he himself was known as a *mamzer*, or illegitimate child. On another occasion, when Christ says 'No man puts new wine in old bottles'[104] – apparently an innocuous enough axiom – he may actually have been mocking John's greater age and apparent staleness as a religious teacher, for wine bottles were made of animal skins, similar to those that the Baptist famously wore. In other words, it was impossible for John to teach anything fresh and interesting – the implication being that he, Jesus, could provide just that.

The unthinkable
Why did Leonardo hate the Holy family so much that he risked a heretic's terrible death by incorporating outrageous and blasphemous symbols in his works? Why did he portray little Jesus apparently pulling the ears off the lamb that represented the Baptist, and depict Jesus' limb cutting across its vulnerable neck? And then there is the disciple in the Last Supper who is thrusting the John gesture into Christ's oblivious face as if hissing 'Remember John' . . .

Perhaps there is a clue in one of the passages excised from St Mark's Gospel, which resurfaced in the innocent Clement's letter found at Mar Saba. It is the one that seems to indicate the identity of Jesus' female Beloved: 'And the sister of the youth whom Jesus loved and his mother and Salome were there, and Jesus did not receive them.'

However, there may well be a second, considerably more significant deduction to be discerned in those three lines. 'Salome' is mentioned. Jesus is known to have had a female disciple of that name: indeed in the Gnostic *Gospel of Thomas* she appears in a bizarre little scene in which she and Jesus exchange religious ideas while both lying with some intimacy on her couch.[105] Her name also crops up in the list of female disciples in the New Testament, but only once.

Of course there is another Salome connected with biblical events, although contrary to popular opinion she remains resolutely anonymous in the Gospels. In fact, Herod's step-daughter who dances the dance of the seven veils and demands the Baptist's head is only named in Josephus' *Antiquities of the Jews* – which is strange, for if Josephus knew her identity, the Gospel writers must also have known it. Yet for some reason they not only omit to mention her name, but the redactors (or editors) of the New Testament thought to remove the otherwise innocent enough verse that ended up in Professor Morton Smith's hands at Mar Saba in which she is named as part of Jesus' inner circle, a friend of his mother and the Magdalene. But why was Salome's very identity deemed so potentially disastrous to the Christian cause as to be edited out of the New Testament?

Perhaps a resonance is found in her legendary (but sadly non-biblical) Dance of the Seven Veils. As Barbara Walker points out, ' . . . the Dance of the Seven Veils was an integral part of the sacred drama, depicting the death of the surrogate-king, his descent into the underworld, and his retrieval by the Goddess, who removed one of her seven garments at each of the seven underworld gates.'[106] This association with the sacred seven is repeated in Mary Magdalene's 'seven devils', allegedly cast out of her by Jesus – and which the Gospel writers are keen to mention at any given opportunity. But we have seen how they, and the male disciples, had no idea about the significance of either the anointing or the anointer, and so the sacred drama, once again, becomes garbled and dismissively sexist. Because it involves female power, the sacred seven is transmuted into either a strip-tease or possession by demons. *Jesus* understood, but when did the likes of Saint Peter ever let their Master's wishes get in the way of their own god-making ambitions?

However, the concept of the ritual killing of John begs several key questions, the answers to which, once again, suggest a shocking reversal of what Christians consider good and evil. Was John himself involved to the extent that he knew the nature of his role, and his inevitable end? If so, did he accept this unenviable destiny?

We have seen how scholars now suggest that the biblical scene where the Baptist falls ingratiatingly at Jesus' feet, hailing him as 'the Lamb of God' is unlikely to have happened because the two men were known to have been rivals. As the New Testament is essentially propaganda on behalf of the Jesus cult, obviously they would want to misrepresent John as the submissive, inferior sect leader – no matter how dignified and superior he might actually have been. Yet there is another, perhaps equally valid, interpretation.

In this hypothetical scenario John *does* fall at Christ's feet to acknowledge him as 'the one who is to come' – a phrase as ambiguous as our modern equivalent, meaning either the prophesied one or one who is to follow as John's own successor. Of all his thousands of followers, the Baptist singles out Jesus Christ as the one who will carry on his work among both Jews and gentiles, perhaps running the international organization from the old headquarters in Alexandria, in Egypt. He baptizes the younger man to set the seal on the beginning of his mission, knowing that the Magdalene will similarly mark out the moment when the end is nigh by anointing him as Christ. In this scenario perhaps the older man deliberately provokes Herod in some way in order to get himself locked up and ritually slain at the hands of the ruling family, or perhaps Salome simply arranges it all. But then something happens. Something shocking and traumatic.

While in jail, John suddenly seems to have changed his mind about Jesus, sending a message out saying, 'Art thou he that should come, or do we look for another?'[107] Significantly, however, he seems to have been inspired to harbour such doubts by something he had heard about Jesus' *actions*, for his words are preceded by 'Now when John had heard in the prison the works of Jesus, he sent two of his disciples [to ask Jesus] . . .'[108] It is immediately after this – and in response to it – that Jesus stresses his superiority to the Baptist, saying: 'What went ye out into the wilderness to see? . . .[109] A prophet? Yea, I say unto you, and more than a prophet . . .' And it is then that he takes that sly dig at John as noted above, the almost incredible direct insult of 'Among them that are born of women there hath not risen a greater than John the Baptist . . .'[110] As we have seen, 'born of women' was, and is, a well-worn Middle-Eastern insult, meaning fatherless, or 'bastard' – in both senses of the word, as in the modern British use. With the old prophet in jail, the last sacred king about to be slaughtered, was the successor taking the golden opportunity to insult and demean him? Was Jesus making John the Baptist a laughing stock? We have also seen how Christ gibed about not putting new wine in old bottles – as bottles were made of animal skins such as the Baptist was famously known to wear, this is another crack at his expense. So was John languishing in jail, about to meet his pre-planned demise, with the sudden fatal certainty that he had chosen the wrong successor? As we will see, his chosen successor was very different from Jesus Christ . . .

There are many other questions, most of them deeply disturbing. What, or whom, did Salome really want John's head for? It seems that the old prophet's death was by no means the end of him, and even his physical remains were to suffer a chequered history.

Grave suspicions

Of course it is enormously difficult to piece together the dramas of 2,000 years ago, but certain aspects of John's death still raise suspicions. He was a political prisoner of great status, yet apparently he was executed on the whim of a stripper who specifically asked for his *head*. As beheading was not a common method of execution in Judaea – the Jews tended to stone criminals and outlaws whereas the Romans employed the considerably crueller method of crucifixion – there is a distinct sense of ritual to the Baptist's death. For what purpose, or for whom, did Salome really want John's head?

After John's death, Jesus' mission began in earnest, but as his fame as a healer and exorcist spread, King Herod was afraid that he was possessed by the spirit of John, saying '. . . John the Baptist was risen from the dead, and that is why miraculous powers are at work in him'.[111] Bizarrely and shockingly, Herod may have had a point – at least as far as Jesus' own beliefs were concerned. For as biblical scholar Carl Kraeling wrote in the 1950s, 'John's detractors used the occasion of his death to develop the suggestion that his disem-

bodied spirit was serving Jesus as the instrument for the performance of works of black magic, itself no small concession to John's
power.'[112]

To Christians the very mention of magic is abhorrent. Christ
came to sweep away all the blasphemous and futile trappings of the
occult, so firmly associated with pagan cults. Yet this interpretation
is a modern projection: the early Christians, while of course fulmi-
nating against their enemies the pagans, were just as much involved
with the occult – perhaps more so, if one considers Jesus' miracles.
Outside the cosy world of faith the harsh reality is that the early
Christians cast spells in the name of Jesus and that Christ himself
was not averse to practices that would certainly earn excommuni-
cation from modern fundamentalist groups.

More significantly, the Carpocratian leader Marcus (see the
beginning of this chapter) was described by the appalled Bishop
Irenaeus as:

A perfect adept in magical impostures, and by this means
drawing away a great number of men, and not a few women, he
has induced them to join themselves to him, as to one who is
possessed of the greatest knowledge and perfection, and who has
received the highest power from the invisible and ineffable
regions above.[113]

We recall that the Carpocratians were reputed to possess initiatory secrets of a sexual nature, which they claimed originated with
Mary Magdalene, Martha and Salome – and which Clement of
Alexandria tacitly acknowledged as being authentically the rites of
Jesus himself. If the sex rituals were originally approved and even
encouraged by Christ, what about the magic practised by Marcus
and his followers?

Morton Smith, in his *Jesus the Magician* (1978) claims that
Jesus' popularity lay in his clever use of Egyptian magic. First he
would intrigue the inhabitants of whatever village he passed
through by putting on a dramatic show of casting out devils and
healing the sick, then he would move in with his teaching and hook
the people. His writing in the sand, walking on the water and so on
were, Smith asserts, mainstays of the itinerant Egyptian sorcerers,

who also employed hypnotic – and possibly *narcotic* – techniques. But did Jesus' ambition go well beyond simply garnering the oohs and ahs of a few backwater peasants? Did he also have his eye on John the Baptist's huge international empire?

According to Matthew 11:18, the Jews believed of John that 'he had a demon', although this may not have referred to his being possessed by one, but rather that he had one over which he had power as an occult 'servitor', similar to the Middle Eastern *djinn*.[114] Again, the practice of what amounts to black magic is not something that sits comfortably with the accepted image of the Baptist, but then we now know that the real man was very different – a married man with children, a bitter rival of Jesus, whose favourite was the Church's hated Simon Magus, a renowned sex magician.

In this light perhaps it is not so astounding that John 'had a demon' or slave-spirit, even though traditionally the means to acquire this dubious slave was to obtain a body part of a murdered man, although magically speaking the optimum power was achieved by murdering the man oneself . . . This is particularly interesting in the case of the Baptist's own execution. Was it some kind of ritual slaying, a blood sacrifice necessary to clear the way for the incoming sacrificial king? What was the mysterious Salome's real role in demanding John's head?

Morton Smith redefines Herod's words above as: 'John the Baptist has been raised from the dead [by Jesus' necromancy; Jesus now has him]. And therefore [since Jesus-John can control them] the [inferior] powers work [their wonders] by him [i.e. his orders].'[115]

Jesus was not averse to what others would unhesitatingly define as necromancy: the Jews roundly denounced his raising of Lazarus as trafficking with demons. Even if it were merely a ritual and not a literal recall to life, it still took place in a tomb – abhorrent and unthinkable to the orthodox. It was immediately after this event that the Jews planned Jesus' downfall.

Did Jesus (for so long believed to be the epitome of divine love and righteousness) or at the least his followers actually arrange for the Baptist to be killed? Certainly, Australian theologian Barbara Thiering believes so, as the Jesus cult was the only obvious candidate to benefit from his death.[116] But was it merely a political assassination, to clear the way for Jesus to take over? After all, John's cult, the Mandaeans, still claim that Christ 'usurped' and even 'perverted' the Baptist's following. But if it was also a ritual murder, could it have been motivated by the dark desire to enslave his soul by possessing a part of him? Christ's contact in the palace was presumably Salome, although possibly aided and abetted by another female disciple listed in the New Testament, Joanna, wife of Chuza, Herod's chief steward. On the orders of Herodias Salome demanded John's *head* – although her identity was suspiciously obscured by the writers of the gospels.

That anyone could even contemplate such a scenario – Jesus Christ being implicated, perhaps knowingly, in the murder of the Baptist, not to mention possibly being deeply involved in what amounts to black magic – will no doubt be profoundly shocking to many people even outside the Christian community. Curiously, however, much of this theory has been in the public domain for years: for example, Morton Smith's *Jesus the Magician* was first published in 1978, and Barbara Thiering aired her idea that the Jesus movement might have been behind John's death in the early 1990s. Yet none of this filtered out much beyond the cultish circles of 'alternative seekers' or perhaps the more open-minded theologians (usually American) into the wider world, although Ms Thiering's admittedly somewhat strange book came in for a hard time, being largely dismissed as 'fantasy'.

The same wall of stony ignorance surrounds the Christian community on the subject of the Gnostic Gospels, about which ordinary believers continue to be kept in the dark. But why should they care about these long-lost texts, when theologians sneer about their 'dubious' authenticity and refuse even to contemplate central questions such as their depiction of the relationship between the Magdalene and Jesus, the row with Peter, and the status of women as apostles in the early Christian movement? Clearly it is very much in the interests of today's devotees to ignore the uncomfortable picture of the Gnostic texts, but there is only so long they will be able to maintain this lofty stance as more people read them for themselves.

If Jesus Christ is believed to be God Incarnate then no evidence that he was the contrary will make any kind of impact, except cause disgust. Faith cannot be argued away, and in many ways, whatever the historical Jesus was really like, he has now achieved such archetypal status as the ultimate Good, that perhaps one should simply avoid becoming engaged in such arguments. Yet although one might agree with Jeffrey Burton Russell, who writes: 'Any religion that does not come to terms with evil is not worthy of attention',[117] when faced with the fact of the anti-Jesus Johannites such as the Mandaeans, who have traditionally denounced Christ in the most immoderate terms, tough questions have to be asked. Not about the universal evils such as torture and starvation, but the whole concept of Jesus' goodness, so widely accepted even among non-Christians in the West as to be deemed a holy truth set in stone. But, to a mainstream Christian it is the Johannites who are evil and 'perverted', just as the Baptist's favourite, Simon Magus, has been vilified since the earliest Christian times.

Yet of course it is of prime importance to uncover great historical wrongs – no matter how uncomfortable they may be to our cultural and religious certainties – for only in doing so can humanity ever move forward. And if that involves revisiting and radically revising the character, motives and deeds of Jesus called the Christ, then it must be done unflinchingly, for old prejudices and even basic concepts of right and wrong will have to be revised. As the early Christians were so fond of denouncing their rivals as tools of Satan, perhaps it is time to redress the balance – especially as the persecution of those whose beliefs were different remains an indelible scar on the human psyche.

PART TWO

Legacy of the Fall

CHAPTER FOUR

Synagogues of Satan

❧

After Constantine's Edict of Milan effectively anathematized all forms of Christianity other than the new Roman Church, heretics such as the Carpocratians persisted in following their consciences with either enormous courage or foolhardiness amounting to insanity, depending upon the extent of one's sympathy for martyrdom. Most of them were wiped out swiftly and mercilessly, but as the years progressed, certain heterodox beliefs succeeded in simmering away, by their very existence nibbling at the security and complacency of Rome. Perhaps it is no coincidence that these 'evils' usually involved some reverence for the Feminine, provoking Peter's organization to a wrath that echoes in infamy to this day. In particular, one area was to prove a persistent headache for the Pope – the south of France, the area largely encompassed by the Languedoc and Provence.

Pockmarked with caves, its high blue skies riven by the sharp peaks of snow-topped mountains, it is a beautiful but unforgiving landscape, which in the Middle Ages provided a safe haven for many with less than orthodox religious views, such as the Cathars, whose meetings were known to the Church as 'Synagogues of Satan'. As Jean Markale comments in his *Montségur and the Mystery of the Cathars* (1986), in the caves 'there are devils that hold their Sabbaths there in the company of witches. These are the only beings who have no fear of entering such places. Caves represent the forbidden world. And consequently it is also an alluring world.'[1] Whether there really were witches in those caves is beside the point: the land as a whole already had a reputation for paganism and heresy even before the terrible events of the thirteenth century, but after that time it was nothing less than the land of Satan to the Church.

This was where, in the twelfth and thirteenth centuries, there arose a Christian cult whose members although known as *les bonshommes* ('good men', or 'good people') to the locals, were in the eyes of Rome 'Luciferans'. The successors to the Gnostic Bogomils of Bulgaria, the Cathars[2] (meaning 'pure'), attempted to reinvent what they perceived to be the simple lifestyle and worship instigated by Christ, renouncing the Church as the corrupt 'whore of Babylon', together with all its panoply and hierarchy. They eschewed the use of specially dedicated church buildings, choosing to worship in the open or in private houses – after all, Christ neither built churches nor exhorted his followers to do so – and adopted an ascetic lifestyle, eating a simple, 'fishertarian'[3] diet, and even sparingly of that. They aimed to become *perfecti* or *parfaits* ('perfects'), men and women who had renounced all earthly pleasures, including sex – procreation being especially abominable to them because it prolonged the soul's contact with the hated material world.

As Gnostics, the Cathars truly abominated the physical realm, and this is where most modern readers will part company with them (except for woolly-minded New Agers who tend to venerate them as a species of cosy fellow travellers). High-minded and essentially decent though the heretics undoubtedly were in a society riddled with the most heinous corruption and hypocrisy, they took their hatred for earthly existence to ultimately distasteful extremes. Basically they institutionalized anorexia in the form of the *endura*, a slow fast to the death, which they believed was almost as 'good' a death as martyrdom – although very soon they were to have ample opportunity to indulge their longing for the latter mode of transition to the spiritual realm. (Without a 'good' death, the Cathars believed they were condemned to be reborn until they could be martyred and then escape finally to the realms of pure spirit and Light.)

Of course relatively few Cathars made the grade as 'Perfects':

their rank and file, the *credenti* ('believers'), developed their own peculiar version of righteousness. Some preferred sex outside marriage, for example, because then they were only committing the single sin of intercourse rather than the two sins of intercourse and (probably) procreation. As Markale notes:

> To the Cathar . . . to sin was to submit to the world. There was no distinction between venal and mortal sins; all sins were mortal.
> . . . Every sexual union involved the flesh and ran the risk of prolonging Satan's work indefinitely . . . They made no distinction between legitimate and illegal unions, free love, homosexuality, adultery, incest or even bestiality.[4]

Rumours abounded about the *credenti's* sexual abuses – after all, if one was damned equally for the usual heterosexual coupling and a gay encounter or even a fling with a goat, why not indulge all appetites? They might as well be hanged for a sheep as for a lamb (or a goat). And if creating babies was so evil, then why not use sodomy as the means of contraception? While wild stories always circulate about any self-contained and heterodox sect, whether justified or not, human nature being what it is, almost certainly there would have been *some* truth in these rumours.

Because *anything* material was anathema to them, the Cathars even had their own version of the Lord's Prayer, substituting 'Give us this day bread beyond substance' for 'Give us this day our daily bread'.[5] Tinkering with the words of the only prayer believed to be given to us by Jesus himself was beyond the pale to orthodox Christianity (even though there is evidence that the Lord's Prayer actually originated with John the Baptist, not Christ at all.)[6]

Clearly, this was bad enough as far as the all-powerful Church was concerned – vegetarianism itself was known as 'the Devil's banquet',[7] and of course their rejection of the Church hierarchy marked them out as heretics anyway – but the Cathars' beliefs and lifestyle went considerably further than that.

As Gnostics, they believed that Jesus was the Son of Light, not the Son of God. He and Satan were both the sons of God the Father, the two manifestations of a divinity that is both good and evil.

There had been two Jesuses: one of matter, who was the lover of Mary Magdalene,[8] and one of pure spirit who could never have been crucified – which is why the Cathars refused to accept the traditional symbol of the crucifix, although they had their own form of the cross, the *rosace*, 'signifying the solar Christ'.[9] In fact, according to Jean Markale, there is evidence that the Cathars built their citadels dizzyingly high on the very top of needle-like mountains because they sought to be close to the sun and stars – a worrying association with ancient pagan rites to the Church. They also rejected the concept of an eternal Hell, the threat of which had long been the Vatican's most powerful weapon in keeping its flock in line: the Cathars believed that even the Devil could be saved.

However, above and beyond all that, for many of the clergy the heretics' days must be numbered because they possessed a secret Gospel of John, which they claimed contained Christ's initiatory teachings. The existence of such a book spelt extreme danger for an organization that had long thought itself safe from the influences of the Gnostic gospels. But, equal to all of the above in degrees of horror for a majority of the Pope's men was surely the fact that the Cathars had female preachers – worse, they ranged about the very land where, according to legend, none other than Mary Magdalene herself had taught.[10]

True 'Luciferans'?
Only too predictably, the fanatical Reverend Montague Summers rails against the 'Cathari', claiming 'They openly worshipped Satan, repudiating Holy Mass and the Passion, rejecting Holy Baptism for some foul ceremony of their own',[11] quoting an anonymous Inquisitor as evidence of their Devil worship. Clearly, Summers is useless as an objective source, but even in the twentieth century he did provide an insight into the mindset of those who sought to exterminate the Cathars. (He also denounces them as 'incendiaries' and 'terrorists', which is startlingly at odds with the view of even most ordinary non-Cathars of the time, who admired and even supported them even in the face of terrible danger to themselves. Besides, the Cathars were sworn pacifists.) However, was Summers' accusation based on a garbled version of the truth? Were the Cathars not Satanists but actually Luciferans?

A major problem in assessing the truth about the heresy is that few records survive other than the accounts of their enemies, but dedicated researchers have been able to piece together beliefs that would certainly not have won the Cathars many favours with orthodoxy. As Yuri Stoyanov notes in his classic *The Hidden Tradition in Europe* (1994):

> In the Catholic records descriptions appear of 'Luciferan' sects in whose belief the traditional . . . Cathar dualism of the evil demiurge of the material world and the transcendent good God appeared in reversed form, and where Lucifer was revered and expected to be restored to heaven, while Michael and the archangels would duly be deposed to hell.[12]

However, Stoyanov is careful to add, 'Whether such dualism "of the left hand really existed as a derivation from decadent forms of Catharism or was formulated in the inquisitorial imagination is still being debated."'[13] And, of course, Lucifer equates with Satan here.

One researcher to whom there was no debate – and a very different undestanding of 'Lucifer' – was the mysterious Otto Rahn, who became obsessed with the last Cathar stronghold of Montségur, in the foothills of the Pyrénées, where approximately 200 *Perfecti* met a fiery death in 1244 after holding out against the Crusaders for ten months. Rahn spent many months in the 1950s combing the area for clues that might link the Cathars with the Holy Grail, making friends with the locals – although certainly not impressing all of them[14] – and perhaps crow-barring in the facts to fit his own hypotheses.[15]

In his 1937 book *Lucifer's Court*[16] Rahn argues that what are seen as interrelated groups – Cathars, Knights Templar,[17] the Troubadour movement and so on – were all part of a Gnostic religion centred on Lucifer, also known to them as 'Lucibel', or his European equivalent such as Apollo, the solar deity. Rahn also linked the medieval blossoming of 'Lucifer's Court' to Nordic myths, attempting to create a religion derived from European, rather than Middle Eastern, roots.[18] In Rahn's hypothesis, what links all these groups together is the Holy Grail, since it has been associated separately with both the Cathars and the Knights Templar.

Rahn's university thesis was on the subject of the thirteenth-century poet, Wolfram von Eschenbach, author of *Parzival*. Although the major German poet of the Grail romances, he claimed he used sources from southern Europe – the Languedoc and Spain. His Grail is not a recognizably Christian symbol, such as a great chalice filled with Christ's blood as in later tales, but a *stone* linked, if not with Lucifer directly, then at least with fallen angels, although Wolfram himself is not explicit on this point.

In search of the Grail

In the early 1930s Rahn became friendly with Maurice Magre,[19] a member of the mysterious secret society, the Fraternity of the Polaires, an occult group keen to be associated with an ancient Nordic tradition. They claimed to be in contact with unknown 'masters' in Agartha, 'the invisible initiatory centre',[20] but Magre was to resign from the group dramatically. Some believe Rahn was a Polaire, which may have been the case as, initially, he hero-worshipped Magre, who originally urged him to carry out extensive research 'on the ground' in the Languedoc, rather than burying his head in the Bibliothèque Nationale.

Magre introduced his German friend to many local people, one of whom, Arthur Cassou – 'an old Ariège sage'[21] – told him the legend of the aristocratic Cathar heroine Esclarmonde, claiming that she had hidden the Grail in some safe location before the fall of Montségur.

Rahn believed that Eschenbach was inspired to write his Grail romance by the Cathar story, citing the similarities between his hero Parzival, whose name means 'pierce well' and the heroic Viscount of Carcassonne, Trencavel – 'cut well'. Other characters were matched with real people from that time and place, including the Fisher King Anfortas[22] with Ramon-Roger de Foix. And of course what else could the fictitious 'Montsalvage' ('Mount Haven' or 'secure mountain') be other than Montségur? Moreover, Montsalvage is protected by a 'Fountain Salvage', which Rahn linked to the fountain of Fontesorbes, while the forest surrounding Montsalvage, 'Briciljan' in the tale, must be the wood known as Priscillien. Rahn noted triumphantly: 'Yes: only the Cathar fortress of Montségur, in the Ariègois Pyrénées, could have been the invio-lable temple of the Grail.'[23]

To Rahn, the Grail was one of several stone tablets inscribed with runic writing, although he elaborated 'The Grail is triple: it is a book of knowledge, a symbolic cup containing that knowledge and a stone …' He believed it was a green stone, similar to the legendary emerald stone of the Hermetic master Hermes Trismegistus on which the greatest occult secrets are engraved. Rahn saw it as an emerald of 144 facets (twelve times twelve, the number of perfection), or 144 smaller stones inscribed in emerald. This stone had fallen from Lucifer's crown when he fell to earth – onto Montségur.

As Arnaud d'Apremont writes in the Introduction to the French edition of *Lucifer's Court*:

> Now, if for common mortals, Lucifer is synonymous with the devil, with Satan, it was not the same for Rahn. For the latter, Lucifer was Lucibel, the light bearer, Abellio, Belenos, Baldur, Apollo . . . A highly pure and luminous figure. Rahn . . . wanted to see himself recognized as a 'Light-bearer', a Lucifer.[24]

He adds: 'There is nothing there that couldn't be written by Rahn the Cathar or Rahn the pagan.' Rahn himself claimed that as the stone that fell from Lucifer's diadem, the Church claimed it, 'in order to christianize it'.[25] The stone is believed to bestow near-immortality: perhaps the literal-minded Rahn was seeking it as a gift for his Führer – in which case we must be very grateful for the fact that apparently he failed to find it.

Rahn believed that:

> the Old and New Testaments, even if they speak of different 'anti-gods', have a single and unique knowledge. The Old Testament curses the 'fair star of the morning'; the New Testament reveals to us in the [apocryphal] Apocalypse of John, that a certain 'king and angel of the abyss' bears 'in Greek the name of Apollyon'.

He explains: 'Apollyon, angel of the abyss and prince of this world, is the luminous Apollo.' He links the two by citing the fact that the Greek for morning star is *Phosphorus* (or 'Light-bearer'), which 'passed for the faithful companion, the announcer and representative of Apollo, seemingly the sun,[26] the greatest light bearer, and that Apollo himself was confused with the fair "Star of the Morning", the sun.' Of course the Church would consider an ancient solar god to be synonymous with Satan in any case.

Rahn believed that the crusade against the Cathars represented the war between 'the Cross and the Grail', and that the *Perfecti* held the power of Lucifer in the form of the green stone. This is presumably the product of an over-heated romantic imagination, but there is reason to believe that the Cathars did possess a 'Grail', although it may have been neither a stone nor a cup . . .

An unholy Grail

What is (or was) the Holy Grail, according to the medieval accounts? The earliest of the stories is Chrétien de Troyes' unfinished *Perceval* (or *Le conte del Graal*), written in the 1180s, but whether he died or simply gave up with it is not known. It concerns a grail (or *graal*), introduced in this scene: 'Two more youths appeared carrying candelabras followed by a fair maiden who held a bejewelled, golden grail in both her hands.' It only becomes *the* Grail as the story develops, and the only significance of the definite article is that it is *this particular* Grail that is at the centre of events. And neither is it a holy grail: although the story is set against a Christian background (how could it be otherwise?), Chrétien's *graal* is given no religious significance, and certainly makes no connection with Jesus. It is simply an object with magical properties.

There is little mystery about the nature of Chrétien's *graal*. Although later writers seem to have been unaware of the meaning of the term, Chrétien clearly felt he had no need to elaborate because he assumed his audience would be familiar with a *graal*. Unromantically, the word is probably a variant of the Old French *gradal*, meaning a type of serving dish. He describes it specifically as *scutella lata et aliquantulum profunda* – 'a wide and slightly deep dish' – in other words, something like a platter or salver, a conclusion supported by the fact that it magically produces food (in this version only for the Fisher King, but in later versions for the whole court). Its magical or mystical properties make it important, not the fact that it is a grail. (Just as the significance of a story about a magic teapot would lie in the fact that it was magic, not that it was a teapot.)

Chrétien's tale was both popular and unfinished, presenting an irresistible challenge to other poets to compose their own versions, so the story – and the Grail – underwent a rapid process of evolution. The focus shifted away from Perceval, the hero of the Grail quest becoming Gawain (probably because Chrétien's story breaks off in the middle of a subplot in which he features) and then Galahad, a newly invented, annoyingly perfect character who basically seems like a thinly-disguised Jesus.

The development of the Grail into the Cup of Christ happened quickly. In an anonymous continuation of *Perceval*, written within a decade or so of Chrétien's original, the author fused it with quite separate legends – which, according to British author Andrew Collins,[27] date back to the eighth or ninth centuries – of Joseph of Arimathea bringing a cup containing Jesus' blood to Britain. Presumably this was inspired by the concept of the Grail as a vessel, the author casting around for something similar to link it with Jesus.

This line was followed by Robert de Boron in *Joseph d'Arimathie*, written in the 1190s or very early 1200s. This is when it becomes the Holy Grail – *sangreal*: Robert was aware of the pun of 'San greal' and 'Sang real',[28] although in his version the latter meant 'true blood'. A major, influential telling of this version of the Grail story was the *Queste del San Graal*, part of a vast Arthurian cycle composed by Cistercian monks between 1215 and 1235 (in which Galahad makes his first appearance).

Clearly all this represents the Christianization of the Grail, and the development of the Grail story into a Christian morality tale. Whether this was a deliberate attempt to undermine the heretical elements of the original, or simply the result of the permeation of Christian thought throughout all medieval art and literature, is impossible to tell. (The legends of Joseph of Arimathea were not entirely devoid of the whiff of heresy, since the legend also claimed that Joseph carried secret teachings of Jesus, which he passed on to his family. Besides, the Grail quest never really lost its Gnostic flavour, with the hero finding his way to the divine through his own endeavours; but perhaps this was damage limitation by the Church.)

It was this line that went on to influence Mallory's *La Morte d'Arthur* and even the Steven Speilberg/Harrison Ford classic, *Indiana Jones and the Last Crusade*.

However, this was quite different from the line taken in the other major retelling of the Grail story, Wolfram von Eschenbach's *Parzival*, written between 1200 and 1210, therefore in parallel with the 'Christ's Cup' concept. It would be interesting to know whether Wolfram was aware of, and deliberately ignored, the Christianized continuations of Chrétien's tale.

A slight ripple was created by the anonymous *Perlesvaus*, written between the 1190s and 1220s, as the author – a cleric of some kind – claimed that he found the story in a book at Glastonbury Abbey, though most scholars believe this was just an attempt to gain credibility. Sitting between the Christianized version and Wolfram's, it is clearly based on Robert de Boron's version of the fused Grail/Joseph of Arimathea tale and, on the surface, follows the same Christian morality tale, but it has some very interesting heretical elements – an emphasis on severed heads, alchemical references and Gawain's parallel quest for the sword that beheaded John the Baptist.

In *Parzival*, the *Gral* is described as a stone. Why Wolfram transformed Chrétien's dish or salver in this way is unknown – it has been suggested that he simply misunderstood the French word (he made other mistakes in translation, for example rendering 'carving dish' as 'carving knives'). However, his Grail does have the property of miraculously producing food and drink, so there is still the connection with a serving dish. Wolfram gives the Grail many other magical abilities – those who see it cannot die for a certain length of time, and instructions from Heaven appear on it.

However, if Wolfram's reason for making the Grail a stone remains unknown, at least we know where his idea originated: the medieval German poem *Alexander*, itself derived from popular legends of the Emperor Alexander, many variants of which circulated in the Middle Ages. Wolfram is known to have been familiar with *Alexander* and several elements of *Parzival* are clearly inspired by it. Most importantly, Alexander receives a miraculous stone – it changes weight and in some versions has rejuvenating properties – which is even described in some Latin copies as *lapis exilis* ('small stone'), which presumably became corrupted into Wolfram's term for the Grail, *lapsit exillis*. So Wolfram, too, has merged Chrétien's Grail story with a separate legend.

Wolfram links the origins of the Grail – its being brought to earth – with the 'neutral angels', i.e. those who took neither side in the war between God and Lucifer, although there is some ambiguity about whether the neutral angels or another group were responsible for bringing it down to earth (see below). In any case, since the angels departed it has been protected by an order of knighthood, explicitly described as Templars, and a bloodline of Grail kings.

Wolfram claimed not only to know the proper ending to the story, but also to have had access to a more authentic version than even Chrétien – although if Chrétien based his story on *Peredur*, then this claim is clearly false. Wolfram states that his version derived from the works of the 'heathen' Flegetanis, via Kyot of Provens:

> There was a heathen named Flegetanis who was highly renowned for his acquirements. This same physicus was descended from Solomon, begotten of Israelitish kin all the way down from ancient times till the Baptism became our shield against hellfire. He wrote of the marvels of the Gral. Flegetanis, who worshipped a calf as though it were his god, was a heathen by his father. How can the Devil make such mock of such knowledgeable people, in that He Whose power is greatest and to Whom all marvels are known neither does nor did not part them from their folly? For the infidel Flegetanis was able to define for us the recession of each planet and its return, and how long each revolves in its orbit before it stands at its mark again. All human kind are affected by the revolutions of the planets. With his own eyes the heathen Flegetanis saw – and he spoke of it reverentially – hidden secrets in the constellations. He declared there was a thing called the Gral, whose name he read in the stars without more ado. 'A troop left it on earth and then rose high above the stars, if their innocence drew them back again. Afterwards a Christian progeny bred to a pure life had the duty of keeping it. Those humans who are summoned to the Gral are ever worthy.' Thus did Flegetanis write on this theme.

The wise Master Kyot embarked on a search for this tale in

Latin books in order to discover where there may have been a people suited to keep the Gral and follow a disciplined life. He read the chronicles of various lands in Britain and elsewhere, in France and Ireland; but it was in Anjou that he found the tale.[29]

As we have seen, the original Grail was a large dish or salver, but what inspired Chrétien with that idea?

Perceval is modelled on the Celtic folk tale *Peredur, Son of Efrawg*, part of the celebrated collection of Welsh tales known as the *Mabinogion*. The Grail itself is derived from the severed male head carried on a platter that features in that tale.

Peredur is entertained by the lord of a castle, a lame knight, who turns out to be his uncle:

Thereupon he could see two youths coming into the hall, and from the hall proceeding to a chamber, and with them a spear of exceeding great size, and three streams of blood along it, running from the socket to the floor. And when they all saw the youths coming after that fashion, every one set up a crying and a lamentation, so that it was not easy for any to bear with them. The man did not, for all that, interrupt his conversation with Peredur. The man did not tell Peredur what that was, nor did he ask it of him. After silence for a short while, thereupon, lo, two maidens coming in, and a great salver between them, and a man's head on the salver, and blood in profusion around the head. And then all shrieked and cried out, so that it was hard for any to be in the same house as they. At last they desisted therefrom, and sat as long as they pleased, and drank.[30]

The fact that Chrétien's tale lacks an ending reveals that the writers of the continuations were not familiar with *Peredur*, as both the Christianizing writers and Wolfram add endings that are quite different from the Celtic original. In fact much of the traditional mystique of the Grail romances derives from trying to provide explanations for the miraculous elements that, in the original Welsh tale, are entirely unnecessary. In particular, there is the mystery of the nature of the Grail, and of the Question that will lift the enchantment on the Fisher King.

The serpent – taken to be the embodiment of wickedness – successfully tempts Adam and Eve to eat the forbidden fruit. Yet in discovering evil, they also discovered good, and their Luciferan spirit of enquiry was ignited, which led to all human progress.

William Blake's *Glad Day* encompasses the joy of being human, acknowledging the endless challenges in which the real Lucifer revels.

The ancient Egyptian god Set, destroyer and avenger – but was he also the model for the Israelites' Yahweh?

The Egyptians' magical child-god Horus, defier of the evil Set, Horus is the nearest Egyptian equivalent to the bright 'Son of the Morning', Lucifer, who challenged Yahweh and lost – or so we are told . . .

The Roman goddess Diana Lucifera – the illuminator or enlightener. The church hated and feared pagan goddesses for their power and the inspiration they offered to ordinary women.

Pan, the beautiful god of nature, caressing the sacred snake of wisdom. In his mature guise of horns and hooves he became the Christians' model for the Devil.

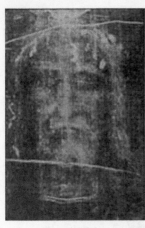

The face of the man on the Shroud, seen in an extraordinarily detailed photographic negative. Does the image behave like a photograph because that is what it is?

Portrait of the man on the Shroud. But is this really Jesus Christ, or the face of the great Luciferan artist and illusionist, Leonardo da Vinci as depicted below?

Da Vinci's preliminary sketch for *The Virgin and Child with St Anne*. Is the baby Jesus blessing John, or is he steadying his head to take a blow? Leonardo the Luciferan imbued many of his works with profoundly heretical messages about the superiority of the Baptist. Note the severed head hidden in the landscape at the top right-hand corner.

D. G. Rossetti's depiction of Mary Magdalene shows a flame-haired passive beauty. Known to her devotees in France as 'Mary Lucifer' – the light-bringer – her red hair signified sexual energy, perhaps the main reason that red-haired women were believed to be witches.

Goya's famous *The Witches' Sabbath* superbly evokes the sinister horror of a coven's worship of the goat-like Devil. Unfortunately most of the more lurid accounts of the Sabbath came from the imagination of 'witches' under torture.

Ein erschröckliche geschicht/ so zu Derneburg in der Graffschafft Reinstepn am Hartz gelegen/ von dreyen Zauberin/ vnnd zwapen Mafien/ In etlichen tagen des Monats Octobris Jm 1 5 5 5. Jare ergangen ist.

No one knows exactly how many so-called 'witches' were tortured and burned in Europe over at least 300 years. Estimates vary wildly between 5 million and a hundred thousand! But most of the accused were completely innocent of trafficking with the Devil.

Dr Dee's maverick assistant Edward Kelley and an accomplice seek to learn the future from a magically-reanimated corpse. Luciferan daring can often lead to dangerous or distasteful activities – the price we pay for being enthralled by extreme possibilities.

Sir Isaac Newton, alchemist and pioneering scientist, embodiment of the Age of Enlightenment, when the light of Lucifer finally began to sweep away the darkness of superstition.

In *Peredur* these are coherent parts of the overall plot. On that first occasion in his uncle's hall, Peredur fails to ask the identity of the severed head and what the procession is all about, and therefore misses (temporarily) his destined path. After going on to have many more, unrelated adventures (the basis of the perils encountered in the Grail quests), he is visited at Arthur's court by a hideous black-skinned woman – the original of the 'loathly damsel' of the Grail stories – who upbraids him:

> Peredur, I greet thee not, for thou dost not merit it. Blind was fate when she bestowed favour and fame upon thee. When thou camest to the court of the Lame King, and when thou sawest thou there the squire bearing the sharpened spear, and from the tip of the spear a drop of blood, and that running as it were a torrent as far as the squire's grip – and other marvels besides thou sawest there, but thou did not ask after their meaning nor the cause of them. And had thou so asked, the king would have had health and his kingdom in peace. But henceforth strife and battle, and the loss of knights, and women left widowed, and maidens without succour, and all that because of thee.[31]

In *Peredur*, the 'meaning and cause' that the hero fails to establish has a much more direct significance than in the Grail romances: the dead man whose head is borne on the salver is Peredur's cousin, slain by the witches of Caer Loyw, who have also cast a spell on the kingdom. Peredur's task is to avenge him. Indeed, it has been prophesied that he will do so, but because he failed to find out that the man was a kinsman the fulfilment of the prophecy has been thrown into doubt. When he does find out, and slays the witches, their enchantment is lifted. In the story's own terms all this makes perfect sense.

However, in the Grail stories these elements have become detached from the plot and taken on a transcendental character. The 'unasked question' becomes a mystical quest in its own right, and the mere speaking of it lifts the enchantment. (In *Perceval* the question is, 'Whom does the Grail serve?' – because this tale is unfinished we never find out what the answer is – and in *Parzival* it is, 'Dear Uncle, what ails you?')

The object in *Peredur* on which Chrétien de Troyes based his *graal* is the severed head on a salver. This is supported by the conclusion that his *graal* was some kind of shallow serving dish. However, Chrétien has chosen to omit the more significant part of the 'prototype Grail' – the head – and highlight the mundane part, the dish. Clearly, Chrétien has deliberately chosen to change or obscure this aspect of the Grail, but why?

The severed head motif was common enough in Celtic mythology and folklore, so it is hardly significant to find it in *Peredur*. However, in a Christian context, the severed head on the platter makes an obvious association with John the Baptist, and it seems to have been this association that appealed to Chrétien. But then it is odd that he should obscure the very aspect of the tale that seems to have attracted him in the first place and would make sense of the platter.

If Chrétien deliberately sought to obscure the severed head, the connection with the Baptist and the existence of the historical Johannite heresy might provide an explanation for this. (If Chrétien were a Johannite, and modelled *Perceval* on *Peredur* specifically to produce a Johannite work, the question remains about where he learnt about the heretical cult of John. Chrétien originated, as his name suggests, from the northern French town of Troyes, which was not only a centre of learning, but also the court of the Count of Champagne, who 'sponsored' the founding of the Templars. Troyes was the site of the first Templar preceptory in Europe.)

The military order of the Poor Knights of Christ, or the Knights Templar, became enormously rich, powerful and arrogant, especially in France, and were consequently ruthlessly suppressed in the early fourteenth century, amid accusations and confessions – admittedly extracted from them by the application of hideous torture – of blasphemy. It was said that they worshipped, among other idols, a bearded severed head called Baphomet, and that they spit and trampled on the cross. In *The Templar Revelation* we investigated these claims and were astonished to discover that there might indeed have been some basis in fact. For the Templars, it seems, encountered 'the Church of John in the East' – the Baptist's followers, or the Mandaeans, whom we have already discussed. According to the likes of Summers, they 'infected' the Christian knights with their heresy, although it would appear that only the inner circle was so contaminated. The rank and file – the vast majority of the Templars – were simply Christian warrior-monks with little or no idea of what the upper hierarchy believed or practised. In the context of the Mandaean 'contamination', the rumours of spitting and trampling on the cross, not to mention revering a bearded severed head, suddenly make perfect sense, tortured confessions or not.

When seen in Johannite terms, Chrétien's choice of *Peredur* as his model becomes even more significant. The 'secret' of the Grail lies in the identity of the beheaded man, and it is his death that has brought ruin and sterility to the kingdom, which recognizing his true identity and avenging his death will reverse. (Perhaps there is even significance in the fact that the dead man is a cousin of the main protagonist: John and Jesus were said to be cousins.)

None of this chain of reasoning would have been obvious to Chrétien's audience *unless* they knew his source, so it becomes a neat way of passing on the Johannite message in 'coded' form. Perhaps this is why Chrétien failed to finish the story, or perhaps, having removed the all-important head, he was stuck for an ending. In *Peredur* it centres on working out whose head it is.

All this Johannite heresy is lost in the Christian 'branch': the Grail becomes an explicitly Christian symbol, and the quest a Christian spiritual process. It was this branch that became the most familiar version. Wolfram, however, remained largely true to the Johannite line.

However, although there are specific references to Jesus as Christ, and to conventional Christian teaching and doctrines, in Wolfram's story, by the standards of the time and culture they are noticeably few – perhaps just the bare minimum to avoid raising suspicion. It has been noted by many scholars that Wolfram has deliberately minimized the role of the Church and clergy, to the point of removing certain characters and situations that appear in *Perceval*. Conventionally, this is explained by the idea that it was Wolfram's intention to write a morality tale aimed specifically at the knightly caste (to which he himself belonged), encouraging them to a greater spirituality. He therefore tried to show how *they* could change their ways without necessarily having recourse to the clergy. But while this may or may not be correct, the significant point is that Wolfram's marginalization of the Church is so conspicuous that scholars feel a need to explain it (although, of course, they have no reason to suspect that Wolfram was trying to deliver a heretical message).

On the other hand, there are many references that *appear* to be Christian, but which make more sense in Johannite terms: the frequent use of the term 'baptized men' to describe the keepers of the Grail (although they are very occasionally called 'Christians', as in the above quotation concerning Flegetanis); a somewhat evasive appeal to 'He whom painters still depict as the Lamb, with the Cross between His hooves', and so on.

Tobias Churton has argued for a Sabian 'Arabic' influence on Wolfram's work[32] – the name of one of the great Sabian scientists, Thabit ibn Qurra, even crops up, out of the blue, in *Parzival*. Such an influence would have come via Moorish Spain, so Wolfram's invocation of Flegetanis and Toledo makes sense. If equating the Sabians of that period with the Mandaeans is accepted (a link Churton would reject), then the source of the Johannite elements becomes clear.

But if Wolfram was aware of the hidden Johannitism of the Grail story, why did he change the Grail itself from a salver into a stone (although, as noted above, he kept the connection with the provision of food)? Is this, too, open to a Johannite interpretation?

Wolfram has Trevrizent explain the origins of the Grail to Parzival:

> When Lucifer and the Trinity began to war with each other, those who did not take sides, worthy, noble angels, had to descend to earth to that Stone which is for ever incorruptible. I do not know whether God forgave them or damned them in the end: if it was His due He took them back. Since that time the Stone has been in the care of those whom God appointed to it and to whom He sent his angels.[33]

But then, at the end of the story Trevrizent admits:

> I lied as a means of distracting you from the Gral and how things stood concerning it. Let me atone for my error [. . .]. You heard

from me that the banished angels were at the Gral with God's full support till they should be received back into His Grace. But God is constant in such matters: He never ceased to war against those whom I named to you here as forgiven. Whoever desires to have reward from God must be in feud with those angels. For they are eternally damned and chose their own perdition.

So it has gone from 'God forgave them' to 'I don't know what happened to them' to 'God damned them'. It has been suggested that this reversal was the result of Wolfram being censured by his local priesthood for the earlier comments. (*Parzival* is thought to have been composed in parts, which were circulated as they were completed, so a correction would have to be issued for any 'doctrinal error' spotted in an early part.)

Whatever the reason, the twist makes the Grail an object belonging to condemned and damned angels, who God-fearing folk 'must be in feud with' – maybe not as bad as Lucifer and his hordes, but nearly so.

So, although Wolfram fails to link the Grail and Lucifer directly, it could be argued that he does so indirectly, by association with the fallen angels (who, if God did damn them, must have ended up in Hell and therefore be subject to Lucifer in his Satanic mode anyway).

Undoubtedly, in medieval symbolism, John the Baptist was associated with the Morning Star, although the thinking behind this is obvious and conventional – the Morning Star heralds the coming of the sun as the Baptist heralded the coming of Christ. In the thirteenth century Jacob de Voragine would write in his *Golden Legend* (in Granger Ryan and Helmut Ripperger's translation) concerning John the Baptist:

For the Father calls him an angel, and says of him: 'Behold I send my angel, and he shall prepare the way before my face.' But angel is the name of an office and not of a nature; and therefore he is called an angel by reason of his office, because he exercised the office of all the angels. First, of the Seraphim. Seraphim is usually interpreted fiery because the Seraphim set us afire, and they themselves burn more ardently with the love of God; and in Ecclesiasticus it is said of John: 'Elias the prophet stood up, as a fire, and his word burnt like a torch'; for he came in the spirit and power of Elias. Second of the Cherubim. Cherubim is interpreted the fulness of knowledge; and John is called the morning star, because he put an end to the night of ignorance and made a beginning of the light of grace. [It goes on to compare John to various groups of angels . . .][34]

So there is a tenuous association of ideas that links John and Lucifer, via the Morning Star, but this stops far short of actually equating the two, as some did in the Middle Ages. However, in his book on the Templars, Michel Lamy quotes Jacob de Voragine's last sentence as: '*John is called Lucifer or the morning star . . .*'

In context, Lamy's version makes sense. Jacob is comparing John to angels, and without a reference to an angel the connection between the Cherubim and the Morning Star is a *non sequitur*. And there is the other, albeit tantalisingly circumstantial association of ideas mentioned earlier: the Morning and Evening Stars are, of course, really the same – more accurately, the planet, Venus. The Morning Star was linked with Lucifer and the Evening Star with the planet Venus, which the heretics associated with Mary Magdalene.[35] So if we accept Lamy's curious translation of John being Lucifer, then perhaps the story of the stone falling from Lucifer's *head* is not so far off the mark.

In any case, according to the Inquisition, the Cathars owned the head of John the Baptist . . . Surely of all possible types of 'Grail', that is the one that the Church would have really loved to have seized from the heretics.

The Cathars' own view of John was somewhat confused: they took the idea from their precursors the Bogomils that the Baptist was 'a demon', surreally, 'forerunner of the AntiChrist'.[36] And in the Cathars' holy book, the *Book of John* (*Liber Secretum or Secret Book*) Jesus announces that John the Baptist is an emissary of Satan, the lord of the physical world, despatched to earth to sabotage his mission. But of course this is merely an exaggerated version of what is already in the standard New Testament: as we have seen, Jesus appears to have roundly insulted the Baptist at least twice. Clearly the Cathars realized that the two men were bitter enemies, but assumed – as indeed most Christians would – that Jesus must unequivocally and eternally be on the side of right.

Whatever their beliefs about the Baptist, perhaps they still inherited his head from some other Gnostic group, keeping it to maintain its magical enslavement. Perhaps, too, it was part of the fabled 'Cathar treasure' that four *Perfecti* allegedly carried away the night before the others gave themselves up to the Crusaders. If so, they had also removed the Johannites' most sacred 'Grail': perhaps that is why so many Templars were so friendly towards them, despite papal urgings to the contrary.

With the martyrdoms of the Cathars of Montségur the scene was set for a shift in papal thought: now heresy was intimately linked with Devil-worship, with the horrors of *witchcraft*. There was no need for the newly-formed Inquisition to kick its heels in idleness now the field was wide open for an even greater crusade.

The terror begins

Colin Wilson comments in his book, *The Occult* (1973): 'Christianity was an epidemic rather than a religion. It appealed to fear, hysteria and ignorance.'[37] However, this definition largely depends on the particular manifestation of Christianity in question. The calm, probity and intellectual capacity of the itinerant Cathar preachers was notably at odds with the decadent lifestyle of the higher Catholic clergy, and the often staggering ignorance of the parish priests, equipped to do little more than say the Mass and preside over the usual offices such as burying the dead. But then came Dominic de Guzmán, a fanatical Spanish cleric who aimed to use the Cathars' own methods against them – and in doing so, he unleashed a virtual apocalypse upon at least 100,000 poor wretches, and caused suffering and hardship to many millions more ordinary people for generations. Under the flag of his new order, the Dominicans, he created the Holy Office, otherwise known as the Inquisition, a word that should – but these days rarely does – evoke the same concentrated shudder in the minds of all decent people as does the terrible term 'Gestapo'. They are not dissimilar, except the latter was a very brief manifestation of evil compared to the lengthy reign of the Inquisition – in fact, it still operates today, but under the less emotive name of the Congregation for the Doctrine of the Faith.[38]

This speech of Dominic's to the people of the Cathar country, dating from the 1200s, reveals a hint of the horrors to come:

> I have sung words of sweetness to you for many years now, preaching, imploring, weeping. But as the people of my country say, where blessing is to no avail, the stick will prevail. Now we shall call forth against you leaders and prelates who, alas, will gather together against this country . . . and will cause many people to die by the sword, will ruin your towers, overthrow and destroy your walls and reduce you all to servitude . . . the force of the stick will prevail where sweetness and blessing have been able to accomplish nothing.[39]

Despite the unflinching harshness of this warning, 'dying by the sword' would no doubt come to seem like an outright luxury compared to the atrocious methods of death meted out to thousands by his henchmen.

Deeply involved with Simon de Montfort, Dominic finally settled his headquarters at Toulouse (Carcassonne proving too hostile), where he founded the Order of the Preaching Friars, or the Dominican Order, in December 1216. Three years later he and his monks were on the move again: Toulouse had proved too hot to hold them. Giving the Languedoc up as a very bad job, the Dominicans spread to various locations, including Paris and, of course, Spain. By the time of Dominic's death in 1221, his movement was riding high, with a hundred houses – and its success was assured when the Dominican-friendly pope, Gregory IX, began his reign in 1233.

A year later two Inquisitors were officially appointed at Toulouse, centre of Cathar country – previously too hostile for the Dominicans to make their base. Now they were back, and they were in charge, with new and terrible powers from the pope himself. However, the Inquisitors by no means enjoyed unmitigated success, as Guillaume Pelhisson discovered after having several living heretics burnt, and, for good measure, also 'certain deceased persons . . . dragged away and burnt'.[40] The people rebelled and set upon the Inquisitor, beating him badly. Outraged, Guillaume remarks apopleptically: 'They beat, wounded and killed those who pursued them . . . many wicked things were done in the land to the church and to faithful persons.'[41]

An unedifying story illustrates the fanaticism and dehumanization of the new masters of bodies, if not souls. In 1234 Dominic was canonized – as Michael Baigent and Richard Leigh remark in their 1999 book *The Inquisition*: 'Few saints can have had so much blood on their hands'[42] – and while the Dominicans at Toulouse were preparing to celebrate the event, news arrived of a dying woman's heresy. As she lay on her deathbed, apparently she had received the Cathar version of the last rites, the Consolamentum. The Inquisitors, including the Bishop of Toulouse, rushed to her bedside, where they found her steeped in Catharism and obdurate in her heresy. 'Forthwith, the bishop . . . by virtue of Jesus Christ condemned her as a heretic. Moreover, the vicar had her carried on the bed in which she lay to the count's meadow and burned at once.'[43] As Baigent and Leigh remark dryly, 'Thus did the Dominicans of Toulouse crown their celebration of the newly sainted Dominic's feast day with a human sacrifice.'[44]

Shortly afterwards, the Dominicans were expelled from Toulouse by an outraged populace, but their revenge on that city, and on the neighbouring countryside, was so atrocious that its fall-out reverberates to this day in an impoverished land still suspicious of the Church of Rome. First, to establish that their power transcended even the safe haven of the grave, the Inquisition had the bones and putrescent bodies of prominent heretics dragged from their graves and burnt 'to the honour of God and the Blessed Virgin, His Mother, and the Blessed Dominic, His Servant [who] . . . most happily brought about this work of the Lord.'[45]

One of the most zealous (and therefore most vicious) of the early Inquisitors was himself a former Cathar, the Dominican friar Robert '*le bougre*' ('the Bulgar'), also known as 'the hammer of the heretics'. He sent many thousands to the stake in both Flanders and France, in 1239 consigning 183 of his former co-religionists to the flames in Mont-Aimé *en masse* as 'a fiery propitiation of God'. (But perhaps even Yahweh at his sourest would stop short of demanding such an offering. And there is no record of the Devil doing so, either.) That particular horror is notable for the fact that the local bishop offered them the solace of the Consolamentum before they died.[46]

Although there had been isolated cases of the execution (or exile) of heretics in the past, now the Inquisition proved a well-oiled, highly dedicated machine, a conveyor belt for tipping whole communities into Hell. However, because of a long-standing ecclesiastical tradition of not actually causing heretical blood to be shed, more or less ingenious ways of torturing and despatching the accused were devised that would keep bloodshed to a minimum, such as the thumbscrew and the rack. As Baigent and Leigh put it succinctly: 'Devices of this kind would seem to have been contrived to cause maximum pain and minimum mess.'[47]

Fire was the answer to the Inquisitors' prayers. From the point of view of the Church it has several major advantages. It is relatively bloodless. It has a unique capacity to evoke terror: the very thought of flames near one's vulnerable flesh induces an immediate atavistic fear, and the real thing is satisfyingly excruciating – particularly if produced by lighting slow-burning green wood, or setting the fire a fair distance beneath the heretics. And, ultimately, it is very cleansing, a purgation of the filth of heresy. As an afterthought, it could be argued that fire cleanses the heretic's soul, although mostly they were led to believe their only possible destiny was eternal hell fire. Suffering beyond imagining in life was to be followed by considerably worse – including the prospect of the spiritual desolation of being for ever removed from the love of Christ. Even the Nazis or the henchmen of Pol Pot contented themselves with mere mortal agonies.

However, the Cathars were relatively soon despatched, as we have seen, culminating in the conflagration of 210 *Perfecti* beneath the citadel of Montségur in 1244. Although pockets of Catharism survived – and may, in some form or another, continue to survive to this day – the Inquisition had done its worst and triumphed. But even so, it had hardly hit its stride. Dominic's men had a much older and more widespread enemy in its sights, a more virulently hated opponent of truly primeval standing – *women*.

Perhaps it should come as no surprise that the priests of Peter's Church should campaign tirelessly and fanatically against females – after all, the Magdalene had complained to Jesus that he 'hates me and all the race of women' – but the ferocity and insanity involved still have the power to rock both heart and soul.

Their excuse was, of course, witchcraft, not only evil-doing and heresy, but also Devil-worship – the deliberate act of aligning oneself with Satan, often, allegedly, by actually signing a pact with the Prince of Darkness himself.

The story of how the Inquisitors dealt with the accused is not for the squeamish, but must be faced if the nature of persecution and the dire potential of bigotry and hatred is ever to be fully understood. Although despicable in the extreme, the Nazis' reign of terror against the Jews and Stalin's atrocities against 20 million of his own people[48] only present part of the picture of man's inhumanity to man. The depredations of the medieval Church provide the missing link in the history of sadism – man's inhumanity to woman.

It is here that the Reverend Alphonse Joseph-Mary August Montague Summers enters the story proper – as, if nothing else, a cautionary tale about the limitless capacity of even an educated and intelligent bigot for believing the most arrant and dangerous nonsense. Yet he is no fire-and-brimstone character from the pages of the medieval Inquisition, although no doubt he would have loved to be: Summers died as recently as 1948, a pitiless and fanatical opponent of anything or anyone that smacked of heresy or challenged the smallest detail of Catholic belief. He will be quoted extensively, for although well-balanced modern readers may be tempted to dissolve into giggles simply because of his 'over the top' pompous and self-satisfied style, in fact he is a profoundly serious object lesson. The twentieth-century Summers possessed the same thought-processes and emotional responses as his brothers-in-spirit, the monks and priests of the medieval Inquisition, with hardly an iota of difference. Chillingly, even the jacket blurb of the 1960s reprint of his infamous book *The History of Witchcraft* (1925), states:

He was not ashamed of the great excesses committed in the 17th and 18th centuries, on the contrary, he vigorously defends everything the church ever did to extirpate witchcraft and heresy.

Interestingly, Summers notes: 'All the heresies, and the Secret Societies of heretics, which infested Europe during the Middle

Ages were Gnostic . . .'[49] Just like Mary Magdalene and John the Baptist. Just like Jesus himself, in fact.

It is no accident that the first 'witches' accused of attending the diabolical Sabbat to fall foul of the Inquisition were in fact Cathars and their maidservants from the Toulouse and Carcassonne area. In 1335 sixty-three people were tortured to extract confessions: chief among them was Anne-Marie de Georgel, who declared – apparently also speaking for the others – that they understood this world to be a battleground between the god of Heaven and the Lord of this world, and as they considered that the latter would triumph, they supported him. This may have seemed like Satanism to the accusing clerics, but it was, of course, simply Gnosticism – although as far as they, and the later Summers, were concerned, there was no great difference between the two. Another young woman admitted to the crime and sin of serving 'the Cathari at supper'.[50]

Inherently unclean

Excavating beneath the story of the original witchfinders and the thoughts of Summers, the full horror of a world gone mad is revealed. But it is more even than that: it is a living nightmare where the torturers and killers do so in the name of the highest good, and the 'evil' accused are, for the most part, utterly innocent of all great wrong. This was truly a time when Satan walked the earth – in the guise of the God of Love.

While there will undoubtedly be many who object to the witch trials being depicted as primarily a sustained outrage against women, there is no doubt whatever that the witch hysteria 'provided a focus for sexist hatred in male-dominated society'.[51] It had not escaped the notice of the Inquisition that the hated Cathars practised an almost unique form of spiritual egalitarianism of the sexes, and that their influence had helped foster a great flowering of secular arts in the south of France, including the artful songs of the Troubadours, and the cult of the Lady – clearly a resurrection of ancient goddess worship. (The Troubadour's insistence of *loving* individual women was quite new to most people – nothing in the classical world was remotely similar.) Everywhere they looked in the Languedoc and Provence, the men of the Church must have blanched at the unavoidable echoes of the unacceptable 'Apostle of the Apostles' – Mary Magdalene, whose memory they were so eager to malign, and whose cult they were intent on destroying.

It must not be forgotten that women, whether accused of witchcraft or not, were widely believed – certainly by the Church patriarchy – to be naturally polluted and unclean. In this, they accepted the Rabbinical tradition that claimed Eve first menstruated only after she had fornicated with the snake – her firstborn, Cain, being widely seen as the child of the serpent, not Adam. Today orthodox Jews refuse to shake hands with a woman in case she is menstruating, while rural communities across Europe still hold that a woman with her period will turn milk or wine sour and blunt knives. Saint Jerome thundered 'Nothing is so unclean as a woman in her periods; what she touches she causes to become unclean.' In the seventh century, Bishop Theodore of Canterbury forbade menstruating women to take communion or even enter a church – as did the French synod of Meaux. Even in the twentieth century a Scottish medical textbook quoted the old rhyme: 'Oh! Menstruating woman, thou'rt a fiend/From which all nature should be closely screened.'[52] As Barbara Walker points out, religious women especially were ordered to detest their own bodies, citing the Rule for Anchoresses: 'Art thou not formed of foul slime? Art thou not always full of uncleanness?'[53]

The association between the vileness of 'witchcraft' and menstruation was reinforced as far as the Montague Summers of this world were concerned by the – admittedly extreme – rites of Gnostic groups such as the Ophites and the Carpocratians (whom we have discussed previously). When reading the following passage by Epiphanius, it is instructive to recall that the Carpocratians claimed to have received sexual secrets (akin to those of the Ophites) from Salome, Martha and Mary Magdalene – and that Saint Clement confessed that he knew this to be true.

> . . . the wretches mingle with each other . . . after they have consorted together in a passionate debauch . . . The woman and the man take the man's ejaculation into their hands, stand up . . . offering to the Father, the Primal Being of All Nature, what is on their hands, with the words, 'We bring to Thee this oblation, which is the very Body of Christ'.

... They consume it, take housel of their shame and say: 'This is the Body of Christ, the Paschal Sacrifice through which our bodies suffer and are forced to confess the sufferings of Christ.' And when the woman is in her period, they do likewise with her menstruation. The unclean flow of blood, which they garner, they take up in the same way and eat together. And that, they say, is Christ's Blood. For when they read in Revelation, 'I saw the tree of life with its twelve kinds of fruit, yielding its fruit each month,[54] they interpret this as an allusion to the monthly incidence of the female period.[55]

Clearly Evensong was once rather more colourful than it is today. However, as we shall see, devotees of the Black Mass revived the sacrament of the semen and menstrual blood, although they may not actually have realized that they were reinstating an original Christian ritual (if, indeed, the Carpocratians, Simon Magus and Clement of Alexandria were right). Perhaps they merely wanted to shock. In any case, this sort of rite is also found in Tantrism, where consuming the living substances of sex and reproduction were believed to be of a higher kind of spirituality than eating the dead god, even when transubstantiated into, or represented by, the bread and wine – 'although the colour symbolism was the same'.[56] (Interestingly, both Catholics and the later Protestants denounced witches as cannibals.)

To the Tantrics, the officiating priestesses, who were expected to menstruate in order to benefit from the extra flow of lunar power, were symbolized by the colour red. Is this why Mary Magdalene was traditionally portrayed as boasting a thick red mane of hair, despite the fact that as an Egyptian or Ethiopian – or even, as widely supposed, a Judaean – her hair would have been extremely dark? And one must not forget that in the Middle Ages women with the symbolic red hair were believed to be witches, and often burnt as such.

It was long believed that demons were born of menstrual blood – including the legendary basilisk with the fatal look. However, not all cultures despised the monthly flux: 'the very word taboo, from Polynesian *tupua*, "sacred, magical", applied specifically to menstrual blood.'[57] And even some European peasants believed it had curative powers – stained rags scattered on fields were believed to bless them with greater fertility. But in general the western view was – and to a large extent, still is, one of abhorrence.

Both the Catholic and Anglican hierarchies of the late twentieth century argued against the ordination of women on the grounds that a menstruating woman would 'pollute' the altar. Walker notes wryly: 'This would not preclude ordination of post-menopausal women, but different excuses are found for those.' She adds: 'The holy "blood of life" used to be feminine and real; now it is masculine and symbolic.'[58]

In the Middle Ages certain areas associated with the Feminine were proscribed by the Church, including wells, groves and caves, all of which had become indelibly linked with goddess worship and which – unsurprisingly – became denounced as the haunt of witches and demons. Any similar place was categorized as *cunnus diaboli*, 'devilish cunt', and was therefore avoided by all God-fearing folk.

After the Cathars and associated heretics were effectively erased from the map, the Inquisition's feeding frenzy needed more fuel, and what worse or more disgusting heretics were there than witches, actual self-confessed worshippers of Satan? How convenient, too, that most of the accused were women! As Mary Daly writes in her *Beyond God the Father* (1973):

> The spirit of the Church in its contempt for women, as shown in the Scriptures, in Paul's epistles and the Pentateuch, the hatred of the fathers, manifested in their ecclesiastical canons, and in the doctrines of asceticism, celibacy, and witchcraft, destroyed man's respect for woman and legalized the burning, drowning, and torturing of women . . .
>
> Women and their duties became objects of hatred to the Christian missionaries and of alternate scorn and fear to pious ascetics and monks. The priestess mother became something impure, associated with the devil, and her lore an infernal incantation, her very cooking a brewing of poison, nay, her very existence a source of sin to man. Thus woman, as mother and priestess, became woman as witch . . .[59]

Abandon hope, all ye . . .

Citing the biblical authority of Exodus 22:18 'Thou shall not suffer a witch to live' – although the *kasaph* of the original text actually means 'seer' or clairvoyant, ironically in the same paranormal category as the exclusively male prophets – the Holy Office waded into the bloody fray, arresting, interrogating and murdering countless people.[60] But of what were they accused?

Many were simply ugly old women, no doubt senile and unpleasant, or who those had fallen foul of their neighbours. Their constant mumbling was taken as the invocation of devilish spells – or even a direct prayer to Old Nick himself. Conversely, a particularly pretty girl was often accused of witchcraft, often by jealous peers or a thwarted would-be lover, especially if he was a priest. Denunciations of witchcraft represented the ultimate in harassment and bullying: human nature being what it is, the temptation was tragically too great to pass up an opportunity of settling old scores when the Inquisitors came to town.

One woman was arrested because she quarrelled with her neighbour, who then saw a snake in her garden. If horses bolted, crops failed, butter stubbornly remained milk, children sickened, women miscarried, there was always a handy witch to blame. Another woman was convicted and burnt because she had rowed with a drunk at a tavern, who – how strange! – found himself up all night vomiting. Yet another poor wretch found herself facing the flames because she had been seen pulling off her stockings – and shortly afterwards her neighbour became lame. Two Scottish 'witches' were hanged because they had treated, and *cured* an ailing child. As Barbara Walker notes:

> Joan Cason of Kent went to the gallows in 1586 for having dry thatch on her roof. Her neighbour, whose child was sick, was told . . . that the child was bewitched, and it could be proved by stealing a bit of thatch from the witch's roof and throwing it on the fire. If it crackled and sparked, witchcraft was assured. The test came out positive . . .[61]

Women with dissimilar eyes or red hair were instantly recognizable as devil worshippers: apart from the symbolism discussed previously, perhaps this was because redheads usually have freckles, and these were often taken as 'witch marks'. The Inquisitors made it known as a fact that witches bore certain special marks on their bodies, where the devil had touched them as an affirmation of their unholy pact, and which remained impervious to pain. Part of the torturers' job was to strip and search the accused for the 'Devil's teat', jabbing a large bodkin into their flesh, which – although it caused great suffering – was not even categorized as torture. Then, with swift sleight of hand, the 'witch pricker' substituted a retractable bodkin and, lo and behold, the mark was found! Of course witch pricking offered the perfect opportunity for all manner of violent sexual abuse, but again, this was deemed the torturer's perk and not part of being 'put to the Question', or torture proper.

At a witch trial in 1593, as the jailer searched a female 'witch' – which of course he did thoroughly – he discovered 'a little lump of flesh, in manner sticking out as if it had been a teat, to the length of half an inch', which he 'perceiving at the first sight thereof, meant not to disclose, because it was adjoining to so secret a place which was not decent to be seen; yet in the end, not willing to conceal so strange a matter'[62] he did show it to others. They all agreed – married men and all – that this was new in their experience, and almost certainly demonic. The woman was convicted and burnt. This 'devil's teat' was, of course, a clitoris. Even physicians believed that no virtuous woman would possess such a thing[63] – an interesting application of the theory of predestination.

At Lille in 1661, the pupils of alleged witch Antoinette Bourignon confessed:

> The Devil gives them a Mark, which Marks they renew as often as those Persons have any desire to quit him. The devil reproves them the more severely, and obligeth them to new Promises, making them also new Marks for assurance or Pledge, that those Persons should continue faithful to him.[64]

The twentieth-century's own would-be Inquisitor, the Reverend Summers, expounds without so much as a flicker of irony on this, 'the most important point in the identification of a witch . . . the very sign and seal of Satan . . .'[65] Nevertheless, in his eagerness to prove his case, Summers is nothing if not thorough in providing a wide spread of sources, which possess a quaint horror for those of more balanced minds. He cites Robert Hink, 'minister at Aberfoill', in his *Secret Commonwealth* (1691), who noted:

> A spot that I have seen, as a small mole, horny, and brown-coloured; throw [sic] which mark, when a large pin was thrust (both in buttock, nose and rooff of mouth), till it bowed and became crooked, the witches both men and women, nather felt a pain nor did bleed, nor knew the precise time when this was doing to them . . .

Summers informs us breathlessly that, 'This mark was sometimes the complete figure of a toad or a bat; or . . . the slot of a hare, the foot of a frog, a spider, a deformed whelp, a mouse'.[66] Note the 'foot of a frog' – a vague description if ever there was one – or that '*deformed* whelp', which might be almost any shape or size: indeed, as many people would have borne some kind of birthmark or blemish on their person, who should emerge blameless?

(Summers also argues that heretics had a particularly loathsome *smell*, as indeed they probably did – terror does generate a markedly acrid sort of sweat. Besides, even a single night in the Inquisition's jails would render the most fragrant somewhat malodorous. However, of course, to Summers Catholic priests often exuded the odour of sanctity, as evidence for which he remarks in utter seriousness 'I myself have known a priest of fervent faith who at times diffused the odour of incense'.[67] Surely it would be a very odd thing if most priests did not 'at times' smell of incense! One may laugh, but this sort of infantilism – nice people smell nice but nasty people smell nasty – smacks too much of Dr Goebbels' anti-Semitic propaganda, lapped up by millions of ordinary intelligent Germans, to be anything other than chilling.)

Summers quotes 'that same authority' on the site of such 'Witch Marks': 'In men it may often be seen under the eyelids, under the lips, under the armpits, on the shoulders, on the fundament; in women, moreover, on the breast or the pudenda.'[68] Ah. But remember that wherever these marks were 'found' they were located by having a skewer-like bodkin, usually about three inches long, rammed into the near-locality 'till it bowed and became crooked'. And this *still* was not officially classed as torture.

Summers explains that the 'Little Teat or Pap' so found on the body of a wizard or witch, and said to secrete milk that nourished the 'familiar' – a demon-possessed creature such as a cat or toad – must be carefully distinguished from the insensible devil-mark. This, for some reason, was a phenomenon more or less exclusive to England and New England, in the days when witch hysteria had moved seamlessly from the Inquisition to the dour Protestant Fathers. (Of course Montague Summers dismisses cases of Protestant exorcism as merely the fantasies of poor afflicted country folk, whereas the Catholic version is always a genuine spiritual feat.)

In 1597 Elizabeth Wright of Burton-on-Trent

> the old woman they stript, and found behind her right sholder a thing much like the vdder of an ewe that giuth sucke with two teates, like vnto two great wartes, the one behind vnder her arme-hole, the other a hand off towardes the top of her shoulder. Being demanded how long she had those teates, she answered she was borne so.[69]

The poor old woman's birthmark or defect effectively signed her death warrant.

If an obvious witch's mark was neither found nor fabricated through the use of the retractable bodkin, there was still no likelihood of the accused escaping. When Bavarian witch-hunter Jorg Abriel failed to find the incriminating mark, he simply announced that the woman looked like a witch and then tortured her until she confessed.[70]

(The Devil's mark can be seen – and no doubt was by Summers and his like – as the satanic mockery of the stigmata, the marks of Jesus' crucifixion that have been witnessed to appear on the side, head, feet and hands of the Catholic devout, and are often associated with sainthood. For example, the Franciscan Capuchin monk Padre Pio of Pietrelcina [d. 1968, aged eighty-one], who was said to have bled from his miraculously wounded hands every day for fifty years and worked many miracles, was canonized by Pope John Paul II on 16 June 2002. However, the phenomenon of stigmata raises some interesting questions: as it is impossible to crucify a man by hammering nails through his palms, as depicted in most religious works of art – the skin would tear and he would fall to the ground – why do stigmatics usually bleed from their palms?)

However, to the Inquisition, the Devil's marks were proof of the greatest sin of all, visiting the Sabbat where they made a pact with the Devil himself. According to received wisdom about such matters, the individual members of a local coven would slip out at night – perhaps leaving their spouses asleep in the marital bed, all innocent of the enormity of their actions, a broom now lying in their place. One by one the witches sloped off to a remote or hidden place, a clearing deep in a forest or a cave (preferably one originally dedicated to a pagan goddess), where they met, feasted, drank and revelled on occasions that were not even saints' days. According to a contemporary French writer, 'Mere clowning and japery are mixed up with circumstances of extremest horror; child-ishness and folly with loathsome abominations'.[71] Here, too, they were supposed to encounter the terrifying figure of Satan himself, rearing up from the shadows in the guise of a great horned goat, usually with a giant phallus which was sometimes even admitted to be artificial, a dildo or *fascinum*. The new witch, no doubt in a pitiful state of fear and excitement, had to affirm his or her dedication to the Devil by kissing his backside, and/or perhaps signing the official pact with their blood. They might then receive the distinguishing satanic mark – although clearly some already had them, having borne them since birth – and the entertainment might then consist of orgiastic coupling before the bedraggled and exhausted coven slunk home and slid once again between the marital sheets. But the evil deed had been done, and their soul was literally no longer their own.

Sometimes, if the Sabbat – and even Summers is careful to state that it was 'wholly unconnected with the Jewish festival',[72] although in the eyes of many medieval people it almost certainly was linked, as anti-Semitism was rife – was far away, the witches would ride on broomsticks. Summers admits the illusion of flying was frequently brought on by the use of hallucinogenic ointment, rubbed on the legs before sitting astride the broomstick. The witch may have gone nowhere except in her imagination, but that was good enough for her accusers. In others cases she was said to ride 'upon certain beasts along with the pagan goddess Diana',[73] which rather says it all.

The satanic pact (of which more later) was always, we are led to believe, a triumph of hope over experience – other witches' experience, that is. For the Devil might hold out any glittering promise, but it was as well to realize he is also 'the Father of Lies' and will always fail even his most stalwart devotees – in the end, when it matters most.

In that, however, the Devil was not alone. Many of the accused witches were promised by the Inquisition that if they confessed they would be released with a fine. When they were condemned to the pyre they shrieked that they had been tricked. Once again there was not much to choose between the Church and Satan himself.

The horror

It is impossible to know how many of the accused were Luciferan challengers of the status quo or real Satanists: clearly some were merely 'wise women' or 'cunning men', local herbalists and casters of spells, while others were probably adherents to a form of the old goddess or fertility god religion: indeed, the descriptions of a typical Sabbat, as outlined above, seem to echo the ancients' celebrations of Diana or Pan. Perhaps some of the 'Sabbats' were simply the equivalent of the modern swingers' party – merry-making, boozing and wife-swapping – or even more innocently, just a spot of dancing and feasting away from the prying eyes of the clergy, or so they hoped. Life was grim, short and brutish enough in those days, in any case, so why not let off steam deep in the forest at night?

However, common sense dictates that some of the accused *were* Satanists, were involved in casting spells to harm others, if for no better reason than that such people always exist, everywhere. Spite and superstition together will always produce 'witches', although not necessarily at an organized level. And ironically, as the witch craze deepened and spread, no doubt there was an exponential increase in the number of genuine Devil worshippers. After all, how could even Old Nick himself be any worse than the Inquisition? Who wouldn't be tempted to side with the opposition as the madness circled ever closer and you could almost feel the sparks of the great fires on your skin? Despite rumours to the contrary, Satan might, just might, prove a loyal master, rewarding the faithful with material support – and even the all-important magical release from jail, rack and pyre.

No one will ever know exactly how many of the recently-estimated 100,000 accused were genuine witches and who was merely in the wrong place at the wrong time – although the records of individual cases make it horribly, pitifully clear that most were just victims. Their own confessions to even the most heinous and blatant Devil worship meant absolutely nothing.

One eyewitness, Weyer, wrote that the condemned 'were slaughtered with the most refined tortures that tyrants could invent, beyond human endurance. And this cruelty is continued until the most innocent are forced to confess themselves guilty.'[74] At Eichstätt in 1637 a woman who was arrested on charges of dealings with the Devil initially 'laughed heartily', declaring she had rather die than admit to any such nonsense, and that she had lived a decent life with her husband and eight children for over twenty years. 'Three weeks later she died under torture, confessing that she was in love with the devil, that she killed one of her children at his bidding, and that at least 45 of her neighbours were fellow Satanists'.[75]

Usually the poorer heretics were killed off first, while – as ever – the rich accused could usually buy their way out of trouble, as the following contemporary account of the persecution in France in 1459 makes clear:

In this year, in the town of Arras and country of Artois, arose, through a terrible and melancholy chance, an opinion called, I know not why, the Religion of Vaudoise. This sect consisted, it is said, of certain persons, both men and women, who, under cloud of night, by the power of the devil, repaired to some solitary spot, amid woods and deserts, where the devil appeared before them in human form – save that his visage is never perfectly visible to them – read to the assembly a book of his ordinances, informing them how he could be obeyed; distributed a very little money and a plentiful meal, which was concluded by a scene of general profligacy; after which each one of the party was conveyed home to her or his own habitation.

On accusations of access to such acts of madness, several creditable persons of the town of Arras were seized and imprisoned along with some foolish women and persons of little consequence. These were so horribly tortured that some of them admitted the truth of the whole accusation, and said, besides, that they had seen and recognized in their nocturnal assembly many persons of rank, prelates, seigneurs, and governors of bailliages and cities, being such names as the examiners had suggested to the persons examined, while they constrained them by torture to impeach the persons to whom they belonged. Several of those who had been thus informed against were arrested, thrown into prison, and tortured for so long a time that they also were obliged to confess what was charged against them. After this those of mean condition were executed and inhumanly burnt, while the richer and more powerful of the accused ransomed themselves by sums of money, to avoid the punishment and the shame attending to it. Many even of those also confessed being persuaded to take that course by the interrogators, who promised them indemnity for life and fortune. Some there were, of a truth, who suffered with marvellous patience and constancy the torments inflicted on them, and would confess nothing imputed to their charge; but they, too, had to give large sums to the judges, who exacted that such of them as, notwithstanding their mishandling, were still able to move, should banish themselves from that part of the country . . . It ought not to be concealed that the whole accusation was a strategem of wicked men for their own covetous purposes, and in order, by these false accusations and forced confessions, to destroy the life, fame [good reputation], and fortune of wealthy persons.[76]

The possibilities for blackmail must have been particularly tempting when the Inquisitors arrived in one's neighbourhood. To demand money rather than make a formal charge of witchcraft would no doubt have occurred to a great many during the witch craze – although it is unlikely that such transactions were recorded.

Inside the torture chamber
According to the Inquisitors' handbook, the *Hammer of the Witches* by one of the most nightmarish partnerships of all time, Heinrich Kramer (1430–1505) and Jakob Sprenger (1436–95) – of whom Summers, their only English translator to date,[77] heartily approves

as 'erudite' – torture was to be known as 'the Question'. It was to be used 'lightly' at first to extract a confession – sometimes, indeed, merely showing the accused the instruments of torture succeeded in this – although what the Inquisitors meant by 'light torture' is not what the victims would have understood. A woman from Constance admitted to causing storms by pouring water into a hole after she 'had first been exposed to the very gentlest questions, being suspended hardly clear of the ground by her thumbs.'[78]

Records often claimed that confessions were given freely, without recourse to torture – *sine tortura et extra locum torturae* – 'without torture and even out of sight of the instruments of torture'. But what this meant in practice was that the victims were simply taken into another room and given the choice of confessing there and then or being returned to the torture chamber and put to 'the Question' without mercy.

One Rebecca Lemp wrote heartrending letters to her husband both before and after torture, revealing that even *in extremis* she had fears for her soul. At first, as she languished in the dungeons, she seemed confident, writing

My dearly beloved Husband, be not troubled. Were I to be charged by thousands of accusations, I am innocent, else may all the demons in hell come and tear me to pieces. Were they to pulverize me, cut me in a thousand pieces, I could not confess anything. Therefore do not be alarmed; before my conscience and before my soul I am innocent. Will I be tortured? I don't believe it, since I am not guilty of anything.[79]

She was tortured, five times, after which she wrote,

O thou, chosen of my heart, must I be parted from thee, though entirely innocent? If so, may God be followed through-out eternity by my reproaches. They force one and make one confess, they have so tortured me . . . Husband, send me something that I may die, or I must expire under the torture . . . Send me something, else I may peril even my soul.[80]

Note that to this poor soul the greater sin would be to confess to crimes of witchcraft, though wholly innocent, than to commit suicide. We do not know her fate, but almost certainly we can guess what happened to her, unless somehow her husband did manage to smuggle her the means with which to end her agonies.

Prisoners of the Inquisition who did kill themselves, died of their injuries or of being eaten alive by rats in the dungeons – which happened often, as their suppurating wounds attracted vermin – were said to have been killed by the Devil, 'for so did Divine justice dispose'.[81] For their part, the Inquisitors were absolved from all sin and culpability: when a victim died under torture, Pope Urban IV urged the Inquisitors to absolve each other. He declared they were innocent in the sight of God.[82]

Although on the whole most 'witches' were women, and poor women at that, some rich men were arraigned, especially in areas where the Inquisition rapidly spiralled out of control, with each successive confession implicating another dozen or so people, and so on.

Elsewhere the richer you were the more likely you were to escape. However, the following extract is from the letter of Burgomaster Johannes Junius, a wealthy man whose property was seized. The note, which was smuggled out of Bamberg prison in 1628, while familiar enough to researchers, never fails to be heartrendingly poignant:

Many hundred thousand good-nights, dearly beloved daughter Veronica. Innocent have I come into prison, innocent have I been tortured, innocent I must die. For whoever comes into the witch prison must become a witch or be tortured until he invents something out of his head and – God pity him – bethinks himself of something. I will tell you how it has gone with me . . . The executioner put the thumb screw on me, both hands bound together, so that the blood ran out at the nails and everywhere, so that for four weeks I could not use my hands, as you can see from the writing . . . Thereafter they first stripped me, bound my hands behind me, and drew me up in the torture [strappado]. Then I thought heaven and earth were at an end; eight times did they draw me up and let me fall again, so that I suffered terrible agony. The executioner said, 'Sir, I beg of you, for God's sake confess something, whether it be true or not. Invent something, for you cannot endure the torture which you will be put to, and even if you bear it all, yet you will not escape' . . . Now, dear child, here you have all my confession, for which I must die. And they are sheer lies and made-up things, so help me God. For all this I was forced to say through the fear of the torture which was threatened beyond what I had already endured. For they never leave off with the torture till one confesses something; be he never so good, he must be a witch. Nobody escapes . . . Dear child, keep this letter secret so that people do not find it, else I shall be tortured most piteously and the jailers beheaded. So strictly is it forbidden . . . I have taken several days to write this; my hands are both lame. I am in a sad plight. Good night, for your father Johannes Junius will never see you more . . . Dear child, six have confessed against me at once . . . all false, through compulsion, as they told me, and begged my forgiveness in God's name before they were executed.[83]

Note that the 'executioner' seemed to have retained a modicum of decency as he begged the old man to invent some confession, although it was made clear that escape was hopeless in any case. And even in his agonies, this good man remarks not only about the danger to himself, should his letter fall into Inquisitorial hands, but also to his jailers, who would be beheaded.

The usual plan was to torture the victims until they confessed to trafficking with the Devil, then torture them further to elicit a list of accomplices, who were then pulled in for questioning, and so the process began again – until whole districts fell to the hysteria. One woman said to her interrogator:

I never dreamed that by means of the torture a person could be brought to the point of telling such lies as I have told. I am not a witch, and I have never seen the devil, and still I had to plead guilty to myself and denounce others.'[84]

When a cleric urged another woman to retract her accusations of innocent villagers, she answered forcibly:

Father, look at my legs! They are like fire – ready to burn up –

so excruciating is the pain. I could not stand to have so much as a fly touch them, to say nothing of submitting again to the torture. I would a hundred times rather die than endure such frightful agony again. I cannot describe to any human being how terrific the pain actually is.[85]

The whole procedure was deliberately calculated to exacerbate the maximum of both terror and pain. No doubt some accused chained up in their cells could hear the shrieks and pleadings of those writhing in the torture chamber – but in any case it is likely that the prisoners would suffer the trauma of witnessing their cell-mates' post-torture distress when they rejoined them in the dungeons. Next the accused would be roughly dragged into the torture chamber and shown the instruments that might at any moment be put into use, and then finally face the Question itself, which might take the form of the *strappado* (as in the case of Herr Junius, above), which involved hauling the accused into the air by the arms, pinioned behind the back, then suddenly letting them drop to a foot or so above the ground. Shoulders and arms were routinely dislocated. Otherwise, flesh was torn from the body with pincers, feet and legs were smashed to pulp in 'the Boot', limbs were broken and sinews torn on the rack, feet and hands were roasted over braziers, besides whippings and beatings administered routinely. One woman had flaming brimstone held to her genitals as she hung in the *strappado*. Most women suffered rape and worse even before they even reached the torture chamber.

That was 'merely' the physical aspect of the torture. Mental torture included the build-up of terror or being forced to witness the rape or torture of close family members, perhaps children under ten (categorized as 'infants'). Usually children were tortured without much preamble because of their susceptibility to the torment of the whole experience, not the least having been wrenched for reasons they could never understand from their families. Usually, though, they were fair game, and soon persuaded, one way or another, to incriminate many others, including their own mothers and fathers. Being tortured on the testimony of your eight-year-old, knowing that this child had suffered abominably, must have added enormously to the victims' agony. Such testimony was acceptable in a witch trial, but in no other kind of court, even at that time.

The records of the infamous Spanish Inquisition, based at Toledo, reveal that

some victims were prevented from confessing until the lust of their tormentors had been gratified. Their torture went on for days or weeks beyond the point where they had wholly broken down, and pleaded to be told what to say, so they could say it.[86]

As the European Inquisitors tended to use the more obviously brutal forms of torture compared to the methods of interrogation utilized in Britain, it might be thought that the English and Scottish witch-finders were generally more compassionate. In fact, this was hardly the case: in Britain tortures such as dunking in water ('swimming the witch'), binding tightly with ropes, sleep deprivation ('walking the witch') and so on were the order of the day. Sometimes the mob devised more hideous means of dealing with the accused. In Catton, Suffolk in 1603, an eighty-year-old woman was set upon by a gang of violent men, who punched and threw her about, flashed gunpowder in her face, and then hurled her with force on a specially constructed seat 'in the which they had stuck daggers and knives with sharp points upwards, [and] they often times struck her down upon the same stool whereby she was sore pricked and grievously hurt.'[87] The vivid mental picture conjured by this terse report summons the not dissimilar image of Nazi bully-boys setting fire to old Jews' beards, or dragging naked middle-aged women through the streets by their hair – images that haunt long after the photograph or film footage has been removed from sight. It comes as a shock, however, to realize that intensely horrible though those particular Nazi atrocities were – and remain in the mind's eye – even they were not quite so disgusting as what happened to that anonymous eighty-year-old woman in the quiet English countryside of the 1600s.

The sheer inventiveness and sadism of the tortures and the fact that most of the accused were women reveals the real agenda of the Inquisition, as expressed by the truly demonic double act, Kramer and Sprenger. Their *Hammer of the Witches* makes it conclusively clear that to them, at least, witchcraft was a gender-specific crime. They write of the evils of women in openly hostile terms, speaking of them being 'so beautiful to look at' but 'contaminating to the touch', with sweet voices that 'entice passersby and kill them . . . by emptying their purses, consuming their strength and causing them to forsake God'. To the authors of the Inquisitorial handbook, a woman is a vampire, and a 'curse worse than the devil'.

The Hammer of the Witches was designed to appear authoritative, being accompanied by a papal bull from Innocent VIII, supporting the book in its campaign – virtually a crusade in itself – to eradicate witches, root and branch. There is also a supportive letter from a group of theologians from the University of Cologne, but recent scholarship has suggested it was partly forged.[88] And other inconsistences indicate that the wider picture of witch-hunting was at least a little different from the accepted view. For example, Kramer claimed to have tried nearly a hundred women in the Tyrol in the early 1480s, half of whom died by fire. But the surviving records tell a different story: Kramer arrived and began inciting the populace to implicate their neighbours. Eight women were convicted and burnt, but both the local archduke and the bishop remained sceptical – the latter calling Kramer a 'senile old fool' and expelling him from the town.

The reason for the bishop's hostility was that Kramer had rarely accused the women of actual diabolism: on the whole they stood trial for using love spells. In the case of Helen Scheuberin, he attacked her on the basis of her promiscuity, the details of which he seemed particularly anxious to hear until the bishop's representative ordered him to stop. The townspeople were so horrified by his blatantly salacious and perverted *raison d'être* that they complained to the authorities, who threw him out. Kramer then took to composing the handbook for more successful witch-hunters, infecting thousands, for generations, with his own brand of sexist sado-masochism. It found a ready audience, however, among Catholics who had always been encouraged to 'offer up their suffering to God' but not their joy, and whose every visit to Church provided yet another encounter with the images of Christ's bloody and terrible death by torture. The implacable wrath and blood lust of the patriarchal God was surely nowhere more evident than in his demand for the crucifixion of his own son.

Kramer drew on several earlier sources, particularly Johannes Dominicus' *Lectiones super Ecclesiastes* (1380), which blames the 'natural' vices of women for their openness to the Devil's influence – greed, carnality and so on. Like Eve, women are light-hearted and therefore easily swayed by demons. Dominicus, however, had never mentioned witchcraft.

On the other hand, another of Kramer's sources, Johannes Nider's *Formaricus* (1435), does associate outright diabolism with women's alleged natural sins – particularly that of insubordination, as evidenced in the rare occasions of their dressing in male clothing or carrying weapons. Pretending to be close to God was particularly singled out for male opprobrium. 'It is presumption, deception and rebellion that are his targets.'[89] In Kramer's hands, however, Nider is misquoted: women themselves become inherently evil, especially their propensity for carnality.

In a lather of the most embarrassingly obvious Freudian fear, Kramer emphasizes the anti-male crimes of women, such as their ability to make penises disappear (if only by means of illusion, the witches' *glamour* – an interesting addendum, rendering such an accusation open to an entirely subjective interpretation). Perhaps this primitive terror of impotence was behind the handbook's stress on the Inquisitors taking precautions against the witch's 'evil eye', such as erecting a screen between themselves and the miscreant in the courtroom. (Although the authorities were assured many times that they alone had the power to withstand the witches deadly glance, few of the accusers felt particularly confident of this.) Another mode of protection was to wear a bag of salt consecrated on Palm Sunday; to avoid making eye contact with the witch, and to cross oneself as much as possible when in their jail. One Peter of Berne was careless, and plummeted down a flight of stone steps – clearly the result of a witch's enchantments, for he tortured her until she admitted it.[90]

Women who nag or usurp male authority were top of the *Hammer's* hit list, for it was assumed that they must be witches. At the same time, husbands had long been actively encouraged to abuse their wives to the last degree. Friar Cherubino's fifteenth-century *Rules of Marriage* said to husbands:

Scold her sharply, bully and terrify her. And if this still doesn't work . . . take up a stick and beat her soundly, for it is better to punish the body and correct the soul than to damage the soul and spare the body . . . Then readily beat her, not in rage but out of charity and concern for her soul, so that beating will redound to your merit.[91]

Saint Thomas Aquinas remarked that a wife is lower than a slave, for at least a slave can be freed, but 'Woman is in subjection according to the law of nature, but a slave is not.'[92] Presumably the 'law of nature' means that as women are generally physically weaker than men, they should and must be bullied. Up until the late nineteenth-century it was legal for a British man to beat his wife as long as the instrument he used – a whip, cane or rod – was not thicker than his thumb, the original 'rule of thumb'. As Walker says, 'Wives had little help from the law; they were legally classified with minors and idiots, and were consigned to the custody of their husbands.'[93] They were *femmes couvertes*, women whose personalities were legally 'covered' by their husbands'. It was in this context that female rebels, children of Lucifer but not of Satan – however mild their actions might seem today – were hounded as witches.

Cunning harm

But another group were perceived as undermining the very fabric of godly society, and were therefore singled out for the harshest of treatment – midwives. Unfortunately, the very word comes from the Anglo-Saxon *med-wyf*, meaning 'wise-woman' or 'witch'. The Church's line on midwives was neatly summed up by Kramer and Sprenger: 'No one does more cunning harm to the Catholic faith than midwives', explaining that they seize the newborn child and baptize him in the name of the Devil with a magical rite by the kitchen hearth.[94] Unsurprisingly, Montague Summers agrees, but he is merely voicing a view that is alive and well, especially in twenty-first-century American fundamentalist circles, for midwives were always associated not only with the mysteries of birth, but also procuring abortion. Kramer and Sprenger's statement, if modified to read: 'No one does more harm to the Christian faith than abortionists', possesses a remarkably modern resonance.

In the ancient world, midwives were highly regarded: in Egypt they were ruled by Isis Hathor in her Sevenfold manifestation, who gave every child its seven souls. 'An earthly midwife is a sort of fairy godmother, with a spiritual tie to each child she brings into the world'[95] – the polar opposite of the demonized Christian midwife. In ancient Rome there were three types of midwife, all associated with the women's temple and linked to the Greek Horae, temple servants on earth, but midwives to the gods in heaven. The *obstetrix* assisted at the birth; the *nutrix* or 'nurturer' taught the mysteries of nursing and encouraged the milk to flow, while the priestesses of Ceres, the *ceraria*, took charge of the religious rituals surrounding the birth. All were honoured members of society.

In Christendom, because women were deemed to be *sacer* or untouchable after giving birth, they were not allowed to enter church for forty days afterwards. Being unclean, only other women could deal with their physical and emotional needs at this time, so female midwives were essential to the wellbeing of both mother and child. But medieval clerics hated them, mainly because they echoed the era of goddess-worship, when women had power over their own lives. The detestation of midwives procuring abortions was not out of compassion for the unborn child, but because it implied a sort of empowered feminine freemasonry.

Women in general were always suspected of using enchantments in everyday life. The Dominican friar Johann Herolt thundered:

Most women belie their Catholic faith with charms and spells, after the fashion of Eve their first mother, who believed the devil speaking through the serpent rather than God himself . . . Any woman by herself knows more of such superstitions and charms than a hundred men.[96]

Spells and potions were the only known cures before the sixteenth century – indeed, the clergy believed that the only way to heal the sick was through exorcism. Yet the great pioneering doctor Paracelsus admitted that witches had taught him everything he knew about healing.[97] However, whereas a male conjuror was permitted to heal by the use of the magical arts, women were put to death for doing the same.

Besides abortion, any form of contraception and the easing of birth-pangs was deemed anathema. In 1559 the Parliamentary

Articles of Enquiry commanded local church officials to report the use of 'charms, sorcery, enchantments, invocations, witchcrafts, soothsaying' or similar *especially in the time of women's travails.*' (My emphasis). Unbelievably, in 1591, the Scottish noblewoman Eufame Macalyne was committed to the stake simply for seeking palliatives for the agonies of childbirth from a midwife. In 1554 midwives were expressly forbidden to use any means to alleviate childbed suffering other than prayers that 'may stand with the laws and ordinances of the Catholic Church'.[98]

Up until the twentieth century the view of the Christian patriarchy was that God had cursed Eve so that she and all women throughout history would give birth in pain, so anything that eased the agony went expressly against the will of God. When women died in their travails, the Church took this to be an example of God's 'continuing judgement on the sex'.[99]

When the nineteenth-century James Simpson initiated the use of ether and chloroform in childbirth, there was a massive outcry across the Christian world. Clergymen denounced it as a 'sinful denial of God's wishes',[100] while Scottish ministers asserted that such pain-control would be 'vitiating against the primal curse against woman'.[101]

Barbara Walker notes the words of a New England minister: 'Chloroform is a decoy of Satan, apparently offering itself to bless women; but in the end it will harden society and rob God of the deep earnest cries which arise in time of trouble, for help.'[102] Walker comments briskly: 'With the usual half-concealed sadism of patriarchal morality, he was really saying that female screams of pain gave God pleasure, and men must see to it that God was not deprived of this.'[103] (As we have seen, it was none other than Queen Victoria who set the seal of approval on the use of chloroform in childbirth, effectively silencing at least the British clergy once and for all.)

In this context it is particularly interesting that Kramer and Sprenger emphasized the importance of making a witch shed tears. Her screams were not enough, she must be seen by the Inquisitor to weep copiously. If a witch failed to shed tears during torture she was guilty, being urged to cry 'by the loving tears shed by Christ on the cross'. She was guilty if she did, of course, because it proved that the devil 'gave her the gift of tears to mislead the judges',[104] round and round in a sickening Kafkaesque whirl of mad logic. Across Europe 'taciturnity' was a crime punishable by burning, although so was virtually everything else a witch was accused of, and in England by *peine forte et dure* – being crushed under a board loaded with heavy weights.

Witches lost everything. Their money and property was instantly forfeit to the Church, which grew fat on the profits of human misery on an unheard-of scale. The accused even had to rely on 'Christian charity' for the bits of mouldy bread that passed for meals in jail and it was usual for the Inquisition to demand payment for the services of the torturer, even for the wood on which the condemned were to burn. If the condemned refused to agree to parting with their money or were in no fit state to do so, their families would have to pay up.

Even the average Christian was contaminated by the Church's perversion of the truth. Although it was once widely accepted that witchcraft was a delusion, after Pope Innocent's reign, it became a heresy *not* to believe in its reality. Anyone who claimed witchcraft was not real must also be ranked as a witch. Inquisitor Heinrich von Schultheis declared: 'He that opposes the extermination of the witches with one single word cannot expect to remain unscathed.'[105]

The flames of hell
Whether a witch confessed or held out, wept or remained taciturn, implicated others or refused to accuse her neighbours, there was usually only one way her torments would end – with yet more torture, on the stake, in front of a baying crowd.

Many of the condemned had been so badly injured during the 'Question' that they had to be carried or pulled in a cart to the pyre: Father Urbain Grandier (whose case will be examined later), who had suffered terribly in the 'Boot', was conveyed to his grisly fate on a hurdle and had to crawl with his shattered legs to the pyre.

Some, especially women, had their tongues ripped out before they were forced on the walk of shame to their deaths to prevent them from shouting out accusations against their jailers. It seemed few cared whether they had been racked or whipped, but the same folk would be horrified if they learnt of sexual abuse.

Although under other circumstances, occasionally miscreants were afforded the mercy of being strangled before being committed to the flames, few received this solace when convicted of witchcraft. As nothing could be worse than trafficking with the Devil, so the death penalty had to take the most hideous form imaginable, affording the mob – whose hysteria effectively blanked out the uniquely abominable stench of roasting flesh – the ultimate delight of witnessing the living hell of another human being. Some witches were disembowelled before being tied to the stake, and, incredibly, even then they sometimes survived long enough to suffer an hour or so of the flames.

Many children died in the fires, being 'imps of Satan', and one woman was burnt because she had given birth to the Devil's child. A French woman gave birth while writhing in the flames, and somehow managed to throw the living baby clear of the inferno. The crowd threw it back.

As the madness swallowed whole swathes of Europe (before being transplanted across the Atlantic to the New World), the accusations became more surreal. A cockerel was immolated for crowing at an inappropriate time (although in fact cocks do crow at all hours of the day, as the accusers must have known full well) – obviously a tool of Satan – and a horse met a fiery end for having been taught how to count by pawing the ground, which was clearly sorcery. But it was on the whole stinking human fat that coated the walls of dwellings in many a village.

In England the preferred method of despatching witches was hanging, in itself something of a craze as the over-zealous Protestant 'Witchfinder General' Matthew Hopkins took command in the seventeenth century. In Scotland, though, witches were usually burnt, the last one to meet such an end being in 1727, although unofficially there were later examples. Even the founder of Methodism, John Wesley, declared 'The giving up of [belief in] witchcraft is in effect the giving up of the Bible.'[106]

Wesley would be pleased – a belief in witchcraft is still alive and well, especially among fundamentalists who view liberals, freethinkers, most other religions and, of course, all pagans as no better than outright Satanists. Legally, however, the situation has changed, although the end of the mass persecution of witches was signalled by the execution of Alice Molland at Exeter in 1684, and the conviction of Jane Walhern in Herefordshire in 1712. However, an interesting potential postscript was suggested by a letter in the

Daily Mail of 9 December 2004 in response to a reader's query about the meaning of an inscription on a tombstone in the old churchyard at Pitsea Mount, near Basildon in Essex, which reads: 'Ann Freeman, died 20th March 1879. Here lies a weak and sinful worm, the vilest of her race, saved through God's electing love, his free and sovereign grace.' Essex man Neil Fisher responded: '. . . local legend has it that the damning inscription . . . reflects the fact that Ann Freeman was the last witch to be tried and put to death in England . . .' He adds: 'For such poignant and powerful words to be put upon a person's place of rest must have been testimony to some alleged evil commitment.' Perhaps the key is the simple word 'alleged'. In any case, she seems to have repented and been 'saved', presumably at the last moment, which is doubtless why she is buried in holy ground. But this poses the question: how many more 'last witches' were there, recorded or unrecorded? How many more are still to suffer? If the firebombing of a pagan bookshop – which also stocked works on Christian mysticism – in the north of England by fundamentalists in the 1980s had resulted in deaths, would they have been the last witches to be 'executed' in Britain?

In fact, the last woman to be arrested under the 1735 Witchcraft Act in Britain was Spiritualist medium Helen Duncan in 1944. Summers spoke for many churchmen (even in the twenty-first century) when he declared: 'Camouflage it how you will, Spiritualism and its kindred superstition . . . [is not a] "new religion" . . . but the old Witchcraft'.[107] The case of Mrs Duncan, which is complicated by evidence of the involvement of British Intelligence, unfortunately lies outside this investigation,[108] but suffice it to say that Summers' righteous fulmination about the 'superstition' and 'charlatanism' of Spiritualism sits uncomfortably with one who accepts without question the authenticity of religious relics and the miracles of the saints.

Having examined the Church's genocide of the Cathars, and its three-century gender-genocide of the witches, it is time to turn to the men who are believed to have made a pact with the Devil, to have sold their souls for material gain and power. But, like the vast majority of the witches, are these also merely misunderstood and maligned?

CHAPTER FIVE

Pacts, Possession and Séance Rooms

While on the whole it was poor uneducated women rather than rich learned men who fell foul of the witch hunters, history abounds with tales – many of them near-apocryphal – about scholarly male sorcerers who sought to traffic with the Devil. But like the illiterate women, many of these men were caught up in a hysteria that engulfed the guilty and innocent alike, and with a dire inevitability they paid the ultimate price.

Undoubtedly, however, there were also serious seekers after all knowledge – most of it being forbidden by the authorities – whose craving for information took them into the murkiest of spiritual byways. These were often solitary men with a reputation for magic who were not above summoning the Devil himself in order to sign a pact in their own blood, one of the more colourful aspects of witchcraft and sorcery.

The pedigree of the pact is perhaps not as old as one might imagine, dating back to two stories that circulated among Christendom as late as the fifth and sixth centuries. The hugely influential Church Father, Saint Jerome, was responsible for the first, the story of Saint Basil, retold by Hincmar of Reims in the ninth century,[1] which goes like this: a man lusting after an attractive girl visits a sorcerer who arranges for him to make a pact with Satan – basically, the girl is his if he sells his soul. Emissaries of the Evil One duly appear and take him into the Presence. Satan asks in a blasphemous parody of the Christian baptism: 'Do you believe in me?' Raging testosterone clearly obliterating common sense, the man responds eagerly: 'Yes, I do believe.' He is then asked: 'Do you renounce Christ?' He acquiesces: 'I do renounce him'. But the Devil refuses to be duped, saying: 'You Christians always come to me when you need help but then try to repent later, presuming on the mercy of Christ. I want you to sign up in writing.'

The deal is done and the girl falls helplessly for the newly fledged Satanist, seeking permission to marry him from her father. Unfortunately, as he has ambitions for her to enter a convent, he refuses. Before they embark upon a sinful liaison the young man comes to his senses and the story of the pact leaks out. In the nick of time, Saint Basil intervenes and the girl's honour remains unsullied.

The other influential pact story – which reached a huge audience across Europe over the course of 1,000 years, 'fathering the Faust legend and indirectly influencing the Renaissance witch craze'[2] – was that of Theophilus, a priest from Asia Minor who refused a bishopric only to suffer demotion at the hands of the incoming bishop. Furious at this unfair twist of fate, he consulted a Jewish sorcerer, who took him to a remote spot to meet the Devil. Theophilus agreed to enter Satan's service in return for his former position in the Church, signing a pact and kissing him as a token of his obeisance. Theophilus duly became rich and powerful, but . . .

As everyone but the pact-signers themselves always seem to know, the deal can only ever end in the bitterest of tears. As agreed, demons turned up on the dot to claim the man's soul, although they were trounced. His terrified prayers had produced none other than the Virgin Mary, who fearlessly marched into Hell itself to retrieve the contract and return it to the sinner to be destroyed. The Virgin begged God for forgiveness for Theophilus, which was granted, and once again the Devil came out of the deal empty-handed.

However, while we would all no doubt congratulate the sinner on his lucky escape, the thought still occurs that it was the man, and not Satan, who proved himself a slippery customer – pact, what pact? Also, if the Devil is so cunning, why is he so often outsmarted by unremarkable mortals? It seems the trick is to sign the pact, enjoy all the advantages and then at the last moment appeal to the

Virgin for help. And if Satan is so desperate for human souls, one would imagine he would at least create the illusion of a fabulously enticing end to the pact-signers' lives, instead of having the newcomers to Hell being seized by foul imps from the Pit.

As the tale of Theophilus spread, as Jeffrey Burton Russell notes, 'it promoted anti-Semitism and the cult of Mary. More significant, it initiated the idea of the pact.'[3] Similar legends did the rounds: such as the story of a student at St Andrews in Scotland who met a 'minister' who assisted him in his academic work in return for a deal signed in blood. Even Sir Francis Drake was said to have used similar means with which to defeat the Spanish Armada. In discussing the farcical element in many of these tales, Russell tells the story of a knight

> who promised to give the Devil his soul if ever he came to a town called Mouffle. The knight, confident that no such town existed, felt perfectly secure. The knight turned to the religious life, became a monk, and finally rose to the position of archbishop of Reims. Eventually he visited his home town, Ghent. There he became seriously ill and to his horror the devil appeared at his bedside to claim him – on the ground that the real, secret name of Ghent is Mouffle.[4]

The concept of a devilish pact became intimately involved in the demonization of Muslims, Jews and heretics – all of whom were seen as conscious agents of the Evil One. One Saracen figure was even known as Abisme, or 'Hell'. The Muslims were accused of worshipping thousands of demons or idols – which is, of course, ludicrous for the most rigidly monotheistic religion in existence. Nevertheless, the ignorant slurs continued to take hold, seriously affecting the treatment of Muslims, Jews and 'witches', all of whom were accused of killing and usually eating Christian babies. One myth, which was to prove very useful to Chief Inquisitor Torquemada, centred on the 'Santo Niño', the 'Holy Child' allegedly ritually killed and disembowelled by Jews in order to cast a spell that would exterminate all Christians. It must have been true: after all, most Jews admitted it – under torture, that is.[5] A variation of witches-as-baby-slaughterers fable was to resurface horrifically

Satanic ritual abuse hysteria that rampaged among fundamentalist social workers in the late twentieth century, doing untold
damage to countless innocent families. (As in the case of the
medieval accusations, the fact that no babies were actually missing
and no pregnancies unaccounted for made not the tiniest dent in the
zealots' mania.)

Mephistopheles laughs

The most famous demonic pact of all is of course that of Faust, or
Dr Faustus, although fiction has long since largely obscured the
little fact that might have been attached to the legend. However, it
seems that there was a real Dr Faust, a rather unimpressive self-
publicist and charlatan, who – like the Simon Magus of legend –
boasted he could out-perform the miracles of Christ. Among his
'wonders' was the ability to produce edible game out of season, and
even simply threatening a group of monks with the attentions of a
poltergeist for serving him sour wine. (The latter was probably on
an off-day.) A pathological braggart, he cheerfully spread rumours
of his pact with the Devil, bolstering his reputation for the dark arts
by announcing to a well-known local man,[6] 'I surely thought you
were my brother-in-law and therefore I looked at your feet to see
whether long, curved claws projected from them.' Either supremely
arrogant or possessed of a death wish, nevertheless all this satanic
posturing merely succeeded in getting him expelled from the city of
Ingostadt. He was lucky. He died, 'scandalously'[7] in 1537, although
probably not as the result of being torn to shreds by demons.

In the play by roistering Jacobean playwright Christopher
Marlowe, *The Tragicall History of Dr Faustus* (1604), the eponymous anti-hero notoriously becomes an addict of arcane power,
declaring "Tis magic, magic that hath ravished me'.

Undoubtedly, just as feeble-minded old women who lived on
their own with a pet cat would invite mutterings of witchcraft –
especially if in their senility they had become none too pleasant to
their neighbours – similarly solitary men with a penchant for dusty
books and scientific experiment would be seen as sorcerers. Given
the popularity of the pact fables and the Faust dramas, the idea of
having a real Satanist on the outskirts of your village would no
doubt really be quite thrilling. Although it is impossible to know

how many of these solo scholars were simply bookish and anti-social old men and what proportion were actually concerned with ritual magic, certain famous names were known to be involved with some very dark arts.

Marlowe's Faustus was described as '. . . falling to a devilish exercise/And glutted more with learning's golden gifts/He surfeits upon cursed necromancy'. Necromancy (from the Greek *nekos*, 'dead' and *manteria*, 'divination')[8] or the conjuration of the dead in order to discover the secrets of past, present and – particularly – future, was a grisly business involving horrible and illegal rituals centred on the exhumation of corpses, in which many seekers after knowledge were said to indulge (although given the practical problems involved, not to mention the traumatic *modus operandi*, probably not many actually did).

Known as 'the Black Art', necromancy can be either divination via ghosts – and, like it or not, some forms of Spiritualism did come within that category – or divination using actual corpses, which obviously involves desecrating graves. As a knowledgeable website notes, as a

> universal practice of great antiquity, only the profoundly initiated, brave and single-minded magician has any chance of success in such a venture, always considered to be extremely dangerous, for not only is a pact with the Devil necessary, but it is thought that the "astral corpse" has an intense desire to live again and could, by absorbing life-energy from living creatures, prolong its life indefinitely, thus, unless he has taken adequate precautions, the magician might be in great danger.[9]

The mage and his assistant set up their magic circle in an appropriately emotive location such as a graveyard or blasted heath, on an astrologically propitious night, and call forth the dead, using the most powerful names of God. Woe betide them if they step from the protective circle, for then the temporarily animated corpse could tear them to pieces and destroy their souls. Even within the hallowed circle they have to be proof against nightmarish screaming and gibbering figures, decked out in rags of putrid skin, eye sockets flickering with a dim and hellish light.

Utterly abominated and proscribed in the Bible, as was all forms of communication with the dead – the classic case is the Witch of Endor[10] – necromancy has had a long and chequered history, according to the differences in attitude of various cultures and generations.

As I have suggested, it is even possible that Jesus' own movement engaged in a variation of necromancy, if indeed, as the evidence may suggest, they seized the head of the Baptist in order to enslave his soul for purposes of divination. It may not be how the modern mind works, but such necromantic practices have a long pedigree.

Wooed, showered with all the glittering prizes of material and intellectual life, the anti-hero of *Dr Faustus* is of course doomed to be ultimately betrayed by the Evil One. But the story of his flight from all that is good and holy was also a colourful morality tale guaranteed to give the groundlings rip-roaring, not to say occasionally terrifying, entertainment.

The Faust of the great German poet and philosopher (and one-time sorcerer) Johann Wolfgang Goethe (1749–1832) is somewhat subtler. He has to battle to maintain his place centre stage against the wit and charm of a particularly charismatic Mephistopheles, who says to God:

> Your pardon, if my idiom is lowly,
> My eloquence up here would not meet with scorn,
> Pathos from me would cause you laughter solely,
> If laughter weren't a thing you have foresworn.[11]

The last line merely makes explicit what churchgoers must have long suspected, however guiltily: judging from the dour and pompous Old Testament, Yahweh does appear to have lost his sense of humour, if indeed he ever had one to lose. The wryly amusing Mephistopheles possesses an instant appeal particularly to a modern, Anglo-Saxon audience to whom a talent to amuse and the expectation to be amused is almost everything. A sense of humour – more particularly a sense of the absurd – is now seen as the epitome of civilization, the antidote to fanaticism and bigotry, the gift that marks humans out from the beasts, and often the one light

in a grim and bleak life. Yahweh smacks rather too muc
boring head teacher pontificating about rules and regulations wime
the whole school sniggers over a private joke: to use a Dickensian
analogy he is the ramrod straight, and downright sinister, cold-
hearted Mr Murdstone against the mercurial, funny and irreverent
Sam Weller.

Goethe's Mephistopheles – although he has his dark moments –
is a brilliant member of the irreverent tradition that had already
produced a long line of capering anti-Establishment court jesters
and had yet to include the likes of Mel Brooks, the Monty Pythons
and Eddie Izzard. With God apparently choosing to present himself
as a sort of unsmiling and ranting Taliban, who can blame those
who prefer to be entertained and even informed by masters of the
subversive art of humour? Surely of all human activities and talents,
humour is the most truly Luciferan, with intellectual enquiry –
particularly science – a close second, as we shall see.

The dynamic between the truly Satanic and the Luciferan can be
see in the horrifying story of the woman arrested for witchcraft,
having sex with the Devil and all manner of puerile nonsense, who
laughed.[12] She could hardly imagine anything more ludicrous than
her being a practising Satanist: but very soon she had been
'persuaded' to 'confess' to anything and everything the truly
Satanic Inquisitors demanded of her. She had been a breath of fresh
air in the foetid witch-dungeon until devoured by the Terror, and
although we do not know her name, we can still sing her praises.

Like Milton's Satan, Goethe's representative of Evil is also sexy,
roguish and attractive: as women have long known and nice guys
suspected, bad boys possess a powerful but elusive allure. With a
casual and flippant air Mephistopheles announces that he merely
observes 'the plaguey state of men', finding 'it boring to torment
them', but nevertheless actively seeks out the rather priggish and
unappealing Faust. In a brilliantly astute line, Mephistopheles notes
that the human, desperate to attain knowledge and assuage his
craving for he knows not what, already 'serves me in a bewildered
way'. Satan's emissary seeks to make Faust lick up dust, 'Just like
the snake, my celebrated cousin'. (Mephistopheles also murmurs
'Omniscient? No, not I; but well-informed.')

Faust, it seems, was already halfway to Hell, being maddened with the frustrations of academic life that promises so much and delivers so little. Like many another solitary thinker and lost soul, he cries: 'Who is my guide? What shall I shun?/Or what imperious urge obey? . . .' Desperate to attain and achieve intellectually and spiritually he muses on where exactly any progress would take him, asking tormentedly: 'Shall I then rank with gods?'

Sorcerers sought to command gods to do their bidding or fought to achieve a sort of illusory godhood for themselves, only maintained by the toughest of personal battles and doomed to an ignominious end. On the other hand, Gnostics and mystics realized that every individual is already potentially divine, believing that this inner deity will only truly blossom with profound spiritual honesty, dedication to the true ideals of divinity, and the harnessing of ecstasy. Faust overlooked the fact of his own godhood in seeking to exert power over the gods; a true recipe for disaster.

Yet Faust was only half of the story: in a literal sense he was 'possessed' by Mephistopheles – *but only when he was ready for the pact*. In other words, like many examples of apparent demonic possession, Faust is flooded with evil only when he invites it in. In the world of the occult it is said that 'like attracts like', and this is the true meaning of the satanic pact. Give yourself up to a harsh and unforgiving god or bigoted mores and that is what will possess you to the neglect of everything that is brighter and better: your mind and soul will be as narrowly confined and implosively consuming as the source you have espoused. Let in the bright spark of the Luciferan principle, and it will know no bounds, for it is essentially about enhancing, expanding and making sense of human potential.

While enjoying the fruits of his new highly-charged intellect, like all Renaissance anti-heroes, Faust suffers from a fatal flaw – in his case a monumental egotism, surely the besetting sin of all dedicated sorcerers. Inevitably there will be a dreadful reckoning, as Mephistopheles rather honourably points out:

> Follow the adage of my cousin snake.
> From dreams of god-like knowledge you will wake
> To fear, in which your very soul shall quake.

He does, however, add famously, 'While there's life, there's hope', although there may not be much hope, one suspects, ultimately for Faust. In fact, his soul is redeemed, largely through the pure love of a good woman, and instead of a hellish climax, there is the sweet sound of hymns of the mystical chorus and a prayer to 'Virgin, Queen of Motherhood' to 'Keep us, Goddess, in thy grace'.

Goethe's intelligent and often humorous work nevertheless contributed to the widespread idea of the reality of the pact, which fuelled countless witch trials. Ironically, many cases of devil-worship, both real and imagined, were born in the heady hot-house atmosphere of religious houses.

Weird sisters

In the medieval and Renaissance world few who entered convents or monasteries had a true vocation for the religious life. Often there was simply nothing else for them to do: girls especially would be forced to take the veil if their families failed to provide the requisite dowry for them to marry, or if they were too independent – too much of a handful – to be accepted in the outside world. But living an enclosed, sexless life all too often induced *acedia*, or the particular sort of 'abysmal apathy'[13] common to the monk or nun's sequestered existence, and out of such fertile soil grew some spectacular episodes of mass hysteria, particularly centring on a belief in possession by demons. Little wonder that single-sex religious houses were veritable hot-beds of the wildest fantasies – which spelt very bad news for some . . .

One infamous case of apparent mass demonic possession took place at Loudun, Vienne, in France in 1634, which became known to a wider twentieth-century audience, first through Aldous Huxley's book *The Devils of Loudun* (1952) and then through Ken Russell's brilliant but astonishingly graphic film, *The Devils* (1971)[14], which showed torture and death at the stake in unflinching detail.

In this alarming story of dark human potential, erotomania took fast hold among the nuns of Loudun, resulting in fits of screamed blasphemies and obscenities together with much abandoned rolling around on the floor and displaying of genitalia. In the great release this afforded the repressed women under their wimples, frustrations of all kinds emerged into the light of day.

The confession of the real-life Sister Jeanne des Anges reveals a profound abhorrence of her religious life, normally hidden beneath the modest submissiveness expected of a nun, besides illustrating the contemporary belief that all such hysteria was the work of possessing demons:

> My mind was often filled with blasphemies, and sometimes I uttered them without being able to take any thought to stop myself. I felt for God a continual aversion . . . The demon beclouded me in such a way that I hardly distinguished his desires from mine; he gave me moreover a strong aversion for my religious calling, so that sometimes when he was in my head I used to tear all my veils and such of my sisters' as I might lay hands on; I trampled them underfoot, I chewed them, cursing the hour when I took the vows . . . More often than not I saw quite well that I was the prime cause of my troubles and that the demon acted only according to the openings I gave him . . . As I presented myself at Communion, the devil took possession of my head, and after I had received the blessed host and half moistened it the devil threw it in the priest's face.[15]

The Mother Superior herself claimed to be possessed by the demons Balan, Iscaron, Leviathan and Behemoth, while the nuns under her care exploded into a mass of writhing, screaming frustrated female flesh. Their exorcist, Father Urbain Grandier, found that with each successive attempt to rid the women of the possessing devils the outbreak became stronger. In the end, Grandier himself was seized by the Inquisition and subjected to the abominable agonies of the Boot, and then his mangled but still living body was committed to the pyre. Somehow, despite his suffering, he managed to maintain his innocence and refused to name any accomplices, but a forged pact with Satan was produced that sealed his fate. It read:

> My Lord and Master, I owe you for my God; I promise to serve you while I live, and from this hour I renounce all other gods and Jesus Christ and Mary and all the Saints of Heaven and the Catholic, Apostolic, and Roman Church, and all the goodwill thereof and the prayers which might be made for me. I promise

to adore you and do you homage at least three times a day and to do the most evil that I can and to lead into evil as many persons as shall be possible to me, and heartily I renounce the Chrism, Baptism, and all the merits of Jesus Christ; and in case I should desire to change, I give you my body and soul, and my life as holding it from you, having dedicated it forever without any will to repent.

Signed URBAIN GRANDIER in his blood.[16]

It never seem to dawn on his persecutors that since the possessions continued after he was burnt to death he was effectively exonerated – perhaps they argued that once possessed, always possessed. Or perhaps they simply ignored the inconvenient fact of Grandier's passing.

(Montague Summers solemnly recounts how Grandier tested positive for a 'Witch Mark': 'two marks were discovered, one upon the shoulder-blade and the other upon the thigh, both of which proved insensible even when pierced with a sharp silver pin'.[17] Summers fully believed that 'the discovery of the devil mark' was nigh to 'infallible proof' of Devil worship, the mark being an indelible brand of 'Satan's own sign manual'.)[18]

The nuns' lewd performances rocketed from strength to strength, drawing large and appreciative audiences. Sister Claire

... fell on the ground, blaspheming, in convulsions, displaying her privy parts without any shame, and uttering filthy words. Her gestures became so indecent that the audience averted its eyes. She cried out again and again, abusing herself with her hands, 'Come on then, fuck me!'[19]

(Had the observers really wanted to avert their eyes, they would hardly have travelled miles to be part of the audience.)

Yet one must exercise caution in layering on modern scepticism too thickly. Father Surin, who arrived at Loudun as an exorcist was himself possessed, and, like Jeanne, described the curious sensation of watching and listening to himself, unable to stop uttering obscenities and blasphemies, in a kind of unholy out-of-the-body-experience. The hysteria may have originated in the most intense sexual frustration and monastic acedia, but it soon took on a life of its own.

Another father confessor who suffered for his charges' hysteria was Louis Gaufridi, a priest of Accoules, near Marseilles, who was jailed in 1611 for 'foulest sorcery' and condemned largely because he, too, was discovered by local surgeons to bear the devil's mark.[20] His accuser was the teenager Madeleine de la Palud, who admitted in court that her allegations were 'all imaginings, illusions, without a word of truth in them' and that she had merely 'swooned for the love of Gaufridi'. As Colin Wilson notes, 'She then began to quiver with erotic frenzy, her hips moving up and down with the movements of copulation.'[21] Gaufridi was also convicted of trafficking with Satan, and condemned to a heretic's death. Once again latent sexual problems had become magnified at the hands of an institutionally celibate and sex-hating organization.

Despite Madeleine's confession, Gaufridi was 'persuaded' to reveal the formula of his Devil's pact, which read:

I, Louis Gaufridi, renounce all good, both spiritual as well as temporal, which may be bestowed upon me by God, the Blessed Virgin Mary, all the Saints of Heaven, particularly my patron S. John-Baptist, as also S. Peter, S. Paul, and S. Francis, and I give myself body and soul to Lucifer, before whom I stand, together with every good that I may ever possess (save always the benefit of the sacraments touching those who receive them). And according to the tenor of these terms have I signed and sealed.[22]

Gaufridi's alleged victim, Madeleine, signed an even more blood-curdlingly blasphemous pact:

With all my heart and most unfeignedly and with all my will most deliberately do I wholly renounce God, Father, Son, and Holy Ghost; the most Holy Mother of God; all the Angels and especially my Guardian Angel, the passion of Our Lord Jesus Christ, His Precious Blood and the merits thereof, my lot in Paradise, all the good inspirations which God may give me in the future, all prayers which are made or may be made for me.[23]

If nothing else, these pacts reveal a real talent on the part of the local officers of the Inquisition for imaginative Devil worship. They also underline the central point that without the Church there could be no Devil worship and even no Devil. The one feeds off the other.

Gaufridi and Grandier were almost certainly innocent of the Satanism of which they were accused and for which they died so horribly, although they may have encouraged the women of the convent to flirt – perhaps a little more than that. However, others, like Faust, were not necessarily so blameless, although the extent to which one apportions sin will depend on one's own spiritual background.

Trampling the cross
Jeffrey Burton Russell explains that the earliest idea of the pact – originally a deal between two more or less equal parties – changed dramatically in medieval times:

> It was now assumed that the person making the pact did so as a grovelling slave, renouncing Christ, trampling the cross, worshipping Satan ... offering the obscene kiss ... Heretics and other evildoers had put themselves under Lucifer's command whether or not they had made a conscious and deliberate submission.[24]

Certain elements in that list echo the alleged blasphemies of the Knights Templar – specifically trampling the cross and renouncing Christ. Almost all historians reject the reality of these accusations, and one can understand why, given the prevalence of confession-by-torture: basically this is inadmissible evidence. But in this case, is it really worthless? As we have seen, the fact of the existence of the 'Church of John in the East', the Mandaeans, who encountered the knights in what is now Turkey, adds an ironic twist to the tale. If the inner circle, or at any rate a high-ranking group, within the Templars did indeed become enthused with (most would say, with Summers, 'infected by') the Johannite heresy, then no doubt they really did spit and trample on the cross and renounce Jesus, seeing him as an impostor, usurper and possibly even accomplice or accessory to the fact of murder. But to many of the initiates, s they were in that time with a fervent belief in the conventions of Christianity – after all, most Templars joined the Order because they were devoted to Christ – such actions must still have seemed blasphemous, even diabolic. Perhaps in their heart of hearts they truly believed themselves to have gone over to the other side, to be Devil worshippers. This echoes the Cathars' concept of the Baptist as a devil: this would make sense if they knew that the two men had been bitter rivals, for assuming (and who wouldn't?) that Christ is without question always and for ever Goodness personified – the cowboy in the white hat as it were, intent on cleaning up the town – John must therefore be Evil, the scowling bar-brawler in the black hat. But as the song says, 'It ain't necessarily so'.

While the Templars' contribution to humanity may not be great – although they did give us the monetary cheque and some stunning Gothic cathedrals – other heretics and Luciferans gave us much more that has proved of lasting value. Indeed, it is true to say that without their intellectual striving, we may well still be in the Dark Ages. Although the true flowering of both these official and unknowing Luciferans was to come much later, in the Age of Enlightenment, its roots were already thrusting through the tentatively promising soil of the Renaissance, nourished in the dark on Mephistophelean magic.

Anti-Christ

When Leonardo da Vinci mused on the painter's power exalting him to the status of the 'Grandson of God',[25] it was both a curious and extraordinarily bold statement, for its implications are nothing if not outrageously heretical. To most people, both then and now, it was and is an unwritten article of faith that Jesus was a lifelong, pure celibate, with no children – so to talk of God possessing a *grandson*, however metaphorically, is astonishing blasphemy. It may be countered that it was merely a clever turn of phrase, virtually meaningless, implying a vague grandeur, nothing more – and that it is pointless trying to analyse it. After all, writers have routinely called themselves the likes of 'children of Nature': in his 1914 *Immanuel Kant* Houston Stewart Chamberlain declared that 'All arts, all sciences, all Thought are "daughters of the Eye"', adding 'and so it is that the painter is "nipote a Dio", "the grandson of God"'. But he completely misses the point. Being a child of Nature is one thing, but even daring to imply, however poetically or metaphorically that Jesus had children was nothing short of extreme heresy. But in any case, this is *Leonardo da Vinci*, a viciously anti-Church heretic: indeed, as a sort of Anti-Christ himself, when he made any remark about the Deity it is surely worth noting.

So what drove Leonardo to make such a dangerously controversial statement, even in the privacy of his own notebooks? What did he really mean by aligning himself with the 'Grandson of God'? Was he claiming kinship with the historical figure of Christ? (Although, judging by his anti-Jesus, wickedly Johannite symbolism, that seems rather unlikely.) Was he perhaps even implying that he knew Jesus had a son? Or was he not referring, however indirectly, to Jesus at all – but to *John*? Clearly he saw the Baptist, as least figuratively, as Son of God, and few Johannites would qualify more in their devotion to the cause to be his 'son' than Leonardo da Vinci. Whatever his motive, likening himself to the grandson of God would not have been the chosen metaphor of a God-fearing, devout Renaissance Catholic – quite the reverse.

In any case, few more Luciferan individuals than Leonardo da Vinci have ever walked the earth, in his audacity, his refusal to set limits on his own potential or imagination, and his constant challenge to received wisdom, especially to the religious establishment of his day.

In *Turin Shroud: In Whose Image?*[26] Clive Prince and I argued that the 'Holy Shroud of Turin' – long believed to bear the miraculously imprinted image of Jesus himself, complete with horrific marks of crucifixion – was a brilliant fake by Leonardo, who not only used his own face for that of Jesus', but created the image using a technique that we now know as *photography*. In fact, we argue, the Shroud is nothing less than a 500-year-old photograph of Leonardo da Vinci . . .

And, with supreme Luciferan genius (although many would call it somewhat warped), he used this pioneering and 'devilish' technique to create the ultimate Christian relic, thus ensuring that the priests of the organization he abhorred kept it safe for posterity. That particular example of Luciferan guile – the ultimate practical joke aimed at undermining the very Church that kept the Shroud alive for believers for centuries – shows real inspiration. How he must have laughed. And the Da Vinci 'Holy Shroud' contains its very own code.

The Shroud of *Turin* was quite clearly a substitute for an earlier alleged relic, an embarrassingly obvious painted daub on display in France in the second half of the fourteenth century, which even the local bishop disowned and named the artist involved.[27] On the other hand, no one could accuse Leonardo's later version of being a blatant painted fake: a projected, *photographic* image had no need of paint.

Even if, as Clive and I believe, the Renaissance Maestro had been commissioned to create this crowd-pulling relic by the Vatican itself,[28] the task he had set himself was not without its dangers. Leonardo had to approach this project with even greater than usual secrecy (although by nature an intensely private man): it would not have been wise to make public the method he used to create a non-painted image, thought by many to be sorcery. In fact it seems he employed a *camera obscura* or pin-hole camera – which he called the *oculus artificialis*, the artificial eye – described in his notebooks in the following terms:

If the facade of a building, or a place, or a landscape is illuminated by the sun and a small hole drilled in a building facing this, which is not directly lighted by the sun, then all objects illuminated by the sun will send their images through this aperture and will appear, upside down, on the wall facing the hole.[29]

Leonardo was constantly in danger even experimenting with a simple pinhole camera: the Church reserved a special antipathy towards what we would recognize as the early experiments in photography, perhaps because it saw the capturing of a lifelike image without brushes and paint as demonic. It must have seemed like magic: it was not merely the 'primitive' peoples who believed that to take someone's photograph was bad luck, for it stole the soul. To the medieval and Renaissance authorities it really did seem as if the new science threatened to 'catch' every nuance of the living being, as if a vital essence had been waylaid by the sorcerer/photographer. As demons notoriously stole souls, why were photographers any different? A lifelike photograph was indeed a magical image, even a sort of graphic version of the demonic pact – the soul frozen in time, captured and possessed.

Even a generation after Leonardo, his fellow countryman Giovanni Battista della Porta was arrested for sorcery after demonstrating a magic lantern by projecting the images of actors onto a wall.[30] However, in della Porta's case, the evidence was already stacked against him: he was a known Hermeticist and alchemist, and founder of the Academy of Secrets, which was disbanded by the Vatican. He managed to extricate himself from jail, but only with the greatest effort – it was a near thing.

To the photographer/alchemist himself the very concept of capturing living images must have seemed magical, and the actual process even more so. In discussing the 'Picatrix' or *Ghayat al Hikam, The Aim of the Wise*, the Arabic book of astrological and magical aphorisms dating from around 1000 CE, Tobias Churton writes:

> Picatrix maintains that the whole art of magic consists in 'capturing' and guiding the influence of spiritus (something like the souls of the celestial world, below intellectus, or the Greek *nous*) into *materia*. The method consisted in making talismans: images associated with the stars, inscribed on the correct materials at the most propitious times (astrology played a part), and in the right state of mind.* The practice demanded a deep knowledge of astronomy, mathematics, music and metaphysics, and formed a kind of mirror to the practice of alchemy. Talismanic magic aimed to get *spiritus* into material form, while alchemy aimed at extracting spiritus from matter in order to change the matter and the mind of the operator.[31]

Churton also adds as a note (to * above): 'Perhaps the conceptual origin of Photography: 'light-writing', from the Greek *photos*=light and *graphe*=writing; making an impression.'[32] Is the Shroud of Turin actually a magical talisman, imbued with the DNA, not of the Son of God, but of the pretender to the rank of Grandson of God? There is real blood on the Shroud, after all, although it may be a mixture of Leonardo's and of certain chosen others. (There is even a suggestion of *female* DNA[33] on the image, which would be in keeping with the artist-photographer's obsession with the Gnostic/alchemical androgyne. This can also be seen in Leonardo's sketch 'Witch with a Magic Mirror', which at first glance simply shows a young woman admiring herself in a hand mirror. But look carefully and you will see that the back of her head takes the shape of an old bearded man – presumably Leonardo himself: not only the opposite gender, but also the end of the age scale of which she represents the beginning.)[34]

Leonardo's experiments into the workings of the *camera obscuras* gave rise to his own increasingly dark reputation. As biographer Maurice Rowden writes:

> In Pavia he worked on his camera obscura, to demonstrate his theory that all vision is determined by the angle at which light falls on the eye: the upside-down image thrown on the wall from the camera's pinpoint of light was a more graphic argument than words, and it was little wonder that he got the reputation of being a sorcerer and alchemist.[35]

Of course Leonardo's penchant for dissecting cadavers, some of which he had specially exhumed, would hardly help – nor would his friendship with Giovan Francesco Rustici, a *known* necromancer, with whom he was shut away for months creating their joint sculpture, *John the Baptist*, which now offers target practice for pigeons outside the Baptistery in Florence. (And which, of course, flourishes the 'John gesture'.)

Apart from his extreme reverence for the Baptist, Leonardo evinced a sort of worship not only for nature but also number – 'let no one read my works who is not a mathematician', he wrote sternly – none of which would endear him to the ecclesiastical authorities, which sought total control over mind and spirit. The whole idea of the universe being controlled by a system other than that approved by the Vatican was naturally anathema. No one could control Leonardo's spirit. Irreverent, as we have seen, to the point of blasphemy, Leonardo would have been delighted by the commission to create the Holy Shroud Mark Two – secretly, of course –

both the egregious heretic and naughty schoolboy in him would have been absolutely tickled to be asked to make the holiest of Christian relics.

Yet there were always more serious and usually considerably more profound and even darker aspects to Leonardo's brilliant jokes, as we have seen with his paintings. In this, he was encapsulating a major principle of the secret Rosicrucian movement, officially still in the future when he died in 1519, but which he seems to have known and approved of. Certainly, occult historian Dame Frances Yates had no doubts that Leonardo exhibited 'a Rosicrucian frame of mind',[36] meaning he encompassed a heretical raft of intellectual pursuits that challenged orthodoxy head-on. Dr Yates also muses, courageously for an academic: 'Might it not have been within the outlook of a Magus that a personality like Leonardo was able to co-ordinate his mathematical and mechanical studies with his work as an artist?'[37]

It was in the early seventeenth century that documents began to circulate among would-be free-thinking intelligentsia. These were the 'Rosicrucian Manifestos' issued from Germany, which described the existence of a secret brotherhood of Magi[38] closely associated with alchemy (and which, it is claimed, would assist the rise of Freemasonry). The Order, consisting largely of alchemists, magicians, Hermeticists and Cabalists, claimed it originated with Christian Rosenkreutz, who had allegedly died at the vast age of 106 and been buried in a fabled tomb kept lit by an eternal but mysterious source of light. As 'Rosenkreutz' means 'Rosy Cross' – which owes little or nothing to the Christian symbol[39] – it seems his story was a metaphor for the continuation of the Rosicrucian 'light' in secret places. If such an organization had existed in Leonardo's day, he might have been an enthusiastic member, but as it was, he probably was not an unknown face at more informal, but basically similar groups of magi and alchemists who wished to preserve secret knowledge away from the eyes of the Inquisition. He also shared another quality with the ideal Rosicrucian – a playfulness and sense of trickery and illusion. In his Foreword to Tobias Churton's *The Gnostic Philosophy* (2003), Dr Christopher McIntosh writes:

The Dutch historian Huizinga, in his classic book *Homo Ludens* [Playful Man], deals with playfulness and its importance in human culture throughout history. This spirit of playfulness is, I believe, an important vein running through the Gnostic tradition ... Churton mentions an early example in the figure of ... Simon Magus.[40]

Acknowledging that Churton's previous book, *The Golden Builders*,

skilfully placed the Rosicrucians within the context of the emerging gulf between science and religion, a gulf which they wished to prevent by creating a universal system of knowledge, linking religion, science philosophy and art. The Rosicrucians embodied this vision in a brilliantly created mythology with a strong element of playfulness.[41]

Therefore Leonardo would have been in every way the perfect Rosicrucian: his scientific, artistic and 'religious' (i.e. Johannite) sensibilities being enriched and enhanced by his essential understanding of jokes and playfulness. This creates a mind that sees immense and often apparently contradictory possibilities in everything, that espies a unifying force beneath all nature – and that particular God is one of laughter, just like Goethe's Mephistopheles, but infinitely more powerful, hopeful and full of light. And it may be significant that a nineteenth-century poster advertising a Rosicrucian salon in Paris depicted Leonardo as Keeper of the Grail ...

Cracking the Da Vinci Shroud Code requires the same sort of off-beat perception – which has absolutely no connection with academic standing or an intimate knowledge of Leonardo's brushwork – that will see for itself the giant phallus made of rocks towering above Mary's head in the *Virgin of the Rocks*, the femininity of the young 'St John' or the disembodied hand clutching a dagger in the *Last Supper*.

To those who eagerly quote the latest desperate outpourings from the usually rather acidulous pens of the remaining 'Shroudies' (those who, despite all the evidence to the contrary, insist on believing that the alleged relic is genuine), let me point out certain key factors about the image on the shroud that prove, even to a child – indeed, *especially* to a child[42] – that it cannot be anything but a fake. First, the height of the man is literally impossible. As it is supposed to be Jesus' winding cloth, there is a front and a back image, roughly joined at the crown of the head – yet the man is two inches shorter at the back than he is at the front, which would indeed be a miracle. Shroudman is actually 6ft 10in at the front and 6ft 8in at the back, although nowhere in the New Testament does it remark about Christ's astonishing height (and uniquely sloping head). Although it is true that the Christian Bible is not much concerned with physical appearance, if Jesus were a giant surely some sort of remark would have crept in, especially in an era when great height was associated with kingship.[43]

There is absolutely no doubt about this: in my capacity as a consultant for the National Museum of Photography, Film and Television's exhibition, 'The Unexplained', in 1999 I, along with Clive Prince had the golden opportunity to put our theory about Shroudman's height to the test. (Previously we had simply done the calculations.) The museum had made the full-length photographic reproduction of the Shroud the focus of a huge, otherwise completely bare room, displaying it on a massive, specially built light-box no more than two feet from the ground. This enabled the visitor to look down at the image, besides being able to stand back at a distance and see it from all angles – much more telling than being crammed shoulder to shoulder in a long line of pilgrims and shuffling along to see no more than a couple of inches of the real thing at roughly eye-height. Conveniently Clive is exactly six foot tall, so we were able to measure the height of Shroudman with some precision, by laying him on the ground beside it, aligned with the top of the head. We also had assistance from the museum staff. And yes, Shroudman is enormously, impossibly tall . . . Of course as a projected image he could be any height at all from tiny to gigantic, although in that case one has to wonder why a genius like Leonardo failed to correct such a blunder. But then, was it actually a mistake – could the ludicrous height actually have been left there *deliberately*?

Remember this is the man who set a giant phallus on the Virgin

Mary's head and got away with it for 500 years; the artist whose 'St John' is a woman and whose *Last Supper* contains a disembodied hand clutching a dagger that virtually no one ever notices. Leonardo was the ultimate psychologist, knowing – even relying on – the fact that people only ever see what they expect or want to see. If that were not true, he would have been in serious trouble virtually before the paint dried on many of his masterpieces. He seems to be creating 'errors' of a particular sort, but not for the masses to notice, because he had no intention for them to do so and was confident that they would miss them anyway, but perhaps to speak profoundly to 'those with eyes to see'.

Here he has created not only an impossibly tall Jesus, but the man's head is apparently *severed*. Indeed, there is a distinct demarcation line at the base of the neck, which can be seen perfectly, like many of the other details, when viewed in photographic negative. Once again, this is beyond reasonable doubt: we had the image run through a computer programme that turned it into a species of contour map,[44] making the discovery that the image does indeed suddenly stop completely at the exact position of the line, picking up again at the upper chest. Why should this be?

One reason was no doubt simply practical. It is obvious that the image of the head at the front was created at a different time from the rest of the front and the whole of the back. The face is actually a different size and scale from the body,[45] being also narrower and proportionately smaller than the head at the back (which is also at a completely different angle).[46] The ears are missing, replaced by curious blank strips between the face and the hair, which gives an oddly neat frame to the face (unlikely were the body supine).[47]

In fact, we discovered very quickly during our experiments that this peculiar foreshortening is simply a side-effect of using a lens in the camera obscura, a sort of fish-eye effect. Leonardo is known to have ground his own lenses, even making himself a rather 'cool' pair of dark blue spectacles. (But again, one wonders why? Why did he need to protect his eyes from intense light and heat? Did he make the glasses specially for his Shroud work, in which – as we discovered for ourselves[48] – when creating similar images, both heat and light must be kept at a maximum for over 24 hours?)[49] The question of a lens led us to make a particularly exciting discovery:

we know Leonardo used one at least in his manufacture of the face of the Shroud of Turin because it can clearly be seen in the dead centre of the face – the bridge of the nose – as a dark circle on the negative and a light circle on the positive image. This is a photograph of the lens itself.[50]

However, this being Leonardo, one layer of explanation will never be enough. Multi-faceted himself, he demands that we engage our brains, hearts and souls (not to mention our sense of the absurd): his unsettling representations striking at the core of the psyche, and sometimes giving a curious twist to the heart. As in his uncompromising satire on Marian virginity, *The Virgin of the Rocks*, his work may often be curiously dark in the literal, artistic sense, but it is also white-hot with anger – and that anger communicates itself loud and clear after 500 years to 'those with eyes to see'.

Considering all the bold and outrageous Johannite symbolism in Leonardo's paintings, was he also saying in his depiction of a very obviously separate head on the Shroud of Turin, that 'one who was beheaded is "over" – morally and spiritually – one who was crucified'? Certainly that would be the neatest and ultimate symbol of the *real* 'Da Vinci code' . . .

It is almost certainly *Leonardo's own face* (see illustrations). He loved putting himself in his works – such as in the bottom right-hand corner of *The Adoration of the Magi* or as Saint Thaddeus/Saint Jude in the *Last Supper*: the joke no doubt being that Saint Jude is patron saint of lost causes. It is even possible to see that Saint Jude's face is very similar to that of Shroudman, from the distinctive hairline to the large, knobbly nose.

Various other devotees to the idea that Leonardo faked the Shroud[51] have suggested that he used his own face out of reverence for Jesus, literally in imitation of Christ. However, even leaving his personal heretical beliefs aside for the moment, from the viewpoint of his time and place that is simply inconceivable. He has represented himself splattered with Christ's holy blood, believed to be sacred and redemptive: to fake it would be absolute sacrilege. It would have been impossible for a believer, a true son of the Church, to have taken such a far-reaching liberty with the face and body of the Redeemer. To have faked Christ's broken and bloody body was neither for the squeamish nor anyone who entertained any hope of ever seeing Heaven. On the other hand, a passionate dyed-in-the-wool 'anti-Christ' would have welcomed the chance to render Jesus not only mortal, but also made in his own image – and Leonardo was quick to take such an opportunity. Not only did he think of himself as Grandson of God, but clearly had ambitions to be his own father! (For the illegitimate artist who suffered at the hands of his half siblings, especially over vexed problems of inheritance, presenting himself as the alleged Son of God would have had an extra piquancy. Unfortunately, this particular association passed Sigmund Freud by.)

Of course, from an objective viewpoint, with the Turin Shroud Leonardo succeeded brilliantly, even though he could never have known that in the late nineteenth century his 'magic' image would suddenly leap into incredible detail when it was photographed for the first time and seen in negative.[52] (Although it seems unlikely, did Leonardo himself have some means of seeing Shroudman in negative? Did he know that he had created such a work of Luciferan genius – or was it merely a shot in the dark, a species of message in a bottle thrown into the seas of posterity with the hope that one day it would be recognized for what it is?)

As for the image of the terribly beaten and nailed body, that presumably came from unholy tinkerings with scourge, hammer and nails behind closed doors with one of the many corpses Leonardo used for anatomical research. This is an actual body that really had been subjected to the great abuses of beating, scourging and the dreadful piercing of hands, side and feet. (The head bears the marks of the Crown of Thorns, but perfectionist Leonardo would have endured the pain for the sake of his heretical art. In fact, the face itself is remarkably free from wounds and certainly far too composed for a man who had allegedly been tortured to death.) The body had truly been nailed upright, for the nail wounds are in the wrists and not the palms, showing a grim practicality. (Incredibly, some Shroudies have even suggested that no one could have known how to recreate the wounds of the crucifixion. Yet surely all one has to do is read the New Testament, which describes what happened to Jesus – and boldly set about some grisly experimentation.) And, although Leonardo never painted a crucifixion, there is an intriguing reference in a note that has long puzzled biographers, dating from *c.* 1489 that refers to a specimen that he had borrowed: '. . . the bone that Gian de Bellinzona pierced and from which he easily extracted the nail . . .'[53] It seems that Leonardo was experimenting with crucifixion for some nefarious purpose of his own.

It is significant that while there is no paint to speak of[54] on the Shroud, there is real blood around the sites of the wounds. A painstaking – not to say nit-picking – genius, Leonardo was unlikely to spoil his masterpiece by splodging it with crude daubs of paint instead of blood. (Similarly, of all fakers a perfectionist of his genius would hardly have used linen straight from the loom for a relic that was supposed to be 1,500 years old.) So it might be said, albeit perhaps melodramatically, that in one sense at least he did sign away his soul to Lucifer in blood.

Faking the 'Shroud' of Turin was, arguably, Da Vinci's greatest hour – certainly as a Luciferan, whether one takes that to mean an agent of the Devil, as would most Catholics and all Shroudies, or merely as a daring experimental scientist. The fake is an astonishing joke – truly a *commedia*, a profoundly serious comment – but in this case, also a brutal nose-thumbing at the Church, even at its founder. As his first biographer, Giorgio Vasari, wrote: 'Leonardo formed . . . a doctrine so heretical that he depended no more on . . . any religion', although perhaps prudently this passage was removed from subsequent editions, being replaced by a brief and unconvincing note about Leonardo's death-bed repentance.[55]

Never officially endorsed by the Vatican, although it has come close once or twice, the Shroud for the most part is kept locked away from prying eyes and the depredations of modern life and the polluting air. From time to time it is displayed in the cathedral at Turin, where no doubt the shade of the old master enjoys the religious raptures of the pilgrims crossing themselves and murmuring devout prayers over a *photograph* of a sixteenth-century Johannite heretic.

Even to a non-Christian, the sheer *chutzpah* involved is breathtaking, almost shocking in both the literal and figurative sense. The image of the Shroud, particularly in minutely detailed negative, induces that peculiar abrupt lurching in the pit of the stomach that marks an encounter with something truly outrageous – as in suddenly seeing for oneself what he did with the dark rocks looming above the Virgin's head. Coming face-to-face with Leonardo's wilful, brilliant and intentionally blasphemous master-piece is a moment of truth that many would rather not experience.

Nor could Leonardo have guessed at another extraordinary side-effect of using his own face as the model for Christ on the Shroud – although no doubt he would have exploded with laughter if he had. Although there had been depictions of Jesus as bearded before the Turin Shroud went on display in the late fifteenth century, after that watershed Christ's appearance in popular art changed specifi-cally to resemble it. Suddenly the divine look was standardized into a very tall (although never quite so tall as Shroudman, for obvious reasons), broad-shouldered man with reddish hair parted in the middle, a long nose and hauntingly beautiful, regular features. In other words, our general cultural perception of what Jesus looked like is none other than Leonardo – another shocking triumph for the inspiration of *The Da Vinci Code*. Just think of all those plaster statues, the countless stained-glass windows and twisted bodies on crucifixes not as images of a first-century Jewish teacher and mage at all, but a fourteenth-fifteenth-century Italian homosexual heretic who hated Christ with all his Johannite heart. Again, there is that disturbing shift in the pit of the stomach, as yet again the founda-tion of our collective unconscious lifts – and shudders slightly.

One day the 'Shroud' may be prominently displayed where it belongs – in a museum of photography or science and technology, where the fruits of the Da Vinci heresy can be freely appreciated for what they are, far away from pilgrims, priests, candles and incense. The Shroud does not deserve to be prayed over, but then perhaps nothing does.

Behind closed doors

Although the authorities' suppression of scientific experiment and intellectual enquiry from the early days of Christianity to the Age of Enlightenment was patchily inconsistent – depending largely on the attitude to learning of each individual pope – it is true to say that in general the Church frowned on too much knowledge, debate and thinking. And it surely is no coincidence that the Latin and Greek for 'knowledge' – respectively *scientia* and *gnosis* – represent the two aspects of learning that it most abhorred. As a blend of much that was anathematized, being a left-handed-gay-vegetarian-Johannite-photographer-aviator-anatomist, Leonardo got away with an enormous amount, due mostly to friends in high places, but even he often thought it prudent to move from place to place quite quickly from time to time. (It was only at the end of his life, in 1513, when Pope Leo X began to express his distaste for Leonardo's anatomical work that he ceased his obsessive dissection in hospitals, charnel houses and graveyards.)

However, although in many ways his contribution to human knowledge and to the annals of heresy was unique, Leonardo was merely the bright blossoming of an ancient tradition of working behind closed doors, away from misunderstanding, the rack and the stake. Usually these secretive scholars were known as 'alchemists', a sort of convenient umbrella term for what we would acknowledge simply as research scientists. Alchemy proper, however, was a complex business, often involving mystical and spiritual exercises, with a strong sexual content: once again, we discuss that sacred sexuality is the background to an eminent esoteric tradition.[56]

True alchemists often positively welcomed their bad reputation as idiotic charlatans who insanely wasted their lives attempting to turn base metal such as lead into pure gold. To be dismissed as one of these empty-headed materialistic 'puffers' could mean being left alone to concentrate on much weightier matters such as searching for the fabled Philosopher's Stone, an elixir that would bestow not only near-immortality, but also supreme spiritual knowledge and wisdom. Every child the world over today knows that one Nicholas Flamel is rumoured to have found this magical substance, thanks to J. K. Rowling's Harry Potter books, but few realize that he really existed. Flamel lived and worked in fourteenth-century Paris with his beloved wife Perrenelle, with whom it is said he achieved the 'Great Work' on 17 January 1382. As a result, rumours still abound that they lived for hundreds of years.

While it is untrue that all popes were equally anti-learning as far as the laity was concerned, the activities of most alchemists were deemed to be inherently beyond the pale. Many sought not only to transmute base metal – be it their own souls or a heap of uninspiring lead – into something purer and finer, but some attempted to blast through all restrictions and enter the truly Luciferan world of creating life in the laboratory. Stories circulated about the original 'test-tube babies', said to be unholy little homunculi, created without the usual procreation specifically to scurry around to do their master's bidding as occult servitors. Needless to say, the homunculi were, at least in the vast majority of alleged cases, the product of over-heated imaginations, but it does reveal that scientists condemned for trying to 'play God' are not unique to the twenty-first century.

However, the great physician and alchemist/sorcerer Aureolus Philippus Theophrastus Bombast von Hohenheim – otherwise known simply as Paracelsus (1493–1541) – declared boldly 'It is necessary to know evil things as well as good; for who can know what is good without also knowing what is evil?'[57] An active Luciferan in this sense, he claimed to have actually made several such little monsters using a process he described as follows:

Let the semen of a man putrefy by itself in a sealed cucurbite with the highest putrefaction of venter equinus for forty days, or until it begins at last to live, move, and be agitated, which can easily be seen. At this time it will be in some degree like a human being, but, nevertheless, transparent and without a body. If now, after this, it be every day nourished and fed cautiously with the arcanum of human blood, and kept for forty weeks in the perpetual and equal heat of venter equinus, it becomes thencefold a true living human infant, having all the members of a child that is born from a woman, but much smaller. This we call a homunculus; and it should be afterwards educated with the greatest care and zeal, until it grows up and starts to display intelligence.[58]

(Sceptics would no doubt point out that some movement was virtually guaranteed in putrefying matter after a certain time – but from nothing more occult than maggots.)

In 1658, Gian Battista della Porta, the sorcerer who was arrested for projecting images using a magic lantern (see above), proposed to show 'how living Creatures of divers kinds, may be mingled and coupled together, and that from them, new, and yet profitable kinds of living Creatures may be generated.'[59] Della Porta aimed to produce through magical means all sorts of animate gimmicks, writing instructions on 'how to generate pretty little dogs to play with'.[60] However, Paracelsus saw a greater practical potential in the little homunculi, writing:

> Now, this is one of the greatest secrets which God has revealed to mortal and fallible man. It is a miracle and a marvel of God, an arcanum above all arcana, and deserves to be kept secret until the last of times, when there shall be nothing hidden, but all things shall be manifest. And although up to this time it has not been known to men, it was, nevertheless, known to the wood-sprites and nymphs and giants long ago, because they themselves were sprung from this source; since from such homunculi when they come to manhood are produced giants, pygmies and other marvellous people, who get great victories over their enemies, and know all secrets and hidden matters.[61]

Even the great Paracelsus clearly had areas of his imagination that were still marked, as on the old maps, 'Here there be Dragons'. It was said that he willed that when he became old, he would be cut into small pieces and buried in horse manure in order to resurrect as a virile young man. Unfortunately, his servant dug him up too soon, and ruined the marvellous plan.

As the self-styled 'Christ of Medicine'[62] – he also gave one of his names to the word 'bombastic', because of his overbearing manner. Paracelsus studied alchemy and chemistry at Basle University before researching minerals, metals and the occupational diseases of miners. Because he believed that 'like acts on like' in minute doses, he is credited with the discovery of homeopathy, as well as inventing 'ether as an anaesthetic and laudanum as a tranquillizer' [and] he was the first to describe silicosis, and 'traced goitre to minerals found in drinking water'.[63] Announcing 'If the spirit suffers, the body suffers also', he was also clearly a pioneer of what we would call holistic medicine. A major influence on subsequent generations of physicians, even his ideas about homunculi were taken seriously.

In 1638 Laurens de Castelan made the point in his 'Rare et

Curieux Discours de la Plante Appelée Mandragore' that although most people rejected Paracelsus' theories his homunculus could still have been 'a bit of diabolical magic' – in other words, it may have been *real*, but created by devilish means. In 1672 the scientist Christian Friedrich Garmann wrote of the evolution of the human egg, musing about the possibility that conception could take place outside the womb, in an article about 'the chemical homunculus of Paracelsus'.[64] And in 1679 Scottish doctor William Maxwell wrote in his *De Medicina Magnetica* that 'just as salts of herbs can reproduce the likeness of the herb in the test tube, so the salt of human blood can show the image of a man – "the true homunculus of Paracelsus".'[65]

It may be significant that it was also claimed to be possible to grow magical, sentient entities inside the wombs of cows. Leonardo's drawing of a perfectly formed human baby curled up inside a cow's uterus has always been dismissed as a typical Da Vinci joke – presumably at the expense of women. Perhaps it was a sly dig at the sanctity of motherhood, but perhaps it was also a comment, satirical or even admiring, on the magical concept of homunculi. Leonardo's own life-like creations – at least those we know about – took the less creepy form of a robot, a true working humanoid automaton, which he built *c.* 1495.[66] Dressed in a full suit of armour, it was designed to open and close its mouth, move its head, sit up and wave its arms, and 'may have made sounds to the accompaniment of automated drums'.[67] Leonardo's pioneering work with robots directly inspired Mark Rosheim's 'mechanical men' or 'anthrobots', and whose work 'has culminated in the electric 43-axis Robotic Surrogate built for NASA Johnson Space Center and intended to service Space Station Freedom. Thus, Leonardo's vision reaches beyond the confines of our planet to explore the universe.'[68]

While making moving machines in the humanoid shape may not have been considered very devilish by sophisticated men of his day, the Church predictably disliked any such object (see below). But as for the notion of attempting to fly off into space it had no place in their learning, as did any real astronomical research. It is as well that Leonardo kept his notebooks to himself, for one bears the scribbled note, perhaps a reminder, to 'make glasses to see Moon up close', anticipating the astronomical daring of Galileo and Copernicus by a generation, neither of whom were exactly revered by the Inquisition.

The tongues of angels

England's most famous mage, Dr John Dee (1527–1606), also received a reputation for sorcery because he designed and built a robot – a mechanical beetle for a play. By then, however, he had established himself as something of an academic prodigy – having gone up to Cambridge University when just fifteen, becoming Greek Under-reader and a fellow of its newest college, Trinity, where he was already rumoured to be engaged in the dark arts.

As visiting scholar to all the great European seats of learning, Dee seized every opportunity to debate the finer points of astrology, mathematics, navigation, theology, even ritual magic – but as always, concentrating on his first love, astrology.[69] It was his astrological work that was to put him in great personal danger.

In 1553 the future Queen Elizabeth I was under house arrest on the orders of her fanatical Catholic sister, Queen Mary (who tortured and burnt her way to earn the title of 'Bloody Mary').[70] Princess Elizabeth summoned Dee to cast her regal sister's horoscope in order to know when Mary might die, but the Queen retaliated by throwing the astrologer in jail for trying to kill her through sorcery. Strangely, at such a time and in the reign of such a monarch, even one who was believed to traffic with devils for purposes of treason survived: he was released in 1555 after having been freed then re-arrested for heresy, over which he also miraculously triumphed. Dee's apparently charmed life was to last – but certainly not for ever.

When Mary died[71] and Elizabeth took the throne in 1558, she appointed Dr Dee as her court astrologer, and – judging by the secrecy that surrounded his many foreign trips as 'agent 007' – perhaps even a major spy, although as ever where the intelligence agencies are concerned, hard evidence remains elusive. With royal favour, Dee's career flourished. He also dedicated his tract on alchemy, *The Hieroglyphic Mind* (1564), to the Hungarian Emperor Maximilian II, thus ensuring his celebrity spread across Europe. In the guise of Prospero in Shakespeare's *The Tempest*, he says happily: 'Now does my project gather to a head: My charms crack not; my spirits obey; and time/Goes upright with his carriage.'[72] It was during this golden time that he began to work with mediums, although the first proved useless for his purposes. The second, however, was to change his life completely over the course of a long and bizarre occult partnership . . .

In 1581 he met Edward Kelley (or 'Kelly'),[73] an occultist, alchemist, magus and necromancer – exactly what any self-respecting magician wanted, although Kelley always seemed reluctant to exploit his gift for mediumship. Ironically, although Dee himself had a raw talent for divination, he found it impossible to open up completely to the invisible world. Kelley may have been the answer to Dee's prayers as magical colleague, but perhaps his reputation for petty crime had not penetrated as far south as the astrologer's home in Mortlake, Surrey, although his cropped ears, mutilated as punishment for passing forged coins, would inevitably be spotted no matter how closely he pulled his black cap close over them. Kelley had a murky background as rogue lawyer, when he was convicted of forging land deals, and other semi-professional crimes. When he first presented himself to Dee, Kelley used the alias 'Talbot', which he maintained from March to November 1582, while he ingratiated himself with the erudite court astrologer. Suddenly Talbot disappears from Dee's diary to be replaced by 'E.K'. Dee's fourth *Book of Mysteries* begins 'after the reconciliation with Kelley'[74] – perhaps the first of the rows and upsets that were to plague their partnership.

However, in 1570 Kelley had acquired an old alchemical document concerning the transmutation of metals, and the story goes that eight years later he successfully turned 1lb of lead into pure gold. Although this would always be a potent prize to dangle before the greedy eyes of kings and princes, it was gold of another sort that he offered to Dee, who coveted intellectual and spiritual wealth far more. The twenty-seven-year-old entered the Dee household as a Mephistopheles to a Faust: charming, persuasive, and corrupting, another snake in Eden.

Kelley used a variety of techniques with which to operate clairvoyantly, including a 'shewstone', something akin to a crystal ball. As Samuel Butler (1612–80) wrote scathingly in his *Hudibras*:[75]

'Kelly did all his feats upon/the Devil's looking-glass, a stone/
Where, playing with him at bo-peep,/He solv'd all problems
ne'er so deep'. Kelley was clearly adept at 'scrying' – using a
polished surface, in his case a convex mirror of obsidian[76] to see
far-off places or times, or as a medium through which to communicate with non-human entities – such as the Archangel Uriel.

(As the Baptist's traditional guardian, perhaps Uriel represented
the idea that John's skull would be used for purposes of divination.
It may also be significant that young boys who were used as clair-
voyants in the early Common Era often had 'Uriel' written on their
foreheads.)

The archangel gave him instructions for forging a protective
talisman, an essential tool for those who engage in the perilous
business of working with entities that might not be all they claim to
be. In later years Dee developed the 'Monas Hieroglyphica', which
he believed to be the ultimate occult symbol.

During the next seven years, Dee and Kelley worked together
obsessively. The mage recorded his angelic conversations, in which
he was taught the 'ancient Enochian language' – believed to be
spoken in Eden before the Fall – besides completely new magical
rituals. While many of his notes are perhaps deliberately obscure,
and others are simply concerned with the finer points of Enochian
grammar, others detail what appear to be authentic predictions. For
example, on 5 May 1583 Uriel gave Kelley a disturbing vision of a
horizon darkened with a huge fleet of ships, later presumed to be
the Spanish Armada of 1588, which perhaps prompted Dee to hex
the enemy vessels. Significantly, the medals struck to commemo-
rate England's escape from the Armada echo the idea of a miracle,
bearing the words: 'God blew his wind and they were scattered'.
Uriel also bestowed another major vision, of a woman being
beheaded by 'a black man' – almost certainly Mary Queen of Scots
at the hands of the black-hooded executioner.

Although their 'workings' were quintessentially magical, underlying them was Dee's fervent desire to return the Christian religion
to a potent unity – but as all he could see all around him were
dissent and schisms, persecution and bigotry, this reunification
would have to be achieved in heterodox ways. Uriel told him:
'These are the days wherein the prophet said, No faith should be

found on the earth. This faith must be restored again, and men must glorify God in his works. *I am the light of God*' [My emphasis].[77] The strongly Gnostic tone is repeated, for example, in the angel Madimi's words to Dee:

And lo, the issue which he giveth thee is wisdom. But lo, the mother of it is not yet delivered. For, if a woman know her times and seasons of deliverance: Much more doth he [God], who is the Mother of all things . . .[78]

Much of the angelic material was colourfully and repetitively apocalyptic in nature, and rarely wasted the opportunity to emphasize the fact that the two men were called and chosen, as in 'You are becoming prophets, and are sanctified for the coming of the Lord.' But the spirits that appeared in the shewstone were not always rigidly dour. Kelley saw a luminous figure declare: 'There is a God, let us be merry. E. K. [Kelley] He danceth still. There is a heaven. Let us be merry. E. K. Now he taketh off his clothes again.'[79]

The angels took over Dee's life. He and Kelley, together with their respective families, travelled widely in Europe on the suggestions/orders of the communicators, finally arriving at Cracow, Poland, in 1587. It was there that the angelic idyll turned terminally sour. On 17 April the angels urged the men to indulge in wife-swapping, which horrified Dr Dee – who worried that the angels might have become demons – but as the injunction was something of a command, they reluctantly complied. Perhaps in all senses, that broke the spell. Although nearly thirty years older than his wife Jane, Dee was devoted to her, often scribbling caring diary notes about her moods and health. Both of them had always been faithful to each other, and this new injunction – which they reluctantly obeyed – proved traumatic. Although still on speaking terms with Kelley, the Dees left him on the continent and fled back to England, where it is said Dr Dee renounced magic for ever, dying an outcast and a pauper in 1608.

(Many sorcerers have died in obscurity and poverty, providing an inevitable and facile cautionary tale for moralists and fundamentalists, but one wonders if the unfortunate magi had simply been too addicted to the delights and challenges of the other-world ultimately to bother to forge much of a life in this one.[80] To be ravished by even the least spectacular magic often means ignoring bills – and the necessity to find the means to pay them[81] – and maintaining social ties. However, many scholars in disciplines other than the occult have also succumbed to the enchanted addiction of learning, but the moralists ignore the inconvenient fact that they, too, died of starvation and destitution, also utterly alone and without even the excuse of soul-devouring demons at hand.)

Even though receiving the equivalent of a knighthood from the King of Bohemia, Kelley's good fortune came to an abrupt end, although – as with much about his life – the precise circumstances are not known. Perhaps he had returned to his previous career as a forger, or the monarch simply tired of his empty promises to produce gold. Kelley was repeatedly thrown in jail, from where he wrote – full of indignation and self-righteousness – to the king, hinting once more that he could create gold for him from base metal. The tone may be seen from the opening passage:

> Though I have already twice suffered chains and imprisonment in Bohemia, an indignity which has been offered to me in no other part of the world, yet my mind, remaining unbound, has all this time exercised itself in the study of that philosophy which is despised by the wicked and foolish, but is praised by the wise. Nay, the saying that none but fools and lawyers hate and despise Alchemy has passed into proverb. Furthermore, as during the preceding three years I have used great labour, expense, and acre in order to discover for your Majesty that which might afford you much profit and pleasure, so during my imprisonment – a calamity which has befallen me through the action of your Majesty – I am utterly incapable of remaining idle. Hence I have written a treatize . . . But if my teaching displease you, know that you are still altogether wandering astray from the true scope and aim of this matter, and are utterly wasting your money, time, labour, and hope . . .[82]

This mixture of indignation, barely veiled accusation and bombast was not well advised. Kelley ended his days trying to escape from jail in 1595.[83]

As for Dee, he seemed increasingly a broken man. Money was a serious problem, although Queen Elizabeth constantly reassured him that one day he would be granted a profitable living. It never came. Then came absolute disaster for such a dedicated scholar: his precious library and laboratory were razed to the ground by a mob who believed him to be in league with the Devil, and despite his royal patronage, it was with such an unenviable reputation that he eked out his last years. Then a double blow: the Queen's great councillor, Lord Burleigh (William Cecil), and Dee's friend and patron, died in 1598, and then the regal Gloriana herself passed on in 1603. For his last three years Dee entered not a single thought in his diary. The sad old man seemed to be living out Prospero's decline:

> Now my charms are all o'erthrown
> And what strength I have's my own,
> Which is most faint . . .
> . . . Now I want
> Spirits to enforce, art to enchant
> And my ending is despair
> Unless I be relieved by prayer . . .[84]

A trite and contrived end for a great magician. He went to join his Queen – and possibly Edward Kelley – on 26 March 1609.

It is easy for twenty-first-century readers to dismiss the angelic dealings of the Dee-Kelley team as foolishness, illusion, the product of suggestibility – even a *folie à deux* – or simply the result of some nifty stage-management from the unscrupulous cropped-eared mountebank. Indeed, unsurprisingly, the first of the angelic messages urged Dee to pay Kelley the then considerable sum of £30 a year as a pension, together with the plain statement 'none shall enter into the knowledge of these mysteries but this worker': similarly, the order to exchange wives coincided neatly with the climax of Kelley's lust for Mrs Dee. But as with many cases of the paranormal, bald scepticism rarely provides the complete answer.[85]

As set down in Dee's *Liber Logaeth*, Enochian (communicated via Kelley from an angel called Nalvage) seems to be a valid language, complete with its own vocabulary, grammar and syntax –

difficult, if not impossible for a non-academic such as Kelley to have invented, at least *consciously*. The problem is that even in the twenty-first century we have little idea about the capabilities of the human unconscious, although the annals of abnormal psychology offer a glimpse of a dark, Luciferan world of immense and labyrinthine possibilities.

Dr Dee was by no means the only person to have received a completely new language under what might be termed paranormal circumstances. In the late nineteenth century, Catherine Elise Muller, a Spiritualist medium from Geneva, Switzerland, proved that while in trance she would produce automatic writing in Arabic, or – through a spirit 'control' called Leopold – speak what she claimed to be Martian. She even drew crude sketches of life on Mars, complete with streets, houses and the latest Martian fashions.

As her fame spread, the renowned Swiss Professor of psychology, Theodore Flournoy, took an intense interest in Catherine – now operating under the pseudonym of Hélène Smith – spending five years sitting in on her séances and recording her 'Martian' outpourings. Applying psychoanalytical techniques, he concluded that she was abnormally imaginative, her fantasies emerging as highly coloured fact during the dissociative state of trance. She may not have been *consciously* cheating, but her *unconscious* mind was. However, Flournoy added that Catherine's exceptional gift for fabrication was probably augmented by *real* psychokinesis (mind over matter) and a certain amount of telepathy – a conclusion that would be far too brave and subtle for today's media-hungry alleged 'parapsychologists', eager to make their names as professional debunkers, a species of televangelists for a particularly aggressive and bigoted form of rationalism.

Moreover, although a Sanskrit expert declared that 98 per cent of Catherine's 'Martian' words could be traced to known languages, he claimed that her outpourings behaved like a real tongue, with authentic grammatical constructions. If a relatively uneducated young woman in the nineteenth century could unconsciously invent a passable language, it is possible that in the heightened atmosphere of a sixteenth-century sorcerer's laboratory, so could Edward Kelley.

As we will see when discussing *The Book of the Law*, produced by ritual magician Aleister Crowley in 1904, inspired or 'channelled' writings usually appear to have originated with another personality or mind entirely, which is why they are so compelling in the first place. Of course these days we know all about dissociation in principle – the apparent splitting of an individual's consciousness to reveal seemingly discrete personalities. The most obvious example of this is multiple personality, where a single person can exhibit such entirely different modes of thinking and expression that other people appear to be trapped, as it were, inside the 'host' body. Although this is understood to be classic dissociation pure and simple, certain related phenomena take multiple personality into the category of 'extreme possibilities' (as *The X-Files*' Fox Mulder would say): for example, while six of the seven personalities obediently slumber after the host takes a strong sleeping pill, the last one refuses to succumb and stays awake. *But how?* In other cases one particular personality might claim to suffer from diabetes – which is confirmed by a blood test, although none of the other personalities test positive when it is their turn to take over . . .

We may label yesterday's magical activity either as fraud or 'abnormal psychology' but that does not mean that by the simple but satisfying act of categorization it is actually tamed or even explained. By their very nature paranormal events are impossible to pin down, even often difficult to interpret.

Back from the grave

Were Dee's magical operations actually demonic, as the mob of arsonists that destroyed his library and laboratory believed? It must be remembered that although he may have thought differently from most of today's mainstream academics,[86] Dee was by nobody's standards a fool. Frances Yates in her book, *The Rosicrucian Enlightenment* (1972), claimed that he was one of the founders of the Rosicrucian movement and that it was essentially English, although Tobias Churton disagrees, saying 'Germany and Bohemia had sufficient Magi (if not so universally brilliant as Dee) of their own to initiate their own movement', although he does admit that the time Dee and Kelley spent abroad 'was a significant influence on the alchemico-magico-apocalyptic reforming philosophy', especially through his *Monas Hieroglyphica* (1564), 'which laid out a complex theory of cosmic unity whose aim was to integrate all knowledge in a cosmic spiritual/mathematical system: an aim implicit in the Rosicrucian endeavour.'[87] Churton could have been describing Leonardo.

Even Dee's non-esoteric achievements are astounding enough: coining the word 'Britannia', he tried to ensure she ruled the waves by drawing up the first comprehensive, long-term plan for the British Navy. The first scholar to apply Euclidian geometry to navigation, he built the necessary instruments to do so, trained several of the greatest navigators of the Age of Discovery, and charted the Northeast and Northwest Passages accurately, without leaving his Surrey home.

Even where his magical work was concerned, Dee was ever on his guard for 'illuders', or low-level (mischievous or time-wasting) spirits that masqueraded as angels. He took command of any ambivalent situations, on one occasion compelling an illuder to confess, and then consigning it to the flames, saying 'Master Kelley, is your doubt of the spirit taken away?'[88]

Yet whenever spirits are involved in any human endeavour, there must remain some questions about both their authenticity and their motives, even if they claim to be angels. In effect, the *modus operandi* of the Kelley-Dee team was closer to Spiritualism – Kelley is often referred to as 'the first medium' – than much previous occult work, which is not without its problems, although perhaps less obviously so than the 'cursed necromancy' itself. Indeed, Kelley (together with a magician called Waring)[89] is said to have successfully raised a corpse from its grave in the churchyard at Walton-le-Dale in Lancashire to command it to predict the future.

Montague Summers is, of course, swift to condemn trafficking with *any* kind of spirits as diabolism pure and simple. He notes apropos of allegations that witches 'flew' to their Sabbats, that '. . . outside the lives of the Saints, spiritistic [sic] séances afford us examples of this supernormal phenomenon.'[90] More in character, he declares forthrightly: 'Camouflage it how you will . . . this "New Religion" [of] Spiritualism and its kindred superstitions . . . is but the old Witchcraft'.[91]

Today when Spiritualists follow their own version of the

Christian religion, and many famous mediums proved their astounding abilities repeatedly under strict conditions, besides giving untold comfort and hope to thousands, it is difficult to conceive of the movement having any possible association with anything devilish. However, even leaving the preconceptions of Summers aside, in the old heyday of 'physical mediums', theirs was a considerably more ambiguous activity, often carrying a distinct whiff of sulphur.

In 1911 twenty-three-year-old Brazilian Carmine Mirabelli was sacked from his job in a shoe shop because the shoes insisted on flying around by themselves. Duly confined to a lunatic asylum for nineteen days, two doctors watched him closely. They concluded that he possessed an extraordinary excess of nervous forces – remarkably similar to the modern idea that poltergeist attacks usually centre on teenagers undergoing particularly tumultuous puberties. Mirabelli's mere presence caused some extraordinary phenomena: inanimate objects moved about and even apparently liquefied. He also produced reams of automatic writing[92] in 30 languages, exhibited extraordinary powers of telepathy and clair-voyance – and was frequently reported to travel instantaneously, by teleportation (basically similar to the mode of transport celebrated in *Star Trek*'s famous line: 'Beam me up, Scottie').

Mirabelli's achievements allegedly included levitating himself nearly seven feet off the ground, an event that was photographed. However, there is some dispute about this: it is now claimed that the photograph has been tampered with to show the medium apparently in mid-air, whereas in fact he was simply standing on the top of a step-ladder – later erased in the finished picture – to indicate how high he *had* levitated.

A leading light of the Brazilian Spiritist movement (devotees of the French medium Alan Kardec), on one occasion, it is said, Mirabelli not only levitated while handcuffed, but as he rose into the air he dematerialized, the handcuffs clattering to the floor. He was discovered behind a locked door. But his most controversial feat was to materialize the dead – apparently more successfully and dramatically than even the practised necromancer Edward Kelley.

At Mirabelli's séances, sometimes held in brightly lit rooms, skeletons would gradually form in the air, clothed horrendously with ragged flesh – and stinking of decay . . . At his most successful, he is said to have eventually materialized solid human beings. In one case the man he apparently conjured out of thin air was clearly of African origin, while on another occasion a dead poet materialized between Mirabelli and a sitter – who not unnaturally is rigid with fear, the whites of his eyes showing like a terrified horse. This poses the important question: Mirabelli's mediumship may have been genuine – but was it *nice*? Was his laudable attempt to present evidence for an afterlife merely conjuring up dark forces? Like many cases from the annals of materialization (or 'physical') mediums, the sheer horror involved surely rendered that form of continued existence akin to the obscene undead, vampires and ghouls. No one would like to think of their loved ones returning for an hour or so to stink of the grave, or indeed, to look forward with any enthusiasm to the prospect of doing so themselves.

Once, when a skull that Mirabelli had merely looked at began to move, the eminent psychiatrist Dr Franco da Rocha noted:

> When I picked up the skull, I felt something strange in my hands, something fluid, as if a globular liquid were touching my palm. When I concentrated my attention further, I saw something similar to an irradiation pass over the skull when you rapidly expose a mirror to luminous rays.[93]

(It should be noted that Spiritualists describe necromancy as *pretended* communication with the dead, for they believe that the dead cannot be forced, under the normal 'rules', to have any contact with the living. Spiritualists themselves believe they merely *invite* the dead to communicate.)

Mirabelli died in 1951 after being hit by a car. But although few researchers took an interest in him during his lifetime, in 1973 the Brazilian Institute for Psychobiophysical Research (BPP) appointed a team to compile a dossier on his extraordinary phenomena. Its members included the British writer-researcher Guy Lyon Playfair, who spread the word in Britain.

Mirabelli's sons, although sometimes highly sceptical of Spiritism, were adamant that their father had made astonishing things happen 'almost every day, any time and any place'.[94] His were united in denying that he had cheated – or, indeed, that he had any motive for doing so.

Yet Theodore Besterman of the Society for Psychical Research (SPR) had no hesitation in denouncing Mirabelli as a fraud, even though he had himself witnessed examples of apparent psychokinesis (mind over matter) in his presence, and seen the medium write a 1,700-word automatic script in under an hour in French – a language he did not know. (He also produced intelligible automatic writing in Hebrew, Japanese and Arabic, just like 'Hélène Smith' and her alleged Martian, and Kelley and Enochian.)

The mysterious movement of objects Besterman ascribed to the use of 'hidden threads', although neither he nor the other members of the research team managed to explain how they could have produced such a variety of phenomena. Despite Besterman's scepticism, however, Professor Hans Driesch of the Society for Psychical Research (SPR) and May C. Walker of the American SPR found Mirabelli 'most impressive',[95] while Guy Lyon Playfair also discovered no evidence of cheating.

Perhaps the last word should be given to Dr Felipe Ache, who hazarded that Mirabelli's strange gifts were 'the result of the radiation of nervous forces that we all have but that Mirabelli has in extraordinary excess.' In other words, perhaps we all have such astounding abilities in latent form, but only certain rare people, with a distinct psychological and perhaps even physiological make-up, will ever possess the weird talent to activate it. If it means conjuring up putrefying corpses, perhaps we should be grateful for that.

Another major case from the annals of the Golden Age of physical mediumship reveals the difficulty in separating apparently genuine phenomena from fraud, at least on a conscious level as far as the medium was concerned. And it shows how dramatic, but often unpleasant, the world of the séance room once was.

Eusapia Palladino remains the most thoroughly investigated medium in the history of psychical research, certainly over a protracted and chronological period. A Neapolitan, she was studied for more than twenty years by at least fifty scientists – many of them internationally acclaimed – from Italy, France, Poland, Russia, England and the US.

Eusapia's life began inauspiciously. Her mother died shortly after the future medium was born in 1854, and her father was murdered when she was twelve. Perhaps this trauma was in some way the cause of the phenomena that surrounded her first attendance at a séance the following year, at which the furniture moved towards her and rose into the air.

Then in 1872 the English wife of one Damiani, an Italian psychical researcher, attended a séance in London at which a spirit calling itself 'John King' came through and informed her that there was a very powerful medium in Naples who was the reincarnation of his daughter Katie King, already a well known haunter of séance rooms herself. The ghostly John King then gave the complete address of the house where this reincarnation could be found. In due course, Damiani followed this up, finding the house – and Eusapia Palladino. Much impressed, as well he might be, Damiani helped to foster the Neapolitan's powers.

Soon she was a sensation in the neighbourhood, but it took twenty years for her talents to reach the notice of local academic, Professor Ercole Chiaia – and thence of the waiting world. In 1888 he appealed for scientists to investigate her gifts in a letter to the eminent criminologist – and extreme sceptic – Professor Cesare Lombroso. This was a critical moment in Eusapia's career, after which nothing was ever the same for her.

The investigations begin
In 1892 Professor Lombroso, together with five scientific colleagues put the medium through her paces at a series of sittings, finally pronouncing himself satisfied that her phenomena were genuine. This was only a start: the following year a seven-man commission of distinguished academics from several fields was set up under Professor Schiaparelli, director of the University of Milan. After a full seventeen sittings, they pronounced her genuine.

Their published report included this pronouncement:

'It is impossible to count the number of times that a hand appeared and was touched by one of us. Suffice it to say that doubt was no longer possible. It was indeed a living human hand which we saw and touched, while at the same time the bust and the arms of the medium remained visible, and her hands were held by those on either side of her.'[96]

Professor Enrico Morselli, who studied Eusapia closely over a long period in his laboratory in Genoa, drew up a list of thirty-nine varieties of phenomena he observed her produce at close quarters and under rigorous test conditions.

Before long, the obscure Neapolitan had become a psychic superstar, famous across the western world. Scientists from as far away as Russia's St Petersburg flocked to Naples to witness her phenomena for themselves – not all credulous fools by any means. Most put her through her paces in a highly critical frame of mind, having searched both her and the premises beforehand very thoroughly. She also visited Rome, Genoa, Palermo, Turin, Paris, Warsaw – and Cambridge, where she was the guest of the Society for Psychical Research (SPR), never known for its credulity.

It was at this point that criticism began to sour Eusapia's career. One of the witnesses was Dr Richard Hodgson, who suspected she was an incorrigible cheat. Although during the experiment he was supposed to control her movements, in fact he relaxed his guard – and Eusapia immediately seized the opportunity to fake the phenomena. As a result, the SPR branded her a fraud, but this created a rift among the international community of psychical researchers: many across Europe declared that they were aware she would fake it if she could, but if denied the opportunity, her phenomena were genuine.

Perhaps tellingly, Camille Flammarion, the leading French astronomer, who also tested Eusapia, noted that as the medium became increasingly tense the phenomena became nastier and more destructive. He wrote:

The sofa came forward when she looked at it, then recoiled before her breath; all the instruments were thrown pell mell upon the table; the tambourine rose almost to the height of the ceiling; the cushions took part in the sport, overturning everything on the table; [one participant] was thrown from his chair. This chair – a heavy dining-room chair of black walnut, with stuffed seat – rose into the air, came up on the table with a great clatter, then pushed off . . .[97]

Because reports continued to be positive about Eusapia, the SPR examined her again, sending the very sceptical team of Everard Feilding, Hereward Carrington and W. W. Baggally out to Naples. But after holding séances at the Hotel Victoria, even they were compelled to admit defeat, concluding that phenomena including the movement of objects, mysterious lights, raps and materializations were due to an agency 'wholly different from mere physical dexterity on her part.' Feilding was moved to write:

For the first time I have the absolute conviction that our observation is not mistaken. I realize as an appreciable fact of life that, from an empty curtain, I have seen hands and heads come forth, and that behind the empty curtain I have been seized by living fingers, the existence and position of the nails of which were perceptible. I have seen this extraordinary woman, sitting outside the curtain, held hand and foot, visible to myself, by my colleagues, immobile, except for the occasional straining of a limb while some entity within the curtain has over and over again pressed my hand in a position clearly beyond her reach.[98]

However, despite this glowing endorsement – and from such a very unlikely source – Eusapia went on to cheat again, and was caught once more. This was during her seven-month tour of the US in 1909, when an investigator managed to get under the cabinet curtain and saw that 'she had simply freed her foot from her shoe and with an athletic backward movement of the leg was reaching out and fishing with her toes for the guitar and the table in the cabinet.'[99]

Yet the contradictions multiplied. Even Herbert Thurston, the great conjuror and scourge of fake mediums (and contributor to Samri Frikell's classic sceptics' guide, *Spirit Mediums Exposed*) had to admit that table levitations in her presence: 'were not due to fraud and were not performed by the aid of her feet, knees or hands.'[100]

Levitation is a particularly interesting phenomenon. Montague

Summers fully believed that while saints reveal their holiness by rising unaided into thin air – the seventeenth-century monk Joseph of Cupertino, later canonized, regularly flew some distance, to the high altar or the tops of trees[101] – anyone else who exhibited similar phenomena must be acting under Satanic power. However, this seems unlikely. Even Summers would have been most perplexed when, some years ago, there was a playground craze for levitation in which groups of schoolchildren would levitate one of their number using a simple, invented pseudo-magical ritual. There is no doubt that it works, and that real people have floated over the heads of their friends without benefit of special effects, trickery or even a safety net. The ability to flout even the law of gravity by just about anyone in the right frame of mind (whatever that might be) removes the phenomenon of levitation from the exclusivity of either the annals of the saints or the history of witches.

However, another of Eusapia Palladino's rare talents takes us back to the unpleasant aspects of physical mediumship, almost to necromancy.

Ingenious ectoplasm

Interestingly, Eusapia herself admitted that she sometimes cheated, explaining – perhaps ingeniously – that sceptics could will her to do so when she was in the highly susceptible state of deep trance. However, many of her admirers suggested that some of the accusations of cheating could be the result of an error – that as the 'ectoplasm' that exuded from her often took the shape of hands and feet, perhaps that is what her accusers saw moving suspiciously.

Ectoplasm was a greyish-white substance, often similar to mucus, that allegedly oozed from all the orifices of the entranced medium, like something that might be more successfully banished by penicillin than an exorcist. The ectoplasm would gradually take the shape of human faces or figures, which sitters often recognized as their deceased loved ones. However, the phenomenon appears to be a thing of the past: sceptics say it no longer appears in séances because fake mediums are afraid modern infra-red photography would reveal their grubby secrets to the world. The eminent astrophysicist and active psychical researcher, Glasgow's Professor Archie Roy, told me many years ago that when he managed to come close to some ectoplasm it 'smelt like B.O.' By no means a sceptic, Professor Roy added, 'Which wasn't surprising, because of where it was kept . . .'[102]

Most known ectoplasm turned out to be nothing more than lengths of cheesecloth, regurgitated, or expelled from other orifices, which says more for the mediums' powers of muscle control than for evidence of the afterlife. However, some photographs of alleged ectoplasm show some other kind of substance – unknown or at least unidentified – at work as a moving and growing hand or face. It seems quite horrible and proves nothing, certainly not the existence of an afterlife, but it could just as easily be paranormal as suspiciously normal.

In the case of Eusapia Palladino, her ectoplasm turned itself into useful rods and levers, known as 'pseudopods', which were seen under conditions of infra-red photography, to raise objects and tilt tables. (And significantly, not even Herbert Thurston suggested that these were real rods and levers, somehow secreted about the medium's person.)

At many of Eusapia's séances, humanoid phantoms materialized, apparently created out of ectoplasm, and *were* seen and felt by investigators. Professor Morselli and fellow researchers witnessed an astonishing example of this on 1 March 1902 in Genoa. The professor examined the medium closely for smuggled aids, then tied her to a camp bed very thoroughly. She remained tied up although in 'fairly good light' six ghostly figures appeared.

Professor Charles Richet, a world-renowned physiologist and Nobel Laureate joined in the general endorsement of her gifts, saying: 'More than 30 very sceptical scientific men were convinced, after long testing, that there proceeded from her body material forms having the appearance of life.'[103] Dr Joseph Venzano would agree: at a séance he held on 16 June 1901, several ghostly hands materialized and stroked the dumbfounded sitters. Then the disembodied hands took hold of Venzano's:

When my hand, guided by another hand, and lifted upwards, met the materialized form, I had immediately the impression of touching a broad forehead, on the upper part of which was a quantity of rather long, thick, and very fine hair. Then, as my hand was gradually led upwards, it came in contact with a slightly aquiline nose, and, lower still, with moustaches and a chin with a peaked beard.

From the chin, the hand was then raised somewhat, until, coming in front of the open mouth, it was gently pushed forward, and my forefinger, still directed by the guiding hand, entered the cavity of the mouth, where it was caused to rub against the margin of the upper dental arch, which, towards the right extremity, was wanting in four molar teeth.[104]

The astounded Dr Venzano recognized the face he had just felt as that of a deceased relative. Unsure of which teeth the man had missing, he checked his dental records – and discovered they were four molars . . .

However, it was only in Italy that Eusapia continued to be praised. After her exposure as a cheat in the US, her fate was sealed in the Anglo-Saxon world. She died in 1918, an enigma to the end, her apparent triumphs still debated today. But despite her cheating and the weirdness of her phenomena, Eusapia represented what may be seen as a typical Luciferan raft of miracle: always ambiguous, equivocal, perhaps shifting rapidly from positive to negative and back again. Professor Richet wrote tellingly:

. . . we are now dealing with observed facts which are nevertheless absurd; which are in contradiction with facts of daily observation; which are denied not by science only, but by the whole of humanity – facts which are rapid and fugitive, which take place in semi-darkness, and almost by surprise; with no proof except the testimony of our senses, which we know to be often fallible. After we have witnessed such facts, everything concurs to make us doubt them. Now, at the moment when these facts take place they seem to us certain, and we are willing to proclaim them openly; but when we return to ourself, when we feel the irresistible influence of our environment, when our friends all laugh at our credulity – then we are most disarmed, and we begin to doubt.[105] May it not all have been an illusion? May I not have been grossly deceived? . . . And then, as the moment of the experiment becomes more remote, that experiment which once seemed so conclusive gets to seem more and more uncertain, and we end by letting ourselves be persuaded that we have been the victims of a trick.[106]

It may be apt at this point to quote Dr Margaret Mead, who declared to the American Association for the Advancement of Science: 'The whole history of scientific advancement is full of scientists investigating phenomena the Establishment did not believe were there.'[107]

To dare to boldly go where man has never even considered being is the mark of the fearless Luciferan, seeker and maker, quester in both triumph and despair. And with the coming of the Enlightenment, a new kind of mage arose and courageously saluted God – but this time made in his own image.

CHAPTER SIX

Do What Thou Wilt

As the West crawled towards the Age of Enlightenment, when the likes of Locke, Voltaire, Newton and Hume's secular religion of rationalism began to draw hearts and minds on its often precarious journey away from the medieval mindset, a wave of both Luciferan invention and discovery and quasi-Satanic decadence was unleashed – although, as Colin Wilson points out, the eighteenth century boasted little actual magic.[1] It was as if, after all those years in the iron grip of the ecclesiastical authorities a dam had broken, and the energy released had to find its own level quickly, be it in the form of exciting new discoveries in chemistry or medicine, or the grim trappings of an orgiastic *faux* Black Mass. Yet the Dark Ages of clerical oppression were not over: the Inquisition still had the power to torture and kill, and 'witches' were still being condemned by both the Catholic and Protestant ignorant – on both sides of the Atlantic.

In Salem,[2] Massachusetts, for one year beginning in 1692 a terrible contagion of witch hysteria swept not one, but twenty-three communities, ending with 141 people arrested – including a four-year-old child who was clapped in irons – nineteen hanged, one legally crushed to death and many more traumatized and robbed of their health, peace of mind and property.

The craziness allegedly began when the Reverend Samuel Parris' slave Tituba instructed his ten- and eleven-year old daughters about voodoo, although that may well be a convenient excuse. In any case, the girls began to convulse and act in ways that could 'only' mean demonic possession – and that, in turn, could only mean terrible news for their community.

As the girls' accusations spread to other localities and the tragic harvest of their hysteria began to fill the jails, one of the accused, John Proctor, wrote a beseeching letter to the authorities, including the now-legendary witch-finder Cotton Mather, from Salem Prison on 23 July, 1692:

The innocency of our Case with the Enmity of our Accusers and our Judges, and Jury, whom nothing but our Innocent blood will serve their turn, having Condemned us already before our Tryals, being so much more incensed and engaged against us by the Devil, makes us bold to Beg and Implore your Favourable Assistance of this our Humble Petition to his Excellency, That if it be possible our Innocent Blood may be spared, which undoubtedly otherwise will be shed, if the Lord doth not mercifully step in. The Magistrates, Ministers, Jewries, and all the People in general, being so much inraged and incensed against us by the Delusion of the Devil, which we can term no other, by reason we know in our own Consciences, we are all Innocent Persons. Here are five Persons who have lately confessed themselves to be witches, and do accuse some of us, of being along with them at a Sacrament [witches' Sabbat], since we were committed into close Prison, which we know to be Lies. Two of the 65 are (Carriers Sons) Youngmen, who would not confess any thing till they tyed them Neck and Heels till the Blood was ready to come out of their Noses, and 'tis credibly believed and reported this was the occasion of making them confess that they never did, by reason they said one had been a Witch a Month, another Five Weeks, and that their Mother had made them so, who had been confined here this nine Weeks. My son William Proctor, when he was examin'd, because he would not confess that he was Guilty, when he was Innocent, they tyed him Neck and Heels till the Blood gushed out of his Nose, and would have kept him so 24 hours, if one more Merciful than the rest, had not taken pity on him, and caused him to be unbound. These actions are very like the Popish Cruelties. They have already undone us in our Estates [seized money and property of the accused], and that will not serve their turns, without our Innocent Bloods. If it cannot be granted that we can have our trials at Boston, we humbly beg that you would endeavour to have these Magistrates changed . . . and begging also and beseeching you would be pleased to be here, if not all, some of you at our Trials, hoping thereby you may be the means of saving the shedding [of] our Innocent Bloods, desiring your prayers to the Lord in our behalf, we rest your Poor Afflicted Servants,

JOHN PROCTOR ETC.[3]

Note that Proctor describes the local people as being 'incensed against us by delusion of the Devil', the complete reversal of how the accusers understood the situation: as experience took its dreadful toll, like all innocent 'witches' Satan was embodied by those who accused them of worshipping him. And, speaking to a solid Puritan audience, Proctor also points out – with total justification – that 'these actions are very like the Popish cruelties'.

Cruelty is no respecter of religion once the Devil is let in to rampage throughout a community via a fundamentalist belief in him, tempered by not a shred of humour, individual conscience or intelligence. Lucifer is not to be found in Salem – but once the Devil has been conjured, he is free to take over minds. And then humans go into swarm mode.

Although Proctor's petition caused the authorities to reconsider their criteria for dealing with 'witches', it came too late for him and his fellow prisoners, who were hanged.

Montague Summers notes that while the godly Salem residents fasted, the witches were supposed to have indulged in 'a Sacrament that day at a house in the Village, and that they had *Red Bread* and *Red Drink*.'[4] He adds: 'This "Red Bread" is certainly puzzling'[5] – but not if seen as the desperate invention of an accused witch eager to placate the authorities with ever more fanciful accounts of satanic goings-on. Summers also asserts that the Rev. George Burroughs, accused by eight witches of 'being an Head Actor at some of their Hellish Rendezvouses' 'certainly officiated at their ceremonies',[6] for several of the residents testified to seeing him do so. By that time, however, sworn testimony, had come to be utterly worthless.

Tellingly, as the hysteria spiralled out of control, the girls' power craze meant they finally overstepped themselves and accused the governor's wife of witchcraft – an unwise move. When writs were issued for slander, the girls fled. Their 'possession' was miraculously over.

Lessons about persecution and injustice were not well learnt: the succeeding centuries saw countless lynchings of poor blacks,[7] while America in the twentieth century suffered the McCarthyite anti-Communist 'witch-hunts' and the later epidemic of accusations of satanic ritual abuse, mainly by fundamentalist Christian social workers. Arthur Miller's classic play *The Crucible* (1953), while outwardly about the Salem witch hysteria, is in fact an allegory for the McCarthyite House Committee on Un-American Activities.[8]

We have seen what a similar hysteria – mass craziness – did to Europe as the Inquisitors' eagerness to exterminate witches wiped out whole communities, especially in France and Germany. However, the Devil need not be invoked as such: Hitler persuaded most ordinary German citizens that all Jews were evil and that any indignity and horror could be inflicted on them because they were *not human*. Yet lesser-known contagions are often more instructive about the extraordinary capacity decent folk have for being blinded – almost literally – by an *idea* that provokes hysteria.

During the Second World War bomb-maddened and half-starved British folk often turned on any strangers in the neighbourhood, believing them to be Nazi spies, with a viciousness that their decent pre-war selves would never have believed possible. Occasionally, however, a kind of madness overrode even their persecution of strangers: on one occasion in remote East Anglia, the mob turned on a man who far from being a new face in the area was actually *one of them*, a neighbour known well to them all. Happening to be out on a Home Guard patrol, he was seized, roughed up, and, despite his desperate and bewildered protestation that he was their long-time neighbour, shot dead. He had spoken to the crowd, reminded them of his identity, and even shown them his papers, but they were so possessed by bloodlust that they literally could not see him as he was. The next day when the red rage had ebbed away, the people were stunned by the fact of a very familiar but very dead man, and the bewildered grief of his traumatized family. No one had any way of explaining what had happened.[9]

His satanic majesty

The last major fling of the English witch-hunters took place in the seventeenth century, as Elizabeth I's successor, James I (1566–1625)[10] spread his own fear – amounting to a phobia – of witches through a land already raw with religious division, plotting and paranoia. His predecessor, while mouthing platitudes about individual consciences, had made it impossible for Catholics to worship legally in her kingdom, and resentment grew among them exponentially. Known as 'the wisest fool in Christendom' (although even that remarkably back-handed compliment is debatable), James had survived the Gunpowder Plot of 1605 when he and his Parliament were targeted by a group of Catholic fanatics, which merely added fuel to the fires of religious intolerance and a heightened atmosphere of suspicion.

Even before Guy Fawkes and his co-religionists attempted to blow up the Houses of Parliament,[11] James had published his *Daemonologie* (1597), providing zealous witch-hunters with plentiful ammunition. In the book, the narrator Epistemon explains what categories of 'unlawful charms, without natural causes' are to be considered witchcraft:

> I mean by such kind of charms as commonly daft wives use, for healing of forspoken [bewitched] goods, for preserving them from evil eyes, by knitting . . . sundry kinds of herbs to the hair of the goods; by curing the worm, by stemming the blood, by healing of horse-crooks . . . or doing such like innumerable things by words, without applying anything meet to the part offended, as mediciners do.

This was a licence to persecute herbalists and traditional healers – be they efficacious or basically harmless, continuing the ancient traditions of folklore. Even if the healer's aim was only to do good, it was still witchcraft. (Many fundamentalist Christians take much the same view about healers today – unless they are of the same persuasion.) Yet what were the poor folk to do in an age when toothache could kill and 'official' medicine was not only often worse than useless but also expensive, and the local wise woman with her mysterious jars of herbs might just provide some relief?

Under James, witches were everywhere, like the later 'Reds under the bed' hysteria of twentieth-century America. The king himself took an active interest in the major cases, even participating in a number of the trials. Not surprisingly with this unofficial royal warrant, the courts were soon full of wall-eyed, deformed and senile old women on their way to the gallows.

In Scotland, the witch mania saw women at Forres bent double into barrels filled with tar, rolled down Cluny Hill and set alight at the bottom. This would have particularly satisfied James, who was convinced he had been cursed by witches during a visit to Forres in 1600. Having fallen ill while in the neighbourhood he had the area searched: a coven was found in the very act of melting a wax image of the monarch. (Somewhat suspiciously perfect timing.) They were tried and rolled down the hill to their deaths. Of course it is perfectly possible that people were trying to kill James with any means at their disposal – including the 'sympathetic magic' of stabbing his image – but whether or not that made them witches or merely desperate to get rid of him must remain open to question.

As his reign progressed, James abandoned his belief in the supernatural abilities of witches, but persisted in seeing them as anti-social elements with subversive potential. Ordinary folk were slower to strip witches of their powers. For, as H. T. F. Rhodes notes in his *The Satanic Mass* (1954):

Witchcraft was not thought less a social and theological danger with the change of religion in Europe [i.e. from Catholic to Protestant]. It is a singular fact that opinions and beliefs concerning it became even less critical.[12]

The Jacobean playwright and cleric Thomas Heywood described in his *Hierarchie of the Blessed Angels* (1635)

ceremonies of the Sabbat where in the worshippers renounce Faith, Baptism and Eucharist, acknowledge Lucifer, and worship him with "contrarie" rites and ceremonies. To this he adds an original piece of embroiderie of his own by reporting that the witches worship their God standing upon their heads.[13]

The contemporary Duke of Newcastle echoed the contradictory nature of the general attitude to witches in a conversation recorded by his servant Hobbes:

> To which my Lord answered, That though for his part he cared not whether there were witches or no; yet his opinion was That the Confession of Witches, and their sufferings for it proceeded from an erroneous belief, viz, That they had made a contract with the Devil to serve him for such Rewards as were in his power to give them; and that it was their Religion to worship and adore him; in which Religion they had such firm and constant belief, that if anything came to pass according to their desire, they believed the Devil had heard their prayers, and granted their requests, for which they gave him thanks; but if things fell out contrary to their prayers and desires, then they were troubled at it, fearing that they had offended him, and not served him as they ought, and asked for forgiveness of their offences. Also (said my Lord) they imagine their dreams are real exterior actions; for example, if they dream they flye in the Air, or out of the Chimney top, or that they are turned into several shapes, they believe no otherwise, but that it is really so. And this wicked opinion makes them industrious to perform such Ceremonies to the Devil that they may worship him as their God, and chuse to live and dye with him.[14]

Hobbes may pour scorn on the poor deluded Devil-worshippers who thanked their god if things went right for them but were troubled and wondered how they offended him if matters took a bad turn, but it could equally be an accurate description about how many Christians actually view their own relationship with God, even today.

'Satan in the suburbs'

If the coming age of the true Lucifer means the western world was flooded with light, then – apart from the usual horrors of war and pestilence – there must have been attempts to harness and celebrate the opposite, the mentally and spiritually befogging darkness of Satan. While it is true that the Inquisition continued its satanic depredations on freedom of thought and spirit, there were those who sought to enter into a more immediate and intimate relationship with the Lord of Hell.

Of course, as we have seen, both the Cathars and the Knights Templar had been accused of being Satanists, but as the centuries progressed groups and individuals emerged from the shadows whose entire *raison d'être* was not merely to indulge in what outsiders would consider dubious and weird rites, but explicitly to worship the Evil One. Many of these Satanists were claimed by one writer to have been priests – some defrocked – but a high proportion simply worked secretly for the opposition.

One of the commonest of their dark rituals was the parodying of the Mass, with the intention of destroying a living person. As H. C. Lea noted in *Materials Towards A History of Witchcraft* (1939):

> Wicked priests employed the mass as an incantation and execration mentally cursing their enemies while engaged in its solemnization, and expecting that in some way the malediction would work evil on the person against whom it was directed. Nay, it was even used in conjunction with the immemorial superstition of the wax figurine which represented the enemy to be destroyed, and mass celebrated ten times over such an image was supposed to ensure his death within ten days.[15]

Despite the evidence of repeated experience, Devil-worshippers were seen as richer, healthier and happier than Christians, and this myth may have fostered the occasional outbreak of somewhat pathetic half-hearted Satanism. In his *Tableau de L'Inconstance des mauvais Anges* (1613), Pierre de L'Ancre – admittedly a Catholic bigot – declares unequivocally '*La plus grande partie des Prestres sont Sorciers*' ('The majority of priests are sorcerers'.)[16] He also believed that it was poverty that drove them to the Black Arts, although boredom and sexual frustration may well have been important factors, as we saw in the case of flamboyant possession in the religious houses.

As ever, secret societies or at least groups operating under conditions of secrecy are inevitably accused of wild orgies of the most ingeniously perverted kind imaginable. And just as inevitably, especially where Satanism is concerned, some of those rumours will be true. Indeed, the Black Mass as we know it today was invented – admittedly a somewhat dubious honour – by the seventeenth-century alchemist, abortionist and poisoner, Catherine La Voisin, who studded it with sexual sacrileges.

Montague Summers describes the diabolical activities at La Voisin's Paris home[17] (although his credulity and callousness make him hard to read and even harder to like, his scholarship is not always questionable):

It was in 1666 . . . [that] night after night . . . at the house of the mysterious Catherine la Voisin the abbé Guibourg was wont to kill young children for his hideous ritual, either by strangulation or more often by piercing their throats with a sharp dagger and letting the hot blood stream into the chalice as he cried: "Astaroth, Asmodée, je vous conjure d'accepter le sacrifice que je vous présente!" (Astaroth! Asmodeus! Receive, I beseech you, this sacrifice I offer unto you!) A priest named Tournet also said Satanic Masses at which children were immolated . . .[18]

(Poor Asherath – 'Astaroth' – has fallen a long way since her days as consort of God.)

For once, it seems that La Voisin and her confederates did use dead babies in their satanic rites, although they may not have been murdered specially. Apart from doing a brisk trade in harmless stuff such as cosmetics and love philtres, she branched out into a highly lucrative sideline as abortionist, once again underlining the connection – this time almost certainly real – between diabolism and abortion. From there for this highly ambitious and ruthless woman it was but a short step to providing poison for wives who urgently wished to be widows, together with all the evocative paraphenalia of Devil-worship.

La Voisin's expertise was called upon by the cream of Parisian society – even Madame de Montespan, one of King Louis XIV's mistresses, who desired to be raised to what she considered her rightful place as his consort. When La Voisin was arrested and horribly tortured, a veritable Satanic network was revealed of at least 246 people of high social standing, many of whom thought it prudent to suffer voluntary exile, while others of their class were jailed. Thirty-six of the 'lower orders' were executed. Incriminating pages were removed from the archives, and the king forbade any mention of Madame de Montespan in connection with the scandal, although it did her little good: after the death of the queen in 1683, Louis took the good Catholic Madame de Maintenon as his wife.[19]

Child-killing in the name of Satan had become something of a cliché in France – which, for some reason, seems to have had more than its fair share of Satanists in the past, although now the United States is catching up rapidly. Perhaps it is France's long history as the heartland of heresy[20] that provided such fertile soil: the heretics perhaps coming to believe their own bad publicity, with a Gallic shrug accepting their fate as 'natural' Satanists.

Perhaps the most shocking satanic individual of medieval times was another Frenchman, Joan of Arc's marshal, Gilles de Laval, Maréchal and Baron de Rais,[21] a sexual pervert who derived ecstatic pleasure from the torture and butchery of children. In 1440 he was accused of the abduction and murder of 140 named children, but some estimate the number as high as 800. However, he was not always criminally insane, or if he was he hid it well: as a young man he had been remarkable for his absolute piety and generosity towards the Church.

At just twenty-four years old he was a national hero, due to his heroic exploits at the side of La Pucelle ('The Maid', or Joan of Arc); later he became Maréchal (Marshal) of France. After Joan's burning as a witch and the end of his martial exploits, Gilles retired to his country estates – and began his life as a serial sex murderer.

A homosexual, Gilles would lure a handsome lad into his castle, hang him by his heels, but before he lost consciousness he would be taken down and reassured. Nothing horrible was really going to happen: it was all just a game. This was pure sadism, for then the bewildered boy would be violently raped, after which Gilles or one of his henchmen would cut his throat or slice off his head. The corpse continued to exert an irresistible allure, however, and Gilles piled necrophilia on to the horrors he had inflicted on the living boy, by slitting open the stomach and sitting among the intestines to masturbate. He also indulged in variations on this theme, for example procuring two boys, one of whom had to watch the other being tortured and killed while waiting his turn.

Gilles' intense bouts of sadism were like an attack of madness: he would collapse after each individual abomination and not regain consciousness for many hours. His fellow monsters meanwhile would cut up the corpses and burn them. However, they were not always very thorough, and it was their laxity that brought disaster to Gilles' insane bloodlust.

Having recklessly overspent, Gilles was desperate for money, and alchemy seemed like a promising solution, even though it was illegal. A magician named François Prelati impressed upon him that the only way to make alchemical gold was by selling his soul to the Devil, which he always refused to do, but had no scruples when told that in any case he must sacrifice boys in order to stand a chance of benefiting from the magical gold. Their rituals were often distinguished by violence both within and without the protective circle from invisible forces, and once by the hallucination of a monstrous green snake.

By 1440 the local authorities and the Inquisition had a list of forty-seven charges against Gilles (the indictment was forty-nine paragraphs long), including conjuration of spirits, heresy and sexual perversions against children – and human sacrifice to demons. Although he himself was not tortured, presumably because of his high status, his servants were 'put to the Question', but not one of his 500 attendants were required to give evidence in court. Gilles was not allowed to defend himself nor employ counsel. Begging for forgiveness and asking for the prayers of the onlookers – who openly wept at his plight – he was strangled and his body burnt. His two associates were burnt alive. The Church became phenomenally wealthy after seizing his land and property.

The terrible blood-spree of Gilles de Rais forms a grim background to J. K. Huysmans' *Là Bas* (*Down There*, 1891),[22] which discursively tells the story of a vampiristic sexual relationship in contemporary Paris, but which is famed for its apparently authentic description of a black mass. In his *tour de force*, *The Occult*, Colin Wilson writes of the critical scene:

The altar boys are ageing poufs, covered with cosmetics. The chapel is dingy and damp, with cracked walls. The face of Christ on the cross is painted so that it laughs derisively. [The] Canon . . . pours out . . . invective on the Crucified: 'Thou hast forgotten the poverty thou didst preach, thou hast seen the weak crushed . . . thou hast heard the death rattle of the timid . . .' The women then begin to have convulsions in the manner of the Loudun nuns. One of the aged choir boys performs an act of fellatio on [Canon Docre, who] ejaculates on the host and tosses it to the convulsed women; he also apparently defecates on the altar. Huysmans' language is not explicit, but ordure obviously plays a central part in the mass.[23]

Wilson sagely notes that uppermost in the black mass is the 'desire of the participants to *shock themselves* out of their normal state of dullness.'[24] Yet even so, their activities never reach beyond a puerile attempt to upset bourgeois sensibilities – with their emphasis on undoing all the accepted ideals of cleanliness – and, of course, an equally childish attack on the Church. As Colin Wilson says: 'The "blasphemies" sound completely harmless to anyone who is not a Catholic and who does not accept that disbelief in the divinity of Christ involves eternal damnation.'[25] This sort of back-street Satanism was described perfectly by the twentieth-century British philosopher Bertrand Russell as 'Satan in the suburbs'.

One of the most intriguing of the French 'Satanists' was Eugène Vintras (1807–75), who established his Church of Carmel – also known as the Oeuvre de la Miséricorde (Work of Mercy), in the early 1840s. Clearly a charismatic figure, Vintras appealed to high society, but soon his movement was accused of Satanism, largely because his rites were highly sexual in nature. Worse, Vintras was embroiled in a massive political scandal centred on Charles Guillaume Naundorff (1785–1845), who claimed to be the 'lost' King Louis XVII, believed by most to have died during or shortly after the French Revolution in the 1790s. Naundorff and Vintras publicly backed each other, the latter ending up in what was clearly a show trial accused of fraud. After five years in jail, Vintras fled to London, as France was rapidly becoming too hot to hold him. A former member of his Church of Carmel, one Father Gozzoli published a pamphlet accusing him of organizing the most debauched orgies imaginable – and Gozzoli seems to have possessed a particularly lurid imagination. In 1848 the sect was declared heretical by the Pope and all its members excommunicated, whereupon they established themselves as a totally independent entity, with both male and female priests, rather like the Cathars.

What is especially interesting is that both Vintras' Church of Carmel and the Naundorff supporters were a shadowy sect called 'the Saviours of Louis XVII' – otherwise known as the *Johannites*. A complex and elusive group, they were primarily concerned with the restoration of the monarchy in France, although they supported less obvious individuals and causes. These particular Johannites appear somehow to have 'stage-managed' visions of the Virgin at La Salette in 1846, probably as part of a wider campaign to elevate the Feminine, first by emphasizing the role of Mary the Mother, then through more overtly sexual means and active hostility to the Church. Vintras' own link with the Johannites was through the evocatively named 'Sister Salome' (Madame Bouche), but on his death the Order passed to the keeping of the scandalous Abbé Joseph Boullan (1824–93), who had set up the Society for the Reparation of Souls in 1859 with the much younger Adèle Chevalier, whom he had seduced at the convent at La Salette. Matters escalated from highly controversial to outright shocking when Boullan extended his sex rites to the animal kingdom, and rumours spread like wildfire that he and Chevalier had sacrificed their own child during a Black Mass in 1860: interestingly, neither was even arrested for such an offence, although they were convicted of fraud.

The plot thickens, however. After serving a custodial sentence, Boullan of his own volition presented himself to the Inquisition in Rome, but even they could find no fault in him. He was free to return to Paris,[26] where he threw himself into leading Vintras' Church of Carmel into ever increasing scenes of wild sexual licence, first declaring himself to be the reincarnation of John the Baptist. This may have inspired his portrayal as 'Dr Johannes' in Huysmans' *Là Bas* – also one of Boullan's aliases – although it would be quite wrong to assume that he was the villain of the piece. In fact, he was a friend of Huysmans who depicted him as a crusader *against* Satanism, though much maligned by the Church. But to this day there are major questions to be answered about Boullan. As we wrote in *The Templar Revelation*:

> While in Rome Boullan wrote his doctrines down in a notebook (known as the *cahier rose*, overtly after the colour of the cover), which was found by . . . Huysmans among his papers after his death in 1893. The precise details of the contents are unknown – though it was described as a 'shocking document' – and it is now locked away in the Vatican Library. All applications to see it are refused.[27]

Was Boullan actually a sort of *agent provocateur* for the Vatican, infiltrating a heretical group in order to undermine it? Certainly it is very odd that, despite all the melodramatic and salacious rumours, he was only convicted for fraud and the Inquisition could find no fault with him. But if not a Vatican agent, perhaps he knew some great secret that he could wield as blackmail even against the might of Peter's Church. Perhaps it was connected with what may well have been the *real* John the Baptist, and the sex rites of the original Christians, including Jesus and the Magdalene . . . To most ordinary Christians, that would seem like Satanism.

Orgies in the caves

Secret and semi-secret societies mushroomed in the eighteenth and nineteenth centuries, perhaps inspired by the new wave of Romanticism, revolutionary politics or the radical thinking that would produce embryonic trades unions, but they were more likely to concentrate on drinking and leching, with a hefty pinch of pseudo-Satanism thrown in for added spice. In England, the most famous of these clubs for the terminally bored was the Order of the Friars of Wycombe, or The Monks of Medmenham, the Order of the Knights of West Wycombe, or – most famously but inaccurately – the Hellfire Club.

It was founded by Sir Francis Dashwood (1708–81), a well-established MP and former Treasurer to George III and Postmaster General: the epitome of the successful English gentleman. On the obligatory Grand Tour of Italy, he had come to hate the Catholic

Church and, having met the legendary 'Bonnie Prince Ch[...] exiled Prince Charles Edward Stuart – he was enrolled as a Jacob[...] agent. He went on to become involved in various Rosicrucian, neo-Templar and Masonic Lodges. In 1738 Pope Clement XII had prohibited Freemasonry and excommunicated all the Italian brotherhood on pain of being handed over to the Inquisition, but Dashwood remained in contact with the Italian lodges. As a young traveller through France he had been an observer at a Black Mass, which intrigued him, but only at the more puerile level of insulting the Church.

Back in England he founded the Society of the Dilettanti, one of the many London clubs devoted to phenomenal alcohol consumption and whoring. In 1746 he founded the Order of the Knights of Saint Francis, which met at the sixteenth-century George and Vulture pub in the City of London, made famous in Charles Dickens' riotous first novel, *Pickwick Papers* (1836–7). They met in an upper room, the focus of which was 'an everlasting Rosicrucian lamp', a massive crystal globe surrounded by a gold snake with its tail in its mouth, and topped by silver wings – a profoundly Gnostic design, which also appeared on the font Dashwood later presented to West Wycombe Church.

It was close to West Wycombe in Buckinghamshire that Dashwood and his cronies established their infamous 'Hellfire Club', at Medmenham Abbey on the River Thames near Marlow in 1751. Dashwood lavishly renovated the former medieval monastery – no expense was spared – complete with the now infamous motto carved over the entrance 'Do as thou will'. The temple to hedonism was complete with a priapic statue and a voluptuous statue of Venus in the well-tended gardens. As she was bending over, a clumsy newcomer would find himself already in a compromising position before he had even entered the house.

Two ancient deities of Silence – the Egyptian Harpocrates and the Roman goddess Angerona – adorned the Abbey's sumptuous dining room, perhaps as a reminder to the Order's members never to speak of the goings-on there in the outside world. Pagan gods were everywhere in Dashwood's life: one whole wing of his house, designed by Robert Adam, was a replica of a Temple to Bacchus, while Ariadne, Dionysus and a whole host of cavorting satyrs frolicked over the ceiling. Statues of other ancient deities graced the gardens, which some said were laid out in the rather graphic shape of a naked woman.

In 1750 Dashwood enlarged the honeycomb of tunnels and caves under West Wycombe Hill in which to hold the Order's meetings, although word spread that they took the form of orgiastic couplings. As occult writer and Dashwood expert Mike Howard explains:

These caves featured individual 'cells' for the 'monks' to enter-tain their female guests . . . An underground stream, known to the monks as the River Styx had to be crossed to give access to the Inner Sanctum, a circular room where so-called "Black Masses" were said to be performed.[28]

Heavily made-up prostitutes from London were delivered by the carriage-load to act as officiating masked 'nuns', while high-born ladies offered their naked bodies as altars for the Black Mass. Most people would dismiss the activities of Dashwood's circle as a fairly unimaginative attempt to stave off *ennui* by indulging in a little light whoring and blasphemy in excitingly spooky surroundings. However, there appears to be more to it than that. One of the leading 'Friars' was John Wilkes, who declared: 'No profane eye has dared to penetrate the English Eleusinian Mysteries of the Chapter Room [the inner sanctum] where the monks assembled on solemn occasions . . . secret rites performed and libations to the *Bona Dea* [the Good Goddess].'[29] While many, if not most, of the Medmenham 'monks' – whose number included some extremely well-known names, such as the Prince of Wales and possibly even the American statesman and scientist Benjamin Franklin (1706–90) – probably enjoyed their naughty caperings at an adolescent level, some clearly observed them in a more ancient spirit. It is significant that the so-called 'Hellfire Caves' dated back to prehistoric times, known locally as 'pagan catacombs', with an altar to an unknown deity nearby. Mike Howard concludes:

As one nineteenth-century writer put it, 'Sir Francis himself officiated as high priest . . . engaged in pouring a libation from a communion cup to the mysterious object of their homage.' From the available evidence, it is safe to surmise that this 'mysterious object of their homage' was, in fact, the Goddess and that Sir Francis Dashwood and his merry monks were not Satanists but followers of the pagan Mysteries.[30]

However, the enactment of the Black Mass – if indeed it were anything more than rumour – suggests not only a reverence for the ancient gods of fertility and sensual indulgence, but also an active detestation and mockery of Christianity. When Dashwood paid for the renovations of his local church, the result was 'an Egyptian hall' that gave 'not the least idea of a place sacred to religious [i.e. Christian] worship'.[31]

However, once again, we find what was basically a Luciferan outbreak of orgiastic high spirits and pagan joy in sexuality being deliberately contaminated with *faux* Satanism. Perhaps rumours of the Black Mass were encouraged simply to keep away prying eyes, but it seems that some did indulge in that tasteless and ultimately pointless activity. Did they, perhaps, like some Knights Templar, Johannites and other Luciferans believe in their heart of hearts that they were indeed as evil as they stood accused? Christianity was, and to some extent still is, a most potent form of conditioning, and to subvert its teachings is for many brought up in the faith a very grave step, no matter how loud and brittle their pseudo-Luciferan bravado.

Last of the magicians
As the Enlightenment took hold of hearts and minds, science progressed by leaps and bounds, aided not only by a new secular freedom but by the astonishingly under-estimated mass drug of choice – caffeine. Tea, coffee and chocolate poured into the coffee shops and homes of the West, kick-starting a whole new level of energy and enquiry. Foremost among that blossoming of exciting new talent was, of course, Isaac Newton, who came second in a recent survey of the world's most influential people – after Mohammed (1) but before Jesus Christ (3).[32] He is seen as the epitome of the no-nonsense rationalist, the atheistic scientist *par excellence*, but – as with Leonardo – nothing could be further from the truth.

At the end of the entry on Newton in *Chambers' Biographical Dictionary* (1990), very much as an apologetic afterthought, there is a passage of just three-and-a-half lines about his religious and esoteric interests, beginning: 'Newton was also a student of alchemy . . .'[33] He was indeed: as the economist John Maynard Keynes remarked after reading Newton's previously lost notebooks (which were 'of no scientific value'): 'Newton was not the first of the age of reason. He was the last of the magicians.'[34]

Born in 1642, Newton was to write over a million words on the subject of alchemy, although the Royal Society declared they were 'not fit to be printed'. He is most famous for his discovery of the Law of Gravity in 1665 or 1666, the fall of an apple in his garden suggesting the earth's irresistible pull.

In his specially constructed laboratory on the edge of the fens near Cambridge, Newton obsessively studied the construction of telescopes and the refraction of light through prisms, which led him to build reflecting telescopes, although they were to be considerably refined by William Hershel (1738–1822) and the Earl of Rosse (1800–67).[35] In the near-literal sense of the word, Newton was a true Luciferan, for he believed that light – his lifelong fascination – embodied the word of God, echoing the obsession of the Gnostics and esotericists with Light as both metaphor and actuality.

One of Newton's servants recorded:

> He very rarely went to bed until two or three of the clock, sometimes not till five or six, lying about four or five hours, especially at springtime or autumn, at which time he used to employ about six weeks in his laboratory, the fire [furnace] scarce going out night or day. What his aim might be I was unable to penetrate to.[36]

From his writings, we now know he was striving to create the Philosopher's Stone that would convert base metals into gold. Perhaps it was this unusual hobby that prompted him to accept the occupation as Director of the Royal Mint, with the responsibility of looking after England's store of gold, instead of accepting a Cambridge professorship.

An eccentric scientist to his fingertips, Newton is said to have only laughed once in his life – when he was asked what use he saw in Euclid. He nearly ruined his eyesight by sticking a knife behind his eyeball to induce optical effects. A tortured and introverted homosexual, his only romantic involvements appear to have been with younger men, one of whom induced a nervous breakdown. Obsessed with the apocalyptical interpretations of the Old Testament Book of Daniel, he wrote on the subject extensively, and as a vehemently anti-Catholic Puritan he saw himself as a kind of prophet. As F. E. Manuel writes in his *The Religion of Isaac Newton* (1974):

> The more Newton's theological and alchemical, chronological and mythological work, set by the side of his science, the more apparent it becomes that in the moments of his grandeur he saw himself as the last of the interpreters of God's will in actions, living on the fulfilment of times.[37]

Despite this, he was more heterodox than orthodox in his theology, subscribing to the Arian heresy, which upheld the theory that Jesus was not divine. But it was his passion for alchemy that primarily drove him. As Michael White notes in his Isaac Newton: *The Last Sorcerer* (1997):

> Newton was motivated by a deep-rooted commitment to the notion that alchemical wisdom extended back to ancient times. The Hermetic tradition – the body of alchemical knowledge – was believed to have originated in the mists of time and to have been given to humanity through supernatural agents.[38]

That body of esoteric knowledge was known as the *Emerald Tablet*, and its guardian was the legendary Hermes Trismegistus, inspiration throughout the ages to the likes of Nicholas Flamel and, one assumes, Leonardo da Vinci. Isaac Newton translated the Tablet:

> It is true without lying, certain and most true. That which is Below is like that which is Above and that which is Above is like that which is Below to do the miracles of the Only Thing. And as

all things have been and arose from One by the mediation of One, so all things have their birth from this One Thing by adaptation. The Sun is its father; the Moon its mother; the Wind hath carried it in its belly; the Earth is its nurse. The father of all perfection in the whole world is here. Its force or power is entire if it be converted into Earth. Separate the Earth from the Fire, the subtle from the gross, sweetly with great industry. It ascends from the Earth to the Heavens and again it descends to the Earth and receives the force of things superior and inferior. By this means you shall have the glory of the whole world and thereby all obscurity shall fly from you. Its force is above all force, for it vanquishes every subtle thing and penetrates every solid thing. So was the world created. From this are and do come admirable adaptations, whereof the process is in this. Hence I am called Hermes Trismegistus, having the three parts of the philosophy of the whole world. That which I have said of the operation of Sun is accomplished and ended.[39]

It is easy to understand how even his short passage might obsess and even madden generations of seekers after alchemical truth. Newton cautioned fellow alchemist-scientist Robert Boyle (1627–91) against letting the uninitiated into their secret hot-house world 'if there be any verity in the warning of the Hermetic writers. There are other things besides the transmutation of metals which none but they understand'.[40]

Some authorities[41] suggest Newton (who was knighted in 1705) may have actually achieved the fabled Great Work – after all, secrecy is no proof of failure, especially in such an intensely private discipline as alchemy. Look at how Leonardo triumphed behind closed doors, although his natural secretiveness did little to prevent the spread of rumours about his 'sorcery'.

However, in the case of the British scientist Andrew Crosse, such a reputation – and worse – was to cost him a very promising career and the prospect of being fêted throughout history as the discoverer of something very strange, perhaps even the creator of life itself . . .

One who, according to his second wife, 'delighted in whatever was strange and marvellous', Andrew Crosse was born in 1784 in the west of England and grew into a clever, questing young man.

Probably because his father knew Benjamin Franklin and Joseph Priestley, both pioneers of the new science of electricity, Crosse was fascinated by it from the age of twelve. After some wasted years as a typical 'lad-about-town', he settled down to experiments into electro-crystallization in partnership with George John Singer. But then in 1837 something happened that remains bewildering to this day, as Crosse explains:

> In the course of my endeavours to form artificial minerals by a long continued electric action on fluids holding in solution such substances as were necessary to my purpose, I had recourse to every variety of contrivance that I could think of; amongst others I constructed a wooden frame, which supported a Wedgwood funnel, within which rested a quart basin on a circular piece of mahogany. When this basin was filled with a fluid, a strip of flannel wetted with the same was suspended over the side of the basin and inside the funnel, which, acting like a syphon, conveyed the fluid out of the basin through the funnel in successive drops: these drops fell into a smaller funnel of glass placed beneath the other, and which contained a piece of somewhat porous red oxide iron from Vesuvius. This stone was kept constantly electrified ...
>
> On the fourteenth day from the commencement of this experiment I observed through a lens a few small whitish excrescences or nipples, projecting from about the middle of the electrified stone. On the eighteenth day these projections enlarged, and stuck out seven or eight filaments, each of them longer than the hemisphere on which they grew. On the twenty-sixth day these appearances assumed the form of a perfect insect, standing erect on a few bristles which formed its tail ... On the twenty-eight day these little creatures moved their legs ... After a few days they detached themselves from the stone, and moved about at pleasure.[42]

What on earth were the acari, or tiny mites? Further experiments only served to reinforce the mystery. Crosse recorded after the third attempt at replication:

> I had omitted to insert within the bulb of the retort a resting place for these acari (they are always destroyed if they fall back into

the fluid from which they have emerged). It is strange that, in a solution eminently caustic and under an atmosphere of oxihydrogen gas, one single acarus should have made its appearance.[43]

Strange indeed.

Having involved the steady and methodical W. H. Weeks to attempt to replicate the experiments – whose first concern was to ensure that no extraneous insect eggs fell into the equipment – matters were progressing well. But then Crosse made the mistake of discussing his discovery with the editor of a local newspaper, when all hell broke loose. Had this mad scientist actually created life in his secret laboratory? Who was this mere man to play God? Although eminent scientists such as Michael Faraday (1791–1867) went to some lengths to defend Crosse, Mr Weeks ruined it by solemnly announcing that the experiments had indeed 'given birth' to living creatures.

Bewildered and hurt, Crosse retired to his rural laboratory, only to find himself a social pariah: the local vicar even carried out an exorcism on the locality. Crosse's innocent and objective discovery had marked him out as a Mephistophelean dabbler in the Black Arts. Although he returned to his research – intending to construct 'a battery at once cheap, powerful and durable',[44] and worked on the preservation of food and the purification of sea water through the use of electricity – he remained a broken man, an object of ridicule and superstitious fear.

Before he died from a stroke in May 1855 he said: '. . . the utmost extent of human knowledge is but comparative ignorance'.[45] The inscription on his gravestone reads:

Sacred to the memory of
ANDREW CROSSE/THE ELECTRICIAN . . .
HE WAS HUMBLE TOWARDS GOD
AND KIND TO HIS FELLOW CREATURES

– perhaps a dig at those who thought him very arrogant towards God, and those who were less than kind to him.

To this day, no one is sure what the acari were, and Crosse is largely forgotten except in books about mysteries. But this true scientist may be remembered in much more sensational form: in 1814 the poet Robert Southey (1774–1843) visited his friends Mary and Percy Shelley after having discussed his experiments with Crosse himself. The three friends spent some hours on the subject. And the Shelleys attended a talk given by Crosse that same year. Four years later Mary Shelley (1797–1851) produced her first novel, *Frankenstein*, about an eccentric scientist who creates life in his laboratory through the use of electricity . . . Was this a particularly bizarre case of life following art, or a nasty attack of the Cosmic Joker? Although sceptics might claim Shelley's novel put the idea of creating life in Crosse's head, all the evidence suggests that his mystery was genuine. But in any case, his is the classic case of the Luciferan martyr, persecuted by the mindless mob for honestly investigating a scientific anomaly.

Sons of the Widow

On Saint John the Baptist's Day (24 June) 1717 the Grand Lodge of English Freemasonry was formed, taking what had been a truly secret society concerned with the preservation of sacred knowledge into a new semi-secret era that some might argue saw it degenerate into little more than a well-refreshed dining club.

An 'Invisible College' of Masons had existed in 1645,[46] but if as certain authors[47] claim, they were the rightful descendants of the Knights Templar, then obviously they possessed a much longer pedigree. Indeed, an alchemical treatise dating from the 1450s specifically uses the term 'Freemason',[48] and researcher John J. Robinson cites evidence of Masonic lodges as far back as the 1380s.[49] But as the seventeenth and eighteenth centuries passed, it became clear, according to one writer, Robert Lomas, that the Freemasons were at the forefront of a Luciferan explosion of unprecedented scientific invention and discovery and intellectual progress, with the formation of the Royal Society in 1660, 'the oldest and most respected scientific society in the world'.[50] Under the auspices of Freemason Sir Robert Moray, the aims of the Society were to be:

> To overcome the mysteries of all the works of Nature for the benefit of human life[51] . . . and this is the highest pitch of human

reason; to follow all the links of this chain, till all secrets are open to our minds; and their words advanced, or imitated by our hands towards the settling of an universal, constant and impartial survey of the whole Creation.[52]

Predictably, the Masons have suffered their fair share of abuse and outsiders' paranoia, especially from zealous Catholics and, more recently, fundamentalist Christians, who see 'the Brotherhood' as a sinister conclave of either quasi-Devil worshippers or outright Satanists. A quick glance at the host of fundamentalist websites devoted to this subject will soon reveal the gist of their attitude. According to American scientist and Masonic writer S. Brent Morris, their fulminations usually begin with the words: 'On July 14, 1889, Albert Pike, Sovereign Pontiff of Universal Freemasonry, addressed to the 23 Supreme confederated Councils of the world the following . . .'[53] They go on to quote Pike's alleged declaration:

If Lucifer were not God, would Adonay, whose deeds prove his cruelty, perfidy and hatred of man, barbarism and repulsion for science, would Adonay and his priests calumniate him? Yes, Lucifer is God, and unfortunately Adanay is also god. For the eternal law is that there is no light without shade, no beauty without ugliness, no white without black, for the absolute can only exist as two gods: darkness being necessary to the statue, and the brake to the locomotive.

Thus the doctrine of Satanism is heresy; and the true and pure philosophical religion is the belief in Lucifer, the equal of Adanay; but Lucifer, God of Light and God of Good, is struggling for humanity against Adanay, the God of Darkness and Evil.[54]

There have been no shortage of others willing to condemn Pike for the worship of Lucifer. The French commentator Jules Bois wrote in 1902:

It is surprising, the sacrilegious Gospel of Albert Pike. He divides Christ's existence into two parts: in the first, he classes his doctrine in a way rational, natural (Christ was then, for him,

the envoy of the 'Good God', that is to say Lucifer). In the
second, he had the mystic exaltation . . . such as his affirmation
that he is himself the son of God and equal to the father . . .
According to Albert Pike, Jesus had signed a pact with Adonai
. . . [where] a desire for solitary divinisation had intoxicated him,
rendering him unreasonable and in human. From then, Lucifer
abandoned him and, in exchange for his apostasy, had inflicted
on him by the people the torture due to thieves.

I believe that, with this example, we touch the centre of Lucifer.[55]

However, according to Brent Morris and many other modern
Masons, all this and similar commentary is slander, based on a hoax
perpetrated by 'Leo Taxil' (Gabriel Antoine Jogand-Pages). He
publicly confessed his deception in 1897,[56] although that part of the
story is usually overlooked by those eager to brand Masons as
Satanists. Brent notes that rabbis, bishops and other men of God are
among those who should have been taught 'this disgusting
"Luciferian doctrine"' if it existed, and it 'is inconceivable there
would not have been mass resignations'.[57]

Some Catholic zealots and fundamentalists also tend to quote
Madame Blavatsky in the same breath as the Taxil slander: this nineteenth-century Russian visionary and founder of the Theosophical
Society has a perhaps not entirely deserved reputation for charlatanism – but her monumental writings have been most influential on
many to this day, including various secret societies. For example, she
wrote: 'Lucifer represents . . . Life . . . Thought . . . Progress . . .
Civilization . . . Liberty . . . Independence . . . Lucifer is the Logos, the
Serpent, the Saviour.'[58]

In this light, it is worth examining Madame Blavatsky's writings
more closely in order to understand the esoteric tradition she represented. In her *Isis Unveiled: A Master-Key to the Mysteries of
Ancient and Modern Science and Theology* she quotes the Vatican's
Ecumenical Council of 1870: 'Let him be ANATHEMA . . . who
shall say that human Sciences ought to be pursued in such a spirit
of freedom that one may be allowed to hold as true their assertions
even when opposed to revealed doctrines'.[59] She adds: 'Christianity
is on trial, and has been, ever since science felt strong enough to act
as Public Prosecutor.'[60] Although temptingly – and endlessly –

e, just two more of her little gems will have to suffice here: she notes that the ancients were 'too enlightened to believe in a personal devil'[61] and 'Hell and its sovereign are both inventions of Christianity, coëval with its accession to power and resort to tyranny . . .' With a contemptuous flourish, she adds: 'Sad degeneration of human brains!'[62]

While the Masons indignantly deny Pike's alleged devotion to Lucifer – and there is no reason to doubt that Taxil did perpetrate a hoax intended to slander them – one is left wondering why they are quite so upset. As we now know there is absolutely no need to equate Lucifer with Satan, and in any case, the quotations given above reflect almost pure Gnosticism. In fact, for an organization that prides itself on mystical understanding and tolerance one is left hoping that they do secretly honour the real Lucifer, whose attributes would have made him the perfect patron for the Royal Society.

Indeed, the Masons take religious tolerance particularly seriously, as the following extract from a letter to myself from Masonic writer Robert Lomas makes very clear:

> No man truly obeys the Masonic law who merely tolerates those whose religious opinions are opposed to his own. Every man's opinions are his own property, and the rights of all men to maintain each his own are perfectly equal. Merely to tolerate, to bear with an opposing opinion, is to assume it to be heretical, and assert the right to persecute, if we would, and claim our toleration as a merit.
>
> The Mason's creed goes farther than that; no man, it holds, has any right, in any way, to interfere with the religious belief of another. It holds that each man is absolutely sovereign as to his own belief, and that belief is a matter absolutely foreign to all who do not entertain the same belief; and that if there were any right of persecution at all, it would in all cases be a mutual right, because one party has the same right as the other to sit as judge in his own case – and God is the only magistrate that can rightfully decide between them.[63]

Robert Lomas points out, therefore, that 'Freemasonry is not liked by organized religions because it is tolerant of any and all religious beliefs. And shows no favouritism to any. *So Freemasonry does not encourage devil worship but neither does it condemn it.* [My emphasis].[64] Of course to Christians this in itself would be tantamount to devil-worship.

Leaving aside the Taxil hoax, do Masons have any connection with Lucifer? The Bright Morning Star is, according to Lomas, 'a key feature in both the First Degree Tracing Board and Third Degree Ceremony', key initiations intended to change the Mason's entire outlook in radically profound ways, as he explains in a Masonic paper:

The process of initiation is one of regeneration. It means Developing your inmost essence, first to birth and then to full growth. This involves a rejection and mystical death of all the lower principles that obstruct your growth. This is the path traced through our three Degrees.

The first stage involves refining your gross sense-nature, killing your desire for material attractions and developing indifference to the allure of the outer world.

The second involves disciplining and clarifying your mind till it becomes pure and strong enough to respond to a spiritual order of life and wisdom. That is why in our Second Degree the discovery of a sacred symbol in the centre of the building shows a first glimpse of your personal centre. This knowledge is followed by a desire to wipe from your heart all obstacles to complete union with this centre.

The third stage, the 'last and greatest trial', involves the voluntary dying of your sense of ego and separation from the universal life-essence. As your limited personal ego dies you become conscious of a bright morning star within you lightening your mental horizon.

This is the great secret of Masonry: by instruction and discipline each of you can achieve conscious realization of the unity of your centre.

But why is such a theory a secret? It is because it can only be understood as a personal experience. The experience must be prepared for in secret, be realized in secret, and it remains incomprehensible and incommunicable to anyone who has not lived it.

Masonry leaves you free to follow your own religion, in the sure knowledge that every religion leads ultimately to one centre. It is a preparation for what can be realized in its fullness only by initiation.[65]

Many of those who attack the Masons are outraged that they dare even use the names of pagan gods, as in the following extract from the notes of 'ultimate Masonic guru'[66] Walter Leslie Wilmshurst (d.1939), writing about the meaning of the term 'Son of the Widow':

All initiates have a common mother. In Egypt she was called Isis, the universal widow. Do not be frightened of a so-called pagan name. Names change but reality endures. Later she came to be called . . . the Mother of us all . . . [the] Craft we speak and think of as our mystical and beloved Mother. She, like the Goddess, is a widow, widowed of her Grand Master and guiding hand. She too stands draped in veils, dark and forbidding without, yet shining and glorious within . . .[67]

Once again we see a healthy regard for tolerance, a Gnostic application of the meaning of the Goddess as God and – whether 'official' or not – a profound comprehension of the high Luciferan qualities of enlightenment and scientific enquiry that are, unfortunately, routinely, even predictably, denounced as Satanic. As always, this is a very sad commentary on bigotry and human stupidity, but the mistaken identity of Lucifer as synonymous with the Devil has unfortunately only too often been reinforced by the often confused tenets of modern 'Satanism'.

Wickedest in the world
With a practising Satanist[68] on board Royal Navy frigate *HMS Cumberland* perhaps one might expect ill luck to dog its wake (although some might say heading for the Gulf is quite bad enough). Twenty-four-year-old Leading Hand Chris Cranmer from Edinburgh had read a book by the late Anton LaVey, founder of the Church of Satan, and realized that he must have been an instinctive Satanist all along.[69] The story was greeted with delight by the media

– the irresistible headline 'The Devil and the deep blue sea' appearing in at least two newspapers[70] – but less so by the representatives of the old guard.[71] After all, his new religion declares:

> Satan represents indulgence instead of abstinence; Satan represents vengeance instead of turning the other cheek; and Satan represents all of the so-called sins, as they all lead to physical, mental or emotional gratification.[72]

However, a Satanic spokesman was careful to point out 'We do not murder children, kill animals or do weird things to virgins.' And to Satanists, 'stupidity is very, very bad.'[73]

(The decision by the Royal Navy to permit Cranmer to practise his religion at sea means that if he is killed in action, he could be buried at sea by a priest of the Church of Satan.)

It is not difficult to be seduced by LaVey's easy style and irreverent gibes at the established religions, especially for those who have suffered at their hands. To such people after years of genuflection and watching one's every thought for sinfulness the apparent blasphemy of LaVey's description of the crucifixion as 'pallid incompetence hanging on a tree' can be not only delightfully liberating in its rebellious daring, but also profoundly thought-provoking. After all, in essence Jesus was a failed Messiah – no Jew would accept him as such when he met his end so shamefully as a crucified criminal. And he predicted he would return within the lifetime of his apostles . . .

In his *Satanic Bible* LaVey waxes lyrical about his Lord Satan, who is to him 'the spirit of progress, the inspirer of all great movements that contribute to the development of civilization and the advancement of mankind. He is the spirit of revolt that leads to freedom, the embodiment of all heresies that liberate.' So far, so Luciferan.[74]

In 1969 on the last night of April – the old witch festival of Walpurgisnacht – the sixteen-year-old LaVey was inspired to launch his Church after observing the hypocrisy of church-going men lusting after showgirls, announcing 'I knew then that the Christian Church thrives on hypocrisy, and that man's carnal nature will out! . . . Since worship of fleshly things produces pleasure, there would be a temple of glorious indulgence . . .'[75]

In his job as photographer for the San Francisco Police Department he was confronted with the worst sights possible, but to him more sickening was the endless litany of people saying, 'It's God's will.' In fact, just like the officiating priest in Huysmans' Black Mass, LaVey's Satanic libertinism was perhaps surprisingly underpinned by a real sense of injustice, a railing against God's apparent obliviousness to human suffering. The fact that this arch-Satanist does not wallow in the almost unimaginable sort of human degradation frozen by his camera for the police department, but is horrified by it, reveals if anything a lack of real evil.

His jokey, irreverent style is undeniably appealing, although often rather adolescent. He writes: 'Martin Luther dreamed up Protestantism while sitting on the toilet, and we know what a big movement that became.'[76] But LaVey was deadly serious about his Satanism, explaining carefully however that to worship the Devil means being brave and proud, and to cynically acknowledge Man's basic egoism and instincts. 'Man is the only animal who must be continually reminded of existence. Any sensation will do.'[77]

However, LaVey's new version of an old religion (or anti-religion) was by no means merely a temple to libertinism made more shocking with satanic invocations. The Church of Satan is brutal about the weak or those who simply get in one's way (although it must be said that Jesus' 'Blessed are the meek for they shall inherit the earth' can be seen as a cynical politician's ploy – after all, the Meek are the very people who would never complain if they failed to get it!) In the opening chapter of *The Satanic Bible*, LaVey thunders: 'Cursed are the weak, for they shall inherit the yoke!' and 'Cursed are the poor in spirit for they shall be spat upon!'[78]

The Satanic Bible ends with a section on the 'Enochian Keys', the very magical formulae taken from Meric Casaubon's 1659 biography of John Dee, although that godly magician would no doubt be horrified at what they have become at the hands of the Church of Satan. LaVey declares that Dee's 'angels' were only believed to be so 'because occultists to this day have lain ill with metaphysical constipation'. The quality of the Enochian words and their 'barbarous tonal qualities' create a 'tremendous reaction in the atmosphere',[79] but in doing so they open the doors to *Hell* . . .

As LaVey began to attract a huge following, not unnaturally rumours spread about his activities: that he served up a human leg at a banquet, that he cursed movie star Jayne Mansfield and she was duly decapitated in a car crash, that real demons appeared at his command . . . Then, inevitably, came the backlash – not from the godly, for they had already voiced their opinions long and hard, but from the media. A little research had discovered that LaVey had never been a police photographer, had never had an affair with Marilyn Monroe as he claimed, and although he had denounced the infamous British occultist Aleister Crowley as a 'poseur par excellence [who] worked overtime to be wicked',[80] the general view among serious occultists was that this was somewhat rich coming from him.

LaVey died in 1997, controversy still dogging his memory as his associates – and even his daughter – line up to besmirch his name, which quaintly, is still possible even where a Satanist is concerned.

With the media's soubriquet of 'Wickedest Man in the World' Aleister Crowley (1875–1947) was and still is regarded by 'nice' people with a shudder, although most people, nice or otherwise, know very little about that astonishing magus. Certainly he is a Mount Olympus to LaVey's traffic-calming hump both intellectually and spiritually, although he was by no means an unmitigated joy or a consistently golden inspiration either as a man or a role model.

A talented poet, one of the world's top mountaineers (he is Chris Bonnington's hero), an erudite writer, adept yogi and gifted pornographer, Crowley is largely remembered for adopting the biblical title of 'the Great Beast 666', after his grandmother – a member of the puritanical Plymouth Brethren – insisted on using it of him, quite seriously. But as occult historian Francis X. King wrote in the Introduction to *Crowley on Christ* (1974):

> Crowley was much more than a black magician, although he did once crucify a toad; he was much more than a sexual athlete, although he did on one occasion or another indulge in almost every perversion from sodomy to coprophilia . . .[81]

'Never dull where Crowley is!'

After a mercurial relationship with various magical and secret societies (including the Freemasons), he chose to pursue sex magic (or his preferred 'magick') with the enthusiasm of the Carpocratians or Simon Magus in partnership with either fellow male magi or his serial 'Scarlet Women'. Believing himself to be the reincarnation of Eliphas Levi, he strove for the ultimate magical experiences, even seeking to conjure his Holy Guardian Angel, which he managed partly through the mediumship of his wife Rose in Cairo in 1904. As Francis X. King wrote, '. . . he was much more than a "satanic occultist", although he did identify Aiwass, his "Holy Guardian Angel" with Satan, the Christian Devil.'[82]

Like all dedicated magicians, Crowley sought to obey the ancient injunction to *Know Thyself*, to discover and implement his True Will. His encounter with Aiwass can be seen as the climax of that quest, the confrontation of his inner self as an external force. (He wrote in his *Magical Record*, July 1920: 'I want to serve God, or as I put it, Do My Will, continuously: I prefer a year's concentration with death at the end than the same dose diluted in half a century of futility.')[83]

The result of this climatic angelic encounter was the *Book of the Law*, which – without actually terrifying him – disconcerted Crowley so much he kept trying to lose it, but somehow it always returned. In September 1923 he recalled the quintessence of the 'Cairo Working', writing: 'The Secret was this: the breaking down of my false Will by these dread words of mine Angel freed my True Self from all its bonds, so that I could enjoy at once the rapture of knowing myself to be who I am.'[84]

When writing on the subject of the Tarot card, the Hanged Man, for his *Book of Thoth* (1944), he quoted Aiwass from the *Book of the Law*: 'I give unimaginable joys on earth: certainty, not faith, while in life: upon death: peace unutterable, rest, ecstasy; nor do I demand aught in sacrifice.'[85] Always opposed to the concept of the dying-and-rising Christ as redeemer, he writes: 'This idea of sacrifice is, in the final analysis, a wrong idea.'[86] He also made the point: '. . . Judaism is a savage, and Christianity a fiendish superstition.'[87] (Indeed, up to the Cairo Working Crowley had been largely Buddhist in spiritual outlook, but then Aiwass' insistence that existence was 'pure joy' seriously eroded the concept that life was ultimately nothingness.)

However, the third chapter of the *Book of the Law* changes gear, predicting – even encouraging – mass brutality, bloodshed and death: 'Mercy let be off: damn them who pity! Kill and torture; spare not: be upon them!' Yet, as Tobias Churton points out, it is the alternate voice of a Crowley 'contemptuous of the mush and mire of Edwardian sentimentality',[88] a world that was quickly to be blown to pieces in the carnage of the First World War. 'It is the voice of every place where the True Will is silenced; where the individual walks in fear of the mass'.[89]

Sometimes Crowley could rise to the noblest heights, and when he did, few could match his pure Luciferan sentiments, as in:

. . . Redemption is a bad word; it implies a debt. For every star [individual] possesses boundless wealth; the only proper way to deal with the ignorant is to bring them to the knowledge of their starry heritage. To do this, it is necessary to behave as must be done in order to get on good terms with animals and children: to treat them with absolute respect; even, in a certain sense, with worship.[90]

And, music to the ears of the confined and frustrated Edwardian woman, the *Book of the Law* opens with a clarion call to end false modesty and throw open the gates of womanhood. Aiwass/Crowley writes:

We do not fool and flatter women; we do not despise and abuse them. To us a woman is Herself, as absolute, original, independent, free, self-justified, exactly as a man is . . . We do not want Her as a slave; we want Her free and royal, whether her love fight death in our arms by night . . . or Her loyalty ride by day beside us in the Charge of the Battle of Life . . .

But now the word of Me the Beast is this; not only art thou Woman, sworn to a purpose not thine own; thou art thyself a star, and in thyself a purpose to thyself. Not only mother of me art thou, or whore to men; serf to their need of Life and Love, not sharing in their Light and Liberty; nay, thou art Mother and

Whore for thine own pleasure; the Word to Man I say to thee no less: Do what thou wilt. Shall be the whole of the Law![91]

At least that was the theory. Crowley's Scarlet Women tended to have grave mental problems – Rose, for example, died of alcoholism – and what a pity that he could bring himself to show so little respect for his fellow human beings in general, displaying a marked infantile exhibitionism by defecating on hostesses' drawing-room carpets, and offering 'love' cakes (made of faeces) to his own guests. His desire to shock by cultivating a sensational image often reduced the would-be Master of the new Aeon to the mental age of about three. In that, but only in that, LaVey's sneering dismissal of Crowley as a 'poseur par excellence' hits the mark. And another aspect of his sheer nastiness (after all, he had a lot to live up to as the Great Beast) was his fondness for cursing people[92] with a real deep-down viciousness mixed with a show-off arrogance, a sort of dark and dirty swagger of the soul. ('Never dull where Crowley is!' he wrote of himself.)[93] This is what Tobias Churton, a great admirer of the Gnostic magician Crowley calls 'his frequently stupid, frequently selfish and frequently delightful, magical self'.[94]

Ever one for assuming the guise of the 'laughing master' – like Simon Magus – Crowley declared, tongue in cheek, but still really, really meaning it: 'I have been taxed with assaulting what is commonly known as virtue. True, I hate it, but only in the same degree as I hate what is commonly known as vice.'[95]

Moralists often rub their hands with glee over the story of Crowley's life – from Victorian gentleman to pitiful, poverty-stricken heroin addict in a boarding house at Hastings in 1947, begging his doctor for just one more fix[96] – but he had long recognized that 'attainment is insanity'. Despite appearances, this was not the pitiful death of a failed shaman: as real appreciation of his life and works continues to grow exponentially, it becomes ever clearer that there was little that was truly failed about The Great Beast.

His legacy is astounding. He left behind him a corpus of writings that improve with the keeping, and certainly do not become contemptuous with familiarity, indeed quite the reverse. Where this present enquiry is concerned, Crowley had a particular legacy to bequeath to future generations of seekers, although paradoxically he would have hated to think of it in these terms. But it was Aleister Crowley who gave would-be Luciferans *the rules*.

By its very nature, striking out into the unknown towards the bright light of the Morning Star is as fraught with danger as any pilgrim's progress. Even buoyed by the noblest of ideals, there are dangers aplenty, not the least the temptation of frolicking naughtily in the soft light of black candles to celebrate orgiastic *faux*-Satanism. The real thing, after all (by any other name) is and always will be a form of outright criminal insanity – the evils of a Hitler or a Saddam Hussein being beyond even the imagination of most people. Ordinary folk are simply not cut out to be true Satanists because like it or not, they possess a conscience and an intense disgust for the disgusting. Satanism in the suburbs may be an interesting diversion, but with its emphasis on dirt and darkness it can never provide the way to the Light. But whereas we all have to find our own path, and to some extent therefore make our own maps, these 'rules' of Crowley's provide a sound basis for a well-lived life.

Everyone knows Crowley declared: 'Do what thou wilt shall be the whole of the Law', usually, and inaccurately, taking it to be a licence for depraved hedonism, but in fact his creed goes on: 'Love is the Law, Love under Will'. He adds: 'Every man and woman is a star' – echoed in diluted form in LaVey's 'Each child is a minute Renaissance man'[97] – explaining that in his system, 'The sin against the Holy Ghost is to hinder another star from following its true will'. All too often, however, each individual 'star' hinders his or her own path to their true will.

As Colin Wilson says, 'Man is not small – he's just bloody lazy.'[98]

The Lucifer Key

'The Mystery of Sorrow was consoled long ago when it went out for a drink with the Universal joke.'

Aleister Crowley

Let the Light shine in! Let Lucifer shed light on the grubby little corners of the mind, the delusions, the illusions, the hypocrisies and grinning horrors within. As in the greeting to the Masonic initiate: 'Let the Brother see the Light!' Let the Sister also see the Light!

To the Gnostics Light is All – just as to Jesus the Light was in Mary Lucifer, his 'All' – but this must be balanced by an acknowledged Darkness. To the Christian Jesus Christ is 'the Light of the World', although this will be denied with more or less vehemence not only by those of other religions such as Judaism, but was also denied and still is by the Gnostic Mandaeans, to whom only John the Baptist deserved the title 'High King of Light'. Ironically, at the time of writing, both Christians and Mandaeans are suffering at the hands of the same Islamic fundamentalists in Iraq.[1]

Let the light shine in! Let it sweep away the curse of all and *any* form of fundamentalism – 'From our commitment to ideals comes our excuse to hate'[2] – as well as thought-police and political correctness. Instead, shine on good humour, the ability to laugh long and immoderately, especially at ourselves, and a highly developed sense of the absurd. Become your own 'laughing master', intoxicated with the joy of living. Without humour and alertness freedoms are eroded, then only the pompous, the stupid or, much, much worse, abominable dictators will certainly triumph – and the world has had quite enough of them.

In December 2004 British comic actor Rowan Atkinson ('Mr Bean') reacted strongly against a proposed law banning incitement to religious hatred, as a threat to free speech. He said:

> The right to offend is more important than the right not to be offended. Freedom of expression must be protected for artists and entertainers and we must not accept a bar on the lampooning of religion and religious leaders.
>
> There is an obvious difference between the behaviour of racist agitators who can be prosecuted under existing laws, and the activities of satirists and writers who may choose to make comedy or criticism of religious belief, practices or leaders just as they do with politics.
>
> It is one of the reasons why we have free speech.[3]

Indeed, it is, but the way things are going on both sides of the Atlantic, we may not have free speech very much longer. As aspiring Luciferans we must keep watch on the incremental erosion of all our hard-won rights and freedoms. Use freedom of speech while it lasts to ensure that it will. It is not enough to fall back on evoking the mysterious and elusive 'democracy' that the West is so eager to force-feed to others. It has to be seen to work well in practice in the land of the Mother of Parliaments and the Land of the Free first. Luciferans speak up, or you may soon be denied any kind of a voice at all.

The Light in action
Lucifer is the god of progress and intellectual enquiry, not only the divine inspiration behind the spiritual enlightenment of the Gnostic and the heretic and the lover of God in all his/her forms: it was through Lucifer's spirit that humanity first climbed down from the trees and has represented the flow of progress ever since. But Lucifer may be more than a metaphor for rebellion, enlightenment

and advancement – as the pure creative and motive light s/he may actually be the key to life itself . . .

Over the past fifteen years scientists, largely in Europe and Asia, have made a major discovery. The DNA within the nuclei of all cells of living creatures contains biophotons or ultra-weak proton emissions – in other words, *light*. While it is invisible to the naked eye, it can be detected using new equipment developed by German scientists.

As German science writer Marco Bischof declares in his ground-breaking *Biophotons – The Light in Our Cells* (1995): 'A dynamic web of light constantly released and absorbed by the DNA may connect cells, tissues and organs and serve as the organism's main communication network and as the principal regulating instance of all life processes.' He suggests that 'the holographic biophoton field of the brain and nervous system, and maybe even that of the whole organism, may also be the basis of memory and other phenomena of consciousness . . .'[4]

And, excitingly for we Luciferans who refuse to delineate between 'good' and 'bad' science[5] – between honest enquiry and well-funded research that, while paying lip-service to the wildest theories of quantum physics, derides research into the possibilities of continuing consciousness after death – biophotons even possess implications for the unconventional. Bischof writes that 'The "prana" of Indian Yoga physiology may be a similar regulatory energy force that has a basis in a weak, coherent electromagnetic biofield.'

Lucifer is on the move, inside you and me, chattering between cell and cell, rousing the cohorts of the life-force, keeping us alive and wonderful. Every man and woman is a star – and now we know we have our own inner Tinkerbell light.

But for those who insist on confusing Lucifer with Satan and then indulging in a spot of Devil-worship behind the lace curtains of suburbia, a word of warning. We now enter the world of 'extreme possibilities'.

Just imagine

In his article on sailor-turned-Satanist Chris Cranmer (see page 242),[6] Colin Wilson – about whom there is nothing remotely prissy or prudish – warned of the very real pitfalls of Satanism. He cites the case of celebrated photo-journalist Sergei Kordiev and his wife who in 1959 became involved in a Satanic circle in Burnham-on-Crouch, Essex. After undergoing the usual colourful initiation ceremony, complete with a pact signed in their own blood, all seemed to go wonderfully for them, both financially and career-wise. But then they were forced to witness the rape of a girl – she was being punished for betraying the group's secrets – at a Black Mass, where all the Satanists had to drink the blood of a cockerel, specifically sacrificed for the purpose. Shaken and seriously regret-ting their involvement, the Kordievs later discovered that the man to whom the girl had betrayed their secrets had dropped dead of a heart attack at precisely the same time as the Black Mass was being performed. When they left the group their luck changed for the worse. Kordeiv came close to bankruptcy and his wife had a break-down. And one night his studio was wrecked by a mysterious force, even though no one had broken in. It seems they also had a polter-geist to contend with.

Colin Wilson's other cautionary tale is perhaps more sensational. He cites author John Cornwell's research into good and evil,[7] during which he found a teacher who had been drawn into a Satanist cell, who at his initiation was 'told to beg the Devil to take posses-sion of him, at which point his teacher said: "If you want to see the Devil, look over there."

'The man looked round and saw a man-sized crow, its wings covered in slime. Then it opened its beak, and bloody male sexual organs emerged. The man collapsed in terror.

'Even with the help of a priest, it was a long time before the man regained his sanity.'[8]

A blood-chilling story indeed, but although one feels for the victim's experience of abject terror, had it really never crossed his mind that volunteering to become involved with a Satanist group might lead to such an encounter with a creature from the Pit, if not Old Nick himself? What in hell's name did he expect? Even Satanism in the Suburbs can occasionally spring some unwelcome surprises – and would be very tame if it didn't.

Whether this was 'merely' diabolically clever hypnotism or truly a creature from the Abyss hardly matters. The damage was done. In fact, it may have been neither an hallucination nor the real thing, but a curious entity from the last frontier – of inner space.

Occultists and mystics have long known that visible beings called *tulpas* can actually be *created* by the human mind if one concentrates long and hard enough. It helps to be specially trained and mentally prepared, for otherwise that way madness could well lead.

A classic *tulpa* story is that of the early twentieth-century traveller Madame Alexander David-Neel. Having developed a passion for Buddhist art she was visited in her temporary Tibetan home by a local painter who specialized in painting 'wrathful deities'. She was astounded to witness a misty form behind him of one of these terrifying entities, especially when she put out her arm and felt as if she were 'touching a soft object whose substance gave way under the slight push'.[9] The artist confessed that he had been engaged in rituals to conjure the god whose outline she had just seen.

Fascinated, Madame David-Neel decided to create her own *tulpa* – a fat, jolly monk. Being nothing if not thorough, she went into retreat for a matter of months to concentrate her mind on this exercise in 'extreme possibilities', and after some time began to get brief flashes out of the corner of her eye of a monk-like shape. Time passed and she concentrated further, and gradually her monk became more lifelike and solid. But then he changed from being the fat and jolly being she had set out to create, into a leaner figure that was, 'troublesome and bold'. But to pre-empt all suggestions that solitude and obsession had affected Madame David-Neel's mind and that she was simply hallucinating, an unlooked-for break-through occurred when a local herdsman stopped by – *and mistook her monk for a real man*. Now quite malevolent, he had to go, but the process of 'collapsing' him took six months of concentrated effort. If she had let him run amok, gaining strength and solidity, who knows what he might have done?

Over the centuries brave and learned men and women have sought to conjure all manner of beings, from angels to devils, and many have succeeded in conjuring *something*, although they often wished they hadn't. Whether the entity came from their own minds as a hallucination from their psyche like a tulpa or thoughtform, or whether it actually came from another dimension hardly matters.

Conjuration is an enormous responsibility, not only for your own health and peace of mind, but also for those around you, possibly for years.

As a Luciferan you will do as you will (for it is the whole of the Law, Love under Law, Love under Will), but my advice is if and when you work with the unknown don't *dabble* in the occult. Do it properly! Read everything you can, not only about magic but also about the powers of the mind, prepare mentally and physically, and set up a support team in case of problems. Most importantly, never lose your sense of humour: it is your greatest protection for all manner of horrors from all manner of sources. Act like an intelligent child: open to the possibilities of the phenomena but willing to cut short the experiment if it goes wrong. The minute there's a problem, switch on the light, go to the pub, watch a funny programme, laugh. Or, and this is by far the best advice, forget all about it and go to the pub and laugh anyway. You have no need to conjure anything.

Luciferanism, paganism, hedonism and atheism may be seen as a continuation of the Enlightenment, a rebellion against the centuries of ecclesiastical repression and outright lies and a genuine desire to set foot in a brave new world. Like all new and audacious endeavours there will inevitably be dangers and dead ends, and once the old certainties and the paralysis of blind faith have been removed, opportunities for major mistakes and even crimes. But in seeking their own paths towards the Light, such questers are not aligning themselves with evil.

However Satanism proper is dangerous because it unbalances the psyche, and concentrates the mind on subjects and images that are only normally found in the more colourful works of Hieronymus Bosch. Of course other pursuits also unbalance the psyche: anything that we concentrate on to the exclusion of all else induces the same intensity of tunnel vision, be it compulsively playing computer games or compulsively studying medicine or theology. The key is the compulsivity, the addiction. Everyone knows that chemicals such as alcohol or crack cocaine ruin mind, body and spirit, but the mind itself can become addicted to negative influences, as in gambling, shopping or pornography. Satanism, however, actively invites in the world of real and endless nightmares. Concentrating on the worship of evil inevitably engenders a mind capable of what most of us – non-religious, ordinary decent folk – would automatically reject not only as the apotheosis of immoral and anti-social activities but actually also deeply distasteful and unattractive.

Although it is common to enjoy a minor thrill when touring the grimmer sideshows of waxwork exhibitions, for example, or standing gawping at a traffic accident or watching a graphic movie about Jack the Ripper, there are usually limits to our willing association with horror. Once we have indulged in a burst of catharsis, we return to the mundane and the humorous, recapturing a sort of human balance and reactivating our conscience – arguably the inborn system of checks and balances that requires no religion or political creed to regulate our would-be excesses and dampen the wilder enthusiasms of our inner demons. But true Satanists are essentially unbalanced by choice, having voluntarily switched off their consciences: indeed, to serve their Lord and Master they often find themselves compelled to kill the innocent in cold blood.

In January 2005 the British media splashed the story of 16-year-old Luke Mitchell Dalkieth in Scotland, whose enthusiasm for 'Antichrist superstar' Marilyn Manson and Satanism – he covered school exercise books with mantras such as 'Satan master lead us into hell' – led directly to the murder of his 14-year-old girlfriend Jodi Jones. Other fans of Manson include the Dylan Klebold and Eric Harris who killed 25 of their classmates at Columbine High School, Littleton, Colorado in 1999.[10]

Satanism is dangerous because it fosters a belief in personalized evil, in *the* very real and omnipresent, Devil. But this is also precisely one of the major reasons why religion, especially fundamentalism, is also dangerous, with a similar addiction to the power of evil, against which one must be on guard every split-second of the day. Such concentrated belief in Satan – from either a Satanist or fundamentalist Christian – may as an extreme possibility create him as a sort of tulpoid thoughtform, however briefly. Or if there is already such an objective being, the belief itself may summon him, for doesn't he feed on fear? And fear is the key. Unbounded it can turn any of us into monsters.

Some fear is good: the adrenaline rush of blended fear and

excitement got our hairy ancestors out of the trees into open plains and encounters with much bigger hairier creatures, ending in the eating of one by the other. That's Luciferan fear – which throws open the door to progress, which sniffs the coming catastrophes in the air and has the fortresses built, the food and vaccines stockpiled, archives secured and museums built before our heritage falls to the Philistines . . . But there's the other darker fear, which grows in the night and swamps all humour, discernment and rationality, all things of the Light. As Lucy Hughes-Hallett notes in her *Sunday Times'* review of Joanna Bourke's *Fear: A Cultural History*:

> She discriminates between anxiety (usually rooted in guilt) and fear (which has an identifiable object) and she demonstrates how the one can be converted into the other by the identification of a scapegoat.[11]

Scapegoating bleakly links the Jewish Holocaust with the great witch holocaust – indeed, anti-Semitism and anti-witch/women have always had much in common, from their both being accused of being unashamed baby murderers and eaters to being in league with the Devil. It is fear of chaos that drives rational and decent folk to demonize other rational and decent folk. In their unbridled madness the Nazis singled out the Jews as scapegoats to atone for the rise of Bolshevism and the dire economic privations of post-1918 Germany, while the 'witch' hysteria actually arose after a wave of anti-Semitism in medieval Europe – second choice scapegoats, lined up to atone for hostile weather conditions, famine and the Black Death. God could not be blamed – although as Hughes-Hallett goes on to note: ' . . . many people, it seems, find it easier to accept a catastrophe inflicted by a vindictive God than to come to terms with a piece of random bad luck'[12] – so he must have permitted the Devil to do his worst, as a test to see if the righteous could weed out his emissaries with all the brutality at their disposal . . .

As we have seen, the witch holocaust should serve as a lasting warning against fostering superstition and a belief in devils. As the old saying goes: 'Speak of the Devil and he will appear'. Believe fanatically in the Devil and he will appear, possibly in the form of your once innocent next-door neighbour, who you then deem it your duty to have arrested, tortured and burnt. If you think those days are behind us, think again.

However, merely ridiculing the witch trials of old – having a good old laugh at the ludicrous and uneducated posturings of Kramer and Sprenger and the mumblings of the senile accused – can itself be dangerous, being a form of nervous denial hinting at half-buried fears that could easily erupt as a new incarnation of witch-baiter and burner. As Erica Jong says at the end of her extraordinary book *Witches* (1981):

> When we laugh at the figure of the witch, when we laugh at our ancestors for believing in her evil, when we laugh at those who warn us of the grim morals of the witch-hunts, we bring a renewed siege of witch-hunting that much closer.
>
> In her rattling cart, blindfolded, gagged, bound, on the way to the torture chamber, the gallows, the stake, the witch is trying to tell us something. She is trying to warn us. Hear her. She may be you – next time.[13]

Inside all of us seethes a host of demons, which for our health and the well-being of society should be controlled and denied any strength or potential to grow. We do not need to exorcize them in the name of Jesus Christ or any other god, god-man, guru or political leader, but we do need to apply common sense and conscience before the demons are out of the bag and causing mayhem.

The signs are all around us. Ordinary decent British folk feel justified in spitting at veiled Muslim women; American and British soldiers of both sexes and all sizes have themselves photographed torturing Iraqi prisoners, smiling hugely; television programmes and plays are banned because they threaten the beliefs we so neurotically cling to as if our lives depended upon it, although we would be horrified to discover that they don't . . . In other words, we feel justified in turning into complete fascist dictators because we are Us and they are Them and – heaven forfend! – never the twain shall meet except in the Inquisitors' court.

Them and Us. Us and Them. Nazis and Jews. Red Army and intellectuals. Witches and Christians. Jews and Arabs. Freethinkers and any sort of fundamentalist, and so it goes on, a litany of terror producing more terror . . . We are always in the Right and They are always in the Wrong. We have God on our side, they are spawn of Satan – and even to argue against us, or for them, is proof of their intimacy with him.

The Devil is extremely useful because he proves the existence of God, and can take all the blame for God's failures to regulate and soften our hard everyday existence. Create the Devil in our own image and He will oblige by creating hell on earth.

But viewed through the bleak prism of history, surely God is much more of a failure, especially given his alleged omnipotence. While Satan's henchmen successfully follow their job descriptions – they're only obeying orders, after all – by spreading terror, agony and death across the globe, what has God achieved? True, faith and that highly attractive sense of belonging bestows a sense of inner peace on individuals, enhancing their physical and emotional health, but personal radiance and an aura of smugness and judgementalism has done little for humanity as a whole. We know where Satan's earthly hell is – just look around you – but where is God's heaven on earth? Even, or perhaps especially, the 'holy' cities, home of the self-appointed henchmen of the Lord, stink to high heaven with corruption, hypocrisy and the ongoing death of the soul that seeps cancerously across the globe. Where is the modern paradise? Washington DC? Salt Lake City? Vatican City? Jerusalem? Or is it perhaps in the old Eden, modern Iraq?

If the millennia have taught us anything, it is that we can only count on ourselves and each other for help, support, love, forgiveness and practical assistance such as medicine and sanitation – although of course those human-on-human miracles include the barely understood hidden powers of the mind, which sometimes manifest as apparently paranormal abilities. It is dangerous to invest one's entire psyche in either God or the Devil, for really there is very little difference, as they are mutually supportive and endlessly mutually generating. Where would God be if there was no Devil for his worshippers to be terrified of? Where would the Devil be without God's worshippers to be so terrified of him? Just like humanity's relationship with the God of the patriarchal modern religions, God's own relationship with Satan is symbiotic, the belief of each in the other keeping themselves alive.

If one wants or needs a God, there is always the bright light of humanity, the key to life and progress – *Lucifer*. Now there's a deity worth inventing with all the explosive power of our collective imaginations. But of course he, she or it already exists, sitting quietly, gloriously bursting with creative and illuminating light in every cell of our bodies, waiting at the core of our being to be summoned to make us gods, but perhaps equally happy to be banished once we have become divine – as long as we remember that we created Lucifer in the first place . . .

Notes and References

Introduction

1. Eliphas Levi, *The Mysteries of Magic*, Paris, 1861, p. 428.

Chapter One   Satan: An Unnatural History

1. Professor Karl W. Luckert, *Egyptian Light and Hebrew Fire*, New York, 1991, p. 47.
2. Lynn Picknett and Clive Prince, *The Stargate Conspiracy: Revealing the Truth behind Extraterrestrial Contact, Military Intelligence and the Mysteries of Ancient Egypt*, London, 1999, p. 9.
3. Barbara G. Walker, *The Women's Encyclopedia of Myths and Secrets*, New York, 1983, p. 9.
4. Alister E. McGrath, *A Brief History of Heaven*, Malden, MA, USA, 2003, p. 43.
5. *Ibid.*
6. See Lynn Picknett, *Mary Magdalene: Christianity's Hidden Goddess*, London, 2003 and also Lynn Picknett and Clive Prince, *The Templar Revelation: Secret Guardians of the True Identity of Christ*, London, 1997.
7. Isaiah 51:3. Most biblical quotations throughout will be taken from the New International Version (1973).
8. Ezekiel 28:13.
9. 1844.
10. 'Man' will be used as a synonym of 'human' and therefore includes 'Woman'. Absolutely no insult is intended to either sex.

11. Luke 23:43.
12. Song of Songs 1:16.
13. *Ibid.* 4:12.
14. *Ibid.* 4:15.
15. McGrath, p. 46.
16. Genesis 3:1.
17. Genesis 3:4-5.
18. *Ibid.* 3: 6-7.
19. *Ibid.* 3:11.
20. Genesis 3:14–15.
21. Aleister Crowley, *The Book of Thoth*, London, 1944, p. 86.
22. *Ibid.*, p. 100.
23. *Ibid.*, p. 96.
24. Among other things, as the raw material for countless luxury goods such as handbags.
25. Genesis 3:16.
26. Marilyn Yalom, *A History of the Wife*, New York, 2001, p. 15.
27. Genesis 3:13.
28. John Milton, *Paradise Lost*, 1667, IX, 171–2.
29. Jean Markale, *Montségur and the Mystery of the Cathars*, trans. Jon Graham, Paris, 1986, pp. 115–16.
30. Milton, 'The Argument', *Paradise Lost*.
31. Walker, p. 384.
32. Homer Smith, *Man and His Gods*, Boston, 1952, p. 376.
33. Walker, pp. 384–5.
34. Isaiah 14:12–15.
35. *Assyrian and Babylonian Literature, Selected Translations*, 1901, p. 304.
36. Milton, 1:144.
37. Jean Doresse, *The Book of Enoch*, trans. R.H. Charles, London, 1984, quoted in Tobias Churton, *The Gnostic Philosophy*, Lichfield, Staffordshire, 2003, p. 48.
38. For example, St Jerome.
39. Raphael Patai, *Myth and Modern Man*, 1972, p. 147.
40. H. R. Hays, *In the Beginnings*, 1963, p. 85.
41. Sir E. A. Wallis Budge, *Amulets and Talismans*, New York, 1968, p. 144.
42. Markale, p. 210.
43. Revelation 12:7–9.
44. *Ibid.* 12:4.
45. Genesis 6:1–2. This cryptic allusion has provided some of the wilder theories about divine spacemen colonizing Earth by mating with the indigenous women.
46. 1 Corinthians 11:10.
47. *Vita Adae et Evae (The Life of Adam and Eve)*, 14:3.
48. Elaine Pagels, *The Origin of Satan*, New York, 1995, p. 49.

49. *Ibid.*
50. Markale, p. 117.
51. See *Ibid.*, p. xix.
52. Jeffrey Burton Russell, *Satan: The Early Christian Tradition*, New Haven, 1981, p. 86.
53. Luke 10:18.
54. See Russell, p. 129.
55. Jack Lindsay, *The Origins of Astrology*, New York, 1971, p. 94.
56. Russell, p. 27.
57. *Ibid.*, p. 28.
58. Joshua Trachtenburg, *The Devil and the Jews*, New Haven, 1943, p. 103.
59. See Alister E. McGrath, *A Brief History of Heaven*, Malden, M., USA, 2003, p. 76.
60. Romans 5:11.
61. Walker, p. 75.
62. 1 Corinthians 15:57.
63. McGrath, p. 79.
64. Walker references G.G. Coulton, *Inquisition and Liberty*, Boston, 1959, p. 19.
65. Walker, p. 76.
66. Many people believe the precursor to have been the Essene cult, the radical Jewish sect found mainly at Qu'mran in Judaea. In fact, there is no compelling evidence that either John the Baptist or Jesus were affiliated with the Essenes. Indeed, certain aspects of their life disqualified them from an intimate link. We know from other sources – such as John the Baptist's followers, the Mandaeans of modern Iraq – that the Baptist was a married man with children, whereas the Essenes frowned on connubiality. Jesus' own lifestyle would have shocked the Essenes, for even the non-Essenes in his time and place were horrified by his tendency to consort with sinners, publicans and tax gatherers – all considered 'impure' and contaminating by the sect.
67. Russell, p. 86.
68. This quaint, not to say desperate, explanation was actually put to me by an Anglican minister in Bristol in the early 1990s. He said he had learned about the life cycles of the other gods at theological college, but dismissed them as 'unimportant'.
69. Ignatius, Epistle to the Trallians, 4.2.
70. Russell, p. 37.
71. Jean Daniélou, *The Origins of Latin Christianity*, London, 1977, p. 69.
72. Quoted in Russell, p. 42.
73. Robert M. Grant, *Gnosticism: A Source Book of Heretical Writings from the Early Christian Period*, New York, 1962, p. 15.
74. Robert McL. Wilson, *The Gnostic Problem*, London, 1958, p. 191.
75. Milton, 1:145–8.

76. *Ibid*.
77. Russell, p. 122.
78. See the *Catholic Encyclopedia*'s entry for 'Baptism'.
79. Walker, p. 818.
80. *Ibid*.
81. *Ibid*.
82. Edith Hamilton, *Mythology*, Boston, 1940, p. 70. Quoted in Walker, p. 818.
83. Leviticus 4:31.
84. Walker, p. 818.
85. Jean Markale, *Montségur and the Mystery of the Cathars*, p. 137.
86. Milton, 1:258–9.
87. *Ibid*., 1:263.
88. Tertullian, *Adversus Marcionem*, 2.10.
89. Jeffrey Burton Russell, *Lucifer: The Devil in the Middle Ages*, New York, 1984, p. 54.
90. For example, see Tobias Churton, *The Gnostic Philosophy*, Lichfield, 2003, p. 331.
91. R. O. Faulkner, *The Ancient Egyptian Book of the Dead*, Spell 149, p. 144.
92. Walker, p. 910.
93. Rollo Ahmed, *The Black Art*, London, 1936, p. 34.
94. Plutarch, *Isis and Osiris*, xxi–xxvi.
95. Genesis 3:8.
96. Luckert, p. 130.
97. *Book of the Dead*, 307: 544–5.
98. Luke 10:18.
99. There is no better introduction to these Gospels than Elaine Pagels' *The Gnostic Gospels*, London 1982. See also Picknett, Chapter Four.
100. Werner Foerster, *Gnosis: A Selection of Gnostic Texts*, Oxford, 2 volumes, 1972–4. *The Gospel of Philip*, 2:79.
101. Russell, p. 58.
102. Revelation 12:7-9.
103. *Ibid*.

Chapter Two   The Devil and All Her Works

1. Jean Markale, *Montségur and the Mystery of the Cathars*, p. 196.
2. Jeffrey Burton Russell, *Satan: The Early Christian Tradition*, New York, 1981, p. 96.
3. Jeffrey Burton Russell, *Lucifer: The Devil in the Middle Ages*, New York, 1984, p. 76.

4. Barbara G. Walker, *The Woman's Encyclopedia of Myths and Secrets*, New York, 1983, p. 542.

5. Rossell Hope Robbins, *Encyclopedia of Witchcraft and Demonology*, New York, 1959, p. 127.

6. Walker, p. 960.

7. A. T. Mann and Jane Lyle, *Sacred Sexuality*, Shaftesbury, 1995, p. 137.

8. Robbins, p. 127.

9. Jeffrey Burton Russell, *Witchcraft in the Middle Ages*, New York, 1972, p. 75.

10. Robbins, p. 127.

11. Walker, p. 433.

12. William G Denver, 'Asherah, Consort of Yahweh? New Evidence from Kuntillar "Arjund", *Bulletin of the American School of Oriental Research (BASOR)*, Vol. 255 (1984), pp. 21–27.

13. See Lynn Picknett, *Mary Magdalene: Christianity's Hidden Goddess*, London, 2003, pp. 152–3.

14. Salonon Reinach, *Orpheus*, New York, 1930, p. 42.

15. *Ibid.* Walker is quoting from Sir E. A. Wallis Budge, *Gods of the Egyptians*, New York, 2 vols, 1969.

16. William Powell Albright, *Yahweh and the Gods of Canaan*, New York, 1968, pp. 121 and 210.

17. Walker, p. 66.

18. André Lemaire, 'Who or What was Yahweh's Asherah?', *The Biblical Archaeology Review*, Vol. 10, No. 6 (Nov/Dec 1984), p. 42. He quotes the discovery of an inscription that reads: 'Blessed be Uriyahu by Yahweh and his Asherath'.

19. Walker is quoting from *Larousse Encyclopedia of Mythology*, London, 1968, p. 74.

20. Walker, p. 66.

21. Exodus 23:19 – 'Do not cook a young goat in its mother's milk'.

22. Raphael Patai, *The Hebrew Goddess*, Detroit, 1990, p. 38.

23. Walker, p. 66.

24. Kings 14:23.

25. Raphael Patai, *The Hebrew Goddess*, Detroit, 1990, p. 50.

26. 2 Kings 21:3.

27. 1 Kings 11:4–6.

28. Milton, 1:435–45.

29. Picknett, pp 134–40.

30. Walker, p. 552.

31. *Ibid.*

32. *Ibid.*, p. 416.

33. *Ibid.*

34. Geraldine Thorsten, *God Herself: The Feminine Roots of Astrology*, New York, 1981, p. 336.

35. Rollo Ahmed, *The Black Art*, London, 1936, p. 44.

36. Patai, p. 68.

37. *Ibid.*, p. 96.

38. Robert Briffault, *The Mothers*, New York, 1927, Vol. 2, p. 605.

39. Jacobus de Voragine, *The Golden Legend*, London, 1940, p. 776.

40. Henrich Kramer and James Sprenger, *Malleus Maleficarum* [*Hammer of the Witches*], London, 1971, p. 66. Originally published in 1485.

41. Ahmed, p. 118.

42. *Proverbs*, 8:1-11.

43. *Ibid.*, 14:33.

44. Patai, p. 98.

45. Tinkerbell was Peter Pan's fairy companion in J.M. Barrie's classic play *Peter Pan* (1904). Whether consciously or unknowingly, Barrie included a great many occult ideas. Magic – such as the ability to fly – ceases when children grow up; intense belief makes anything happen, such as bringing Tinkerbell back to life; and Peter muses 'Dying must be an awfully big adventure'.

46. *Ibid.*, p. 111.

47. Walker, pp. 237–8.

48. Sir E. A. Wallis Budge, *Gods of the Egyptians*, 2 vols., New York, 1968, 2nd vol., pp. 126 and 141.

49. S. Angus, *The Mystery Religions*, London, 1968, p. 139.

50. Walker, p. 749.

51. Ezekiel 8:14.

52. Briffault, vol. 3, p. 94.

53. Arthur Edward Waite, *The Book of Ceremonial Magic*, New York, 1977, pp. 186–7.

54. John Milton, *Paradise Lost*, 1:421.

55. Milton, 1:421–78.

56. Aleister Crowley, *The Book of Thoth*, London, 1944, p. 105.

57. *Ibid.*

58. The definition is taken from the *Universal Dictionary*, Boston, 1986.

59. Sir James Frazer, *The Golden Bough*, 1922, pp. 717 and 769.

60. Robbins, p. 512.

61. Walker, p. 765.

62. *Picnic at Hanging Rock*, (1975), starring Rachel Roberts and Anne-Louise Lambert, directed by Peter Weir.

63. Leo Vinci, *Pan: Great God of Nature* (London), 1993, p. 16.

64. *Ibid.*, p. 272.

65. Isaiah 13:21.

66. *Ibid.*, 34:14.

67. Leviticus 17:7, quoted in Vinci, p. 272.

68. Quoted in Vinci, pp. 14–16.

69. Geoffrey Ashe, *The Virgin*, (London), 1976, p. 145.

70. 1 Corinthians 10:19–21.

71. *Ibid.*, 10:22.

72. Vinci, p. 43, quoting ancient sources.

73. Walker, p. 58.

74. Liz Greene, *The Dreamer of the Vine*, London, 1980, p. 31. This book will greatly appeal to fans of *The Da Vinci Code*.

75. Montague Summers, *The History of Witchcraft*, London, 1926, p. 91.

76. Kramer and Sprenger, p. 24., quoted in Walker, p. 432.

77. Euripedes, *Medea*, 1171–2, quoted in Summers, p. 201.

78. Summers, p. 202.

79. Quoted in *Ibid.*, pp. 765–6.

80. 'Timewarp House and the literary treasure buried under the dust' by Bill Mouland, *The Daily Mail*, February 24, 2005.

81. Patricia Merivale, *Pan the Goat-God*, Cambridge, Mass., 1969, p. 64.

82. *Ibid.*, p. 488.

83. Walker, p. 70.

84. *Ibid.*, p. 1043.

85. John Holland Smith, *Constantine the Great*, New York, 1971, p. 287. Quoted in Walker, p. 1045.

86. Also Massa, *The Phoenicians*, Geneva 1977, p. 101. Quoted in *ibid*.

87. *Ibid.*, p. 1043.

88. Sir E.A. Wallis Budge, *Gods of the Egyptians*, London, 1969, vol. 1, p. 24.

89. *Assyrian and Babylonian Literature, Selected Translations*, New York, 1901, p. 4.

90. Michael H. Harris, *History of Libraries of the Western World*, London, revised edition, 1985, p. 30.

91. Elizabeth Pepper and John Wilcock, *Magical and Mystical Sites*, New York, 1977, p. 159. Quoted in Walker, p. 401.

92. Jane McIntosh Snyder, *Lesbian Desire in the Lyrics of Sappho*, New York, 1997, p. 8, quoted in Marilyn Yalom, *A History of the Wife*, New York, 2001, p. 25.

93 David Lance Goines, 'Inferential Evidence for the Pre-Telescopic Sighting of the Crescent Venus', www.goines.net/Writing/venus.html.

Chapter Three   A Woman Called Lucifer

1. Michael Jordan, *Mary: The Unauthorized Biography*, London, 2001, p. 171.

2. Tobias Churton, *The Gnostic Philosophy*, Lichfield, Staffordshire, 2003, p. 88.

3. Irenaeus, *Adversus Haereses*, I.XV.6. quoted in Churton, p. 79, note 45. He adds: 'The poem may be by Irenaeus' teacher, Pothinos who, according to Irenaeus was taught by Polycarp, who knew John the Apostle.'

4. *Ibid.*, p. 89.
5. Understandably, Irenaeus was not a Gnostic favourite. One of their texts – *The Apocalypse of Peter* – refers to orthodox bishops as 'dry canals' who issue inflexible and militaristic orders but offer no pastoral care or mystical revelation.
6. Churton notes (p. 90): 'Irenaeus never envisioned Christianity as a sect or as a religion among other religions' – a common enough state of mind among Christians today, to whom being described as a member of a sect is particularly offensive. Even the description of the early religion as a cult is viewed with distaste, even though technically accurate.
7. Irenaeus, *Adv. Haer.* 1.13.3.
8. Jean Markale, *Montségur and the Mystery of the Cathars*, p. 173.
9. Benjamin Walker, *Gnosticism: Its History and Influence*, Wellingborough, 1983, p. 119.
10. *Ibid.*, p. 139–40.
11. *Ibid.*, p. 140–41.
12. *Ibid.*, p. 141.
13. Montague Summers, *The History of Witchcraft*, London, 1926, p. 22.
14. Churton, p. 88.
15. Lynn Picknett and Clive Prince, *The Templar Revelation: Secret Guardians of the True Identity of Christ*, London, 1997, p. 318.
16. *Ibid.*
17. Walker, p. 91.
18. The identification of the Magdalene with Mary of Bethany is controversial, but to me the evidence is persuasive. See Picknett and Prince, pp. 63, 78, 139, 305–6, 331–7, 341–2, and Lynn Picknett, *Mary Magdalene: Christianity's Hidden Goddess*, London, 2003, pp. 47–8, 50, 53–8, 60–2, 210.
19. John 11:32.
20. *Ibid.*, 11:25.
21. Walker, p. 91.
22. *Ibid.*
23. Mark 14:51.
24. *Ibid.*, 14:52.
25. Walker, p. 91, quoting Morton Smith, *The Secret Gospel: the Discovery and Interpretation of the Secret Gospel According to Mark*, New York, 1974, p. 140.
26. *Ibid.*
27. Smith, p. 140.
28. Marilyn Yalom, *A History of the Wife*, New York, 2001, p. 13.
29. Andrew Alexander, the last section in his column entitled 'America's Real Gift to the World – Moronocracy', the London *Daily Mail*, Friday, 5 November 2004.

30. *Ibid*.
31. Dedicated to 'All those who have suffered at the hands of the Church'.
32. See Picknett, Part Two, Chapter Six: 'Black, but Comely . . . .'
33. Mark 14:3–5.
34. Luke 7:36–50.
35. Mark, 14:6–8.
36. *Ibid*., 14:9.
37. John 12:1-8.
38. Luke 7:36–50.
39. Peter Redgrove, *The Black Goddess and the Sixth Sense*, London, 1989, pp. 125–6.
40. *Ibid*.
41. Acts 2:17.
42. See Picknett, pp. 61-2, 64–6, 82, 147, 231.
43. Luke 8:1–2.
44. *Ibid*., 8:3.
45. See David Ayerst and A.S.T. Fisher, *Records of Christianity*, Volume 1: In the Roman Empire, Oxford, 1971, pp. 144–6.
46. Cyril of Jerusalem, *Catechetical Lectures*, 4.36.
47. David Tresemer and Laura Lea Cannon, Introduction to Jean-Yves Leloup's translation of *The Gospel of Mary Magdalene*, Rochester, Vermont, 2003, p. xi. Their own reference is given as 'James Carroll, Constantine's Sword, New York, Houghton Mifflin, 2001.'
48. *The Pistis Sophia*, translated by G.R.S. Mead, Kila, MT, USA, 1921, Second Book, 72:3.
49. G. R. S. Mead, *Pistis Sophia*, Kila, MT, USA, 1921, Second Book, 160.
50. For example, see Luke 4:38–9, in which Simon's mother-in-law is healed by Jesus. 'Peter' was Simon's nickname, meaning 'rock'. It has been suggested by Michael Baigent and Richard Leigh that it may have been the equivalent of Sylvester Stallone's 'Rocky' – expressing Simon's rough side.
51. Mead, Book Five.
52. Mark 16:9.
53. Luke 8:3.
54. *Ibid*., 12:27.
55. Susan Haskins, *Mary Magdalen*, London, 1993, Chapter III.
56. Leloup, 10:5.
57. *Ibid*., p. 37 (p. 17 of the original text).
58. *Ibid*., p. 39 (p. 18 of original text).
59. *Pistis Sophia*, First Book, 36.
60. *Ibid*., Second Book, 72: 3.
61. *Ibid*.
62. *Ibid*., 28.
63. Picknett, pp. 67–8.

64. I am indebted to Clive Prince for a fruitful discussion on this subject, and for the 'office' analogy.
65. Morton Smith, *Jesus the Magician*, London, 1978, p. 25.
66. Picknett and Prince, 112–13; Picknett 39–41.
67. *Che non ha potesta in un medesimo tempo di dire diverse cose.*
68. Lynn Picknett and Clive Prince, *Turin Shroud: How Leonardo da Vinci Fooled History*, London, 2000, p. 194.
69. Timothy Freke and Peter Gandy, *Jesus and the Goddess: The Secret Teachings of the Original Christians*, London, 2001, p. 45. See also www.BelovedDisciple.org.
70. *Ibid.*
71. John 14:23.
72. See www.BelovedDisciple.org.
73. *Ibid.*
74. John 19:25.
75. Jusino's website.
76. Leloup, p. 37 (p. 17).
77. Layton, *Gospel of Thomas*, 114:18–20.
78. *Ibid.*, *Gospel of Philip*, 48.
79. John 13:23–26.
80. *Ibid.*, 18:15–16.
81. *Ibid.*, 20:2-10.
82. *Ibid.*, 21:7.
83. *Ibid.*, 21:20–23.
84. See Desmond Stewart's *The Foreigner*, London, 1981, p. 108.
85. Mark 10:46.
86. Luke 7:44–47.
87. See Picknett and Prince, Chapter One: 'The Secret Code of Leonardo da Vinci', and Picknett, Chapter One, 'The Outsiders'.
88. In the Sainsbury Wing of the National Gallery, Trafalgar Square, in central London.
89. Luke 7:19.
90. John 1:28. Of John's alleged declaration that he was not the Christ, this passage reads: 'This all happened at Bethany *at the other side of the Jordan*', (My emphasis). Perhaps this comes into the category of 'protesting too much'.
91. G.R.S. Mead, 'Simon Magus: An Essay', London, 1892, p. 10.
92. Picknett and Prince, p. 417.
93. André Nataf, *The Wordsworth Dictionary of the Occult*, trans., John Davidson, London, 1994, p. 182. Originally published in Paris, 1988, as *Les maîtres de l'occultisme*.
94. *Ibid.*
95. Rollo Ahmed, *The Black Art*, London, 1936, p. 53.
96. Walker, p. 938.

97. Mead, p. 10.
98. *Ibid.*, pp. 28ff.
99. Karl W. Luckert, *Egyptian Light and Hebrew Fire*, New York, 1991, p. 299.
100. *Ibid.*, 305.
101. Quoted in Mead, p. 19.
102. Francis X. King, ed. *Crowley on Christ*, London, 1974, p. 15.
103. Luke 7: 28 and Matthew 11:11.
104. This passage appears in the otherwise lost Gnostic *Gospel of the Egyptians*. However, we are indebted to Clement of Alexandria who once again innocently included a quotation from this text in his *Stromateis*.
105. Layton, *Gospel of Thomas*, 61:23–33.
106. Walker, p. 885.
107. Matthew 11:3.
108. *Ibid.*, 11:2.
109. *Ibid.*, 11:9.
110. *Ibid.*, 11:11.
111. Mark 14: 14.
112. Carl H. Kraeling, *John the Baptist*, London, 1951, p. 160.
113. Irenaeus, *Adv. Haer.* Book I. XIII.
114. A Muslim taxi driver told me that Islamic mystics traditionally fast and pray in the desert for 40 days, after which they have the power to summon and use djinns as their occult slaves. Although the average Muslim is wary of such practices, apparently this is not seen as evil.
115. Morton Smith, *Jesus the Magician*, London, 1978, p. 42.
116. Barbara Thiering, *Jesus the Man*, pp. 84–5 and 390–1.
117. Jeffrey Burton Russell, *Lucifer: The Devil in the Middle Ages*, (New York), 1984, p. 307.

Chapter Four Synagogues of Satan

1. Jean Markale, *Montségur and the Mystery of the Cathars*, trans. Jon Graham, 2003. Originally *Montségur et l'énigme cathare*, Paris, 1986, p. 66.
2. For a detailed background to the Cathars, see Markale; Yuri Stoyanov, *The Hidden Tradition in Europe*, London, 1994; Lynn Picknett, *Mary Magdalene: Christianity's Hidden Goddess*, London, 2003, and Lynn Picknett and Clive Prince, *The Templar Revelation*, London, 1997.
3. The Cathars only ate fish because they believed that fish procreated asexually.
4. Markale, p. 173.
5. *Ibid.*, p. 176.
6. See Picknett, p. 184.
7. The reasoning behind this was that as God had given humanity dominion

over all the animals, it was blasphemy not to reinforce that superiority by eating them. It is significant that to this day, among all the countries of Europe, it is the Catholic lands that have the worst reputation for animal welfare.

8. At Béziers, 20,000 townspeople willingly died at the hands of the Crusaders rather than renounce their belief that Jesus and the Magdalene were lovers. It is all the more remarkable because this is not a belief that would naturally appeal to Cathars and therefore is unlikely for them to have invented. Presumably they learnt it from a secret gospel similar to those found at Nag Hammadi in 1945.

9. Markale, p. 160.

10. See Picknett, pp. 91, 93–7, 196, 215–16, 221, 232–3 and de Voragine, pp. 153–5.

11. Montague Summers, *The History of Witchcraft*, London, 1926, p. 23.

12. Yuri Stoyanov, *The Hidden Tradition in Europe*, London, 1994, p. 189.

13. *Ibid*.

14. According to Jean Markale, Rahn was discovered faking some inscriptions and was duly punched on the nose by an outraged local historian!

15. It must be remembered that Rahn was a Nazi, although his earlier research in the Languedoc was relatively untouched by his later unpleasant ideology. His theses are included here in the spirit of Lucifer – i.e., fearlessly citing any interesting research no matter what its source rather than throw the politically correct baby out with the bathwater. After all, on certain points, he may have been correct!

16. Otto Rahn, *Luzifers Hofgesind: Eine Reize zu den guten Geistern Europas*, 1937, tranlated into the French as *La Cour de Lucifer: Voyage au coeur de la plus haute spiritualité européene*, Paris, 1994. I am greatly indebted to Clive Prince for his hard work in translating key passages from the French for me.

17. For an in-depth examination of the history and beliefs of the Templars, see Picknett and Prince.

18. Of course as a Nazi, Rahn would have infinitely preferred a great religion to have Nordic or Germanic rather than Middle Eastern (Semitic) roots.

19. Rahn, p. 15 of the Introduction to the French edition by Arnaud d'Apremont, translated by Clive Prince.

20. *Ibid*.

21. *Ibid*.

22. For those who appreciate what may well simply be a coincidence – or perhaps a Cosmic Joke – 'Anfortas' is an exact anagram of 'For Satan'. Of course it would be considerably more impressive if in French.

23. Rahn, p. 18.

24. *Ibid*., p. 21.

25. *Ibid*., p. 22.

26. *Ibid.*, p. 91.
27. For details, see Andrew Collins' haunting and important book *21st-Century Grail*, London, 2004.
28. For the classic exposition of the theory that 'sangreal' actually means 'holy blood' see Michael Baigent, Richard Leigh and Henry Lincoln, *The Holy Blood and the Holy Grail*, London, 1982. For the fictional version par excellence, there is, of course Dan Brown, *The Da Vinci Code*, New York, 2003.
29. Wolfram von Eschenbach, *Parzival*, London, 1980, pp. 232–3.
30. *The Mabinogion*, trans. Gwyn Jones and Thomas Jones, London, 1949, p. 192.
31. *Ibid.*, p. 218.
32. Tobias Churton, *The Golden Builders*, Litchfield, 2002. See also Picknett, Appendix.
33. Wolfram, p. 240.
34. *Ibid.*, p. 396.
35. Andrew Collins, *21st-Century Grail*, London, 2004.
36. Father Philippe Devoucoux du Buysson, in *Dieu est amour*, no. 115 (May 1989), quoted in Picknett and Prince, p. 123.
37. Colin Wilson, *The Occult*, London, 1973, p. 272.
38. Michael Baigent and Richard Leigh, *The Inquisition*, London, 2000, p. xv.
39. Marie-Humbert Vicaire, *Saint Dominic and His Times*, trans. Kathleen Pond, London, 1964, p. 146. Quoted in Baigent and Leigh, p. 17.
40. Walter L. Wakefield, *Heresy, Crusade and Inquisition in Southern France 1100–1250*, London, 1974, p. 208.
41. *Ibid.*, p. 212.
42. Baigent and Leigh, p. 19.
43. Wakefield, p. 216.
44. Baigent and Leigh, p. 25.
45. Wakefield, p. 224, quoted in Baigent and Leigh, p. 26.
46. Stoyanov, p. 178.
47. Baigent and Leigh, p. 28.
48. See Lynn Picknett, Clive Prince and Stephen Prior, *Friendly Fire: The Secret War Between the Allies*, Edinburgh, 2004, pp. 54–5, 56–61.
49. Summers, p. 20.
50. H.T.F. Rhodes, 'Black Mass', *Man, Myth and Magic*, London, 1971, No. 10, pp. 274–8, quoted in Lynn Picknett and Clive Prince, *The Templar Revelation: Secret Guardians of the True Identity of Christ*, London, 1997, p. 86.
51. Barbara Walker, *The Woman's Encyclopedia of Myths and Secrets*, New York, 1983, p. 1079.
52. Ronald Pearsall, *The Worm in the Bud*, New York, 1969, p. 209, quoted in Walker, p. 643.
53. Vern L. Bulloch, *The Subordinate Sex*, Chicago, 1973, p. 176, quoted in *ibid*.
54. Revelation 22:2.

55. Joseph Campbell, *The Mask of God: Creative Mythology*, New York, 1970, p. 159.

56. Walker, p. 640.

57. Charlene Spretnak (ed.), *The Politics of Women's Spirituality*, New York, 1982, p. 269, quoted in *ibid.*, p. 644.

58. Walker, p. 644.

59. Mary Daly, *Beyond God the Father*, Boston, 1973, p. 69.

60. Although a precise number can never be known, the total number of 'witches', both male and female, who suffered and died at the hands of the Church has been drastically downgraded from estimates as high as 5 million to around 100,000. Yet given the relatively scanty population of Europe during that time, and the fact that whole villages were decimated and never recovered, it is still a large number. And it need hardly be said, even the revised figure is 100,000 too many.

61. Walker, p. 1079.

62. Barbara Rosen, *Witchcraft*, New York, 1972, pp. 296–7.

63. Walker, p. 170.

64. Antoinette Bourgignon, *La Vie extérieure*, Amsterdam, 1683, quoted in Summers, p. 71.

65. My notes at this point read incredulously: 'Is he *mad*?' After a while, I gave up making similar comments. It would have taken far too much time.

66. Summers, p. 71, references Delrio. *Disquistiones magicae*, 1. V. sect. 4. T. 2. '*Non eadem est forma signi, aliquando est simile leporis uestigio, aliquando bufonis pedi, aliquando araneae, uel catello, uel gliri.*'

67. Summers, p. 45.

68. *Ibid.*, p. 226.

69. *The most wonderfull . . . storie of a . . . Witch named Alse Gooderidge*, London, 1597, quoted in Summers, pp. 75–6.

70. Rossell Hope Robbins, *Encyclopedia of Witchcraft and Demonology*, New York, 1959, p. 42.

71. Ribet, *La mystique divine*, III. 2. *Les Parodies diaboliques*: '*Le burlesque s'y mêle à l'horrible, et les puerilités aux abominations.*' Quoted in Summers, p. 110.

72. Summers, p. 111.

73. *Ibid.*, p. 121.

74. Robbins, pp. 500 and 540.

75. Peter Haining, *Witchcraft and Black Magic*, London, 1971, p. 103.

76. Sir Walter Scott, *Letters on Demonology and Witchcraft*, London, 1884, pp. 166–8.

77. Apparently there are problems with his translation, although another one is in the pipeline.

78. Heinrich Kramer and Jakob Sprenger, *Malleus Maleficarum (Hammer of the Witches)*, 1485.

79. Robbins, pp. 303–4.

80. *Ibid*.

81. *Ibid*., pp. 18 and 508.

82. G.G. Coulton, *Inquisition and Liberty*, Boston, 1959, pp. 154–5, quoted in Walker, p. 1006.

83. C. L'Estrange Ewen, *Witchcraft and Demonianism*, London, 1933, pp. 122–3.

84. Robbins, p. 501.

85. *Ibid*.

86. Walker, p. 1005, referencing Jean Plaidy, *The Spanish Inquisition*, New York, 1967, p. 157.

87. Robbins, p. 509.

88. See, for example, www.nd.edu/~dharley/witchcraft/Malleus.html.

89. *Ibid*.

90. Henry Charles Lea, *The Inquisition of the Middle Ages*, New York, 1954, unabridged version, 1961, pp. 815 and 831, quoted in Walker, p. 1080.

91. Terry Davidson, *Conjugal Crime*, New York, 1978, p. 99.

92. Amaury de Riencourt, *Sex and Power in History*, New York, 1974, p. 219.

93. Walker, p. 593.

94. Kramer and Sprenger, Part 1, q. xi: *Nemo fidei catholicae amplius nocet quam obstetrices*.

95. Robert Knox Dentan, *The Semai: A Nonviolent People of Malaya*, New York, 1968, pp. 96–8.

96. Bulloch, p. 177.

97. Wolfgang Lederer, *The Fear of Women*, New York, 1968, p. 150.

98. *Ibid*.

99. Walker, p. 656.

100. *Ibid*.

101. Andrew D. White, *A History of the Warfare of Science with Theology in Christendom*, 2 vols., New York, 1955, vol 1, p. 319.

102. Walker, p. 656, quoting George B. Vetter, *Magic and Religion*, New York, 1973, p. 355.

103. *Ibid*.

104. *Ibid*., p. 1008.

105. Robbins, p.108.

106. Summers, p. 63.

107. *Ibid*., p. 256.

108. For a particularly thought-provoking analysis of the Helen Duncan affair, see Manfed Cassirer's *Medium on Trial: The Story of Helen Duncan and the Witchcraft Act*, Stanstead, 1996.

Chapter Five   Pacts, Possession and Séance Rooms

1. According to Jeffrey Burton Russell in *Lucifer: The Devil in the Middle Ages*, New York, 1984, p. 80 (note): 'Hincmar interjects the tale into his *Divorce of Lothar and Teuberga*, written about 860 (MPL 125, 716–25).'
2. *Ibid.*
3. *Ibid.*, p. 81.
4. *Ibid.*, p. 82. Russell adds in note 41: 'Since *mouffle* is colloquial French for "slob" an element of anti-Flemish prejudice seems present here.'
5. Jean Plaidy, *The Spanish Inquisition*, London, 1967, p. 171 ff.
6. Johannes Weir.
7. Goethe's *Faust*, *Part One*, 1808, translated by Philip Wayne, who also wrote the Introduction to the 1949 Penguin Edition, p. 15.
8. It is through its Italian form, *nigromancia*, that it came to be known as 'the Black Art'.
9. www.satansheaven.com/necromancy.htm.
10. 1 Samuel 28.
11. Goethe, *Faust*, p. 40.
12. See in previous chapter.
13. Lewis Mumford, *Interpretations and Forecasts*, New York, 1973, p. 302.
14. *The Devils*, 1971, directed by Ken Russell, starring Vanessa Redgrave and Oliver Reed.
15. T. K. Oesterreich, *Possession, Demoniacal and Other*, New York, 1966, pp. 49–50.
16. Grillot de Givry, *Witchcraft, Magic and Alchemy*, New York, 1971, pp. 118–19.
17. Montague Summers, *The History of Witchcraft*, London, 1925, p. 73.
18. *Ibid.*
19. Rossell Hope Robbins, *Encyclopedia of Witchcraft and Demonology*, New York, 1959, p. 316, quoted in Barbara Walker, *The Woman's Encyclopedia of Myths and Secrets*, New York, 1983, p. 811.
20. Summers, p. 73.
21. Colin Wilson, *The Occult*, London, 1973, p292.
22. 'À Aix, par Jean Tholozan, MVCXI', quoted in Summers, p. 82.
23. *Ibid.*
24. Russell, p. 299.
25. See Houston Stewart Chamberlain, *Immanuel Kant*, Berlin, 1914.
26. Published in paperback in 2000, subtitled: 'How Leonardo Da Vinci Fooled History'.
27. Thomas Humber, *The Sacred Shroud*, New York, 1978, p. 120.
28. It is know that he had a mysterious room in the Vatican, in which he built a 'machine made of mirrors'. No one would have been any wiser but for the

German mirror-makers he employed on the project – they were foreign because they wouldn't understand much of what was going on – who, convinced he was practising sorcery, locked him in the room and ran away. Such was Leonardo's controlled physical strength that he merely lifted the heavy door off its hinges and strolled away. But what was the 'machine made of mirrors'? In the experiments conducted into Leonardo's possible *modus operandi* by Clive Prince and his brother Keith in the early 1990s, it soon became obvious that any device that concentrated heat and light would be very useful in producing an image using a very simple pinhole camera – a *camera obscura*, one of which we know from his notebooks that Leonardo built.

29. *Codex Atlanticus*.
30. See Josef Maria Eder's 1945 *History of Photogaphy*.
31. Tobias Churton, *The Golden Builders – Alchemists, Rosicrucians and the first Free Masons*, Lichfield, 2002, pp. 34–5. I am indebted to Clive Prince for finding this for me.
32. *Ibid*. and ditto.
33. *BSTS Newsletter* 42 (January 1996), pp. 6–8, reproduced from *Avenire*, 7 October 1995.
34. Picknett and Prince, pp. 187–90.
35. Maurice Rowden, *Leonardo da Vinci*, (London), p. 1975, p. 117.
36. Picknett and Prince, p. 167.
37. Frances Yates, *Giordano Bruno and the Hermetic Tradition*, London, 1964, p. 435.
38. The history of the Rosicrucian Manifestos and the growth of the movement is told in Frances Yates' *The Rosicrucian Enlightenment*, London, 1972, which includes full translations of the original text. Another excellent book on this subject is Tobias Churton, *The Golden Builders*.
39. C. J. S. Thompson, *The Lure and Romance of Alchemy*, New York, 1990, Chapter XXII.
40. Dr Christopher McIntosh, Foreword to Churton, *The Gnostic Philosophy*, p. xii.
41. *Ibid*.
42. Clive Prince and I remain indebted to the insights of Abigail Nevill, who at the age of eleven, inspired us to really look at the Shroud image with a child's eye – and suddenly a great deal fell into place. See Picknett and Prince, pp. 136–7, 157, 235, 240, 242, 245, 252.
43. I am indebted to the research of Steve Wilson for this interesting fact.
44. Thanks to the computer wizardry of Andy Haveland-Robinson, who had no particular axe to grind and viewed our project with complete objectivity.
45. As Abigail Nevill asked when viewing the Shroud image in negative: 'Why is his head too small? And why is it on wrong?'
46. The head at the back is thrown backwards, the hair falling away from the face. At the front the chin is level.

47. Actually the hair appears to have been lightly touched up or painted in using the light-sensitive chemicals that created the photograph. When Clive and Keith Prince discovered that the fish-eye effect renders the hair invisible, that's what they did.

48. Of course Leonardo had the strong sunlight of Italy if he cared to use it, although as this work was undoubtedly of the highest secrecy, he would have chosen to create the Shroud behind closed doors, probably in the Vatican (see note 28, above). We had no such possibilities, having only a garage in grey and unromantic Reading, Berkshire, for our experiments, and a strong UV light bulb or two.

49. See Picknett and Prince for instructions on how to recreate *all* the so-called 'miraculous' characteristics of the Shroud using the simplest of methods. However, you do need an abundance of light – and time! We were the first researchers ever to publish details of our own Shroud recreation, although at roughly the same time Professor Nicholas Allen was completing his similar photographic work in South Africa.

50. For a time we were annoyed at the image of the lens appearing on our experimental 'Shrouds' – until we checked with the image of the Turin Shroud and saw it in exactly the same spot! Then, of course, we were overjoyed.

51. Such as Maria Consolata Corti. See Picknett and Prince, pp. 161–3, 331.

52. In 1898 a lawyer from Turin, Secondo Pio, took the first photographs of the Shroud, which was being displayed as part of the celebrations to mark the fiftieth anniversary of the unification of Italy. Seeing the Shroud in negative was a true epiphany for Pio: previously a lukewarm Catholic, after seeing all the intricate detail of the horrific crucifixion leap into life, he abruptly became passionate about his religion. Unfortunately, like millions of others, he had been duped by possibly the world's greatest psychological conman. The Shroud of Turin is not testimony to the truth of the Christian faith, but quite the opposite.

53. Serge Bramly, *Leonardo: The Artist and the Man*, London, 1992, first published as *Leonardo da Vinci*, Paris, 1988, p. 445.

54. Although the image was clearly not created with paint, there is a small amount of pigment on the cloth, probably due to the custom of laying religious paintings on it to imbue them with extra holiness.

55. Giorgio Vasari, *Lives of the Artists*,1550. This is quoted at the beginning of Chapter Five of Picknett and Prince, 'Faust's Italian Brother'.

56. See Picknett and Prince, *The Templar Revelation*, p. 198.

57. Paracelsus, *De Natura Rerum*, 1572, Book 3.

58. *Ibid*.

59. Gian Battista della Porta, *Natural Magik*, 1658, Second Book.

60. *Ibid*.

61. Paracelsus.

62. André Nataf, *The Wordsworth Dictionary of the Occult*, London, 1994, p. 161.

63. *Ibid.*
64. Lynn Thorndike, 'A History of Magic and Experimental Science', New York, 1929, vol. VIII, p. 629, quoted in Clara Pinto-Correia's online essay 'Homunculus: Historiographic Misunderstanding of Preformationist Terminology', www.zygote.swarthmore.edu/fert1b.html.
65. *Ibid.*
66. The robot was a result of Leonardo's studies in anatomy, which are described in the Codex Huygens.
67. See www.w3.impa.br/~jair/e65.html.
68. *Ibid.* This online article is sponsored by the Istituto e Museo di Storia della Scienza, Florence, and The Science Museum, London.
69. Dee himself had what is believed to be the perfect astrological chart for an occultist, being born with the Sun in Cancer and his ascendant in Sagittarius.
70. Montague Summers indefensibly describes 'the work of rehabilitation so nobly initiated by Queen Mary'. Summers, p. 22.
71. Nevertheless, Dee persuaded Queen Mary to establish a national library, bestowing on it 4000 of his own books. It would ultimately become the British Museum.
72. William Shakespeare, *The Tempest*, Act V, Scene 1, *c*.1608.
73. Elizabethan spelling was notoriously inconsistent, even for personal names.
74. See www.johndee.org/charlotte/Chapter6/6p1.html. This is extracted from a page from The Alchemy Website, www.levity.com/alchemy/kellystn.html.
75. This appeared in three parts from 1663 to 1678.
76. Their magic mirror can now be seen in the British Museum.
77. From the *Fama Fraternitatis*, quoted in Churton, *The Golden Builders*, p. 99.
78. Ed. Meric Casaubon, *A True & Faithful Relation of what passed for many years between Dr John Dee and some Spirits*, London, 1657, quoted in *ibid*. Churton notes: 'Casaubon took his material from Dee's diaries, chiefly from those of 1583–4'.
79. Churton, p. 100.
80. The important and stunning 1997 film, *Photographing Fairies*, starring Toby Stephens, Emily Woof and Frances Barber, and directed by Nick Willing, makes this point quite clear. The main character even fails to defend himself against an unwarranted charge of murder because fairyland calls so strongly to him. 'Death is merely a change of state. The soul is a fresh expression of the self. The dead are not dust. They really are only a footfall away.'
81. Godfather of British esotericism, John Michell, believes that the gods are reluctant to give occult researchers money because it would make them 'slack'!
82. *The Stone of the Philosophers*, ascribed to Edward Kelley, which was included in the booklet *Tractatus duo egregii, de Lapide Philosophorum, una cum Theatro astonomniae terrestri, cum Figuris, in gratiam filiorum Hermetis nunc primum in lucem editi, curante J. L. M. C.* [Johanne Lange Medicin Candidato], Hamburg, 1676, translated by L. Roberts.

83. Some say 1595 or 1597.

84. Shakespeare, Epilogue.

85. I myself grew up in a seriously haunted house in the back streets of York. I was about sixteen before I realized that not everyone has a poltergeist! Since those far-off times I have researched and studied the paranormal and have concluded that although many people report ghosts etc out of a desire to cause a stir, or perhaps even to get rehoused by the local council, most have seen something or someone from another dimension. An underlying belief in the reality of intrusion from elsewhere underpins my *The Mammoth Book of UFOs* (2001), while the strange crossover between a belief in the paranormal and the intelligence agencies is the main theme of my book, co-authored with Clive Prince, *The Stargate Conspiracy: Revealing the truth behind extraterrestrial contact, military intelligence and the mysteries of ancient Egypt* (1999).

86. Although, interestingly, not all and not on all points. There are modern scholars who privately pursue alchemical, Gnostic and magical studies, but who for obvious reasons – mainly academic funding – would never go public.

87. Churton, *The Golden Builders*, p. 100.

88. www.johndee.org/charlotte/Chapter7/7p1.html.

89. His companion is often erroneously said to have been John Dee himself.

90. Summers, p. 6.

91. *Ibid.*, p. 256.

92. Automatic writing is a common product of dissociation, deliberate or unconscious. One's hand writes apparently by itself, sometimes in another handwriting style, conveying messages that appear to come from another personality, and giving information that the person holding the pen seemingly could not have known.

93. Guy Lyon Playfair, 'This Perilous Medium', *The Unexplained*, pp. 2934–7, c.1981.

94. *Ibid.*

95. *Ibid.*

96. Roy Stemman, 'The Phenomenal Palladino', *The Unexplained*, pp. 2241–5, c.1981.

97. *Ibid.*

98. *Ibid.*

99. *Ibid.*

100. *Ibid.*

101. Suffering from intense religious rapture, Saint Joseph (1603–63) was questioned by the Inquisition, but released. Considered to be simple-minded – as a child he was known as 'open-mouth' – he lacked the concentration for the most menial of tasks.

102. Personal conversation between myself and Professor Roy in the early 1980s.

103. Stemman.

104. *Ibid*.

105. Parapsychologists of the 1980s had a term for this phenomenon: 'retrocognitive dissonance', meaning the further one moves away in time from witnessing even the most spectacular phenomena, the more one is liable to doubt them.

106. Charles Richet, 'On the Conditions of Certainty', PSPR p. 14, No. 35, 1899.

107. Dr Margaret Mead, quoted in Archie E. Roy in *A Sense of Something Strange*, Glasgow, 1990, p. 20.

Chapter Six   Do What Thou Wilt

1. Colin Wilson, *The Occult*, London, 1971, p. 372.

2. Ironically, as we have seen, 'Salem' is Semitic for 'peace' – other variations including 'shalom'. 'Jeru-salem' means 'House of Peace'. Shalem was the Hebrew Evening Star, twin to Shaher, or Lucifer, the Morning Star.

3. For the verbatim petitions of this and other convicted witches awaiting execution at Salem, see www.law.umkc.edu/faculty/projects/ftrials/salem/SAL_E&P.HTM.

4. Montague Summers, *The History of Witchcraft*, London, 1926, p. 146.

5. *Ibid*.

6. *Ibid*.

7. Typically, a mob would capture a black man accused of raping or abusing a white woman, and then proceed to beat and torture him publicly, setting fire to him, gouging out his eyes and/or cutting off his fingers, toes or genitals. Members of the crowd would be invited to participate in the torture. Eventually the victim would die of his injuries or be hanged or burnt to death. None of this was usually seen as cruel or anti-Christian: indeed, young people were encouraged to watch and even take part, almost as a sort of initiation into adulthood.

8. *The Crucible* by Arthur Miller was first produced on Broadway in 1953 but was not received well. However, a year later a new production won critical acclaim, setting the seal on the play as a modern classic.

9. *Bombers and Mash*, by Raynes Minns, London, 1980, p. 66.

10. As Elizabeth had no children, ironically the throne went to James, son of Mary Queen of Scots, whom she had had executed. James was the first king of that name in England, but James VI of Scotland.

11. More properly known as the Palace of Westminster.

12. Henry T.F. Rhodes, *The Satanic Mass*, London, 1954, p. 44.

13. *Ibid*.

14. Quoted in *Ibid*.

15. H.C. Lea, *Materials Towards a History of Witchcraft*, Philadelphia, 1939, p. 101.

16. Of course if one analyses what is believed to happen during the mass in the form of transubstantiation – i.e., the bread and wine become Jesus' actual flesh and blood – all priests are sorcerers. This is high magic: indeed, some commentators have had no hesitation to denounce it as black magic.
17. In the Beauregard.
18. Montague Summers, *The History of Witchcraft*, London, 1926, p. 89.
19. *Ibid.*, pp. 160–1.
20. Lynn Picknett and Clive Prince, *The Templar Revelation: Secret Guardians of the True Identity of Christ*, London, 1997, p. 108.
21. Also written 'Rays', 'Rayx' or 'Retz'.
22. Joris Karl Huysmans, *Là Bas*, Paris, 1891, is available in English as *Down There*, trans. Brendan King, London, 2001.
23. Wilson, p. 448.
24. *Ibid.*, p. 449.
25. *Ibid.*
26. Richard Griffiths, *The Reactionary Revolution*, London, 1966, pp. 129–35.
27. Picknett and Prince, p. 226, referencing Griffiths, p. 131.
28. Mike Howard, online article for the discussion group Talking Stick South: 'The Hellfire Club', //easyweb.easynet.co.uk/~rebis/ts-artic4.htm.
29. Quoted in *ibid*.
30. *Ibid.*
31. Quoted in *Ibid*.
32. *The Wall Street Journal Bookshelf*, 19 February 1998, p. A20.
33. Chambers' *Biographical Dictionary*, general editor Magnus Magnusson, Edinburgh, 1990, p. 1077.
34. *Wall Street Journal Bookshelf*, p. A20.
35. William Parsons, 3rd Earl of Rosse, Irish astronomer, born in York.
36. A. Cockren, *Alchemy Rediscovered and Restored*, New York, 1941, p. 82.
37. F. E. Manuel, *The Religion of Isaac Newton*, Oxford, 1974, p. 62.
38. Michael White, *Isaac Newton: The Last Sorcerer*, Addison Wesley, 1997, p. 49.
39. D. W. Hauck, 'Isaac Newton the Alchemist', www.alchemylab.com/isaac_newton.htm, p3.
40. *Ibid.*
41. Such as B.J.T. Dobbs in *The Foundations of Newton's Alchemy* Cambridge, 1984.
42. Paul Begg, 'The Man Who Created Life', *The Unexplained*, c.1981, p. 1767.
43. *Ibid.*
44. *Ibid.* Actually, the first dry-cell battery was produced by Georges Leclanché in1868.
45. *Ibid.*
46. Frances Yates, *The Rosicrucian Enlightenment*, London, 1972, Chapter XIII.

47. See Picknett and Prince; Michael Baigent and Richard Leigh, *The Temple and the Lodge*, London, 1989, and John J. Robinson, *Born in Blood*, London, 1990.

48. Lewis Spence, *An Encyclopaedia of Occultism*, London, 1920, p. 174.

49. Robinson, pp. 55–62, quoted in Picknett and Prince, p. 165.

50. Robert Lomas, *The Invisible College,* London, 2002, p. 3.

51. Thomas Spratt, *A History of the Royal Society*, quoted in *ibid*., p. 79.

52. *Ibid*.

53. S. Brent Morris, 'Albert Pike and Lucifer: The Lie That Will Not Die', short talk Bulletin (Masonic). I am indebted to Robert Lomas for providing the text of this talk.

54. 'Do Freemasons worship Satan/Lucifer?', www.geocities.com/endtime deception/worshipprint.htm, citing the alleged 'Instructions to the 23 Supreme Councils of the World, July 14, 1889. Recorded by A.C. De La Rive in La Femme de l'Enfant dans la FrancMaçonnerie Universelle on page 588'.

55. Jules Bois, *Le monde invisible*, Paris, 1902, pp 168-170. I am indebted to Clive Prince for finding and translating this for me.

56. See for example, Alec Mellor, 'A Hoaxer of Genius – Leo Taxil', (Richmond, Va.,), 1964, pp. 149–55.

57. Morris.

58. H.P. Blavatsky, *The Secret Doctrine*, London, 1888, pp. 171, 225, 255, 888 (vol. II), quoted on website cited in note 54 above.

59. Helena P. Blavatsky, *Isis Unveiled*, London, 1876, Vol. II, p. 2.

60. *Ibid*., p. 292.

61. *Ibid*., p. 482.

62. *Ibid*., p. 507.

63. Private email to me from Robert Lomas, 19 November 2004, quoting Masonic ritual.

64. *Ibid*.

65. *Ibid*.

66. *Ibid*.

67. *Ibid*.

68. Chris Cranmer: he threatened to sue the Royal Navy for religious discrimi-nation if not allowed to worship on board.

69. It must be stressed that Satanism is by no means synonymous with modern witchcraft, or *Wicca* – largely the nature-based pre-Christian religion, which honours both a god and a goddess. Unfortunately, Wicca as such lies outside the scope of this book.

70. Such as 'The devil and the deep blue sea: Navy gives blessing to sailor Satanist' by Helen Carter in *The Guardian*, Monday 25 October 2004. I am indebted to the staff at the Meghna Grill NW8 for very kindly providing this article for me.

71. Ann Widdecombe, former Tory Minister and Catholic convert said: 'Satanism is wrong. Obviously, the private beliefs of individuals anywhere – including the armed forces – are their own affair, but I hope it doesn't spread . . . There should be no question whatsoever of allowing Satanist rituals aboard navy ships. God himself gives free will, but I would like to think if somebody applied to the navy and said they were a Satanist today it would raise its eyebrows somewhat.' Quoted in *ibid*.

72. *Ibid*.

73. *Ibid*.

74. Anton Szandor LaVey, *The Satanic Bible*, New York, 1969, Introduction.

75. *Ibid*.

76. *Ibid*.

77. *Ibid*., p. 50.

78. *Ibid*., p. 34.

79. *Ibid*., p. 155.

80. *Ibid*., p. 103.

81. Francis X. King, (ed.), *Crowley on Christ*, London, 1974, Introduction.

82. *Ibid*.

83. Quoted in Tobias Churton, *The Gnostic Philosophy*, Lichfield, 2003, p. 302.

84. Taken from Crowley's *Commentary on the Book of the Law*, written at the Hotel du Djerid at Nefta in Tunisia, September 1923. Quoted in Churton, p. 310.

85. Aleister Crowley, *The Book of Thoth: (Egyptian Tarot)*, York Beach, Maine, 1944, p. 96.

86. *Ibid*.

87. Ed. John Symonds and Kenneth Grant, *The Confessions of Aleister Crowley*, London, 1978.

88. Churton, p. 319.

89. *Ibid*.

90. Symonds and Grant.

91. Aleister Crowley, *The Book of the Law*, quoted in Churton, p. 318.

92. By a coincidence I have met two people whose relatives were cursed by Crowley. My agent, Jeffrey Simmons, told me that his father received a curse from the Great Beast, which fortunately had no effect except to disgust everyone who heard about it. Another cursee was *Fortean Times*' co-editor Paul Sieveking, whose father Lance was cursed by Crowley. Again, it failed.

93. Churton, p. 304.

94. *Ibid*., p. 315.

95. *Crowley on Christ*, p. 106.

96. It is said that when he refused, Crowley cursed him to die within two days of his own (imminent) death. The doctor duly gave up the ghost on schedule.

97. LaVey, p. 76.

98. Wilson, p. 27.

Epilogue   The Lucifer Key

1. December 2004. It is estimated that there are about 15,000 Mandaeans left in Iraq, but they are officially classed as 'a people in danger' by the United Nations. They were largely left alone under Sadam's regime: it was only after the Invasion that their troubles really began.

2. Howard Blum, *The Lucifer Principle*, New York, 1995, p. 330.

3. 'Mr Bean defends the right to laugh', the *Daily Mail*, Tuesday, 7 December 2004. The proposal would ban anyone from using language that might offend someone on the grounds of their religion. Those found guilty would face up to seven years in jail.

4. Marco Bischof, *Biophotons – The Light in Our Cells* (1995), quoted on www.transpersonal.de/mbischof/englisch/webbookeng.htm.

5. Surely the only truly bad science is that which is pursued by a closed mind with preconceptions and a secret agenda.

6. Colin Wilson, 'Devil and the deep blue sea', *Daily Mail*, Tuesday, 26 October 2004.

7. For what became his book *Powers of Darkness, Powers of Light*.

8. Wilson/*Mail*.

9. Francis X. King, 'The Word Made Flesh', *The Unexplained*, c. 1981, p. 1693.

10. 'Obsessed with drugs and death, a descent into evil', by Peter Allen and Grace McLean, *The Daily Mail*, 22 January 2005.

11. Lucy Hughes-Hallett, 'Be very afraid', *The Sunday Times Culture*, March 6, 2005, p. 51.

12. *Ibid*.

13. Erica Jong, *Witches*, (London) 1981, p. 172.

Acknowledgements

As usual, a great many kind, supportive and especially tolerant friends and colleagues have contributed, directly or indirectly, to the gestation and writing of this book. The following in particular have in one way or another succeeded in keeping up the authorial spirits and getting the show on the road.

Special thanks to:
Clive Prince, my friend and colleague *par excellence*, for his unwavering support and comfort, readiness to point out when anxieties are needless and the efficacy of Thai curries for most ills, not to mention his generous discovery and translation of various French passages and provision of elusive references. It's been the best decade ever!

Debbie Benstead, for inspiring me to write this book in the first place with her enthusiasm for the *real* Lucifer, and for her rightly fabled generosity as a hostess. I don't think we're there yet, though . . .

Sheila and Eric Taylor, whose enduring kindness and northern hospitality know no bounds, and whose comfort in times of stress or distress puts a very different face on the world. Such true life-enhancers are few and far between.

Craig Oakley, an old and very understanding friend, who knows all about the years that led inevitably to this book.

Jeffrey Simmons, my agent and friend, for his support.

Nigel Foster, without whose kindness *The Secret History of Lucifer* would literally never have been produced.

Robert Lomas, for his generous contribution to the section on Freemasonry – and all at a moment's notice!

Graham Philips, for his good advice. And just for being himself.

Yvan Cartwright, for his good-natured hospitality, humour and nagging about a web site. There will be one, one day . . .

At Constable, Krystyna Green, Gary Chapman and Sarah Moore. Thanks for your patience and good humour – not to mention an unusual willingness to stretch deadlines.

Charles and Annette Fowkes, old friends whose hospitality and encouragement is much appreciated.

My York friends: David Bell, Moira Hardcastle and Richard Hardcastle for always being interested and supportive, plus silly giggling and mulled wine experiences and much, much more over more years than any of us care to remember.

All the talented and congenial 'NoNamers', in appreciation of many excellent discussions and lots of laughs, especially Andy and Suzie Collins, Ian Lawton and Caroline Wise.

Lou Tate – lovely to be back in touch after all this time!

Thanks too, to Jayne Burns; Christy Fearn; Carina Fearnley; 'Giovanni'; John Glasscock; Hannah R. Johnson; Octavia Kenny; Jane Lyle; and John and Joy Millar.

The staffs of the British Library and St John's Wood Library.

AND FOR DECADES OF INSPIRATION – WHO ELSE BUT COLIN WILSON?

Select Bibliography

There are hundreds of books on Lucifer, the Devil/Satan, evil and allied subjects, but these are just a sample of the more invaluable texts.

(Where possible, the paperback editions are given. Other titles can be found in the Notes and References.)

Ahmed, Rollo, *The Black Art*, Arrow Books Ltd, London, 1966. First published in 1936.

Baigent, Michael, and Richard Leigh, *The Inquisition*, Penguin, London, 2000.

Baigent, Michael, Richard Leigh and Henry Lincoln, *The Holy Blood and the Holy Grail*, Jonathan Cape, London, 1982; revised edition; Arrow, London, 1996.

Birks, Walter and R. A. Gilbert, *The Treasure of Montségur*, The Aquarian Press, London, 1990.

Blavatsky, H. P., *Isis Unveiled*, Theosophical University Press, Pasadena, CA., 1988, originally published 1876.

——*The Secret Doctrine*, Theosophical University Press, Pasadena, 1888.

Blum, Howard, *The Lucifer Principle: A Scientific Expedition into the Forces of History*, Atlantic Monthly Press, New York, 1995.

Bramly, Serge, *Leonardo: The Artist and the Man*, Michael Joseph, London, 1992; first published as *Léonard de Vinci*, Éditions Jean-Claude Lattés, Paris, 1988.

Campbell, Joseph, *The Mask of God: Creative Mythology*, Penguin, New York, 1959.

Churton, Tobias, *The Golden Builders: Alchemists, Rosicrucians and the First Free Masons*, Signal Publishing, Lichfield, 2002.

——*The Gnostic Philosophy*, Signal Publishing, Lichfield, 2003.

Collins, Andrew, *Twenty-first Century Grail: The Quest for a Legend*, Virgin, London, 2004.

Crowley, Aleister, *The Book of Thoth*, Samuel Weiser, Inc., York Beach, Maine, 1944.

De Troyes, Chrétien, trans. Burton Raffel, *Perceval: The Story of the Grail*, Yale University Press, New Haven, USA, 1999. Originally published in the 12th century.

De Voragine, Jacobus, *The Golden Legend: Readings on the Saints*, trans. William Grayer Ryan, 2 Volumes, Princeton University Press, 1993.

Drower, E. S., *The Mandaeans of Iraq and Iran: Their Cults, Customs, Magic, Legends and Folklore*, Clarendon Press, Oxford, 1937.

Frazer, Sir James G., *The Golden Bough: A Study in Magic and Religion*, Macmillan, London, 1922.

Freke, Timothy and Peter Gandy, *Jesus and the Goddess*, Thorsons, London, 2002.

Godwin, Malcom, *The Holy Grail: Its Origins, Secrets and Meaning Revealed*, Bloomsbury, London, 1994.

Harpur, Patrick, *Daimonic Reality: Understanding Otherworld Encounters*, Penguin Arkana, London, 1995.

Haskins, Susan, *Mary Magdalen*, HarperCollins, London, 1993.

Huysmans, J. K., trans. Terry Hale, *The Damned*, Penguin Classics, London, 2001. First published in Paris as *Là Bas* (*Down There*), 1891.

Institoris, Henricus, *The Malleus Maleficarum of Heinrich Kramer and Jakob Sprenger*, Dover Publications, New York, 1971.

James I and Paul Tice, *Demonology*, Book Tree, New York, 2002. First published in London, 1597.

Jones, Gwyn and Thomas Jones (trans. and ed.), *The Mabinogion*, J. M. Dent & Sons, London, 1974.

Jong, Erica, illustration by Joseph A. Smith, *Witches*, Granada, London, 1988.

Josephus, Flavius, *The Jewish War*, trans. G. A. Williamson, Penguin, London, 1970.

King, Francis (Ed.), *Crowley on Christ*, The C. W. Daniel Company Ltd., 1974.

LaVey, Anton Szandor, *The Satanic Bible*, New York, Avon Books (HarperCollins), 1969.

——*The Satanic Rituals*, Avon Books, New York, 1972.

——*The Devil's Notebook*, Feral House, Los Angeles, 1992.

Layton, Bentley, *The Gnostic Scriptures*, SCM Press, London, 1987.

Lévi, Éliphas, *The History of Magic*, trans. A. E. Waite, William Rider & Sons, London, 1913; first published as Histoire de la magie, Germer Baillière, Paris, 1860.

Lomas, Robert, *The Invisible College: The Royal Society, Freemasonry and the Birth of Modern Science*, Headline, London, 2002.

Luckert, Karl W., *Egyptian Light and Hebrew Fire*, State University of New York Press, New York, 1991.

Mann, A.T., and Jane Lyle, *Sacred Sexuality*, Element Books, Shaftesbury, 1996.

Markale, Jean, trans. Jon Graham, *Montségur and the Mystery of the Cathars,* Inner Traditions, Rochester, Vermont, 2003. Originally published as *Montségur et l'énigme cathare* by Éditions Pymalion/Gérard Watelet, Paris, 1986.

Mead, G. R. S., *Pistis Sophia*, Kessinger Publishing Company, Kila, MT, USA, 1921.

——*Simon Magus: An Essay*, Theosophical Publishing Society, London, 1892.

McGrath, Alister E., *A Brief History of Heaven*, Blackwell Publishers, Malden, MA, USA, 2003.

Milton, John, ed. Christopher Ricks, series Ed., John Hollander, Introduction by Susanne Woods, *Paradise Lost and Paradise Regained*, Penguin Books, London, 2001. First published in 1667.

Nataf, André, *The Occult*, W & R Chambers, Edinburgh, 1991; first published as *Les Maîtres de l'occultisme*, Bordas, Paris, 1988.

Pagels, Elaine, *The Gnostic Gospels*, Penguin Books, London, 1982.

——*The Origin of Satan*, Vintage Books, New York, 1996.

Patai, Raphael, *The Hebrew Goddess*, (3rd Ed.), Wayne State University Press, Detroit, 1990.

Picknett, Lynn, *Mary Magdalene: Christianity's Hidden Goddess*, Robinson, London, 2003.

Picknett, Lynn and Clive Prince, *The Templar Revelation: Secret Guardians of the True Identity of Christ*, Corgi, London, 1998.

——*The Stargate Conspiracy*, Warner Books, London, 1999.

——*Turin Shroud: In Whose Image? How Leonardo da Vinci Fooled History*, Corgi, London, 2000.

Pike, Albert, *Morals and Dogma*, Lightning Source UK Ltd., London, 2004.

Rahn, Otto, *La Cour de Lucifer*, Éditions Pardès, Puiseaux, 1994. Originally published as *Luzifers Hofgesind*, Verlag für ganzheitliche Forschung und Kultur, Berlin, 1937.

Redgrove, Peter, *The Black Goddess and the Sixth Sense*, Paladin, London, 1989.

Rhodes, Henry, T. F., *The Satanic Mass*, Arrow Books, London, 1954.

Robinson, John A. T., *The Priority of John*, SCM Press, London, 1985.

Rowe, Joseph (trans.) *The Gospel of Mary Magdalene*, Inner Traditions, Rochester, USA, 2002.

Rudolph, Kurt, *Mandaeism*, E. J. Brill, Leiden, 1978.

Russell, Jeffrey Burton, *Witchcraft in the Middle Ages*, Cornell University Press, Ithaca and London, 1972.

——*Satan: The Early Christian Tradition*, Cornell University Press, Ithaca and London, 1981.

——*Lucifer: The Devil in the Middle Ages*, Cornell University Press, Ithaca and London, 1984.

Smith, Morton, *Clement of Alexandria and a Secret Gospel of Mark*, Harvard University Press, Cambridge, Mass., 1973.

——*The Secret Gospel: The Discovery and Interpretation of the Secret Gospel According to Mark*, Gollancz, London, 1973.

——*Jesus the Magician*, Victor Gollancz, London, 1978.

Stoyanov, Yuri, *The Hidden Tradition in Europe*, Arkana, London, 1994.

Summers, the Reverend Montague, *The History of Witchcraft*, The Mystic Press, London, 1925.

Walker, Benjamin, *Gnosticism: Its History and Influence*, The Aquarian Press, Wellingborough, Northants, 1983.

Walker, Barbara, *The Woman's Encyclopedia of Myths and Secrets*, HarperCollins, San Francisco, 1983.

Welburn, Andrew, (Introduction and Commentary), *Gnosis: The Mysteries and Christianity: An Anthology of Essene, Gnostic and Christian Writings*, Floris Books, Edinburgh, 1994.

White, Michael, Isaac Newton: *The Last Sorcerer*, 4th Estate, London, 1998.

Wilson, Colin, *The Occult*, Hodder & Stoughton, London, 1971.

Wolfram von Eschenbach, *Parzival*, (trans. A. T. Hatto), Penguin, London, 1980. Originally published in the early 13th century.

Vinci, Leo, *Pan: Great God of Nature*, Neptune Press, London, 1993.

Yalom, Marilyn, *A History of the Wife*, HarperCollins, New York, 2001.

Yates, Frances, *The Rosicrucian Enlightenment*, Routledge & Kegan Paul, London, 1972.

Index

abortion 159
Abriel, Jorg 147
'acari' 235–6
Accoules 176
Ache, Felipe 206
Acts of the Apostles 75
Adam 4, 9, 12, 20, 36
Adam and Eve myth 4, 7–9, 10, 11–13,
    14, 28, 32, 33, 36
Adonis 58
Agartha 122
Ahab, King of Israel 42, 45
Ahmed, Rollo 102
Ahriman 18–19
Ahura-Mazda 18, 19
Aiwass (Guardian Angel) 246–7
alchemy 181, 183, 191–2, 195, 196, 199,
    225, 232–3
Alexandria 100, 102, 104, 108
Amen-Ra 50
Anchoresses, Rule for 141
angels 17, 20
Anne, St 94
Anne-Marie de Georgel 140
anti-Semitism 148, 167, 258
Antiquities of the Jews (Josephus) 98, 107
Aphrodite 61–2
apocatastasis 28
Apollo 121, 123–4
Apollos (Alexandrian) 100
Apostles, Acts of the 101

Apremont, Arnaud d' 123
Aquinas, Thomas, St 24, 159
Arcadia 56, 57
Arian heresy 233
Arras 150–1
Artemidorus 53
Artemis (Diana) 55
Ashe, Geoffrey 54
Asherah/Ashereth 18, 35–6, 38–42, 43,
    44, 48, 59, 61, 62
Ashteroth-Karnaim 62
Astarte 50, 58
Aster 22, 58
Astraea ('Starry One') 58
astrology 195
Atkinson, Rowan 252
atonement 23–4
Atum 3, 14
Auf-Ra 60
Augustine, St 11, 22

Bacchus 93
Baggally, W.W. 209
Baigent, Michael 84, 137, 138
Bamberg prison 153
baptism xiii, 24, 66
Basil, St 165, 166
Basle University 193
Besterman, Theodore 206
Bethany 73, 74, 91, 92, 93, 99–100
Beyond God the Father (Daly) 143

Béziers 84–5
'Big Bang' 3–4
biophotons 253
Bischof, Marco 253
Black Goddess, The (Redgrove) 75
Black Masses 142, 223, 225–6, 227, 229,
　230, 231, 254
Blake, William 28
Blavatsky, Madame 239–40
Bogomils 118, 134
Bohemia, King of 199
Bois, Jules 238–9
Book of the Dead, The 31
Book of John 134
Book of Mysteries (Dee) 196
Boullan, Abbé Joseph 227–8
Bourignon, Antoinette 145
Bourke, Joanna 258
Boyle, Robert 234
Brazilian Institute for Psychobiophysical
　Research (BPP) 205
Brent Morris, S. 238, 239
Brown, Dan xiii, 84, 190
Brown, Raymond E. 88–9
Budge, E. A. Wallis 48
Bulgaria 118
Burnham-on-Crouch, Essex 254
Burroughs, Revd George 217–18
Butler, Samuel 196–7
Buttiglione, Sr 71
Byron, Lord 57

Cabbalists 9, 183
caffeine 231
Cain 141
Cambridge University 195
camera obscura 180, 182, 186
Canaanites 39
Cannon, Laura-Lea 77
Carcassonne 140
Carmel, Church of 226–7
Carpocrates of Alexandria 64, 66
Carpocratians 64–70, 83, 90, 91, 110,
　117, 141
Carrington, Hereward 209
Casaubon, Meric 244
Cason, Joan 144
Cassou, Arthur 122
Castelan, Laurens de 193–4
Cathars 117–24, 134–8, 140, 143,
　164, 178
Catton, Suffolk 156

Cecil, William, 1st Baron Burghley 200
Ceres, priestesses of 160
Cernunnos 54
Chamberlain, Houston Stewart 178–9
Champagne, Count of 130
cherubim 44–5, 134
Cherubino, Friar 158–9
Chevalier, Adèle 227
Chiaia, Ercole 207
child-killing 223, 224, 227
childbirth 10–11, 12, 46, 160–1
Chrétien de Troyes 124–5, 127, 129,
　130, 131
Christians/Christianity 21, 24, 30, 47,
　110, 117
　attitude to sex 11, 60, 65
　and Genesis 6, 7, 13–14
　and necromancy 170
　persecution of 26
　and Satan 22, 23
　sex rites of 62, 68–9, 70–1, 89–90, 91,
　　99, 110, 141–2, 228
Church of Satan 242–5
Churton, Tobias 64, 67, 103, 132, 181,
　183–4, 202–3, 247, 248
Claire, Sister 175
Clement XII, Pope 229
Clement of Alexandria 28, 63–4, 67,
　68–9, 90, 99, 106, 110, 141
Clementine Recognitions 102–3
Cleopatra, Queen of Egypt 59–60
Clergyman's Daughter, A (Orwell) 52–3
Collins, Andrew 125
Cologne, University of 157
Columbine High School 257
conjuration 256
Consolamentum 137
Constance 152
Constantine I, emperor of Rome 26,
　76–7, 117
contraception 160
convents 173–6
Copernicus 195
Cornwell, John 254
Cracow, Poland 198
Cranmer, Chris 242–3, 253
creation myths 3–4
Crete 60
Cromwell, Oliver 51
Crosse, Andrew xv, 234–7
Crowley, Aleister 9–10, 50, 103, 104–5,
　245–9

The Book of the Law 201–2, 246, 247
Book of Thoth 246
Magical Record 246
Crowley on Christ (King) 104, 245, 246
Crucible, The (Miller) 218
Crusaders 121
Cumberland, HMS 242
Cyril of Jerusalem, St 61, 77
Cyrus, King 5

Da Vinci Code, The (Brown) xiii, 84, 190
Daemonologie (James I) 219
Daily Mail 164
Dalkieth, Luke Mitchell 257
Daly, Mary 143
Dance of the Seven Veils 107
Daniel, Book of 233
Darkness *see* Light and Darkness
Dashwood, Sir Francis 229–31
David-Neel, Madame Alexander 255
Dee, John xiv–xv, 195–6, 197, 198, 200,
    202–3, 244
della Porta, Giovanni Battista
    181, 192–3
demiurges 27, 30
demons
    demonic possession 173–6
    our own demons 259–60
Denver, William G. 38
Devil *see* Satan
'devil marks' *see* 'witch marks'
Devils of Loudon, The (Huxley) 173
Devils, The (film; Russell) 173
Diana 55, 58, 62, 149
Dilettanti, Society of the 229
Dionysus 25, 37, 84
divination 169
Dominic de Guzmán 135–6, 137
Dominican Order 135, 136, 137
Drake, Francis 167
Dreamer of the Vine, The (Greene) 55
Driesch, Hans 206
Duncan, Helen 164
dusii 56

ectoplasm 210–11
Eden, Garden of
    Man's expulsion from 6–7, 11–13,
        14, 59
    as Paradise 4–5, 6, 7
    search for location 5–6
    serpent in 6–8, 9–10, 12, 13, 33

Egypt, ancient 9, 14, 33, 45, 59–60, 60–1,
    72, 98, 110–11
    baptisms 24
    creation myth 3–4
    gods/goddesses of 31–2, 39, 47–8, 66
Egyptian Light and Hebrew Fire
    (Luckert) 103
Eichstätt 150
Elizabeth I, Queen of England 195, 200
Emerald Tablet 233–4
endura 118
Enlightenment 30, 178, 215, 231, 256
Enoch, Book of 17
Enochian language 197, 200–1
Ephesus 55, 98, 100
Epiphanes (son of Carpocrates) 66
Epiphanius 102, 141–2
erotomania 173–6
Esclarmonde 122
Ethiopia 72
Eve 4, 8, 9, 10, 11, 14, 34, 35, 36, 59, 61,
    141, 161
Evening Star (Venus) 58, 59, 134
evil *see* Good and Evil
executions 109, 136, 137, 138, 162–3
Exodus
    5:3 32
    22:18 143–4
exorcism 24, 160
Ezekiel 28:13–15 17

Fall, the 8, 12, 13, 14, 21
Faraday, Michael 236
Faust (Goethe) 170–3
Faustus, Dr 102, 168–9, 170, 171–2
Fawkes, Guy 219
fear 257–8
Fear: A Cultural History (Bourke) 258
Feilding, Everard 209
Feminine Principle 34, 44, 50, 60, 62,
    117, 143, 227
Fisher, Neil 164
Fisher King 49, 124, 128
Flamel, Nicholas and Perrenelle 191
Flammarion, Camille 208–9
Flanders 137
Flournoy, Theodore 201
Formaricus (Nider) 158
Forres, Scotland 220
France 117, 130, 137, 150, 218
Frankenstein (Shelley) 13, 237
Franklin, Benjamin 230, 235

Frazer, J.G. 58
Frederick, Prince of Wales 230
free speech 252
Freeman, Ann 164
Freemasonry xv, 183, 229, 237–42, 251
Freke, Timothy 87
French Revolution 226
Freya 52
Friars of Wycombe, Order of the 228
Furniss, Father 15

Galahad 125
Galileo Galilei 195
Gandy, Peter 87
Garmann, Christian Friedrich 194
Gaufridi, Louis 176, 177
Genesis, Book of 4, 5, 7, 18, 20, 35
George and Vulture pub 229
Germany 218
Gian de Bellinzona 189
Giovan Francesco Rustici 182
Gnostic Philosophy, The (Churton) 183
Gnostics/Gnosticism 19, 26–7, 64, 65, 83,
    118, 140, 172, 184, 240, 251
  and Good and Evil 27, 33
  and Jesus 119–20
  and Lucifer 28–9
  secret gospels of 33, 63–4, 68, 78, 81, 82,
    84, 112, 120
  and the serpent 10, 33
Goat of Mendes 54
God (Yahweh) 6, 7–8, 27–8, 46–7
  and Adam and Eve 9, 10, 13, 14, 20,
    28, 33
  as a failure 260
  lack of humour 170–1
  nastiness of 4, 21, 28
  Set as prototype 31–2, 33, 34, 45, 47
  two god theory 30
  wife of 35–6, 38–42, 43, 44, 59, 61, 62
gods/goddesses xiii, 58–62, 104
    Christian parallels 24–5, 47–8
    demonization of 47, 49, 53–5, 79
Goethe, Johann Wolfgang 170–3
Goines, David Lance 62
Golden Age 57
Golden Bough, The (Frazer) 58
Golden Builders, The (Churton) 184
Golden Legend (Jacob de Voragine)
    133–4
golems 13
Good and Evil 30, 33, 63

gospels
  reworking of 88–9
  variety of 76–8
Gozzoli, Father 226
Grahame, Kenneth 58
Grandier, Father Urbain 162, 174–5, 177
graves, desecrating 169
Great Mother 39, 42–3
Great Revelation (Simon Magus) 104
Greece, ancient 29, 50, 79
Greene, Liz 55
Gregory I, Pope 72
Gregory IX, Pope 136
Guillaume Pelhisson 136–7
Gunpowder Plot 219

Hammer of the Witches, The
    (Kramer/Sprenger) 151–2, 156–8,
    159, 161
Harris, Eric 257
Hecate ('Wise Crone') 45–6
Heinrich von Schultheis 162
Helen of Troy 102
Hell 14–16, 24, 28, 42–3, 120, 138, 166
'Hellfire Caves' 230
Hellfire Club 228–31
heresy 24, 135, 136–8
Hermeticism 181, 183, 233, 234
Herod, King 95, 97, 99, 108, 109, 111
Herodias 37, 95, 97, 112
Herolt, Johann 160
Hershel, William 232
Heywood, Thomas 220–1
Hidden Tradition in Europe
    (Stoyanov) 121
Hierarchie of the Blessed Angels
    (Heywood) 220–1
Hieroglyphic Mind, The (Dee) 195
Hincmar of Reims 165–6
Hink, Robert 146
History of the Wife, A (Yalom) 71
History of Witchcraft, The (Summers) 139
Hitler, Adolf 218
Hobbes (servant) 221
Hodgson, Richard 208
Hogg, Thomas J. 57
Hokma ('Wisdom') 45, 46
Holy Blood and the Holy Grail, The
    (Baigent/Leigh/Lincoln) 84
Holy Grail 121–34
Homo Ludens (Huizinga) 184
homosexuality 71

homunculi 192–3, 194
Hopkins, Matthew ('Witchfinder General') 163
Horace 53
Horae 160
horns, lunar 62
Horus 33, 47
Howard, Mike 230–1
Hubristika festival 43
Hudibras (Butler) 196–7
Hughes-Hallett, Lucy 258
Huizinga, Johan 184
humour 170–1, 257
Huxley, Aldous 173
Huysman, J.K. 225
Hypatia 61

Ignatius, St 23, 25
ilim 36
Immanuel Kant (Chamberlain) 178–9
incubi 37–8, 56
Ingostadt 168
Innocent VIII, Pope 157
Inquisition (Holy Office) 28, 56, 134, 174, 177
  and the Cathars 135–40
and heretics 136–8
  Spanish Inquisition 156
  and witch trials xv, 142–58, 161–3, 171, 218
Inquisition, The (Baigent/Leigh) 137, 138
Irenaeus, Bishop of Lyon 24, 64–6, 87, 110
Isaac Newton: The Last Sorcerer (White) 233
Isaiah 15–16, 17, 53
Ishtar-Mari 47, 48
Isis xiii, 24, 31, 32, 33, 47–8, 58, 60, 66, 79, 242
Isis Unveiled (Blavatsky) 239–40
Isis-Hathor 62
Israelites 32, 45

Jacob de Voragine 133–4
Jacobites 229
James I, King of England 219–20
Jerome, St 11, 17, 141, 165
Jerusalem Temple 41, 44
Jesual the Son 19
Jesus Christ 5, 7, 23–4, 25, 33, 47, 62, 66, 68, 69, 72, 110–13, 119–20, 251
  crucifixion of 92

and John the Baptist 94, 97–101, 105–6, 108–9, 111–12, 134
  and the Last Supper xiv, 86, 87–8, 89
  and Lazarus 69–70, 89–90, 91, 111
  and Mary Magdalene xii–xiii, 62, 69–70, 72–5, 78–81, 82–90, 91–2
  'old god' prototypes 24–5, 47–8
  and pagan cults xiii
  possible sex rites of 68, 69, 70–1, 89–90, 91, 99, 110, 228
  Second Coming 23, 25–6
  and Simon Magus 105
Jesus and the Goddess (Freke/Gandy) 87
Jesus the Magician (Smith) 110, 112
Jews/Judaism 7, 14, 18, 21, 22–3, 44, 69–70, 141, 167, 218, 258
Jezebel 42
Joan of Arc 224
Job, Book of 31
Joel (prophet) 75
Johannes Dominicus 157–8
Johannes Nider 158
Johannites 130, 131, 132, 177, 179, 227
John the Baptist xiii, 102–3, 104, 119, 130, 134–5, 178, 179, 228, 251
  and Jesus 97–101, 105–6, 108–10, 134, 170
  killing of 37, 107–8, 109, 111–12
  Leonardo's depiction of 93–7
  as the Morning Star 133–4
John Paul II, Pope 147
John, St (the Evangelist) 34, 72, 73, 76, 82, 85, 90, 101, 104, 105
  Gospel of 74, 84, 87, 88, 89, 99
  as Lazarus 90, 91, 105
John, The Gospel of 120
Jones, Jodi 257
Jong, Erica 259
Jordan, Michael 64
Jordan, river 98, 101
Joseph d'Arimathie (Robert de Boron) 125
Joseph of Arimathea 125
Joseph of Cupertino 210
Josephus, Flavius 5, 98, 107
Judaea 109
Judas 21
Jude, St 96, 187
Junius, Johannes 153–4
Jusino, Ramon K. 88, 89

Kardec, Alan 204

Kelley (or 'Kelly'), Edward 196–7, 198, 199, 200, 201, 202–3
Keynes, John Maynard 232
King, Francis X. 104, 245, 246
Klebold, Dylan 257
Knights of St Francis, Order of the 229
Knights Templar 121, 130–1, 135, 177–8, 237
Knights of West Wycombe, the Order of the 228
Kordiev, Sergei 254
Kraeling, Carl 109–10
Kramer, Heinrich 151–2, 156–7, 157–8, 259

La Bas (Huysman) 225, 227–8
La Salette 227
La Voisin, Catherine 223–4
Lady, cult of 140
Lamy, Michel 134
L'Ancre, Pierre de 222
languages 200–1
Languedoc 122, 136, 140
Laval, Gilles de 224–5
LaVey, Anton 242, 243–5, 248, 249
Lazarus 69–70, 89–90, 91, 101, 111
Lea, H.C. 222
Lectiones super Ecclesiastes (Dominicus) 157–8
Leigh, Richard 84, 137, 138
Lemp, Rebecca 152
lenses 186–7
Leo X, Pope 191
Leonardo da Vinci xiii–xiv, xv, 85–7, 93–7, 194
  as 'Grandson of God' 178–9, 181, 188
  heresies of 85–7, 93–7, 106, 178–90, 191
  Adoration of the Magi 95–6, 187
  John the Baptist (sculpture, with Rustici) 182
  Last Supper xiv, 86–7, 93, 94, 106, 184, 186, 187
  St John the Baptist 93–4, 184, 186
  Virgin and Child with St Anne (cartoon) 94–5
  Virgin and Child with St Anne (painting) 95
  Virgin of the Rocks xiv, 96–7, 184, 185–6, 187, 190
  'Witch with a Magic Mirror' 182
Levi 82

Levi, Eliphas xi–xii, 246
levitation 204, 209–10
Leviticus 53
Liber Logaeth (Dee) 200
Light and Darkness 27, 33
Lilas (Satan's wife) 46
Lilith 36–7, 38, 60, 61
Lille 145
Lincoln, Henry 84
Loki (Scandinavian god) 29
Lomas, Robert 237, 240–2
Lombroso, Cesare 207
Lord's Prayer 119
Loudon, convent at 173–6
Louis XVII, 'King of France' 226, 227
Lucifer xi–xii, 20, 32, 35, 43, 44, 61, 121, 124, 133, 252–3, 261
  fall of 14, 15–22, 29, 30, 33, 123
  Gnostic admiration for 28–9
  and the Masons 238–40
  as the Morning Star xii, 16, 39, 58, 134
  as synonym for Satan xv, 22, 30, 242, 253
Luciferanism xiv–xv, 61, 66, 118, 120, 121, 171, 172, 178, 179–80, 189, 192
  and the Light 251–3
Luckert, Karl 3, 31, 32, 34, 103
Luke, St 73, 76
  Gospel of 33, 73, 74, 81, 84, 91–3
Lyle, Jane 37

Macalyne, Eufame 161
McCarthyite 'witch-hunts' 218
McIntosh, Christopher 183–4
McKenna, Stephen 53–4
Madimi (angel) 198
Maenads 55
magic 101, 102, 104, 110–12
Magnificat 99
Magre, Maurice 122
Maintenon, Madame de 224
Manasseh, King 41
Mandaeans 101, 106, 112, 113, 130, 131, 132, 177, 251
Mann, A.T. 37
Mansfield, Jayne 245
Manson, Marilyn 257
Manuel, F.E. 233
Mar Saba discoveries 63, 68, 89–90, 99, 106, 107
Marcion 30
Marcus (Carpocratian leader) 64–6, 110

Mari-Ishtar (Great Whore) 75
Mark, St 73, 76
  Gospel of 73, 80, 84, 91, 106
  Secret Gospel of 63–4, 68–9, 70, 90
Markale, Jean 12, 18–19, 21, 117-18,
  119, 120
Marlowe, Christopher 168, 169
Martha (sister of Lazarus) 72, 78, 99,
  110, 141
'Martian' language 201
martyrdom 25, 26
Mary: The Unauthorized Biography
  (Jordan) 64
Mary I, Queen of England 195
Mary, Queen of Scots 197
Mary Magdalene xiii, 5, 68, 69, 107, 110,
  120, 134, 141, 142, 228
  anointing of Jesus 70, 73–6, 91–2, 108
  and Jesus xii–xiii, 62, 69–70, 72–5,
    78–81, 82–90, 91–2
  and the Last Supper xiv, 86–8, 89,
    90, 93
  as 'Mary Lucifer' xii, 85
  and pagan goddesses xiii, xv
  role in resurrection 72, 80, 81–2
  status as disciple 72–3, 76, 77–82
Mary Magdalene, The Gospel of 77, 81,
  87, 89
Masculine Principle 50
mass hysteria 173
Materials Towards A History of
  Witchcraft (Lea) 222
Mather, Cotton 216
Matthew, St 73
  Gospel of 76, 84, 111
Maximilian II, Holy Roman Emperor 195
Maxwell, William 194
May Day festivities 51–2
May poles 51–2
Mead, Margaret 213
Meaux 141
Medea (Euripides) 56
mediums 196, 203–13
Medmenham Abbey 229–30
Medmenham, The Monks of 228
Mehen the Enveloper 60
menstruation 141, 142–3
Mephistopheles 170, 171, 172, 184
Michael, archangel 19, 20, 33
midwives 10, 46, 159–60
Milan, Edict of 117
Miller, Arthur 218

Milton, John 11, 12, 16–17, 19–20, 27–8,
  30, 41–2, 49
Mirabelli, Carmine 204–5
Mithras 19, 25
Molland, Alice 163
Monas Hieroglyphica (Dee) 197, 203
monasteries 173
Mont-Aimé 137
Montespan, Madame de 223–4
Montségur 121, 122, 123, 138
Montségur and the Mystery of the Cathars
  (Markale) 117–18
Moray, Sir Robert 237
Morselli, Enrico 208, 211
Moses 32, 45
Muller, Catherine Elise 201
Muslims 31, 36, 167

Nag Hammadi texts 33, 78, 83
Nataf, André 101
Naundorff, Charles Guillaume 226, 227
Nazis 258
Nebuchadrezzar 18
necromancy ('Black Art') 169–70, 204–5
necrophilia 224–5
Nepthys 60
New Agers 20, 54, 118
New Testament 7, 22, 23, 27, 70, 76–7,
  80–1, 97, 98–9, 107, 108, 123
Newcastle, William Cavendish, Duke
  of 221
Newton, Sir Isaac xv, 231–4
Nicaea, Council of 77

Occult, The (Wilson) 135, 176, 225–6
Old Testament 4, 5, 7, 14, 27, 31, 40, 42,
  123, 170
Oldest God, The (McKenna) 53–4
Ophites 33, 141
Origen (Church Father) 22, 28
Origin of Satan (Pagels) 20–1
original sin 12, 33
Orpheus 25, 51
Orwell, George 52–3
Osiris 5, 14, 24, 25, 31, 32, 33, 47, 48,
  49, 51

Pagels, Elaine 20–1
Palladino, Eusapia 206–13
Palud, Madeleine de la 176–7
Pan: Great God of Nature (Vinci) 53
Pan xiii, 50–1, 52, 53–5, 56–8, 149

Paracelsus 160, 192, 193–4
Paradise Lost (Milton) 11, 12, 16–17, 19–20, 27–8, 30, 41–2, 49
Paris 136, 225–6, 227
Parliamentary Articles of Enquiry 160–1
Parris, Revd Samuel 215
Parzival (Wolfram von Eschenbach) 122, 126, 129, 131–3
Passover Plot, The (Schonfield) 92
Patai, Raphael 41, 44, 45, 47
Paul, St 20, 54–5, 71, 98
Pavia 182
Perceval (Chrétien de Troyes) 124–5, 127, 129, 130, 131
Peredur, Son of Efrawg 127, 128, 129, 130, 131
Perlesvaus 126
Persia 18–19, 27
Peter, St 25–6, 78–9, 80, 81–2, 85, 87–8, 89, 104, 105
Peter of Berne 158
Philip, The Gospel of 78, 82–3, 89
Philosopher's Stone 191, 232
photography xiii–xiv, 85, 179–82
'Picatrix' (*Ghayat al Hikam*) 181
Picknett, Lynn 68, 72, 179
    Mary Magdalene xii, 72, 86, 87
    Stargate Conspiracy 3–4
    The Templar Revolution (with Prince) xiii, xiv, 68, 86, 228
    Turin Shroud (with Prince) xiv, 85, 179
Pike, Albert 238–9, 240
Pio of Pietrelcina, Padre 147
Pistis Sophia 78, 79, 80, 82, 88
Pitsea Mount, Essex 164
Plato 22, 58, 66
Playfair, Guy Lyon 205, 206
playfulness 184
Polaires, Fraternity of the 122
Polycarp (Church Father) 26
Porphyry (scholar) 45
Prelati, François 225
Priestley, J.B. 235
Prince, Clive xiii, xiv, 3–4, 68, 85, 86, 179, 185, 228
Proctor, John 216–17
Prometheus 29, 43–4
Prometheus Bound (Aeschlus) 44
Prospero (*The Tempest*) 195–6, 200
Provence 140
Proverbs, Book of 46–7
psychokinesis 204, 206

Puritan Protectorate 51
Pythagoras 66

qedishim 40–1, 59, 84, 105
Queste del San Graal 125

Rahn, Otto 122–4
    Lucifer's Court 121, 123
Rais, Gilles de 225
Ras Shamra 38–9
Raziel, Book of 43
red, significance of 32, 34, 142
Redgrove, Peter 75
Religion of Isaac Newton, The (Manuel) 233
Renaissance 178
Revelation, Book of 19, 33–4, 61
Rhodes, H.T.F. 220
Richet, Charles 211, 212–13
Robert de Boron 125
Robert ('the Bulgar') 137
Robinson, John J. 237
robots 194, 195
Roman Catholics 25, 26, 27, 36, 65, 135
Roman Empire 54, 77
Romantic Movement 28, 56–7, 228
Rome 26, 30, 58, 117, 160, 227
Rosenkreutz, Christian 183
Rosheim, Mark 194
Rosicrucian Enlightenment, The (Yates) 202
'Rosicrucian Manifestos' 183
Rosicrucians 183–4, 202, 203
Rosse, William Parsons, Earl of 232
Rowden, Maurice 182
Roy, Archie 210–11
Royal Navy 243
Royal Society 237–8
Ruah (goddess) 101
Rules of Marriage (Cherubino) 158–9
Russell, Bertrand 226
Russell, Jeffrey Burton 22, 24, 25, 36, 113, 167, 177
Russell, Ken 173

Sabbat 140, 148
Sabia 42
Sabians 132
Sacred Sexuality (Mann/Lyle) 37
St Andrews, Scotland 167
Salem, Massachusetts 215–18

Salome 37, 78, 91, 106–7, 109, 110, 111, 112, 141
Sappho 62
Sata 21–2, 32–3
Satan xi, 6–7, 20–1, 25, 26, 30–1, 33
  and the Jews 22–3
  pacts with 165–7, 168, 172–3, 174–7
  physical models for xiii, 50, 56
  Satan's number (666) 61
  as synonym for Lucifer xv, 22, 30, 242, 253
Satanic Bible (LaVey) 242, 243–5
Satanic Mass, The (Rhodes) 220
Satanism xv, 149, 222–8, 242–9, 253–7
satyrs 52–3, 56
'Saviours of Louis XVII' 227
scapegoats 23, 258
'Scarlet Woman' 34
Scheuberin, Helen 157
Schiaparelli (professor) 207
Schonfield, Hugh J. 92
'scrying' 196–7, 198
Second World War 218–19
Secrets, Academy of 181
Sekhmet 34, 54
Serapis 79, 100
Set (Egyptian god) 31–2, 33, 34, 45, 47, 48
Seth 31
sex 58, 59
  and the Carpocratians 64–8, 141–2
  Christian attitude to 11, 60, 65
  Christian sex rites 62, 68–9, 70–1, 89–90, 91, 99, 110, 141–2, 228
  incubi/succubi 36–8
  rite of horasis 75
Shaher 16, 18, 39
Shaitan 31
Shalem (Shalim) 16, 39
Sheba, Queen of 7, 42
Shekhina 45, 46–7
Shelley, Mary 13, 237
Shelley, Percy Bysshe 28, 57, 237
shewstones 196–7, 198
Sight of Hell (Furniss) 15
Simon de Montfort 136
Simon the Leper 73
Simon Magus ('Faustus') 101–5, 111, 113, 184
Simpson, James 161
Singer, George John 235
Sirius 58
'Sister Salome' (Madame Bouche) 227

Smith, Morton 63, 68, 69, 70–1, 99, 107, 110, 111, 112
snakes/serpents 9, 12, 59–60
Society for Psychical Research (SPR) 206, 208, 209
Society for the Reparation of Souls 227
Solomon, King 7, 41–2, 61
Song of Songs 7, 42
Sophia 45, 47
sorcerers 165, 168–9, 172, 195, 198–9
Southey, Robert 237
Spain 49, 122, 132, 136
Spanish Armada 167, 197
Spiritualism 164, 169, 203–13
Sprenger, Jakob 151–2, 156–7, 259
Stephen, St 97
stigmata 147–8
Stoyanov, Yuri 121
Stuart, Prince Charles Edward 229
Stubbes, Philip 51–2
succubi 37
Sumer 5
Summers, Revd Montague 56, 67, 103, 120, 130, 139–40, 145–7, 148, 151–2, 164, 175, 177, 203, 209–10, 217–18, 223
Surin, Father 175

Tableau de l'Inconstance des mauvais Anges (L'Ancre) 222
Tammuz 25, 47, 48–9, 51, 75
Tantrism 10, 59, 142
Taoism 75
'Taxil, Leo' (G. A. Jogand-Pages) 239
'temple prostitutes' see qedeshim
Tertullian (Christian Father) 11
Theodore, Bishop of Canterbury 141
Theodore (Christian) 64
Theophilus (priest) 166, 167
Thiering, Barbara 111–12
Thomas, St 49
Thomas, The Gospel of 78, 89, 107
Thor 54
Thoth 31
Thurston, Herbert 209, 211
Tiamat 16
Titans 29
Tituba (slave) 215–16
Toledo 156
Torquemada, Chief Inquisitor 167
torture ('the Question') 138, 140, 150–1, 152–6, 162, 174, 225

Toulouse 38, 136, 137
Toulouse, Bishop of 137
Tragicall History of Dr Faustus, The
    (Marlowe) 168, 169
Tree of Life 8, 10, 11
Tresemer, David 77
triple six (666) 61
Trismegistus, Hermes 123, 233
Troubadors 121, 140
Troyes 130
tulpas 255–6
Turin Shroud xiv, 85, 179–80, 181–3,
    184–90
Turkey 177
Tyndale, William 23
Typhon 32

Urban IV, Pope 153
Uriel, Archangel 197–8
Ursula, St 55

Valentine (Egyptian heretic) 33
Vasari, Giorgio 189
Vatican 80, 120, 180, 181, 189, 228
Vaudoise, Religion of 150
Venice 58
Venus (Evening Star/'Lucifera') 58,
    59, 134
Venzano, Joseph 211–12
Victoria, Queen 10–11, 161
Vinci, Leo 53
Vintras, Eugène 226, 227
Virgin Mary (Mary the Mother) 78, 83,
    99, 166–7, 227
Virgin, The (Ashe) 54

Walhern, Jane 163
Walker, Barbara 15, 23, 24, 29, 38, 39,
    43, 48, 59, 61, 107, 141, 144,
    159, 161
Walker, Benjamin 65
Walker, May C. 206
Walton-le-Dale 203
Waring (magician) 203
Watchers, the 17
Wedgwood, Ralph 57
Weeks, W.H. 236

Wesley, John 163
West Wycombe 229
White, Michael 233
Wilde, Oscar 57–8
Wilkes, John 230
Wilmshurst, Walter Leslie 242
Wilson, Colin 135, 176, 225–6, 249,
    253–4
Wilson, Robert McL. 27
Wind in the Willows, The (Grahame) 58
Witch of Endor 170
'witch marks' 144–7, 175
witch trials xv, 258–9
    Inquisition 55–6, 135, 139, 140,
        142–59, 161–4, 171
    and James I 219–20
    and Salem 215–18
witchcraft, perceptions of 148–9, 167–8,
    220–1
Witchcraft Act (1735) 164
Witches (Jong) 259
Wolfram von Eschenbach 122, 126, 129,
    131–3
women 247–8
    Church opposition to 138–9,
        140–1, 143
    and demons 20, 38
    early independence of 60–1
    female preachers 120
    as Jesus' disciples 72, 80–1
    seen as evil 6, 10, 13, 34, 36, 59, 61, 62
    seen as unclean 141
Wright, Elizabeth 147
writings, inspired ('channelled') 201–2,
    204, 206

Xenophon 5

Yahweh *see* God
Yahwists 40, 42
Yalom, Marilyn 11, 71
Yates, Frances 183, 202
Yom Kippur 23

Zarins, Juris 5–6
Zeus 16, 29, 44
Zu the Storm Bird 16